Praise for *New York Times* bestselling author Julia London

"It completely charmed me… The chemistry is so delicious. I simply didn't want to put it down."
—Nicola Cornick, *USA TODAY* bestselling author, on *The Princess Plan*

"Secrets, scandals and steamy chemistry—this paperback escape has it all!"   —*Women's World* on *The Princess Plan*

"Julia London writes vibrant, emotional stories and sexy, richly drawn characters."
—Madeline Hunter, *New York Times* bestselling author

"London's observations of gender roles are keen, and her protagonists are eminently likable in their dogged pursuit of their own goals despite societal expectations and political pressures."   —*Publishers Weekly* on *The Princess Plan*

"Warm, witty and decidedly wicked—great entertainment."
—Stephanie Laurens, #1 *New York Times* bestselling author, on *Hard-Hearted Highlander*

"Charming… A fun, touching 'prince meets real girl' Victorian fairy-tale romance."
—*Kirkus Reviews* on *The Princess Plan*

"Charming, witty and warm. This is perfect historical romance."
—Sarah Morgan, *USA TODAY* bestselling author, on *The Princess Plan*

THE DUKE
NOT TAKEN

JULIA LONDON

HQN

ISBN-13: 978-1-335-49820-5

The Duke Not Taken

Copyright © 2022 by Dinah Dinwiddie

Recycling programs
for this product may
not exist in your area.

For questions and comments about the quality of this book,
please contact us at CustomerService@Harlequin.com.

HQN
22 Adelaide St. West, 41st Floor
Toronto, Ontario M5H 4E3, Canada
www.Harlequin.com

Printed and bound in Barcelona, Spain by CPI Black Print

"I'll never love you."
"I wouldn't want it if I had it."
"Then by all means let us marry."
—William Goldman, *The Princess Bride*

THE DUKE
NOT TAKEN

To whomever is the Master of the Iddesleigh School for Undisciplined Girls, if indeed such a person exists, as it would very much appear that the natives are in charge,

I pen this letter as a concerned resident of Devonshire. Your school has become a disruptive presence in what was once a very peaceful valley. Please do not misconstrue this to be a complaint against the education of girls, as it is certainly not that. All children should be afforded a quality education. But one cannot countenance the shrieking and crying and singing that, on a clear day, undoubtedly is heard all the way to the sea. I respectfully request you instill some semblance of discipline in your charges so that peace may once again reign. Thank you.

A Concerned Resident of Devonshire

—

To A Resident of Devonshire, Concerned,

Thank you for your recent letter. We agree the level of noise that rises from our little school each day is inconceivably horrible! How anyone can arrive at afternoon tea without significant head pain is truly a mystery. It hardly needs to be said that our students are incorrigible and, if one can fathom it, are at times more concerned about who is sitting by whom instead of their figures! But rest assured that at the Iddesleigh School, we are working diligently to instill a semblance of discipline.

Kindest regards to you and yours,
The Iddesleigh School for Exceptional Girls.

—

To the Would-be Master of the Iddesleigh School for Ordinary Girls,

This morning, the girls were not in the classroom, where, one would surmise, a proper education would be occurring. No, they were near the river, laughing and chasing geese along the banks, which, I should not have to explain to any adult, presents a hazard in and of itself. On what would have been an otherwise perfect setting for an artist to paint was ruined by all the shrieking and quacking. Your charges should be at their desks. I cannot comprehend how any education is occurring at all.

A Concerned Resident of Devonshire

—

To A Resident of Devonshire, Concerned,

Thank you for another letter! It is indeed perplexing to understand how anything useful might penetrate the brains of these girls because they simply will not stop talking! However, we persevere and endeavor to do our very best. We believe a well-rounded education includes figures, writing, geography, and humanities, which naturally includes an introduction to nature in her purest form. As a painter, you surely appreciate the importance of that. Unfortunately, we have come to understand that when scads of girls are in the out-of-doors, they will sometimes chase geese and shriek while doing so. To chase geese silently would deny their truest nature. Nevertheless, we agree that such activity is indeed a hazard and we have been very stern in our warnings that they will not like the bite of a beak if they persist in this abominable practice.

Kindest regards,
The Iddesleigh School for Exceptional Girls!

CHAPTER ONE

March, 1858
In the capital city of St. Edys
Wesloria

THEY SAID THAT Princess Amelia fell in love with a footman.

"*Another* one?" her sister asked with dismay.

Amelia hadn't actually fallen in *love* with him, but even if she had, she could hardly be blamed, given how bitterly cold and long the Weslorian winter had been. What was she to do, stuck inside Rohalan Palace with nothing to do on days that saw only a few hours of sun? While winds had howled and rain had poured, Amelia had passed days in front of large blazing hearths, as it was too cold to venture very far from them. And on those days, when she couldn't read another word, or eat another bite, or engage in another dreadfully dull conversation, she looked for games to play. But who was there to join her but a lady-in-waiting and a footman or two?

Anyway, did it really matter now? The last footman had been sent off to Astasia Castle, and spring was upon them, and everything was glittery and green and filled with bright sunshine.

But her sister, Justine, the Queen of Wesloria, said, "I can't look at you right now," and had turned her head. "Kissing *footmen*," she repeated, as if mystified by it, as if she and Amelia hadn't spent a good portion of their teen-aged years fantasizing about that very thing.

When her lady-in-waiting, Lordonna, whispered to her that the footman had confessed to the head butler, who had in turn confessed to the prince consort, Amelia had expected there to be some *how-could-yous* and *you-shouldn't-haves* and *promise-me-Amelias* and was fully prepared to promise. She clung to the hope that when she had apologized enough and swore it would not, *could* not happen again, that they would all move on to something far more diverting: the upcoming social season. There would be balls and galas and Amelia was so ready, *so* ready for something new and different, something other than dark, cold rooms. She needed light and outdoors and the warmth of the sun. She needed laughter and gaiety. She needed attention, she needed life. She was withering away without it.

She'd carried her great anticipation into her sister's privy chamber…but her hope had been immediately dashed when she saw who all was gathered.

Justine was seated with her hands gripped tightly in her lap. That was a sure sign of her sister's nerves—which, in fairness, had vastly improved since she'd assumed the throne, but which, in fairness, could still bedevil her. Amelia had never suffered from nerves, thank the saints—boredom was her cross to bear. She was too restless, too full of a compelling need to seek adventure. Everyone talked about Justine's nerves and how crowds distressed her. But no one ever spoke about how distressing it could feel to Amelia when there was very little to do.

Behind her sister stood her very handsome husband, the prince consort, betrayer of sisters-in-law, William Douglas of Scotland. He winced sympathetically when he looked at her, which Amelia did not take to be the best of signs.

"*Amelia*, darling. What have you *done*?"

That nettled tone belonged to none other than her mother, the Dowager Queen Agnes. She was seated at an easel beside a young man who wore a painter's smock. Her mother was not painting, but she was gesturing at the canvas and speaking quietly to the gentleman about what needed to be added to the scene. It was a peculiar talent of the dowager queen, to paint by proxy. If one did not have a talent for art, did one merely commandeer the talent from someone else? Amelia would say no, but no one listened to her.

Her mother was glaring at her. Another ill portent.

The other person in the room was Dante Robuchard, the prime minister. He was standing at the window, pretending to gaze out at the grounds surrounding Rohalan Palace. He'd barely hung on to his political office after a called vote last autumn. Since then, he'd been ever present around Justine, almost as if he believed if he so much as stepped out of the room, someone might quickly call another vote. If Amelia knew how to do those sorts of things, she would.

Taken as a whole, these four individuals were enough to cause Amelia to wish for a tonic. And yet it was the fifth person in the room that made her feel seasick. That person stood before the hearth, hands held over the fire for warmth. And when she turned, she beamed a smile at Amelia and warbled, "Your Royal Highness! How good it is to see you well after all this time!" She sank into a very deep but crooked curtsy.

"*No*," Amelia whispered.

Lady Lila Aleksander. The *matchmaker*. The same woman who had been employed to make a match for Justine three years ago and then had proceeded to oversee a disaster of epic proportions. Not that Amelia had a single complaint about William—well, other than he could be trusted to tell Justine *everything*—but she had taken issue with several of the candidates presented to Justine before she'd realized that her true love had been standing before her the entire time in William. But none of the others had been suitable for a future queen.

"How long has it been?" Lady Aleksander asked with great cheer.

"It's been three years since Justine was coronated," Amelia's mother said.

"And it's been one and a half years since Amelia had the affair with the soldier," Justine added.

"It was hardly an affair," Amelia sniffed. But it had most definitely been an affair.

Justine ignored her. She continued, "And six months since her first flirtation with a footman, but a mere three weeks since her second! *That's* how long it has been."

"All right," Amelia said, her hands going to her waist. "I think we all get your point, Jussie."

"I see you've been well occupied, Your Royal Highness," Lady Aleksander chirped. "In all that time, were there no proper suitors for you hand?"

"Proper?" Amelia had to mull that over. What did that mean, exactly? Proper in Robuchard's view? Or her own? "I rather liked one or two of them."

"Unfortunately, their alliances did not suit the monarchy." Robuchard had decided to join the fray, and his tone suggested that Amelia's failure to secure a match was the worst thing to ever happen to Wesloria. And what did he mean, *'did not suit the monarchy'*? What tripe was that?

"Some things simply cannot be overlooked," he added, supposedly to explain his tripe, as if the gentlemen in question had been treasonous assassins.

"In other words," William piped in, "the attempts to settle a proper match on our Amelia have been unsuccessful due to politics and, well, her strong aversion to so many Weslorian noblemen." He directed his gaze to Amelia, silently daring her to disagree.

"What? Am I to shackle myself to every foppish Weslorian noble who enters the palace? Is that what you want?"

"Ah. I think I see the problem," Lady Aleksander said with a nod to William.

"There is no problem!" Amelia insisted.

Except that there was. Naturally, *they* all assumed the problem was her. They saw her as an incorrigible flirt, unable to keep her hands from footmen. But the real problem was that no one understood her. Justine had understood her before she'd become queen, but since then she'd been so caught up in the royal business that she had very little time for her sister.

It was Amelia's opinion that she was too sheltered. She was six and twenty and had wants and ambitions and desires. She didn't *do* anything here, and she chafed at feeling useless for anything other than cutting a ribbon here or patronizing a charity there. She was the spare heir whose sole responsibility was to wait in the long shadow of her sister until she was needed. If ever.

"Would you like to know what I think?" Lady Aleksander asked.

"*No*," Amelia said at the same moment Justine said, "*Je, please!*"

"I think, Your Royal Highness, that you are deserving of someone who suits your adventurous spirit."

"Adventurous spirit," Amelia's mother drawled. "That's a unique way of describing it."

"Wait…" It was very plain what was about to happen, and frantic, Amelia tried to think of a way to stop it. "You can't possibly be here for me, madam. I am sure you are not, because I am *certain* someone might have mentioned it." She cast an accusing look at her sister.

"For God's sake, Amelia. It's not as if she's come to escort you to the gallows," her mother said crossly.

"*Yet*," Justine muttered.

"And really, darling, you've no one to blame but yourself," her mother added. "What do you suggest we do with you?"

"You don't have to *do* anything with me, Mama! I am a grown woman and I know my feelings and wants quite well. You could simply *ask* what I should like to do. I should like to do something useful. With all due respect, Lady Aleksander, I am not in need of your services."

"I understand," Lady Aleksander said, and Amelia almost sagged with relief. "No one ever thinks they need me. Are those tea cakes?" she asked, pointing at the sideboard.

"They are," Justine said. "I don't know why I thought we'd all sit like civilized people and take tea. I must have been mad. Amelia, darling, Lila has come to help you. Not because you need her, but because our attempts to find a suitable match for you have not been successful. And by the by, you *do* have useful things to do. I just named you to the royal patronage of the new King Maksim Library!"

Amelia had to clench one fist to keep from shouting out in frustration. When she had opened the new library at Justine's request, she'd been the only person in attendance under the age of fifty. Some tea and crumpets had been consumed, but not a single dance or lively tune was played. "That is hardly the sort of occupation I mean."

Justine sighed. She looked around the room. "Will you all excuse us for a moment?"

"Take all the time you need," Lady Aleksander said brightly. "May I try a tea cake?"

Justine stood, grabbed Amelia by the elbow, and marched her out of hearing to the far end of the room. "You're acting like a brat," she whispered hotly, glancing at the others over her shoulder. "Are you really so surprised? You're six and twenty, Amelia. You're kissing *footmen*. Do you intend to carry on until you do something unpardonable that will make you completely unmarriable?"

Amelia's jaw dropped. "And your solution is to sell me to the highest bidder?"

"*Mein Gott*," Justine said, reverting to their mother's native German language, in which she and Amelia were both fluent in swearing. "My solution is to help you find happiness. Someone who can be by your side in this life on *your* terms. Someone who is agreeable to those who love you and your position as a member of the royal family. And really, isn't that what you want? You've always wanted to be married and have a large family. But you dabble in meaningless dalliances."

Amelia gasped. "That's not fair, Justine. I have no freedom here—you know that."

"You might think of it this way, Your Royal Highness."

Both sisters jumped—they had not heard Lady Aleksander approach. "You will be enjoying a social season in England."

Amelia was set to argue, but that last sentence gave her pause. England—and specifically, London—was a different proposition than having a matchmaker drag a handful of suitors to Rohalan Palace in St. Edys. "London?"

"A fine country home," Lady Aleksander said between nibbles. "Very near London."

"A *country* home?" That didn't sound like any sort of social season. That sounded like punishment.

"You'll be surrounded by friends. There will be parties

and balls. All the fashionable things. You recall Lord Iddesleigh?" Lady Aleksander asked.

Iddesleigh! Beckett Hawke, the Earl of Iddesleigh. She remembered him, all right...but he was far too old for her. "He's married—"

"Oh, he is, indeed, and happily. He and his wife and their delightful young family have taken up residence at his country seat. I don't know if you've had the pleasure of visiting the English countryside in the spring and summer, but it's so—"

"What does Iddesleigh and his delightful family have to do with me?"

"They've invited you to come for the summer!"

Amelia flashed a look of irritation at Justine. "They *invited* me, did they?"

"They were so agreeable to the idea!" Lady Aleksander amended slightly. "And Lord Iddesleigh has *assured* me there will be balls and whatnot."

"Whatnot," Amelia echoed.

"Whatnot, Amelia!" her mother said sternly. "Stop repeating everything the lady says!"

Justine put her hand on her arm. "Amelia, listen to me. You will have every opportunity to socialize as you like, and in the event there is a suitable bachelor who captures your fancy, it can happen properly and without the Weslorian newspapers to record every glance and smile."

Well, *that* was certainly appealing. The Weslorian newspapers had made quite a fuss with the rumors about her, reporting that she had loose morals—she probably did—and was childish—she was *not*. They also said she was unlikable. Amelia conceded that could very well be, but Justine said that was rubbish.

Still, Amelia wasn't appreciating this move to send her

out of the country. "Aren't you concerned there will be no one to keep a close watch on me? Have you forgotten that none of you trust me?"

"I trust Lordonna and my friend Lila Aleksander to keep a close watch."

Amelia glanced at the latter.

Lady Aleksander brushed a crumb from her lip and said brightly, "I am coming with you! I will see you settled at Iddesleigh and will make sure everything proceeds smoothly."

"And naturally, we will not send you alone, Your Royal Highness," offered Robuchard. "Wesloria will be well represented in your retinue."

Amelia's head was spinning. They had all discussed this. Behind her back. It was obviously not just Justine's idea. Amelia looked around at all of them. "Am I...am I being *banished*?"

"No!" They all said in unison with varying degrees of emphasis. Except Justine, who said, "Not *banished*."

Amelia stared incredulously at her sister.

At least Justine looked properly sheepish. "I really rather thought you would be pleased—you love England."

"I love *London*."

"You'll be near it." Justine put her arm around Amelia's shoulders. "And there will be more to do there." She leaned in and whispered, "You might also take into account that our mother will not be on hand to offer her frequent opinion."

"What's that?" their mother asked, on cue.

"You remember how pleased everyone in England seemed to be to have a pair of royal princesses?"

Of course she remembered it—how could she forget it?

The two of them had attracted a crowd wherever they went, and Amelia had loved it. Had *thrived* with that attention.

"Only this time, the attention will be solely on *you*."

It could not be said that Justine didn't know her sister well—she knew how often in their lives Amelia had been overlooked, pushed aside, discounted in favor of Justine, the heir. "What if you go to all this trouble and no one suits me?" Amelia whispered. "You know how I fall in and out of love so easily."

"You fall in and out of lust easily, darling. But I don't think you've ever fallen in love. That's another matter entirely. And if you find no one to suit you, you'll be back in St. Edys in time for the Little Season in the fall. Think of this as a change of scenery."

Amelia rolled her eyes. But the idea of something very different appealed to her. Something adventurous, all on her own, without Justine or her mother or anyone else. And she did want to find the gentleman who might be hers. "All right," she said. "I'll go."

CHAPTER TWO

March, 1858
Devonshire, England

THE WINDOWS WERE open to the morning, the air as still as death, the heat, unusual for this time of year, already rising. There hadn't been a spot of rain in weeks, and the whole of the Hollyfield estate seemed to plod along under the weight of it.

Joshua Parker, the Duke of Marley, was in his bed, the coverlet kicked to the floor, his nightshirt flung across the room. His hair was damp against the pillow. He was not asleep as much as he was lying still with his eyes closed, wishing for a breeze.

But then he heard singing somewhere in the distance.

His first thought was that it was angels. Mercifully, they'd come for him at last. Or maybe they were singing a mass for his lost soul as he made his way down to Hades. It certainly felt hot enough.

The sound of angels drew closer, and then began to sound less like angels, and more like children.

Children?

What would children be doing at Hollyfield? There was hardly anyone here at all, save his butler, who was, ironically, named Mr. Butler. And Mr. Martin, his valet. And Mrs. Chumley, his cook, and Miss Halsey, the housekeeper with a somewhat frightful countenance, whom he preferred to address by only her last name to save time. Like him, Halsey did not waste time with extra words. And last, but not least, a lone chambermaid whom he would occasionally see flitting between rooms with a feather duster.

But decidedly no *children*.

When Joshua had been married, Hollyfield had been teeming with staff. You couldn't take a step without bumping into a footman or a chambermaid or a groom. But he'd let most of them go after the duchess had died, because what was the point of all of them then?

The singing drew closer. It annoyed him. For one, the children were not singing in tune. For another, it sounded as if one child was sobbing. And for yet another, one of the children was singing a beat behind the rest of them. What were they singing, a hymn? Who the devil had children singing hymns in the blasted morning?

Joshua sat up and pushed away the damp lock of hair that draped over his eye. The hound at the end of his bed—Merlin—lifted his head and looked over his shoulder at him. Bethan was on the floor, stretched out on his side, his tongue hanging out the side of his snout as he, too, tried to cool off. And Artemis, the cat, was on the windowsill, his back to the scenery, watching Joshua with silent judgment.

Joshua climbed out of his bed and stepped over Bethan to go to the open window. Artemis gracefully leaped from the sill to the floor and walked over Bethan like he was a piece of clothing. Maybe Artemis thought he was—there was much of Joshua's clothing strewn about. He'd not allowed Mr. Martin into his room yesterday.

The singing stopped. So did the crying. Joshua craned his neck to see down the path that ran along the river. He couldn't see anyone and scratched his chin as he stepped back from the window. The moment he did, the singing began again. "*All creatures of our God and king,*" they sang. "*Lift up your voice and with us sing. Al-le-luuuuuu-jah.*"

Bethan lifted his hind leg and began to vigorously attack an itch on his flank.

Joshua slammed the windows shut. Artemis disappeared under the bed, and Merlin snored on.

"Your Grace?"

Joshua looked around, bleary-eyed. His butler, standing just over the threshold, blinked, then affixed his gaze on the ceiling.

"*Thou burning sun with golden gleam,*" the children sang, their voices leaking in through the seams of the window.

"Who are those children?" Joshua growled, hands on hips.

"Children?" Butler asked the ceiling.

"Can you not hear them?" For a brief moment, Joshua wondered if perhaps he'd lost his mind. Sometimes it very much felt as if he might have done.

"Ah, yes, I can just hear them," Butler said.

He was holding a silver tray, Joshua noticed, onto which he had placed a cream-colored envelope. "What's that?"

"This has come from Iddesleigh, your grace."

Not again. Beckett Hawke was proving himself to be a bothersome neighbor. "Does no one observe a leisurely morning anymore? Must all the singing of hymns and delivery of the post be done at the crack of dawn?"

Butler tentatively peeled his gaze from the ceiling, but only for a moment, then pinned it to the mantle. What was the matter with him? Joshua looked down. His drawers were standing open and revealing the flaccid means to any future Parkers. Who could think about their state of dress when children were screeching in his ear?

He walked to the end of his bed and tugged his dressing gown from beneath Merlin's body. He shoved his arms into the sleeves and wrapped it around him. "All right. Give it to me, then," he said, and held out his hand for the offending envelope.

Butler risked a glance, then came forward in a manner one might approach a sleeping giant. Joshua took the envelope from the tray just as the singing started up again. "What the devil?" He stalked to the window and threw it open again.

There they were. Which meant he'd not lost his mind, because those were very real children, a dozen or so of them. All girls, too, in a dizzy array of pastel pinks and yellows and blues. They were holding hands, two by two, following along behind a gentleman wearing a long black coat and black hat with a wide brim. "What is the meaning of this?" Joshua asked, gesturing heatedly at the girls.

The gentleman leading them halted in the path. He said something to them that caused them to stop singing again. He bent down, pointing to something. The girls circled around him to have a look.

Bethan roused himself and stuck his muzzle under Joshua's free hand. Joshua absently scratched the dog's head while Butler inched forward to have a look.

"Ah," Butler said. "Lord Iddesleigh has established a girl's school in the old gamekeeper's cottage."

"A *school?*" Joshua repeated. "A *girl's* school?"

"Yes, Your Grace. I understand that Iddesleigh has a daughter or two."

He had *five.* For God's sake, at some point, a man had

to accept the fact that he'd not produce a son and leave off his wife.

"He and his wife have established a proper school for them and other young girls in the area and brought in a proper headmaster."

"In a gamekeeper's cottage?"

"I believe it is only a temporary location, Your Grace."

Below them, one of the girls suddenly grabbed the dark locks of another one and yanked. That girl shrieked and grabbed the frock of her aggressor. The two began to tussle like drunks at a pub.

"Will you be having tea?" Butler asked, seemingly oblivious to the melee unfolding below.

Joshua watched the gentleman clad in black step in between the girls to separate them. The two girls, whose hair ribbons were hanging at the tips of their hair or had been trampled in the dirt, simultaneously made their case to the gentleman. It was clear to Joshua that the taller one was the aggressor. He wondered if he ought to shout down to the gentleman.

He raked his fingers through his hair then turned from the window to look at the clock on the mantle. It was half past three. *Half past three.* God help him, he ought to feel some shame for rising from his bed at this hour. But he didn't. Not a lick. In fact, he walked back to his bed with the letter in hand and fell onto his back beside Merlin, who immediately shifted around so that he might drape his head over Joshua's torso. "No tea, Butler. Thank you." He broke the seal of the envelope and unfolded it.

It was another invitation to dine. No less enthusiastically given than those that had preceded it, with an insistence that the writer would not accept no as an answer. Joshua handed the invitation to Butler. "No," he said.

He didn't have the time or patience for society. He had enough to think about, and now, to do, what with this girl's school suddenly underfoot. He would have to think strategically, of course. As the Duke of Marley, he could hardly be perceived to be against education for girls. But neither could he be the duke who had to suffer them.

Not after what he'd been through.

Not after what he'd *done*.

No, he'd have to make his feelings known in a more subtle way.

CHAPTER THREE

April, 1858
England

To Her Majesty the Queen, Justine,

Darling sister, I pray this letter finds you in good
health and spirits, as I sincerely hope that at least one
of us is well. I have much to tell you, and I must begin
by declaring Devonshire to have been a dreadful mistake. While I blame you entirely for sending me here,
I'm not angry with you. Really, I'm far more disappointed in myself for having allowed you to convince
me that this was any sort of solution. Could we not
have guessed that Iddesleigh House would prove to
be just as boring as Rohalan Palace, but even worse,
as it is miles and miles from any proper society? It
is not "close" to London at all, but a day away on the
fastest horses. It is so deep into the countryside that
I've had only a few callers in my first days here, and
they were all quite old.

I miss you terribly! I've no one to talk to, really.
Lordonna, as you know, is very quiet and keeps her
opinions to herself. That leaves me with Lila. But
she is presently in London, rounding up the gentlemen she might possibly persuade to traipse all the

way here to attend the ball Lord and Lady Iddesleigh seem very much determined to host in my honor. I am quite pleased by the prospect of a ball. But I am not pleased if the ball is to be attended by only those in their dotage. Who will I dance with?

I imagined Iddesleigh to be a grand English country house, and I blame Lila for it, as she described a large country home. She does tend to paint everything in the rosiest of terms. And indeed, the countryside we passed through on the way here was quite beautiful, with rolling hills bathed in shades of golds and pinks in a setting sun. We passed a few large houses, built in the Georgian manner. Do you remember our tutor, Monsieur Klopec, and his love of architecture? I paid him more heed than I thought, for I recognized the style at once.

I had every reason to believe Iddesleigh would be just as grand as the houses we passed. I pictured massive gardens, and a ballroom that required no less than four chandeliers to light. A county home befitting a visit from a royal princess, if not from Queen Victoria herself. I was filled with eagerness, until near the end of the long procession to reach Iddesleigh, when I had an omen that things would not be as I'd imagined. You will not believe me when I write this, but the Grim Reaper very nearly collected me, not five miles from Iddesleigh! He appeared from nowhere, a rider racing recklessly past the coaches. He was clothed in black and on a prodigious black horse. He rode so close on a narrow spit of road that I feared he would crash into the coach and kill us all. But at the last possible moment, he maneuvered the horse to avoid a collision and thundered past, disappearing down the road. The coach driver shouted terrible things after him, but the rider paid him no mind.

Goodness, but my heart had climbed to my throat in the few seconds it had all taken place, and I could scarcely breathe. I looked at Lordonna, who looked just as frightened as me. I said, who do you suppose that was? She said perhaps it had been Lord Iddesleigh. I didn't think so—what I recall of him was that he was rather amicable and not inclined to rush anywhere.

The rider came and went so quickly and was so dark and menacing that I was instantly reminded of the Grim Reaper. He looked just like the one Hortensia described. Do you remember Hortensia? She was our nursemaid for only a few weeks. I once heard Mama say she'd had bread that lasted longer. But Hortensia was there long enough to impart some wisdom: *Beware the Grim Reaper* was one. *The devil is always watching and sees you now* was another.

Anyway, a few miles after our encounter with the Reaper, we came upon the Iddesleigh house, which surprised me greatly, and not in a favorable way. It is unimpressive in everything but size. Significant parts of it are scaffolded, which, I suppose, indicates various stages of repair, or perhaps even worse—dismantlement. Half the house appears to be the remnants of a medieval castle, and the other half looks to have been added through the years in a confusing mixture of architectural styles that would distress Monsieur Klopec terribly. The grounds are very plain, with only a manicured lawn and bowling green. But no maze, no flower gardens. Not even a fountain or statue to add interest!

My rooms are well enough, I suppose. I've a bedroom, sitting room, dressing room and bath, as well as an adjoining room for Lordonna. The accommodations are perfectly fine, although not as fine as my rooms at Rohalan Palace. The very first night, a terrible rainstorm had caused the roof to leak, dripping water onto the chaise, and in the days that followed, I was forced to endure a horde of workmen pounding away overhead to repair the roof.

The house is so large Lady Iddesleigh required two afternoons to acquaint me with its exhausting entirety. "It's very large," she needlessly pointed out, and more than once. I don't mean to be unkind, but the lady tends to repeat herself. Then she said it was not particularly functional for a large family.

I said I didn't see why not, that there was a wing for everyone who wanted one. And then Blythe said—oh, I am to call her Blythe and her husband Beck, as they insist they be treated like family— Blythe said they were building a new wing for their little brood. I laughed, which I guess I should not have done, as she did look at me curiously. I explained that her brood was not little, but quite large, and I'd never heard of anyone having so many daughters. I daresay she looked offended. I didn't think I'd said anything wrong, but I begged her pardon, and pointed out that I only meant to say that five children was quite a lot. She said she thought it was the perfect amount. I suppose five children is the perfect amount if one intends to mount one's own army and overthrow the queen, but I can see no reason for it otherwise.

Really, Jussie, the daughters are the most interesting thing about Iddesleigh. They range in age from eight to two. Mathilda, who the girls call Tilly, is the oldest. She is quite skeptical of anything her parents say, and she is a bit of a tyrant to her sisters. She rules them much as Mama rules you and me, always telling us what to do. I beg you not to read that sentence to her when she insists you read the entire letter to her.

Maren is next, at seven years, and the quietest of them. Her father said he hoped that meant she was studious, but as her sisters never allowed her to speak, he wasn't confident that was the case. Maisie is six, but she claims to be seven, much to the consternation of Mathilda, who simply cannot abide such a demonstrable falsehood. Margaret, who the girls sometimes called Peg-leg Meg—in spite of having two perfectly functioning legs—is four, and the last, little Birdie, only two.

"Birdie?" I said to Beck. "Not Miranda or Mariah?"

He said the letter *M* became tiresome, so they'd advanced to another letter of the alphabet. *B* was the popular choice, and if they have more children, there are many *B* names from which to choose. Lord, Jussie, *more* children? I think they are quite mad!

Oh, and I nearly forgot Alice, a small white dog who follows the girls everywhere they go. But Alice is clearly a male dog, and do you know, I expected the explanation would be so ridiculous that I couldn't bring myself to ask why he was given a female name.

The girls enjoy my things, and they love to try on my jewelry and accoutrements. Their questions and theories of royal life are very entertaining. I allow them to think whatever they like, for the truth is there is not much to admire about the life of the spare heir.

I find their father to be entertaining in his own

way, but I seem to have gotten off on the wrong foot with his wife. I honestly don't know why, as I've endeavored to help in any way I possibly can. It's hardly my fault that a melee occurs each morning when the time comes for the oldest daughters to go to school and the youngest two to go to the nursery. It is so loud and screechy that one morning, I offered to walk the oldest ones to school just to put an end to it. Lord and Lady Iddesleigh are terribly disorganized.

Lila came from London last weekend to tell me about this gentleman and that one. She asked me *again* what I should like in a husband. She is quite excited about the prospect of so many gentlemen desiring to make my acquaintance.

But then she asked if she might offer a piece of advice. Naturally, I was all ears as to what advice she could offer me and begged her to continue. She said that I should not offer my opinion to the Iddesleigh family unless it was specifically requested. I tell you, Jussie, I laughed. I'd done no such thing! And I begged her to please enlighten me as to what I'd done. She said that some parents didn't like to be instructed on how to raise their children. She said she suspected that I, being a royal princess, whose opinion on any number of things is highly sought, probably thought it was sought in that way, too. I asked what the devil she was talking about and she said that I should not have suggested a proper bedtime. Why not, I ask you? Really, if those girls were to bed a decent hour, the mornings would be bearable. It is not *my* fault the Iddesleighs are late to everything—to breakfast, to supper, to church. I explained to Lila I meant merely to help them along.

Lila agreed that of course I was helping, but that sometimes I seemed a little ~~ofishus~~. ~~Oficious~~. I don't know the word she used, but I think she meant entirely too forward? Whatever the meaning, it was not complimentary.

She said that it was quite natural for a royal princess to want to help where she sees a need, but in this, perhaps I ought to turn my attention elsewhere. I asked Lila where I ought to turn my attention, as there is absolutely nothing to occupy me.

Well, never mind, I have solved my own problem. I have taken it upon myself to walk the girls to school each day. It's lovely scenery, and I have discovered I very much enjoy walking.

You won't believe what happened just two days past. I saw the Grim Reaper again! I would not have seen him had I not taken it upon myself to walk the girls to school. And if I hadn't seen him, I would not have returned to the school where, as it happens, I found an occupation quite all on my own away from Iddesleigh. But I must save that news for a later date—I hear Blythe calling for me. I hope it is a caller! I should adore a caller. A *young caller*. I'll write soon.

Yours, A

CHAPTER FOUR

THE WEATHER HAD been lovely since Amelia's arrival at Iddesleigh, but this morning the thick clouds and a fine mist hung over the path to the school. She and the girls donned their bonnets and short coats.

"Are you certain, Your Royal Highness?" Blythe asked, peering out the front door. "I'll have Garrett bring round a carriage."

"Don't be silly. By the time they have the team hitched, we'll be at the school."

"But I'd not like you to catch cold."

It would take more than a fine mist to give her a cold. "I'll be fine!" she insisted. "I like the walk. We all do, don't we?" she asked the girls.

"Yes!" Maisie shouted, and she punctuated that by flying out the open door, running straight for the first puddle she saw.

"Maisie!" her mother shouted, but it was too late. Her daughter had smashed into the puddle with both feet and splashed her coat.

"You see? We'll be fine," Amelia said confidently.

Blythe did not look convinced. But it was no use, because Mathilda and Maren had already gone out, oblivious to the damp, too.

Amelia followed them, gathering up the girls to walk down the lane.

By the time they crowded into the tiny foyer of the school, Mathilda pointed out that Maisie's hem was ruined. "Mama will be cross."

"No she won't," Maisie said.

"Yes she will."

"She *won't*."

"She *will*."

Maren hung her bonnet on a peg in the wall and walked between her sisters without a word, and into the classroom. Beck was right—she was the smartest of them all.

"All right," Amelia said, putting herself between the two girls. "As Maisie's hem will be dry by the time your mother sees it, we can only wait and see how cross she will be."

"See?" Maisie tossed her bonnet behind her, not caring where it landed, before skipping into the classroom. Mathilda sighed loudly and picked it up, handing it to Amelia. "No one *ever* believes me. Mama will be so *cross*." She handed her bonnet to Amelia and walked into the classroom.

Amelia looked down at the two bonnets. She was a chambermaid. She had come all this way to be a chambermaid. She hung the bonnets on wall pegs and turned to go, but very nearly collided with Mr. Roberts, the headmaster.

"Oh! Miss Ivanosen. Good morning."

"Good morning, Mr. Roberts." On the first day she'd escorted the girls, the kindly headmaster had seemed a bit befuddled by her. She'd introduced herself as Miss Ivanosen as a lark, thinking he surely knew who she was. The poor man didn't know. Frankly, he seemed to be befuddled by any number of things, and every day he was in a frantic search for lost items—his eyeglasses, the key to the door.

This morning, his hair was standing on end.

"Are you all right, sir?"

"Oh, very well, indeed, madam, thank you. It's just that I can't seem to find the school bell. Got to have a proper school bell."

"Got to have," she agreed. "Shall I help you look?"

His expression melted into relief. "Would you be so kind?" His gaze moved over her shoulder. Two girls who were just arriving were distraught that there were no pegs left for their bonnets.

Amelia politely moved out of the way.

Now, where would someone put a school bell? Not in the foyer—it was too small. She peeked into the classroom, where girls were standing in clumps of twos and threes, all of them talking at once. Not in here, for someone would surely be ringing it. Probably Maisie.

She returned to a much smaller room that was serving as an office. How anyone could accomplish anything in this room was astounding—it was a complete and utter mess. Papers were stacked inches high on the desk. Books and slates had been piled haphazardly onto a chair. On the floor were various cloaks and boots and fishing gear. A variety of walking sticks in different sizes were propped in one corner. Two empty bird cages hung before the window; the bookcases were stuffed with books; and a hand-knitted one-eyed toy cat stared down at her from a perch on a chest of drawers.

But there, very plainly in view, on top of a pile of papers, was the school bell. Amelia stepped over a bucket to pick it up. She happened to glance at the top paper beneath the bell. It was a letter. It was open, as if Mr. Roberts had intended to read it, but had been called away and left his bell there to remind him. She cocked her head to the side to scan the contents. It was a request from a gentleman seeking to admit his daughter to the school.

She didn't see where they would possibly place his daughter—the students were practically stuffed to the rafters as it was.

Amelia shrugged and walked back to the main classroom. She held up the bell so that Mr. Roberts, from his vantage point at the head of the class, could see that it was found. She placed it carefully on the windowsill, and he waved to her in a show of thanks.

As she exited the school, she heard the bell ring and his voice, clear and strong, announce grandly, "All right, young ladies, it is time for our schoolwork to begin!"

Amelia stepped out onto the path. The mist had receded a bit, she was pleased to see. She could walk a little longer.

Who would have thought she'd enjoy long rambles as she had? She'd never had occasion to walk much in Wesloria—there were always carriages and horses and guards about. But she liked it so much that she'd asked Lordonna to please make the necessary arrangements for her to obtain some sturdy walking boots. Lordonna had said she would do so straightaway, but had looked concerned, as if she privately thought it unseemly for princesses to wander the countryside.

It probably was.

What Amelia loved about her long walks was that in addition to it being something to do, no one bothered her. No one seemed to even *notice* her. Even her two Weslorian guards, who had been dispatched to keep her safe, had concluded there was no harm in her ambling around, and sat outside the stables with the English grooms to play betting games while she wandered.

Amelia always wore a plain brown gown for her walks. It was the only one in her large wardrobe that she could bear to see dirtied or wet. Her shawl and her short coat were equally plain. She delighted in the idea that she must look like a farm girl on her way to market. Maybe one day she'd walk all the way to the village and return with a chicken. How amusing that would be! Would anyone notice her then?

She liked her newfound anonymity. She'd never been free to roam, and when she'd mentioned that to Beck, he'd laughed and said, "You're in Devonshire, Your Royal Highness. Not much happens here."

Most days she meandered along the road, as she was this morning, pausing now and again to lean against the stone fence and look at the sheep. She'd passed them enough that she felt they were friends—not that any of them ever came to the fence to greet her, but still.

The entrance to the school was marked by an old stone archway just at the point where the footpath intersected the main road through this dale. Amelia stepped out onto the road and turned to admire the arch with its cherubs carved into stone. She couldn't imagine why such a modest property would think to install such a heavenly arch. She was studying the cherubs for any clue and didn't realize that a rider was coming at her at a high speed around a curve in the road. By the time she turned to the sound of it, the rider was very nearly upon her. With a cry of alarm, she leaped into a shallow ditch beside the stone fence, her hand going to her bonnet to keep it from being whipped off her head by the swirl of wind the horse left in its wake. Her heart climbed to her throat when she realized it was the Grim Reaper thundering past and kicking up mud onto her gown and her face. The same one that had nearly collided with her carriage.

Amelia shrieked with surprise or fear, which caused the rider to draw up several feet away from her. He turned his mount about and trotted a few feet back to have a closer look at her. He was a large man, his shoulders very broad in his black cloak. He wore a hat pulled low over his brow. He had a dark beard that did not look trimmed. And he did not get down off his horse to assist her. When it became apparent to her he wouldn't, she climbed out of the ditch. For a moment, she thought he wouldn't even deign to speak. But then he said, "Pardon."

Amelia gaped at him. "*Pardon?* That's all you have to say? That is what you would say to someone you accidently bump into at a market stall." She stepped back onto the road. "You might have *killed* me. My body might have lain in this ditch for days before anyone found me."

"A body in that ditch would be seen quite clearly by any passerby."

"You almost ran me over!"

"It may have seemed so to you, but I can assure you, I didn't come near you. The moment I saw you, I veered to the left. Are you hurt?"

"No!" She made a show of dusting road splatter from the front of her gown. "But I am covered in mud from all your veering to the left."

"Again, I apologize." He pointed a gloved finger at her, making a circular motion. "You've something on your cheek."

Amelia reached up to brush mud off her cheek.

"Other one."

She brushed angrily at that cheek. "You should have more care."

"I agree, I should have more care about a great many things. And you should not stand on the road."

He said it as if the fault was entirely hers. "I was not standing in the road, I was walking. I had *paused.*"

"Which would be the standing part of it."

She couldn't believe him. "You may trust, sir, that had I known the Grim Reaper was right around the corner, I wouldn't have paused."

"The Grim Reaper." He snorted. He pulled a watch from his pocket and glanced at it, then slipped it back into his cloak. "Again, I apologize for having startled you. If you are unhurt, madam, I shall leave you to your walking and pausing." And with that, he touched the brim of his hat and spurred his horse on, the two of them chewing up the road and kicking up a spray of mud and water as they banged on down the road.

Amelia was in complete disbelief. She looked down at the mud on her gown. And then, adding insult to considerable injury, it began to rain.

She was much closer to the school than Iddesleigh House, so she turned back toward the school.

A few minutes later she slipped into the foyer and immediately removed her dripping bonnet and coat. Mr. Roberts appeared from the classroom and gaped at her.

"Don't mind me, Mr. Roberts. I was very nearly run over by a rider on the road."

"*What?* Are you all right?"

"I'm fine. Just a bit muddy and wet. May I sit in your office until the rain clears?"

"Yes, of course. You should have some tea to warm you. Come, come," he said, gesturing her to follow him into the office.

He went to the small hearth in the room and removed a pot from it.

"Please don't bother, Mr. Roberts. You have your students."

"The girls are working on their slates. I'll just heat some water for tea."

"It's not necessary. As soon as the rain lets up, I'll be on my way."

He put the pot aside. He hurried to the only chair in the room and cleared it for her. "My apologies for the untidy state of this room. I'm a bit overwhelmed with the number of students. We've six more than we thought we'd have, and I'm afraid I've gotten a bit behind in the necessary paperwork."

They heard giggling from the classroom.

"There is quite a lot of paper," Amelia observed.

He sighed. "Letters of interest, mostly, parents wanting their daughters to attend. I mean to write them all down and take them to his lordship for disposition. But we can't possibly accommodate them without more space and more teachers. There are so many girls already."

"You're not allowed to do that, Tilly!" an unfamiliar voice shouted.

Mr. Roberts stuck his head out the office door. "Eyes on your slates, young ladies! I can see you all very clearly!" He turned back to Amelia. "I beg your pardon, but—"

"Perhaps I could be of service," Amelia blurted. What possessed her? It wasn't like her. But she did like the walk, and she liked the girls, and she liked Mr. Roberts. "I'm an excellent writer, and in more than one language. I could make the list."

Mr. Roberts looked confused. "But you're Lord Iddesleigh's guest."

"For the entire summer. And I've really nothing to occupy me. Please, Mr. Roberts. I should like to help if I can." She was surprised by how much she actually meant it.

"I'm telling Mr. Roberts!" a girl cried out.

Mr. Roberts suddenly lurched toward the desk. "I'm an old fool if I turn down any offer of help." He picked up the letters. "If you could just go through these and tally how many girls are seeking admittance, and from what villages, and their names, of course, I would be most obliged." He rummaged around and found paper, then a pencil.

"There we are. I have all that I need," Amelia assured him. "Go to your students, Mr. Roberts."

"Thank you, Miss Ivanosen. I am grateful." He left her and returned to the classroom. She could hear him gently admonishing a student who'd apparently gotten out of her seat.

Amelia settled into the chair and picked up the stack of letters. The first two were simple requests for information about the school One of them wrote that while his daughter had been educated, her studies had been limited to domestic tasks, and he'd heard that the Iddesleigh School for Girls was teaching sciences to their charges. He wanted his daughter to have the opportunity to understand science.

This surprised Amelia. She'd received the same education as boys—science, languages, arithmetic, astronomy.

Another letter followed that one, all in the same vein. But then she stumbled onto a letter that she had to read twice—first with confusion. Then, with delight and fascination.

The sender, an anonymous resident, wrote to complain about the noise at the school. Amelia couldn't help but laugh. It was indeed rather noisy. The tone of the letter reminded her very much of her Austrian grandmother who, until the time of her death, had never found anything to please her—everything was met with complaint. Her grandmother had been so contrary that Justine and Amelia used to amuse themselves by agreeing with everything the old woman said. *Je*, the servants were terrible. *Je*, the food was bland. *Je*, the troops marching by in formation were too loud.

Amazingly, it delighted their grandmother to be heard. "Do you see?" she'd say to her daughter, Amelia's mother, poking her in the arm. "They *are* too loud."

When Mr. Roberts popped in to check on her an hour or so later, Amelia had sorted the letters into piles. One was a stack of general correspondence. One was a stack of those requesting admittance with a neat list of names she'd made and left on top of the pile for him. As she fit her damp bonnet on her head, she said, "There is one more. It was a letter that arrived unsigned. It's a complaint, I'm sorry to say."

"Oh yes," he said, nodding. "We receive those with regularity." He pointed to a few letters stacked on a shelf behind her. "The author leaves them tacked to the door in the middle of the night."

"Tacked to the door?" What odd behavior. "Who is it?"

"I haven't the slightest idea."

Amelia was now even more convinced it was an old crone living nearby. She tied the ribbons of her bonnet under her chin. "Shall I come round tomorrow and help more?"

Mr. Roberts looked eager, but he said, "I couldn't possibly impose."

"It's not an imposition if I am volunteering. I could answer some of these letters if you like."

"*Would* you? I will shower you with gratitude, Miss Ivanosen. I appreciate very much your help. Thank you."

And she appreciated very much an occupation.

It was settled then.

CHAPTER FIVE

JOSHUA HAD A terrible habit of wandering the countryside late at night, following a moonlit path without any concern for his person. Why would he have any concern? Nothing ever happened here. He wouldn't have thought of his lack of concern at all had not his solicitor, Mr. Darren, been so appalled when Joshua mentioned it. He said a duke walking alone at night was particularly vulnerable to thieves and murderers.

Hollyfield was too remote to interest any bad actors. It would be the height of inconvenience to come all this way, rob a man of his purse, and then ride all the way back to proper civilization. Perhaps they would prefer the gold fixtures at Hollyfield, which were heavy, and would likewise require hauling to some black market. He was convinced that good thieves would think through the orchestration and save their dastardly deeds for another part of the country.

More was the pity because Joshua wouldn't mind an encounter with a thief or murderer. He could do with slamming his fist into a nose or two.

He was not so lucky to encounter a murderer or thief, but something interesting did happen during one of his moonlit strolls that week: he received a reply to one of his many anonymous letters written to the headmaster at the Iddesleigh School for Girls.

It was completely unexpected. He'd been tacking letters

to the door of the school for a month without a single reply. He'd left his latest missive two nights past, and tonight, when he'd brought a follow-up, he'd been astounded to find a letter addressed to "A Resident of Devonshire, Concerned."

It was an odd way to address it, but Joshua hadn't hesitated to take it. He suspected there were more Residents of Devonshire, Concerned, just like him, but he felt confident they were not leaving letters in the exact location he was. He replaced the response with his written follow-up, and then quickly stalked home, lit a candle, and prepared himself to read.

He expected admonishment for his complaints to the school. He expected to be lectured with facts and encouraged to have patience with children in general. His last letter had complained that the girls were being taught botany out of doors and, specifically, in Mr. Puddlestone's garden. It was very nearly a crime, as Mr. Puddlestone had won an award for his effort from the Devon Garden Council, a notoriously hard nut to crack. Joshua had written the headmaster that schoolbooks existed for this very reason, and he didn't think there was any reason they ought to be outside, making flower wreaths for their hair, for God's sake, at Mr. Puddlestone's expense.

He'd happened to be galloping by—another peculiar habit of his, riding hard when the demons chased him— and had spotted the girls picking flowers. He'd pulled up and turned back to have a better look. An older girl was instructing them on the fine art of twisting vines into wreaths, and then, as he watched, plucked blooms from Puddlestone's bush and wove them into the vines. It was an abomination.

Joshua recognized that his view of the world at this stage of his life was not shared by everyone, and therefore, he did not expect any sort of agreement. But wonder of won-

ders, the headmaster apparently agreed with his views...
although he seemed at a bit of a loss as to what to do about
it. Poor bastard was probably persecuted by parents into
allowing the girls to do as they pleased.

He read the letter again.

To A Resident of Devonshire, Concerned,

*We are in receipt of your last letter and have con-
cluded that you are absolutely right. One can only
imagine the disappointment of an author who has put
so much time into creating an instructional book on
botany only to see it discarded and the entire classroom sent outside to look at plants. Is that not the very
reason for books to exist, so that the subject may be
brought to the child and not the other way around?
Alas, during a recent rain the roof sprang a bit of a
leak and our very fine botany book was damaged. The
girls had to go out of doors to complete the lesson. You
wouldn't want them to fall behind in their lessons, I
should think. Unfortunately, as there are no gardens
at their current location—a fact we hope to remedy
one day—they were escorted a short distance to see a
very fine garden nearby, and at Mr. Puddlestone's gra-
cious invitation. The chaplets the girls made turned
out to be quite lovely. Mr. Puddlestone wore one for
tea along with the girls. One can only admire a man
who will wear a wreath of flowers on his bald head.*

*Perhaps this knowledge in some small part will
acquit the girls of their crime?*

Warmest of wishes,
The Iddesleigh School for Artistic Girls

Joshua stared at the letter. No, the girls were not acquitted of their crime. He happened to know that Mr. Puddlestone was very proud of his garden and surely had not intended the flowers to be wasted on such a frivolous endeavor. But as Mr. Puddlestone was a gentleman, he undoubtedly did not allow his true feelings to be known. Isn't that what gentlemen did? They subdued their true feelings and allowed the females in the world to have them all.

He read the letter a third time and dragged his fingers through his unruly hair.

Did the headmaster *really* agree with him? Or was this letter written tongue in cheek? He wasn't sure. On the one hand, his complaint might seem puerile to the casual reader. On the other hand, perhaps the headmaster was a long-suffering gentleman, too. Joshua thought of the letter he'd left tonight, this one complaining of more noise. He would wait and see the reply to that one.

It turned out that he could scarcely bear the wait.

Joshua pulled on his boots at half past one in the morning the following night and strode down the road to the school, another letter in hand. He had thought about it, had concluded that *if* the headmaster was mocking him, he would not be deterred. And if he truly did agree with Joshua's thoughts, then he ought to have them all.

When he entered the small yard of the school cottage, he could see the white vellum tacked to the door. Another one directed to "A Resident of Devonshire, Concerned". His heart began to skip ahead of his feet.

Another letter *agreeing* with him! Yes, they were too loud, the headmaster said. Yes, they were incorrigible, and surely heads hurt across the countryside from all the screeching!

But Joshua's satisfaction quickly turned to dismay. What

was he to do with this letter? He ought to be thinking of ways to *help* the headmaster instead of merely complaining.

He was going about this all wrong. But what was right?

He was seated at his desk, mulling it over one afternoon when Butler entered the room with a letter held out on a silver tray.

The dogs, who had been lazing around Joshua's feet, got up to give Butler a good sniff. Artemis remained curled on top of the estate ledger on Joshua's desk.

"What is that?" Joshua asked, hardly sparing it a glance.

"It has come from Iddesleigh House, Your Grace, delivered by the Earl of Iddesleigh himself. He asked if he might wait for your reply."

Joshua looked at his butler from the corner of his eye. "And you said?"

"I suggested that it would be more efficient to have a reply sent round to Iddesleigh."

"Good man, Butler. As to that, you may reply in the same way you have to the others."

"Would you not care to read it, Your Grace?"

"I don't need to."

"If I may, there is to be a ball—"

"*No*," Joshua stood from his chair. He was ravenously hungry. When was the last time he'd eaten properly?

"To introduce Her Royal Highness Princess Amelia of Wesloria," Butler stubbornly continued.

"*NO*," Joshua said again, a little more loudly. This was a new development, something else he'd be forced to monitor. A European princess had come to call on the Iddesleighs, and Joshua was a bit resentful about it. A fortnight ago, the whole valley had heralded her grand entrance, in a caravan of four coaches, no less. One to carry her esteemed self. One to carry her luggage, and one into which all her servants and minders had been stuffed. He'd passed the coaches laboring along the road that separated Hollyfield from Iddesleigh and would have mistaken it for a funeral cortege, had not the plumes on the coaches been pink. *Pink plumes*, of all things.

As if that weren't enough, he'd heard about her in the village. Mr. Darren had described in proud terms how the princess had come to their little corner of the world for the summer. He said she was a charming woman, with fine looks. Mr. Darren had been fortunate, he said, to have made her acquaintance when he'd called on the earl. He was looking forward, he said, to the ball Iddesleigh planned to host in her honor.

Joshua hadn't wanted to know about any charming woman with fine looks. He'd had no desire to know anyone, to do anything, and at that moment, he was having trouble even thinking about what he wanted to do. But what he didn't want was children and princesses so close to him. Moreover, he didn't know what to *do* about it.

CHAPTER SIX

A KITCHEN GIRL was dispatched to walk with Amelia and the girls to school one morning. The cook had made a batch of tea cakes that he deemed unsuitable for a proper tea, but apparently suitable for a dozen girls.

Miss Collins was a slight thing, around seventeen or eighteen years old. She curtsied twice to Amelia, and then a third time by way of apology when Mathilda informed her only once was required. "Aye, yes, milady," she said to Mathilda. With a curtsy.

Poor thing.

The girls skipped ahead, alternately racing or talking to each other at the same time. Amelia kindly tried to engage the young maid on the stroll. She asked if she'd heard about the ball. Miss Collins said that she had but offered no comment or asked a single question. Amelia asked how she found the work in the kitchens. She said it was good work. Did she do any of the cooking?

"I wash, Your Royal Highness. And I dry."

Well, that was not a topic Amelia knew anything about. So, she tried a different tack. She remarked that the day was fine, and the lane smooth despite recent rains, the trees thick…all to which Miss Collins very amicably agreed.

It was a bit like walking with a ghost.

On their return from the school, they passed under the arch that marked the entrance to the school property and stepped onto the road where Amelia had met the Grim Reaper. "Have a care when you walk here, Miss Collins," she said. "I've seen riders who could trample you."

"Yes, ma'am."

Amelia turned her head to sigh very quietly with the tedium of this stroll, and her gaze landed on the dark mansion on the hill. She'd assumed it was abandoned, which seemed odd, given how large it was. Bigger even than Iddesleigh House. But now she reconsidered. The stone was a dull gray, and even in some spots, entirely black. The windows had no shine to them and looked like gaping maws. There were at least a dozen chimneys, but Amelia had never seen more than one or two smoking.

"What is that house there? An asylum?"

The young woman looked up the hill. "No, Your Royal Highness, that would be Hollyfield. The Duke of Marley resides there. Sometimes."

It was a house. She sincerely hoped it had been more inviting at one time. What had happened to it? *Sometimes*, Miss Collins had said. Amelia mulled this over. Sometimes could mean really not at all. It was like Astasia Castle, one of the royal properties in Wesloria. It was high in the mountains and no one from the royal family ever went there except when there was trouble with the coal barons. Amelia couldn't remember the last time there had been trouble with the coal barons. Honestly, she wasn't sure if there were still coal barons anywhere near Astasia Castle. "Well that at least explains why it looks so deserted and bleak," she opined.

"Yes, ma'am, it's had that look since the tragedy."

Amelia instantly perked up—nothing like a good tragedy to liven things on an otherwise dull walk. Hopefully a lover's murder or a drunken duel, something with a good story behind it. "What tragedy?"

"The duke lost his wife and firstborn in childbirth. They say he never recovered from it. He left Hollyfield after that and I think comes only occasionally."

That was truly a dreadful tragedy, and unfortunately, all too common and heartbreaking. "How terribly sad."

"Yes, ma'am."

Now Amelia understood perfectly what was the matter with that house. It was obviously closed, but probably inhabited by a caretaker. The Grim Reaper must have come from there.

The thought sent a small shiver down her spine.

LILA WAS EXPECTED to return Saturday, and for the sake of everyone in the household, it would not be a moment too soon.

The ball would be held next Thursday, and there was much yet to be done, at least according to Blythe, who used every opportunity to complain to her husband.

Maren, Maisie, and Peg-leg Meg were playing at the far end of the room. Beck was pulling Birdie around the drawing room in a small wagon, and Mathilda was holding Alice and hovering near the bookcases, her eight-year-old ears practically pointed at her parents.

"Like what, darling? Tell me and I will see that it is done," Beck said confidently when Blythe again raised the onerous task of preparing for a ball.

"Like *what*?" Blythe repeated. Her laugh of surprise was abnormally high. "Really, darling do you not know? I went over the list at lunch today."

"Did you?" Beck paused in his stroll around the room

and glanced to the ceiling, as if trying to recall. "Papa, pull!" Birdie shouted at him.

"Yes. I did." Blythe said curtly. "Tell me, dearest, do I perhaps speak too softly?"

Beck laughed jovially. "Hardly so."

"Oh, I see. You think I'm a shrew."

"A *shrew?*"

"You clearly meant *something* by it."

"I meant…" Beck bent down and picked up Birdie. Alice began to bark, and Mathilda dropped him. He raced across the room to Beck and Birdie, and Birdie, favoring the dog, leaned so far forward to see the mutt that her father very nearly dropped her. "Nothing. I meant nothing, darling."

"In ten days, we are hosting a ball for three hundred guests in honor of a royal princess!" She pointed at Amelia in case there was any doubt about which royal princess. "Are you not the *least* bit concerned about preparations?"

"I'm not concerned—"

"Because you expect me to do it all!"

"Of course I don't!" Now Beck's voice was rising. "But you will recall that when I offered my opinion on the menu, you very curtly informed me that you had not asked for it, and I took that to mean my opinion was not wanted unless expressly summoned."

Blythe stared at him. "I asked you not to offer an opinion on the *menu*, Beck. Why would I need your opinion on the menu when I have Mr. Banbridge to do the cooking? But of course I desire your opinion on most other things!"

"Aha, see?" Beck said, pointing at her. "There it is. *Most* other things. How is a man to know which things?"

Amelia glanced at Mathilda. She was inching closer, enthralled by the argument unfurling between her parents.

Beck put Birdie on the floor and she instantly grabbed

Alice by the ear. "But if you want my opinion, it is that everything is proceeding along quite well."

Blythe gasped. "The house is not ready! How can you possibly think this house is ready?"

Amelia saw her opportunity to support Blythe and win back some of her good opinion. "You're absolutely right, madam," she chimed in.

Lord and Lady Iddesleigh, as well as Mathilda, looked at her with surprise.

"I don't mean to interfere, but I've attended a hundred balls if I've attended one, and I agree, there are things that ought to be done."

"Such as?" Blythe asked.

"Well…the scaffolding above the entrance should be removed. It's unsightly, and I know you would like to have an immaculate entrance."

No one spoke. Amelia didn't understand their silence—was she wrong? "It's a bit distracting…don't you agree?"

Blythe slowly turned to face Amelia. "Thank you for the suggestion, Your Royal Highness. However, I don't think one can simply *remove*—"

"You're quite right, Highness," Beck said, and picked up Birdie again and handed the tot to her mother, then stepped between his wife and Amelia. "Which is why we have determined our guests will enter from the terrace. But I will ask the builder what he thinks about your idea. In the meantime, Donovan will be arriving this afternoon—"

"*Donovan!* Thank God, Donovan is coming." Blythe's voice was filled with obvious relief. She placed Birdie into the wagon again.

"Pull, Mama!" Birdie commanded.

"Ask your father," Blythe said.

"You see?" Beck said, sounding also relieved as he

picked up the handle to the wagon. "Donovan will take care of everything, I've no doubt of it."

"Yes, we will be saved by Donovan once again," Blythe agreed.

Beck's smile faltered. "What do you mean by that?"

"Splendid!" Amelia said, before Blythe could answer. "Now that we've sorted it, I think I'll go for a walk. Tilly, would you like to join me?"

Mathilda looked like she would much rather stay and watch the argument take a new turn, as the couple clearly were not sorted at all. But she reached down and scooped Alice in her arms and came forward. Amelia put an arm around the girl's shoulders to lead her from the room. As they exited, she heard Blythe snap, "And will you please stop dragging that thing through the drawing room? Look what you've done to the carpet."

As the day was gray and cool, Amelia and Mathilda donned their cloaks. Mathilda set Alice down when they walked outside, and the little dog scurried down the terrace steps and onto the lawn.

"Shall we walk to the river?" Amelia asked.

"I wish we could go fishing," Mathilda said. "Mr. Roberts said he will take us one day. He said that one should always have the skills necessary to procure one's own food. Do you procure your own food?" Mathilda asked, looking up at her.

"Absolutely. I ask a maid for it every day."

Mathilda giggled.

They walked across the lawn and entered the woods. Alice scampered ahead, his undercarriage turning a muddy brown. Mathilda chattered on about the terrible, horrible thing Ann Simpson had said, and how it had hurt Mary Carlisle's feelings, and *something-something-something*.

Amelia was only half listening, as the tale was meandering along.

They emerged on a wooded bridle path that ran between Iddesleigh and Hollyfield. Mathilda's steady stream of chatter was interrupted only once or twice by something she saw that demanded to be pointed out, such as a red bird, and a clump of mushrooms, which, in fairness, they both wanted to examine.

They came to the intersection of their trail and a footpath to Hollyfield mansion. Amelia paused at the proverbial fork in the road and wished that the choices were a bit more exciting. "Shall we have a look at Hollyfield?"

"I've already seen it," Mathilda said.

"Have you?"

"Yes! You can see it on the walk to school. And when you walk home, too."

"Have you been as close as this?"

Mathilda shook her head. She squinted at the monolith on the hill. "It looks scary."

"Think of it as an exploration. What did Mr. Roberts say about exploration?"

"That the greatest wonders of the world were only discovered because people ventured out their doors to explore."

"Shall we look?" Amelia asked. Mathilda nodded. Amelia called for Alice, and the three of them set off for Hollyfield.

At the top of the hill, a stone wall separated the house from the path. The structure rose up like a mountain behind it. The dark windows made it look as if the house was glaring down at them.

"Do you think ghosts are in there?" Mathilda whispered.

"I'd be terribly disappointed if they weren't," Amelia

whispered back. Just then, they saw someone pass by a window on an upper floor. They both gasped and grabbed each other's arm.

"Was that a *ghost?*" Mathilda whispered loudly.

Amelia was too practical to believe in ghosts. "I think it was the caretaker," she said reasonably, and Mathilda visibly relaxed.

They walked on, reaching a wrought iron gate in the middle of the stone wall. Alice had spotted it and raced ahead to have a look inside, his head fitting neatly through the bars. Amelia and Mathilda stepped up behind Alice to have a look, but when they did, a dog suddenly lunged at them from the other side of the gate, barking ferociously. Alice turned and hightailed it down another path to the river, yapping the entire way. Amelia and Mathilda squealed with shock; she grabbed the girl's hand and together they ran after Alice, into the woods, down a steep decline to the river path.

They were panting when they reached it. Amelia pressed a hand to her chest to keep her heart inside her body.

"Where is Alice?" Mathilda asked in a panic.

Amelia was certain the dog was lost, certain the caretaker was coming, certain they'd have to jump in the river to escape and probably drown, and no one would find their bodies for days, and when they did, her mother would say to Justine, "I *told* you so."

But... Alice came trotting back to them, his snout to the ground. The bigger dog had not chased after them and, in fact, Amelia could just see the top half of the gate from this vantage point, and in that top half was an upright, wagging tail.

"That *scared* me," Mathilda said.

"Me too," Amelia agreed. She turned around, thinking

they would carry along beside the river—but just up the path was a man.

Amelia gasped and grabbed Mathilda, putting a protective arm across her.

He was standing twenty feet from them, his legs braced so far apart that it would be impossible to pass him. He was in his shirtsleeves, which he'd rolled up to reveal thick forearms. The shirt was tucked tightly into tighter trousers. His hat was pulled low over his brow; his beard hid his expression. And he was holding a catch of fish on a pole balanced on his shoulder.

"Name yourself!" Amelia demanded.

"What are you doing here?" he said gruffly in return.

"I could ask the same of you, sir." Amelia pushed Mathilda behind her with the noble thought that if she was going to have to fight, she didn't want Mathilda to be harmed. Alice had no fear, however, and trotted forward to have a sniff of him. "Alice! Come!"

Alice did not come. The man looked down at the dog.

"Come here at once, Alice," Amelia demanded.

"You're not to be on this path. *No* one is to be on this path. This is the property of Hollyfield. Whistle."

"Whistle? And who, pray tell, is that?"

"I mean, whistle for the dog."

So many thoughts flew through Amelia's head that she couldn't quickly form an answer. How dare he presume to tell her to whistle? Who was he, why was he angry that they were here, and was it *really* the property of Hollyfield? She looked around them all, then at him. "Are you certain?"

"Dogs generally will respond to a high-pitched noise such as a whistle, so yes, I am certain."

"Not that. Are you certain this is the property of Hollyfield?"

"Am I…" His voice trailed off. He seemed stunned. "*Quite*," he said stiffly.

Alice trotted away from his inspection of the man and began to make his way back to Amelia.

"Then we beg your pardon," Amelia said.

The man gave her a curt nod.

"But it appears to be a public path," she protested.

He stilled. His gaze pierced hers, and she realized, now that she was looking at his beard and the way he simply stared, that this was the same man who had nearly run her over. *The caretaker?*

"In spite of what it may appear to you, madam, it is not public. It is most assuredly private property."

"Really? But it's outside Hollyfield walls. It would stand to reason that a path beside a river is open to anyone who might need it. Just as you've needed it to fish. I can't imagine it belongs to anyone."

He was staring at her as if he couldn't understand her, and for a moment, she wondered if she might have spoken in Weslorian without realizing it. But no, she'd spoken perfect English.

"Are you an expert in the laws of property?"

Amelia actually chuckled. "It's a theory, and I think a reasonable one. I do think perhaps you should make sure of it before you proclaim it's so."

His head tilted to one side. Then he shifted his weight to one hip. "I don't have the time or inclination to explain why your *theory* is wrong. Or the intricacies of ownership, about which I am quite well versed. Now, if you please, remove yourself from this property." With his string of fish, he gestured at the path they'd just come down.

He wanted them to retrace their steps. That would put him behind them, where Amelia couldn't see him. That didn't seem prudent. She looked down at Mathilda, who had inched out from behind Amelia to stare at the man with a frown on her face. He would have the element of surprise. Would he attempt to kidnap them? She certainly wouldn't be the first princess to be kidnapped. But then again, he didn't seem to know who she was. And surely he'd not want the trouble of kidnapping a young girl. "What do you think?" she asked Mathilda.

"I want to go home."

"Then by all means. Go home. *Now*," the man growled, and gestured to the path again with all his fish.

This was precisely the sort of thing that Justine had warned her about. "You're too impetuous, Amelia," she'd said once. But it was a fact that Amelia did not like to be told what to do, which, she supposed, was born of a lifetime of being a royal princess where people were not allowed to tell her what to do. And yet somehow, there was always someone telling her what she could or could not do. Whatever, she had a regrettable tendency to be aggravated when someone ordered her about. And perhaps a bit impetuous.

"*You* go."

"What?"

"*You* go up the path. We'll go our own way."

"What is the matter with you?" the man demanded.

"Why? What did I say?"

Mathilda grabbed the back of her dress and tried to pull Amelia up the path with her. "I can see by the look on your face that you are displeased, and I intend no offense," Amelia said to the man. "But we mean only to walk. Surely you won't deny us that small pleasure. Rest assured we will leave this sacred land of yours intact and find a public path, but in the meantime, I'm afraid I cannot give you leave to command us."

"What the devil?" he muttered. And then he sighed. "Fine." He took a sudden step forward, and while Amelia wouldn't say it was particularly menacing, she caught Mathilda's hand, and turned, running in the opposite direction, away from him, up the river path. "Alice! Alice, come!" she called over her shoulder.

When they'd gone a dozen feet or so, she turned back to see Alice trotting after them without urgency. The man had disappeared again, presumably up the path to the house.

She pressed her fingertips to her cheeks.

"Who was he?" Mathilda asked.

"That, my dear, was the Grim Reaper in the flesh."

Mathilda gasped.

Amelia looked at the route that went up to the house. "Shall we go and see?"

Mathilda's eyes widened even more. "*Yes*," she whispered.

So it was that they did retrace their steps, back up the incline to the footpath outside Hollyfield's walls.

Amelia reasoned they had nothing to fear. He wasn't a ghost or a soul snatcher, but an inconceivably rude caretaker who had told her she could not be on what she was almost certain was a public path.

She would bring this to Beck's attention and see to it that it was *made* a public path.

Also, wasn't it good manners to address strangers with deference? How could he be certain she wasn't a princess?

They returned to the gate. This time, they grabbed onto the bars and pressed closer to see inside. Alas, there was nothing to see but a mess of an overgrown garden. "Not only is he a menace, but he's a horrible caretaker, isn't he?"

"It looks very bad," Mathilda agreed. Amelia craned her

neck to try and see something of interest. There was nothing. "Oh well. Shall we?" She reached for Mathilda's hand.

They turned back to Iddesleigh House, Alice scampering ahead.

At least she had something interesting to write to Justine.

JUST INSIDE THE WALLS, Joshua stood with his back to the wall. Merlin, who had been patiently waiting for his master to return, was at attention, his gaze fixed on the fish. In other words, he was useless to Joshua, oblivious to the troubles at the gate, guarding absolutely nothing but the fish he wanted.

Joshua cocked his head, listening as the woman and her daughter moved away. He wasn't entirely sure what had kept them from inviting themselves in under some misbegotten "theory" that the house was public property, too. And neither was he entirely clear as to why he was hiding.

Who *was* she? A nursemaid? A farm woman? Where had they come from? She looked vaguely familiar to him. Was she the farm woman who had so stupidly been standing in the road a few days ago? That would certainly explain things. He would ask Butler if he knew of a mad woman who wandered around the countryside with no discernible destination, and…

And dear God, that described him.

Except that Joshua was *not* mad. He was…disgruntled. Disappointed? Unbearable, that's what he was. He didn't need anyone to tell him that he'd become unpleasant. Hell, he could hardly abide his own company.

But he was *not* mad.

CHAPTER SEVEN

LILA HAD NEVER seen Lady Iddesleigh with a disposition other than cheerful until today. When last they'd met, the lady had been smiling and happy to have such an esteemed guest as the princess and had urged Lila to take her time in London.

Today, she looked harried. She had faint new lines that creased her brow.

Over tea, they reviewed the plans for the ball. The guest list was very long—Lila was employing a different approach for Princess Amelia than what she'd employed for her sister. Justine despised large crowds. Amelia thrived in them.

Blythe was clearly distracted. At one point, she stood up and went to the window and gestured for Lila to join her.

Below, on the lawn, Princess Amelia held Birdie on her hip, and with her free hand, she was directing Maisie and Maren to stand back to back. As Lila watched with fascination, the two girls began to walk away from each other, taking ten large steps at the princess's count before whirling around and pointing fingers at each other, making *pew* sounds, and then both falling down.

They were playing at a duel. A *duel*.

She glanced at Blythe from the corner of her eye. Blythe was staring at her daughters. "A lovely afternoon to be out in the sun," Lila tried.

Blythe drew a slow breath, the sort one draws when having something dire to impart. Lila guessed it was along the lines of how she didn't think it appropriate that young girls be taught how to duel. "There are some things I think you should know," Blythe said gravely.

Lila had an inkling of what she was about to hear—she knew that Amelia presented as a bit too queenly at times. But she also understood that Amelia had a queen for a mother *and* a sister and was a royal princess herself. Sometimes commands rolled off the tongue a bit more freely than they ought. Moreover, Amelia had the delightful tendency to speak freely, sometimes without seeming to comprehend how her words would be received by others.

Blythe turned from the window to face her. "Lila... I would never say a word against our revered guest."

"I know you wouldn't."

"But she is prone to interfering."

"Oh?" Lila made herself sound light and unconcerned, but sincerely hoped the princess hadn't done something to get her sent home on the next train. *Please, God, don't let it be a footman.*

"She's wonderful to the girls. *Wonderful*. But she..." Blythe sighed wearily. "One afternoon, I happened upon her and my decorator. She had suggested different wallpaper than I had selected, and my decorator was considering it."

"Oh dear," Lila murmured. She sincerely hoped that was the worst of it.

"Suggestions that were not to my tastes," Blythe added.

"Unforgiveable."

"She does not endear herself to others, Lila. Just yesterday afternoon, at tea, before you arrived, she suggested to my husband and me that in her considered opinion, we ought to let Maisie wear trousers if she likes and insisted there was no harm in it."

Lila winced. "Ah. Well, you know how these princesses can be."

"Yes, Lila, you've said that they are raised to believe that everyone wants their opinion. You also said you had spoken to her."

"I did, Blythe. And I will speak to her again."

Blythe took Lila by the elbow and pulled her away from the window. "She is our honored guest, and naturally we are pleased to help you in your cause, you know that, but my husband and I have discussed it..." She paused.

Oh no. They'd discussed it. *Never* a good sign.

"We've discussed it and we are in complete agreement that she seems restless. She went riding two days past and convinced one of the grooms to accompany her, and without her guards! They were gone for more than two hours! I don't have to tell you how that might appear to some."

"No indeed." God above, Lila desperately hoped that the tales of what had happened in Wesloria had not reached Devonshire...yet. She had to intercept and block a chess move she felt was imminent. "You're absolutely right, she seems restless, and the sooner she settles on a match, the sooner she will have the thing she needs to occupy her time and thoughts. We are so close, Blythe."

"Yes. But until that happiest of days, my husband and I had an idea."

Lila braced herself for the worst of ideas to come tumbling forth.

"We don't want to insult her, of course."

"Of course." Lila's sense of impending doom was growing by the second.

"She does seem to care so much for the children."

"Adores them."

"Do you think she might enjoy some time spent in Bibury with Beck's sister?"

No, no, no, Lila couldn't let that happen. "You want to send her to…where, again?"

"Bibury."

"Oh dear, that seems awfully far away, Blythe. May I suggest an alternative?"

"I don't know, Lila. It's just that—"

"Her Royal Highness will be receiving some callers this week. And the ball is next week. Afterward, there will be people to meet, and gentlemen will call to court her. I suspect she will be too engaged to offer any more advice here. But that's not all—Her Royal Highness informed me that she has helped the headmaster of your school with some correspondence recently."

Blythe's frown deepened. "Once or twice, I think, but—"

"But what if she was to offer her help on a more consistent basis? Perhaps every day when she is not otherwise engaged?"

The expression on Blythe's face was dubious. She went back to her seat and picked up her teacup. "I don't mean to sound inhospitable," she said.

"And you don't," Lila hastened to assure her. "Blythe…" She resumed her seat and leaned forward. "Princess Amelia means well. What she needs is a bit of experience on her own, to learn who she is. She's been rather sheltered, as you can imagine. This may well be the first time that she has been out in the world all by herself."

Lila had said the same thing to Queen Justine—Princess Amelia had never had a true purpose, had never had to rely on herself. And she sorely needed a *purpose*. "You remember your first time to London, don't you?"

"I was never on my own," Blythe said. "I went from my father's house to my husband's house."

"Exactly. She may be a princess, but she is still a young woman and she is on her own here."

Blythe sighed.

"I will impress on her again the need to keep her thoughts to herself."

Blythe glanced at her from the corner of her eye. "Do you think she'll be insulted?"

"Of course not." Lila spoke with far more confidence than she felt. "Would you like to see the list of names I have for her? I was thinking a picnic this week, as some are local."

Blythe's eyes fell to the leather-bound journal Lila had set at the edge of the table. "Who?"

Lila picked up the journal and opened it. "Are you acquainted with Mr. Charles Highsmith?"

Blythe's countenance instantly changed. "Rich as Croesus!" she exclaimed. "I understand his father has invested in the steel industry in America. Who else?"

Lila proceeded to review the entire list with Blythe, confident she had headed off a disaster for the time being.

Lordonna told Lila that the princess liked to walk in the afternoons.

"To where?" Lila asked.

"Nowhere in particular, milady. I think she just ambles."

Ambled, did she?

Lila was waiting for Amelia when she came down, dressed in a drab brown dress and a short gray cloak. Her hair was tightly wound into a bun at her nape. She looked like a kitchen girl on her way to market.

"Lila?" The princess took in Lila's walking garb.

"Care for company? I thought I'd walk with you today. I got in so late last night that I haven't had a chance to fill you in on your prospective matches."

Princess Amelia looked at Lila's boots. Lila slid one forward so she could have a better look. Lila enjoyed a good long walk, and when at home in Denmark walked several miles every day. "I think a walk is important for one's constitution. My husband, Valentin, says I would walk all the way around the earth if I had the time."

The princess nodded approvingly. "I'd never been at liberty to walk as far and in any direction I please until I came here. I like it very much, fortunately, as there is so little else to do here." She gave Lila a look as if Lila had intentionally made Devonshire unexciting.

"Are we out for a leisurely stroll?" Lila asked as they began to walk. "Or do you have a destination in mind?"

"No destination, really. Although I am curious how far and wide the Grim Reaper rides on any given day. I follow different paths just to see if I will encounter him."

"I beg your pardon?"

"I am speaking of the man who very nearly killed me."

Lila gasped—no one had mentioned anything to her.

"No need to gasp like that," the princess said. "He didn't *really* very nearly kill me, but he *could* have, and that's the point. He rides like the devil is chasing him and is inconsiderate of anyone on the road. Or even walking along the river path."

What was she talking about?

"I've worked it all out," the princess said as they reached the road. "He's a caretaker or something at Hollyfield."

"Hollyfield?" This conversation was so confusing!

"Mmm. It's a deserted mansion very near Iddesleigh. A terrible shame, if you ask me, for it looks as if it might have once been very grand. I think the Grim Reaper is a caretaker of some sort there."

Lila's confusion only deepened. "Hollyfield is deserted? But Beck said he'd been sending invitations to Marley there."

The princess looked surprised. "What are you talking about?"

"The Duke of Marley resides at Hollyfield."

The princess stopped walking altogether. "Pardon? Do you *know* him? Are you acquainted?"

"Yes—I arranged his marriage several years ago."

Princess Amelia's mouth gaped with surprise. "But… but he's on the Continent. Or perhaps in America. I can't recall what Miss Collins said, only that he deserted the house after a terrible tragedy. Did you know there'd been a tragedy? He lost his wife and baby. Isn't it awful? Anyway, I'm certain this man is the caretaker. He wears all black and rides a black horse as big as any I've ever seen. And he catches his own fish." She smiled a little and glanced away. "Imagine, catching your own fish. I think I should like to try it sometime." She began to walk again.

Lila was trying to make sense of this. "He's all in black, you say? Perhaps you are seeing a member of the clergy."

The princess snorted. "He is no clergyman, I can assure you. Far too dark and dangerous."

They'd come to the point in the road where Hollyfield was clearly visible. Lila peered at it. She was certain Marley was residing here this summer. But what the devil was the princess talking about, this mysterious dark reaper? "How long have you…" She paused, wondering how best to ask her question.

"Been strolling these roads and footpaths in search of the Grim Reaper? A few days. Because there is simply nothing else for me to do, Lila. I help with the school for an hour or so in the morning. Lord and Lady Iddesleigh are very kind, but… I think not pleased with my presence, and Blythe seems against any sort of help at all. Honestly, it's hardly any different here than it is at Rohalan Palace, other than I am free to walk where I please."

"I think you will feel differently about Iddesleigh after the ball. And Lady Iddesleigh, well…we talked about this, remember? Some ladies of the house do not take kindly to suggestions, no matter how useful they may be."

"I think my suggestions are very useful," the princess said without even a smidge of awareness.

"I'm certain they are. But, as a guest in her home, I suppose we must abide—"

"*Je*, I know. I *know*. No one ever wants my help in anything. I tried to help Justine with a problem she was having with one of her ladies-in-waiting. I think honesty is always best, don't you? But one would think I'd taken the woman out to the courtyard and shot at her, the way she carried on to Justine about me." She clucked her tongue.

"Perhaps your time would be better spent if you had something more to occupy you."

The princess rolled her eyes. "That is what I have said repeatedly, Lila. Perhaps you ought to make notes of our conversations so you don't forget what I've said."

"I will endeavor to be more diligent in remembering."

"All right, then, what have you in mind?"

"You've been so kind to offer the headmaster at the girls' school your assistance. I understand he is bit overwhelmed with the instruction, and two new students will join his classroom next week."

"Mr. Roberts is a bit overwhelmed by everything. Every morning when I walk the girls to school, he is looking for his eyeglasses, or the school bell, or the botany book."

"Perhaps you might offer even more to Mr. Roberts than you have so generously done."

Princess Amelia stared at her. "You mean to *teach* them?" She laughed. "I haven't the slightest idea how to teach them a thing! Unless it was dancing. Oh! I could teach them dancing—"

"I was thinking something more useful to Mr. Roberts."

"In what way?"

"The correspondence and paperwork are piling up. Beck tells me there are applications for students, the business of the parish, bills of lading, and so forth. I think any number of issues come up that he hasn't the least amount of time to address. He needs someone who is clever and quick. I thought perhaps you might be amenable to spending an hour or two every day helping him. That is, until you are occupied with matters of your own."

The princess looked at her curiously. "I don't think my mother will allow you to turn me into a secretary, Lila. She's very particular about how princesses are to behave and what they are to do."

"I wouldn't dream of turning you into a secretary."

"I do like Mr. Roberts very much. I like all the girls, too, although *Lord*, they are so very loud. And you're right, I have little else to do but annoy Blythe, it would seem. To think she has all that house and all those children and cannot appreciate the help I so desperately want to offer."

"To think," Lila agreed. "Now. Would you care to hear about a picnic that is being planned as we speak?"

"That depends. Will there be anyone present under the age of sixty years?"

"Only some very fine gentlemen," Lila said pertly.

Princess Amelia looped her arm through Lila's. "Tell me everything."

To the Headmaster of the Iddesleigh School for Unruly Girls, Who Seems to have Lost his Command of the Classroom,

Sir, once again a perfectly fine afternoon has been abused by the sound of young girls singing quite off-key and far too loudly. It is beyond my comprehension to understand why it is imperative to conduct these singing lessons out of doors. Why are singing lessons necessary at all? Children should be taught singing in church and by way of hymns. Or, in the privacy of their homes under the tutelage of a true musician. Or, at the very least, in the privacy of their own homes so that only their parents are subjected to what can only be described as caterwauling. But as you have disregarded your own four walls and roof to contain what sounds like funeral dirges for seagulls, I respectfully request that such lessons be limited to certain days or hours so that one may plan accordingly.

One cannot help but wonder whatever happened to the wise counsel that children should be seen and not heard? That is the basis for any church service or public event and should be adhered to at your school.

Sincerely,
A Concerned Resident of Devonshire

—

To A Resident of Devonshire, Concerned,

*Funeral dirges for seagulls is an apt description for
our girls and has brought us a hearty chuckle. We
can forgive their awful lack of talent (it is abundantly
clear that there is not a gifted soprano among them)
for they come to the music lessons with such great
enthusiasm and joy. Even the coldest of hearts would
be touched by the look of determination on their an-
gelic faces as they try and make their way through a
song. I suppose we may all count our blessings that
we haven't enough pianos to teach them all to play.
We do beg your forgiveness for the outdoor lesson,
but on that particular day, one of the girls snuck a
kitten into the classroom (for the second time), and
the poor thing was so startled by the idea that fourteen girls wanted to hold her that she clawed her
way free of at least half of them and hid. It became
necessary to clear the classroom so the poor creature could be found. If you are in need of a barn cat,
please do advise.*

*It is our belief that children should be seen and not
heard when appropriate, such as at a church service
as you so wisely point out, or a public event. But we
do pride ourselves on teaching these girls the confidence to voice their thoughts, which will be necessary for their success as adults. We encourage a free
flow of ideas so these girls will learn to speak for
themselves. Wouldn't you agree that it shouldn't be
only boys who are encouraged to be thinkers? However, please do trust we only encourage them to think*

freely when it is appropriate. And never *at church, for heaven's sake. That would be an abomination.*

Yours kindly,
The Iddesleigh School for Musical Girls

CHAPTER EIGHT

Joshua was down to his shirtsleeves, chopping wood. The damp fabric stuck to his back, and he had to pause every so often to wipe his brow. He imagined he looked like a drunk. Probably smelled like one, too, as nothing quenched his thirst quite like an ale when he was at hard work. He *liked* hard work. The harder the labor, the better. He liked the reverberation in his body when he struck a lethal blow with his axe. He liked the pain of the blisters on his palms.

One might wonder why a man who had stumbled into the privilege of being a duke would enjoy hard labor and pain. He had no answer for it.

Stumbling into things was the way life presented itself, he mused. There was Butler, who had stumbled into his profession by way of his name. And here he stood, a duke, who shouldn't have been a duke at all, or a viscount before he'd been a duke. Also unexpected.

It had all happened so suddenly. He was the youngest son of an earl, with no idea he would inherit the viscountcy. But then his older brother had died suddenly when Joshua was fourteen, his father two years after that. He'd inherited the title and the Parker estate. He hadn't known what to do with it, unprepared as he was. But with the help of his mother, he'd managed.

And then, when he was four and twenty, his cousin the duke, hale and hearty, was killed in a hunting accident. His

cousin had not had time to produce issue. His title would
have passed to his living male relative, his uncle, Joshua's
father. But he was gone, as was the duke's eldest son. Joshua
had been the only surviving male heir.

Just like that, he was the Duke of Marley. The very last
thing Joshua would have ever expected. Or wanted, truth-
fully. Unfortunately, by then, it was too late to be a good
duke. He'd already laid waste to his reputation.

All that to say that he liked hard labor, because the more
he pounded out the inconsistencies and disappointments in
his life, the better he felt.

He was thinking of the latest exchange of letters with
the headmaster at the school. He was not quite sure if the
headmaster actually agreed with him or was perhaps hu-
moring him. Either way, he couldn't help but admire the
gentleman for it.

He'd decided, as he'd chopped away at this wood, that
perhaps he would test the headmaster's sincerity. Instead of
registering a complaint, he would put a philosophical question to him. He'd sensed a bit of defensiveness when it came
to his complaints about the girls, and honestly, he could
hardly blame the headmaster. Joshua recognized that the
things he wrote bordered on ridiculous, and thereby proved
to himself again that he wasn't actually mad. Of course he
knew that children would sing off tune or laugh loudly or
put flower wreaths on Puddlestone's head. It wasn't the least
bit fair that he took out his aggravation on the headmaster.

Nevertheless, it was rather convenient, what with all
the anonymity in his approach. It was his cross to bear, as
well as the fact that he couldn't abide the sound of happy
children because—

"Joshua."

Joshua jumped in his skin what felt like a good foot off

the ground. His dogs, snoozing in the sun, leaped to their feet when they heard the male voice and began to bark, and Joshua, midswing, very nearly chopped off a toe. He whirled around.

Miles Smythe, the tall, fit, and very blond Earl of Clarendon, strolled down the path toward him. It was a wonder to Joshua that he looked exactly as he had when they were young lads, but he did. Miles had been his closest friend all his life. Closer than his own brother had been.

Joshua tossed down his axe. "Bethan! Merlin! Heel!" he shouted at the two hounds. Bethan immediately slid down onto his belly, apparently relieved he didn't have to exert himself in the heat of the day. But Merlin trotted forward, tail wagging, to greet a man he knew well. Miles was a friend to all dogs and smiled with delight as he went down on one knee to scratch Merlin behind the ears. That, of course, prompted Bethan to get up and trot forward, too.

Miles was generally agreeable in all things, and happily accepted the lap of their tongues and their exploring noses before rising to his full height. With hands on hips, he surveyed the scene. "Expecting an exceptionally hard winter? Building an ark?"

Joshua glanced around, too. There was indeed quite a lot of wood stacked and scattered about—he hadn't realized how much he'd chopped. "I honestly don't know."

"I never knew you to be inclined to hard labor."

Miles knew him as someone who'd always been inclined to drinking and women and cards with a few horse races thrown in. "The country air has inspired me. I like the work."

Miles smiled. "Far be it from me to fault a man in pursuing his passions."

Joshua wouldn't call it a passion. More like…a need.

"Ale?" Joshua gestured to the pitcher that Butler had brought earlier.

"I would prefer a whisky."

Joshua hesitated. Whisky was in the house. And the house was not...ready for visitors.

"I came through it," Miles said. He'd always had a knack of knowing what Joshua was thinking.

Joshua had been back at Hollyfield for a month, but he hadn't exactly opened his house to habitation. "It's just me, and the place is so large," he muttered.

"I understand," Miles said cheerfully. "But I do think you could do with a few more staff. And perhaps a chimney sweep. I think something might have died in one."

Joshua winced. The house looked as if it had been abandoned to the elements. Rooms unopened, furniture still draped in dust covers. Cold hearths, a layer of grime everywhere, and yes, he, too, suspected an animal had died in one of the chimneys. There was only so much a housekeeper with a lone chambermaid could do in a house as large as his.

Joshua looked up at the house. "I intend to sell it."

"Sell what?"

"Hollyfield."

Miles's mouth gaped with surprise. "But...what of the entail?"

He was speaking, of course, of the provisions contained in the duke's will, the same provision handed down for generations, that in the event an heir is born, the estate must be maintained for the heir's heir. There were a lot of ins and outs to it, but it restricted the current duke's access to draining the estate of funds. "I have no heirs."

Miles squinted at his old friend. "And where will you go? To your mother?"

Joshua snorted. "No." But to where? He hadn't thought that far ahead. "London. Paris. New York. I don't know."

"Mmm. That doesn't sound like the Joshua Parker I've known all my life."

It didn't to Joshua, either. He and Miles used to run together. They were young bucks, attending every assembly, every country house party. They pursued drink and women alike. But then Joshua had married, and Miles had become a responsible earl, and the men they were now were not the men they'd been then. Miles had gotten better. Joshua had...not.

"Let's go in," Miles said. "Butler will have made a room presentable by now."

"Why? What are you doing here?"

Miles smiled. "What is anyone doing in Devonshire? The ball, lad."

"What ball?"

"*What ball*," Miles scoffed. "By the look of you, I'd believe you'd been living in a cave. But I know Becket Hawke, and I know that everyone within a twenty-five-mile radius and beyond has been informed of the ball for the comely, rich Weslorian princess who is in need of a husband.

That must have been the last invitation Joshua had received from Iddesleigh. The one he'd tossed aside, unopened.

"When is it?"

"Next week."

Joshua signaled his dogs. They trotted ahead of him and Miles as they began to make their way to the house. "You're a guest of Iddesleigh?" Joshua asked.

Miles laughed. "God, no. I am a guest of Marley."

Joshua felt a slight swell of panic. "Miles...we are not equipped for guests."

"The hell you aren't. You have a massive house with sixteen guest rooms if there is one. You have at least a few staff, and I know that Butler can round up more if necessary. Just because you're living in misery doesn't mean the rest of the world must live that way. Besides, you're going with me."

Joshua snorted. "I'm not."

"You are."

"I'm in no mood for frivolity and princesses and whatever else."

"What else is society. People other than princesses. Old friends, new friends. Gaming. Wine and cakes. And you may begin to remove the shackles of your hermit life with a picnic this very afternoon. There's just enough time to see you bathed and properly turned out for it. Unfortunately, I don't think there is enough time to see that beard groomed and trimmed. But the rest of you, at least."

Joshua glared at him. "Have you lost your mind? I haven't been to a bloody picnic since I was a lad."

Miles laughed. "Neither have I, but I'm not opposed. The weather is fine. The company may be finer. I have it on good authority that Lord Wexham will be in attendance today."

Joshua's heart bumped into his ribs at the mention of that name. *Sarah.* Lady Wexham now. The woman he'd been desperately in love with before he'd married Diana. The woman who had refused him because of his poor reputation and lack of a title. The woman who had broken his heart, which had plagued him right into a marriage with Diana.

And then, in a stroke of fate, he'd become a duke. Sarah and her parents wouldn't think twice about his reputation now.

"Why is Wexham here? Is life not grand enough in Dorset?"

"Oh, I suppose it is. But his younger brother needs a wife with a sizable fortune and a princess bride would solve his problems."

Joshua shook his head. "I don't want to go. I've no desire to see grown men fawn over a woman in pursuit of her fortune."

"Then don't look. I've already told your valet that you're going and to prepare a bath. I tell you, I saw a bit of a spark in Mr. Martin's rheumy eye."

"Miles—"

"*Joshua*, my old friend." Miles stopped walking. He slung his arm around Joshua's shoulders and smashed him into his side, locking him there. "It's been two years since you lost Diana and the baby. You're young yet, but you won't always be. You can't mourn the rest of your life."

That's what Miles didn't understand. Joshua wasn't mourning—he was punishing himself. But he knew Miles well enough to know he would not accept no for an answer. "You may drag me along to your foolishness, but I will not be good company, and for that, you'll be sorry."

Miles dropped his arm from Joshua as they reached the terrace. "You were never particularly good company, so I'm fully prepared."

Bloody hell. "You may think you have won the day, sir, but I never replied to the invitation to the bloody ball."

Miles laughed. "Then it's a good thing I did it for you."

CHAPTER NINE

FINALLY. AFTER MORE than a fortnight of biding her time, of receiving only doddering neighbors, of writing letters to an amusing old crone, of walking miles and miles all through the countryside, *finally,* something interesting was to happen.

A picnic wasn't exactly what Amelia had hoped for, but it was a start. She would have liked something a bit grander—an assembly, a *soirée musicale.* Not a picnic.

At least there would be younger people and a few gentlemen, Lila had promised. Amelia missed having scores of gentlemen around her. That was the best part of being a princess—she was never at a loss for male attention.

The girls were in her rooms, trying on her gloves and shawls. Amelia had invited them in—she thought it important to teach them the lesson of looking one's best on such occasions as this. "A princess should always look like a princess," she'd said.

"Will you wear a crown?" asked Maisie.

"Or carry a stick?" Mathilda asked.

"I think you mean a scepter, and no. The crown and scepter are carried by the sovereign. As a princess, I will carry only myself, but in a regal manner, of course."

"I want to carry one," Peg-leg Meg said. "I want a ree manner."

"Me too!" Maisie shouted.

"All right. Here's what you do—everyone find something to balance on top of your head."

The girls looked at each other—Mathilda pounced on a discarded shoe. Maren and Maisie found a glove and a hat, respectively. Peg-leg Meg began to wail, so Mathilda plopped a small needlepoint frame on her head and watched it slide down over her eyes.

"Watch me," Amelia said. She lifted her chin. Held out on arm like a dancer, and with the other hand, she daintily lifted the hem of her skirt. She slid one foot along the floor, then the next. "Don't let it fall from you head," she instructed, then turned around to adjust the four of them as they made their way slowly around her salon, their regal manners perched on their heads, following after her like little ducklings. "There, you see? Now you all know how to make a proper impression at the picnic. One never knows when one's future husband may be standing nearby."

"Like Cendrillon?" Maren asked hopefully.

"Who?" Amelia asked.

"Cendrillon was a maid, and the prince found her and made her a princess."

"That's not what happened," Maisie said. "*She* found the *prince* and then he married her."

Amelia frowned thoughtfully. "That sounds a bit like my grandmother's story of Ashenputtel. She said Ashenputtel wished for a prince, and then warned me never to lie, because if I did, I might have to cut off my toes to fit a gold slipper."

The girls stopped walking.

"You don't remember that part of the story? The stepsisters wanted to marry the prince, and so they claimed to be Ashenputtel. But their feet wouldn't fit the dainty slipper of gold, so they had to cut off their toes to make the shoe fit."

The girls looked horrified.

"The moral of the story is that some people will do anything to win. All right then, off with you lot so that I might dress."

The girls bounced out of her room, and only Peg-leg Meg left under protest, quite upset she had to leave her regal manner behind.

Amelia had settled on a gold gown with blue embroidery. It was made of lightweight lawn linen, the perfect fabric for a warm day, and was cinched so tightly at the waist that she looked impossibly svelte. Lordonna arranged her blond hair at her nape in a snood made of gold silk knit so fine that the snood itself was almost indistinguishable from her hair. When she was dressed, Lila came into her rooms, wearing a plain blue cotton dress. "Shall I have the coach brought round, Your Royal Highness?"

"Not for me," Amelia said, taking one last look at herself. "I intend to ride."

"To ride?"

"*Je*, madam. It's not very far, is it, and I think it will make a more notable entry. Don't you?"

Lila laughed. "I think it's already rather dramatic to have a royal princess attend this picnic."

"It certainly is. But nevertheless, I intend to ride. Why not?"

"I can think of a few reasons why not."

"I knew you'd understand." Amelia smiled in a way that she hoped Lila would interpret correctly—she would do as she pleased.

So it was, then, an hour or so later, after everyone else bundled into coaches and drove off, that Amelia and her guards mounted horses. She was given a spirited roan mare to ride, and that delighted her. The horse kept tossing her head, ready to get on with it. Amelia leaned over her neck to rub her face. "I'm ready, too," she whispered.

And they were off, trotting along the road. Today was probably the happiest Amelia had been since arriving in England. She was eager to make new friends. And for once in her life, she'd be entering the fray without Justine by her side. She missed her sister terribly, but she didn't miss always being in her shadow. Justine said it was quite the other way around, that she tended to fade to the background when Amelia was about.

Maybe when they were younger. But people came to see a queen.

This time, they'd come to see a princess.

They spotted the picnic across a meadow on the banks of the river. The carriages were lined along the curving road, and a pair of horses grazed contentedly at the water's edge.

Once, when she and Justine were quite young, they'd witnessed the Duchess of Tartavia race across a field and then fling herself into a dismount. They'd been so impressed that they'd spent an entire summer seaside practicing that very thing. Amelia was an accomplished horsewoman, and made a hasty decision, turning her horse off the road and sending her down the grassy slope into the meadow. She liked that her gold skirt billowed behind her as she gave the roan her head. But she misjudged the roan's spirit, and the horse ran with abandon, even when Amelia tried to pull up on the reins. The people gathered hopped to their feet and began to scatter, as if they thought she would plow right through them into the river. It was at the last minute that Amelia was able to give the horse enough of a pull to stop her from doing just that.

She swung off her horse just like the Duchess of Tartavia had, but she stumbled and righted herself before she fell. She straightened her bonnet on top of her head and looked at the roan. "I had hoped for a bit more cooperation," she said to the horse, then turned to the gathering. "Good day! *Bon dien!*"

For a moment, nothing moved except the edge of the linen tablecloth as it lifted gracefully on a breeze. A flower in one of the vases toppled onto the tabletop. One of her guards, still panting from the chase, took the reins from her.

And still, no one spoke.

"Is something wrong?" Amelia asked.

"Not at all!" Lila came out of her trance and looked frantically around at the guests. Suddenly, everyone was dutifully bowing and curtsying. The girls, who had been playing under an elm, ran forward to curtsy, too, knocking into each other as they did.

Lila and Beck moved forward at the same moment, startling each other. Beck picked up his pace to be the first to reach Amelia. "Your Royal Highness, you gave us a fright. Are you all right?"

"A fright!" She laughed. "I'm perfectly well, thank you. I really did think the horse would yield to my rein, but she had a mind of her own. You know how females are." She chuckled at what she thought was a clever joke. Not a single person laughed.

"Thank the Lord you are unharmed." Beck glanced uneasily at her horse as he cupped her elbow and drew her toward those gathered. "May I make some introductions?"

"Please!"

He began with some familiar faces. Mr. Darren, the solicitor, and his wife. The vicar, Reverend Stevens. Then onto those she'd not met, all of whom she had to greet and make the necessary small talk. Behind the first few to come forward, she could see a few gentlemen and was eager to move on to that portion of the afternoon.

Lila was on hand for that. She first introduced her to Lord Wexham. Amelia was thrilled, as he was *quite* handsome. "A pleasure to make your acquaintance, my lord," she said prettily.

"The pleasure, Your Royal Highness, is mine. My only regret is that my wife is not here to meet you as well. Alas, she is with child."

Amelia suppressed a groan.

Next, Mr. Charles Highsmith, who had kind eyes and was no taller than she. He was an industrialist, and Amelia remembered Justine's warning about men who would want to line their pockets with business in Wesloria. "Find someone who loves *you*, darling, and not your country." She'd paused and held up a finger. "Wait—they should certainly love your country. But not too much. Blast it, you know what I mean."

Amelia knew what she meant.

Next was the affable Earl of Clarendon. He was practiced in the art of bowing low. He was not as handsome as Mr. Highsmith, or as married as Lord Wexham, but he was charming and had a lovely smile. The sort that let you know straightaway you would be friends.

All in all, Amelia was pleased with the gentlemen, and was confident they would at least make for a diverting afternoon. But then Lord Clarendon asked if she'd had the pleasure of making the acquaintance of his friend, the Duke of Marley.

Amelia actually laughed. "*Hardly*," she said, and meant to add that he had been away from Hollyfield, but that she'd certainly met his caretaker. Before she could, however, a contretemps between Maisie and Peg-leg Meg erupted over the perfect stick Meg had found and Maisie wanted. One of the girls screamed and tried to hit the other, which cased Birdie to burst into tears, and people were scampering after the girls to calm them.

Except for Amelia.

And the Grim Reaper. The terrible caretaker. The fisherman who thought he owned a public path.

They stared at each other across a few scattered chairs. Amelia stared with great surprise; he with much less. She was so discombobulated by his presence that she didn't see Mathilda until the girl barreled into her, nearly knocking her to her arse.

"Lady Mathilda!" her father said sharply. "Have a care!"

"Sorry, Papa."

"My apologies," Lila said, returning to Amelia's side. "May I present the Duke of Marley, Highness?"

He clenched his jaw tightly and bowed crisply.

"He is the Duke of Marley?" Amelia repeated disbelievingly. She couldn't quite work this out, for there was no possibility that this man was the duke. "Is that what you said?" she asked, hoping she'd misheard.

"Yes…from Hollyfield?" Lila added uncertainly.

Oh, Amelia knew from where. She couldn't take her eyes from him. He was tall and his eyes were an icy gray blue, a little like moonlight, a little like mountain lakes, a little like rain. His gaze was arresting and his figure inspiring, but the rest of him was…underwhelming. His beard was untrimmed, his hat a bit worn, and his boots unpolished. A *duke?*

"Your Royal Highness, it is an honor." He said the words as if someone was holding a knife to his back.

"You're the Duke of Marley," she said again. But then it dawned on her—this was a joke! Amelia laughed and turned to Lila. "It's a jest, isn't it! Tell me it is—he can't possibly be the duke." She cast her smile at him. "Confess, sir!" she said gaily.

He merely gazed back at her, one brow arched slightly above the other. She could hear others gasping with surprise. Guests began to flutter anxiously and move like so many birds on a limb, uncertain what to make of this scene.

"Your Royal Highness," Lila said, her voice low but filled with alarm. "He is indeed the Duke of Marley. You... you must have thought him abroad, hence your confusion. Isn't that so?" She smiled to everyone gathered around them.

"*I* know who he is," Mathilda said. "He's the Grim Reaper!"

"Exactly so, Tilly," Amelia agreed.

From somewhere nearby, Blythe made a muffled sound of distress. "Lady Mathilda, apologize at once! Lord Iddesleigh? Did you hear what your daughter said?"

"Your Royal Highness, I do beg your pardon," Lila said. "But I would think that the mention of a...a *reaper* of any sort...is a bit unsettling?"

"Is it?" Amelia asked absently. Her gaze was still on this man, this reaper, this supposed *caretaker*. She couldn't have been more wrong about him. It just went to show that one must never judge a person on appearance alone. "My apologies. Tilly, darling, but he's not the Grim Reaper at all! If he were, someone here likely would be dead, wouldn't they?"

"Oh my. Lady Aleksander?" Blythe said, her voice getting uncomfortably high. "Mathilda, darling, come and help your father."

Amelia hadn't meant to be rude, but she was taken aback

by her mistake. She tried to atone by smiling at everyone around her. "My apologies! I have a very vivid imagination—everyone says so. Please accept my sincere apology, Your Grace. It's *quite* obvious you are not any sort of reaper at all, and I have clearly mistaken you for..." She tried to think of a word.

"Death?" the duke drawled.

Precisely. She smiled. "You *do* understand. In my defense, I've only ever seen you dressed in black, riding like the devil himself and leaving bodies in your wake."

His dark brow rose higher. "I can say without equivocation that I have never left a single body in my wake. It does seem that perhaps one should not accuse others of riding like the devil when one very nearly rides over a picnic."

"I beg your pardon," Lila said. "You're acquainted with each other?"

"If by acquainted you mean properly introduced, the answer is no, not until this moment," Amelia said. "But he did nearly run me off a road, not once but twice—"

"*Twice?*" the duke said disbelievingly.

"And attempted to scare me off a footpath."

"By informing you that you were on private property?"

"Goodness! I was certainly not expecting this," Lord Clarendon said jovially. He stepped in between them, smiling warmly at Amelia. "Your Royal Highness, may I offer my arm? I understand there is wine, which I think might serve us all. You must forgive my friend the duke. He's been a bit under the weather. Shall I tell you now that I had the pleasure of meeting your late father once?"

That caught Amelia's attention, although she did have a few questions for the duke. "Did you, really?"

"I did. Lovely man, he was."

"Oh, but he was indeed," she agreed. She took Clarendon's arm and allowed him to steer her away. But not before stealing another glimpse at Marley, who had already moved away, his back to her, as if the odious task of meeting a royal princess was done.

CHAPTER TEN

LATER, WHEN THIS infernal picnic came to its inevitable and disappointing end, Joshua would delight in forcing Miles to admit that it was pointless and ill-suited to his temperament.

And as for *that* one...

He looked at her from the corner of his eye, the woman with the golden hair and ready smile. Imagine, riding up like she was meeting an opposing army and scaring everyone half to death. Although he had to admire her riding skills—it wasn't easy to bring a galloping horse to a precise halt. He was especially impressed because he'd expected her to arrive in a litter with a dozen troops surrounding her like the pampered soul she surely was.

What was the matter with her, calling him the Grim Reaper for a *second* time? Granted, he did not look or feel himself these days, but surely he didn't appear *that* despicable. Miles would have told him if he'd looked like death.

Maybe she was a bit off her head? It was a possibility. Everyone knew European royalty married each other so often it had become a family affair.

He supposed he couldn't fault her for thinking he was someone he was not. He certainly hadn't guessed she was the infamous princess everyone was talking about. She'd been dressed in drab brown with a hood or a hat every time he saw her. He'd thought her a farm woman.

Another surprise to him, once he realized that he had seen her before, was that she was actually quite pretty. Some might even say beautiful.

Which was merely an observation. Nothing there to entice him.

Over the course of the afternoon, he'd watched her surreptitiously. Oh, but she was enjoying herself, wasn't she? She clearly thrived being the center of attention. She was unafraid to appear less than regal by running with the girls, carrying streamers like they were exhorting them to chase her. Nor did she have any qualms about collapsing to the ground in a heap, out of breath, so that any gentleman wanting to speak to her would have to go down onto a knee while she fanned herself. She chatted easily, laughed easily, and, from his vantage point, flirted easily.

But ask her not to use a private path, and by God, the claws came out.

Miles, who returned to Joshua's side only once to doff his coat, had tried to convince him to enjoy the spirit of the day. "Come on, lad. It's a fine day. A bit of laughter might do you good. She's rather diverting."

"No, thank you." Joshua preferred to sulk beneath a tree, his back against the trunk, watching it all unfold while he smugly assured himself he was right to have not wanted to come.

He managed to do just that until the unfortunate moment Lady Aleksander intervened.

He hadn't seen her in years. She'd greeted him when she'd first arrived at the picnic, offering her condolences, smiling in that piteous way everyone smiled when a man had lost his wife and child. He'd brushed it off, had inquired after the health of her and her husband, and being assured that nothing was rotten in Denmark, had wandered off.

But here she came again. "Joshua," she said warmly, and put out her hands as if she meant to grasp his and pull him to his feet. "Or should I say, Your Grace? Goodness, so much has changed for you since we last met. I don't know how you've borne it."

A vast understatement. He was a wifeless, childless duke now. "We are well acquainted, madam. Please, call me Joshua as you once did." He could hardly look her in the eye—she was the one who had introduced him to Diana, had arranged the whole thing after everything had fallen apart with Sarah. She was the one who knew what no one else in the world knew—well, save Diana—that he'd been happy enough with his marital arrangement as those things went. But Diana was no great love of his.

He didn't want to be reminded. He might not be able to help being sullen, but he would not be rude to her. So he sat up and put his hand in hers, and she clasped it firmly, squeezing a little. "It really is so very good to see you after all this time," she said.

He wondered what was so very good about it. "Thank you."

For the record, he'd been no great love of Diana's, either. They'd been…friendly. Bound to duty. She lived a life in a social circle she might not otherwise have enjoyed had she settled for love. He had all the necessary ingredients to produce an heir, and that he did, three times over, two of them ending in miscarriage and the last, well…everyone knew how that had ended.

He and Diana had lived separate lives under the same roof, coming together for meals on occasion, and, of course, to fulfill their duties in procreating.

Lila let go of his hand. "How are you faring? I understand you've been away quite a lot from Hollyfield." Without invitation, she sank down onto the ground beside him, landing with a bit of a grunt, and waving off the hand he hastily put out to help her.

"I am well, thank you. And you?" He'd leave the remark about being away from Hollyfield to flit off in the sunshine and spring air.

"Oh, *very* well. I adore England this time of year. Everything is so fresh and colorful and hope for renewal abounds, doesn't it?" She settled onto one hip, facing him, her back to the antics in the field. "But I've been thinking about you."

Joshua frowned. "I'd advise against it. I'm not good company these days, I'm afraid. I would have thought Clarendon would have told you."

"He hasn't said a word about your company."

"Astonishing," he drawled. Miles was no help to him at all. He sighed and shifted his gaze to the distance. "I think you'd find the day more delightful if you kept close to your ward."

"My ward!" Lady Aleksander laughed. "If you mean the princess, you can surely see for yourself that there is no need for me to be close. She is very good at occupying herself. And others."

Was she? What he knew of her was that she stomped about the countryside and then frightened grown men with her riding.

The group was playing a game of Skittles. The wooden "skittles" stood upright and were arranged in a pattern. Each team tried to knock them down by rolling a ball. Points were assigned for the difficulty of striking one in the pattern. Highsmith and Miles had teamed with the princess, and Mr. and Mrs. Darren, Wexham, and the vicar were on the opposing team. The Iddesleigh girls weren't on any team, because it was a general rule that children should be seen and not heard and certainly not invited to engage with adults in this manner, *or so he would have thought*...but they took turns insisting to the adults that they should be allowed a turn, and in most cases, being granted the opportunity.

"How is your mother?" Lady Aleksander asked. "I remember her with fondness. Such a jovial woman."

Joshua hadn't seen his mother since Diana's funeral. She had looked at her own son as if he'd plunged a knife into Diana's heart. He had plunged something into her, all right, but he hadn't known it would kill her. "I think she is not as jovial as she once was."

"Ah, well. A mother carries the burdens of her children. You know, Joshua, I could help you—"

"*No.*" He spoke with a bit too much force and took a moment to collect himself. "No, thank you."

"I understand your reluctance. But it's different now, isn't it? Many years have passed and I've a list of ladies suitable for the life as a duchess and a companion. You'd—"

"*No.*" A tightness crept up his back and into his neck. "I have no interest in the state of holy matrimony." He leaped to his feet with a huff of impatience. He thrust out his hand, offering to help her up. She hesitantly took it and allowed him to pull her up.

"You're suffering from melancholy," she said. "But that won't last forever. You've been dealt a blow, Your Grace, and I want to help. Will you at least consider it?"

"The blow I have been dealt has been suffered by many others before me. I'm not special or in need of care and nor am I...*melancholy.*" He spat the word as if it was stuck in his throat. Maybe it was stuck deep inside him—all evidence did indeed point to melancholy, and there was nothing he could do to hide it.

"You were heartbroken after Lady Wexham, and then… well."

Joshua looked at her, appalled, and a little terrified that someone would bring that up to him now. "I see." He didn't see anything at all. "Excuse me." He walked off, but he had no place to go except home. He didn't want to draw attention to himself by stalking off across the meadow, bound for Hollyfield without his horse, so he took a seat at the table, his back to all the frivolity, while servants readied it for afternoon tea.

He had no idea how long he must have been sitting there like a stewing gargoyle. Perhaps he drifted away a little, because he was startled by a tug of his arm. He sat up and looked to his right. The smallest Iddesleigh girl had her chubby hand on his knee. She looked up at him with the bluest eyes he'd ever seen. "What?"

She put her foot on top of his and began to haul herself up into his lap without a word.

"I beg your pardon? What are you doing?" he demanded, and held his arms away from his body so that he didn't touch the lass. "I did not invite you to sit here."

But the girl, who was no more than two or three years old, ignored him and single-mindedly carried on with her mission. She exerted herself until she'd settled on his lap, her back against his chest, and plugged her mouth with her thumb.

Joshua sat very still. Surely someone would come and fetch the interloper. Surely someone would call her, or demand he set her on her feet. But no one came. And her body, a warm, solid weight against his, sank into him. Her head lolled to one side as she nodded off.

"What in bloody hell am I to do now?" he muttered beneath his breath. He was a tiny bit frantic. The child moved, and he feared her sliding off his lap onto her head, so he draped his arm loosely around her middle to prevent that from happening.

How long must he hold another man's child when his own child lay in a grave somewhere? Did no one notice a child missing? Was this the sort of supervision the children in this country could expect?

"Oh, look, you've made a friend. Thank *goodness*. I was beginning to fret for you." The princess plopped into the chair next to him in a cloud of gold.

He stared. He would have stood, but he had a baby in his lap who was softly snoring.

"Little Birdie," she said, and leaned forward to stroke the baby's cheek. She lifted her gaze to Joshua, and he was struck with the way the sunlight danced in her eyes. "You do forgive me, don't you?"

"For…?"

"For not believing you were the duke. You really don't look like one."

"I beg your pardon? I look as much like a duke as you look like a princess."

She smiled at him in that way women had of smiling when they thought men were incapable of being anything other than an idiot. "You don't really believe that."

He didn't really.

"I was surprised, I will admit. I'm not the best with surprises. I tend to say the first thing I think. My mother— that's Queen Agnes—she says it is the worst thing about me, the way I blurt things out." She shrugged. "But there is worse," she confessed in a low, conspiratorial voice.

He didn't know what to say. Was he supposed to ask what? The child settled deeper into his lap.

"You know what I mean," she said.

"I don't know that I do."

"Just that we all have a side to us we hope no one ever sees. Don't you have a side like that?"

"Even if I did, I don't think I would discuss it with someone I've only just met."

"Really?" She seemed genuinely surprised. "Then what do you talk about? Everything else seems so...superficial."

"Marley, you've taken to our Birdie. Everyone does."

Iddesleigh's voice boomed so closely that Joshua very nearly dropped the girl. The earl clapped a hand onto Joshua's shoulder.

"I wasn't given a choice," Joshua said.

Iddesleigh laughed. "Words I speak every day." He bent over and scooped up his daughter from Joshua's lap. The space she had occupied filled instantly with the cool, empty wind of nothingness. Iddesleigh draped her over his shoulder. "We're going to have tea," he announced.

Joshua turned to the princess—but she wasn't there any longer. She was on the other side of the table, chattering away as Mr. Highsmith escorted her to a place of honor in the middle of the table.

She was surrounded by attentive adults, all of them hanging on her every word, of which there seemed to be quite a lot. She did not spare Joshua another glance, and he didn't spare her more than three or four, either.

Tea was served, and he tried to hear what she was talking about. Something about her patronage of a poorhouse charity that she viewed as quite important in Wesloria, so much so that she was the grand something-or-other of the ball that raised untold wealth for the charity. "People came from as far as Alucia," she added.

"Impressive," Miles said, because Miles was a generous man and, for all Joshua knew, easily impressed.

"The ball was held at Rohalan Palace," she added. "In the grand ballroom. You've never seen anything like it—it's as big as this meadow and lit with *ten* chandeliers."

"Oh," several people said, nodding at the extravagance of it.

The princess leaned forward, smiling charmingly. "But you'd not believe what happened."

"What?" Lord Wexham asked eagerly.

She glanced around, almost as if she was looking to see if any Weslorians had suddenly appeared to overhear what she would say. And seeing none, she continued, "Some of the most important people in the country had turned out, all wearing their finest. Including one of our most esteemed generals, who had previously expressed suspicion that his wife was unfaithful. Well, that night, he caught her in a compromising position with another of our equally esteemed generals! He *immediately* challenged him to pistols at dawn, or, as we say in Wesloria, *au gots navea,* which means 'honor until death.'"

The ladies gasped. The princess certainly had everyone's rapt attention. She settled back, pleased with her performance. She picked up a fork and sliced off a bit of cake.

"What happened?" Mrs. Darren asked from the edge of her seat.

"Unfortunately," the princess said, holding the forkful of cake aloft. "I couldn't really say, as I am not one to rise at dawn. I'm more of a night person. But as for the duel, who knows, really? Words are always spoken in the heat of a moment, particularly when it comes to ladies' lovers. I heard that wiser heads prevailed…but did they? I never saw either gentleman in St. Edys again." She popped the bite of cake into her mouth.

Someone chuckled with the disbelief Joshua felt.

Joshua looked at the tea before him gone cold. The sun was high now and it was hot. The princess had removed her bonnet at some point. He removed his coat.

"Your sister has only recently ascended the throne," Lord Wexham remarked. "How does she find it? It must be daunting for such a young woman."

The princess's head snapped up. "Daunting? Not in the least. She was well prepared and is a wonderful queen."

Goodness. Was that a smidge of indignation he detected in the princess's voice? Was one not to speculate on the talents of her sister the queen?

"Yes, of course." Wexham cleared his throat. "And how is our old friend Lord Douglas? I've known him for many years."

"*Je*, to hear him speak of it, one would imagine that he knows *everyone* in England," the princess said.

Iddesleigh laughed. "There was a time that I think he did, along with everyone in Europe. Quite an Original he was."

"He is very well, thank you," the princess said. "Attentive to my sister in all regards. She's really very fortunate, I think—we should all wish for someone as devoted."

The group fell to an awkward silence. Joshua didn't like awkward silences. He didn't like it when people around him pondered whether they had the devotion required of a mate.

"What brings you to England?"

Everyone turned their head toward him. No one was more surprised than he that he'd voiced the question out loud.

The princess looked delighted that he had. "Well, I…" She shifted in her seat so that she could see him better at his place at the end of the table. "I suppose my sister thought I would appreciate a change of scenery."

"I have never had the pleasure of visiting St. Edys, but I've heard it's beautiful," Clarendon said.

"Oh, it is," she quickly agreed. "But the winters are long and hard, and one could say after the last one, I was a little...restless."

Another word for badly behaved? Joshua would not be surprised. She had not yet fit any of the many female molds he carried around in his thoughts, little sarcophagi of expectation.

"And we are so pleased to have her visit," Iddesleigh said quickly. "The girls adore her."

Speaking of which, to no one's surprise, the girls had run off instead of taking their tea, but one of them chose that moment to make an appearance. She ran up to the table beside her father, planted her hands on her hips and her legs wide apart. "We're back!" she announced grandly. "We're pretending we are knights and we mean to duel. The princess showed us how."

"How to what, dearest?" Iddesleigh asked mildly.

"How to *duel*, Papa. That's when you put your backs together, then march twenty paces, and then turn and shoot!" She mimicked shooting her father.

The princess laughed. Everyone else stared aghast at the child. Then several of them shifted their stunned looks to the princess.

"What? It's not as if they have pistols," the princess said. She looked around, as if she thought that would appease everyone. "I suppose the tale of the two generals was very much on my mind."

"Mrs. Hughes?" Lady Iddesleigh said, twisting in her chair. "Mrs. Hughes!"

A middle-aged woman hurried forward to take the child

and her intention to duel somewhere else. Perhaps to an empty field at dawn.

Joshua turned back to the group, determined to get to the bottom of why they had to have a princess here at all… but Miles beat him to it. "Marley, my old friend, you've been keeping a secret—you failed to mention you'd made the acquaintance of Her Royal Highness."

"I genuinely wasn't aware that I had."

The princess laughed gaily, as if he had said it to be amusing. "Did you not see my regal bearing?" She made a flourish with her hand and gave him a mock bow of her head.

He cleared his throat. "As I mentioned earlier, you were dressed rather plainly, Your Royal Highness."

"Very true, Your Grace. I will admit that it is hard to bear regally when one is wearing brown muslin."

The guests laughed with her. She smiled at Joshua and her smile was…stirring. He knew that sort of smile. It was employed to draw a man in. An attractive woman hardly had to smile at all to draw a man in. A mere look in his direction. A glance.

Men really were pathetic creatures, himself included.

"Ah, but my plain brown gown has served me well since I arrived at Iddesleigh. I have discovered that I like to walk," the princess continued. "Isn't that something? I've never been made to walk—or allowed to walk very far at all. But here, I am at liberty to walk for miles. Unfortunately, I don't possess the sort of clothing one should have for rambling."

"You've been so kind, Your Royal Highness, walking our girls to school every day," Lady Iddesleigh said.

"It's my pleasure! But one must be awfully careful on

that road. There are reckless riders." She glanced again at Joshua.

Joshua wasn't entirely certain, but he thought he might have flushed a little. He had come awfully close to her, despite his insistence otherwise. "There are hardly any riders at all on the road," he pointed out. "There are so blessed few of us in this valley."

"But the road can be treacherous," Iddesleigh said, agreeing with the princess. "A few too many quick turns, if you ask me. Frankly, I'll be glad when we find a new home for the girls' school."

"You're looking for a new location?" Miles asked.

"We must. We've outgrown the cottage. Who could imagine so many girls would need an education?"

The princess raised her right hand as she took another bite of cake with her left.

"My man is searching for a suitable location. It must be large enough to accommodate a few dozen girls, it must be accessible, and it must have room for growth."

Joshua sincerely hoped that the new location was as far from Hollyfield as possible. Perhaps in Essex. Or Cornwall. Wales. Scotland. Belgium. Wesloria.

"Something nearby, of course," Iddesleigh added.

Damnation.

"Oh, look, they've set up the archery field," Lord Wexham said. "Your Royal Highness, are you as skilled at archery as you are at Skittles?"

She put down her fork and craned her neck to see. "I am adequate. My sister is a much better archer than me—she likes to pretend that the target is our prime minister and aims for right between the eyes."

There was another stretch of silence around the table

as the guests all privately tried to assess the truth in that statement.

"That was a jest," the princess said.

"*Ah*," said everyone.

"A bit of one, anyway," she amended with a shrug. "There are days."

"Archery?" Iddesleigh asked. He rose from the table and shouted for his daughters to come along, they were going to shoot at prime ministers.

"Don't encourage them, darling," Lady Iddesleigh complained.

People began to rise from the table to follow. Everyone but Joshua. He was wondering how he might escape and ride back to Hollyfield. It felt like time to chop more wood. Cords of it. Stacks as tall as the house itself.

The princess stood and paused to pick up her bonnet. Joshua couldn't help but notice the white streak in her hair, a tress that had no color. It was hardly noticeable against her golden blond locks, except when it drifted over her temple as it did now.

Unfortunately, he pondered it too long—she noticed. And when she did, she smiled like a cat who'd just had a bowl of warm milk, sated and full of smug happiness. "Won't you join us, Your Grace?"

"I rather think not. I'd not want to risk your death. Or mine."

Her smile widened.

He rose from the table. "Regrettably, I must return to Hollyfield."

"Oh dear," the princess said. "You must be *terrible* at archery if you need to hurry back to Hollyfield."

He bristled, because she was right.

"Do you really live there?"

What sort of question was that? "Pardon? That is my home, so yes."

"I thought it was closed. Or possibly even abandoned. There's never more than a single light, never more than one smoking chimney. Doesn't it take every hearth to warm such a massive structure?"

He bristled again, because he knew very well it looked abandoned—Butler subtly reminded him every day when he asked if he might remove some furniture coverings or take down the window blinds and let in some air. "It's very much lived in." He sounded a wee bit defensive.

She studied him a little more closely, that smile returning to her lips. "May I ask a question, Your Grace?"

No. "Of course."

"Why have you not come around to Iddesleigh House? I understand you've declined every invitation."

That was the last question he expected. Was it a Weslorian custom to ask questions so directly? A bit of warmth crept up Joshua's neck again. He picked up his coat and slung it over his shoulder and tried very hard not to look into the dancing sparkle in the eyes of the princess. "I've been occupied."

"*Every* time?"

"Yes, Your Royal Highness, every time I've been invited, I've been occupied. My sincere apologies."

"None necessary. I only ask in that it is highly unusual. You'd not believe how eager people are to make the acquaintance of a princess. In Wesloria, it's almost as if they crawl out from rocks and roll down from mountaintops for it."

"One can't help but wonder how you were able to escape your home country at all."

"By the dead of night, under a heavy canvas in the back of a cart."

Joshua stared at her.

She laughed. "That was a jest, too. To be fair, not *every-one* is eager to make my acquaintance. Some are actually afraid. I suppose royalty can be a bit intimidating."

She surely didn't think for a moment that he was *intimidated* by her. "I am most decidedly *not*—"

"Ma'am?" Miles had appeared. "Will you join us in the archer's field?"

"*Je!*" she said brightly. "I would like that *very* much." Her gaze flitted over Joshua. "Good day, Your Grace." She put her hand on Miles's arm and presented her back to Joshua.

Miles shot him a look. Joshua shot one back. "Good day, Your Royal Highness. I'll be on my way to open some doors and light some hearths so that Hollyfield doesn't appear abandoned to you on your walks."

"How very kind! Thank you." She flashed another smile over her shoulder at him, this one full of self-satisfaction, then turned all her attention to Miles.

Joshua watched them walk away to the archery field, her face upturned to Miles, her laughter drifting out over the summer day. He had never met a more self-possessed person in his life. He'd never met a royal princess, either, and perhaps they were all that self-assured and frank. But he was still aghast.

He stalked away, inexcusably miffed by her. She was quite comely, he would give her that, but she was unabashedly full of herself, what with her talk of patronages and balls and all the people desperate to meet her.

And to top it off, there were the five little girls, racing around the table and the field as if they were in the nursery. Absolutely no one in charge of them—all the adults seemed quite ready to let them do as they please.

When he reached his horse, he heard Miles call his name, and against his better judgment, he turned.

Miles jogged up a small incline to him. He paused once to glance back at the archery field. The princess was standing amid Wexham, the vicar, and Mr. and Mrs. Darren, her arm extended, apparently urging them all to stand back. In her other hand she held a bow.

"What is the matter with you?" Miles demanded. "You're as irritable as an old man with a toothache."

"I told you I didn't want to come."

"Yes, but I didn't think you'd behave so badly, Joshua. And you have behaved very badly."

"I am fully aware that I was not able to summon the proper demeanor for this infernal outing. Unfortunately, it seems beyond my ability to amend. That...*princess* is as peacockish as anyone I have ever met, and I can't abide another moment of it."

Miles's brows dipped. "What in the devil are you talking about? I think she's quite charming."

"*Charming?*" Joshua snorted and swung himself up on his horse. "I've had enough."

"So have we all," Miles responded with a dark look for him.

Joshua tried to think of something clever to retort, but his mind was one deep hole at the moment. He rode away, his head full of her sitting prettily, her eyes shining, her smile pointed at him. *You'd not believe how eager people are to make the acquaintance of a royal princess.*

Good Lord.

CHAPTER ELEVEN

To Her Majesty the Queen, Justine,

Dearest Jussie, I am in receipt of your last letter and I am *astounded* Lord Rebane had the *gall* to go around Robuchard and come directly to you on the matter of the rail. Papa always said a snake slithers past in the shadows when no one is watching. But you are very clever to have understood what he meant to do and sent him away.

I am faring well here now that Lady A has deigned to do that for which you've paid her so preciously. At long last, I attended a picnic with at least two gentlemen suitors, and more gentlemen who were not. My heart was racing the entire affair because of one gentleman, but not in the way you would expect. Prepare to be astonished, because that gentleman was someone I've previously mentioned—*the Grim Reaper!* I thought him nothing more than a terrible caretaker when all that time, he was actually a terrible duke!

Lady A asked me afterward what I thought of the gentlemen she'd invited, as she would like to know who suits me and who does not so that she might make the right introductions at the ball. I was forthright with her, just as you told me I ought to be. I told her that Mr. H was pleasant but really too short. Is

that terribly vain? Perhaps it is, but I should not like
to spend an entire marriage looking at the crown of
my husband's head. Lord Clarendon was charming
and kind, and I rather liked him. The kind ones never
suit me. Lord Wexham was handsome but vexingly
married. I asked Lady A why he was invited at all,
and she said that I should want to make the acquaintance of everyone who might be a friend and not just
the bachelor gentlemen, to which I said I had precious
little time for that, that I had acquaintances far and
wide and didn't need more, but what I did not have
was a husband.

She said that perhaps I ought to make time for
Lord Wexham as his wife's younger brother would
be attending the ball. I suppose that was her way of
telling me that the gentleman was taking a good look
at me before they send the young man into the ring.

I am loathe to admit it, but the terrible awful duke
was quite handsome in his own, unrefined way. He
is unkempt, as his hair is too long, and his beard too
thick. He reminded me of someone who had just come
back from expedition or safari who had forgotten how
to live in polite society. He is aloof when he speaks,
and his eyes are the color of slate, and his gaze so
concentrated that it feels as if he is looking all the
way through to the curls at the back of my head. I
couldn't understand why Lady A had included him
at all, and she said she hadn't invited him, but that
he had come with Clarendon, and that she was very
pleased to see him, as he had suffered a grave tragedy
when he lost his wife and firstborn in childbirth. She
said he really was a good man, and perhaps I should
reserve judgment. Why are people forever telling me

to reserve judgment? But it hardly matters now as I am determined I will not see him again. I will strike him from any list of guests she presents.

I am looking forward to the ball next week! I've decided to wear the green and pink gown that you liked so much. I will wear the Ivanosen tiara and all the regalia of royalty. Mama says that if you are to make an appearance, you ought to make it a memorable one.

Lady I was very cross with me for teaching the girls about dueling, but I really don't see why the fuss as it is impossible that any of them will die. The girls argued over their pairings, and who in each pairing would be awarded the plum role of dying. But the girls forget everything when they go on to the next game, so there were no hurt feelings.

I've taken your advice to heart and I am endeavoring to be demure and to keep my considered opinions or suggestions from the lord and lady. From everyone, really. Only a few have slipped out.

The school has been a pleasant diversion. I can't imagine why girls are not educated in greater numbers here. They are so eager to learn everything there is to know. They especially enjoy using the abacus. Girls are taught so very little, Jussie. Reading and writing, and basic mathematics is all they might expect. The most excellent subjects of science and geography and histories are left to the boys. Mr. Roberts told me he considered it a travesty that when girls turned a certain age, all their education turned to needlepoint and household management.

I should end this letter and prepare for bed. School resumes tomorrow and now on the morning walk when I pass the Hollyfield estate, I will peer at it with renewed interest, as it is not abandoned but very much open, which, if you ask me, makes it look like an asylum. I will write again after the ball. Love to William and Mama.

With love, A

To The Headmaster of the Iddesleigh School for Untalented Girls,

As I listen to the jarring music produced by a dozen or more girls singing in inharmonious keys, I wonder, sir, what your thoughts are about children in general. You clearly have an affinity for them as you have chosen to dedicate your life to their education.

In moments like these, I wonder why so many adults are keen to produce children at all. One could take an entirely cynical view and see that the costs of child-bearing are high, beginning with the cost to the physical health of the mother, if she is lucky enough to survive the bearing of them. But further, the cost to educate, to dower, to house and feed and clothe them—is there no limit to the burden of a parent? And for what return? Is a child truly necessary for one's legacy? Or do you suppose it an issue of security? Perhaps there are those who have produced the one person who would be obligated to care for them in old age.

I ponder these things when I cannot sleep, and I find that there is no ready answer. I would that I'd had a child, as it might have informed me better, but alas, that was not to be.

A Concerned Resident of Devonshire

—

To A Resident of Devonshire, Concerned,

What interesting questions you pose! Do you think children should be mute? Wouldn't it be grand if they never uttered a word until they reached their majority? Imagine all the arguments we would be spared if that were so. We confess that there are many arguments at the Iddesleigh School, generally concerning the central question of who has what and who hasn't, or who has said what about who.

As for why adults are keen to have children, we cannot provide a satisfactory answer. We would like to believe it is so they will have someone to love with all their heart. Or to form a family in the absence of one. Or to create another being in the image of a most beloved spouse. Perhaps it is as simple as a desire to make the world a better place by bringing into this world children who will be better than oneself. It's only through the continuation of life that progress is made, is that not so? We were once acquainted with a teacher who said that with every child born, the human race is born again. A lovely sentiment, is it not?

Be assured that while we ponder these important philosophical questions, the girls are working on a musical performance for their parents. We are putting all our hopes and dreams into a notable improvement in their collective ability to hold a tune.

Yours kindly,
The Iddesleigh School for Exceptional Girls

CHAPTER TWELVE

ONE MORNING, A WAGON arrived at Iddesleigh laden with various sundries in bags and boxes. This arrival stirred the house into excitement—not for the contents of the wagon, as Amelia guessed—but because it meant Donovan was coming.

Donovan, the mysterious man whose position in society and in this house was not entirely clear. Amelia had met the gentleman the last time she'd been in England, but only briefly. She and Justine had not been able to determine who or what he was then, either—the Iddesleighs had laughingly called him a governess. But he *had* been a childminder of sorts, and Amelia had assumed that he must have been a bachelor uncle. It had all been very odd, but it was abundantly clear that the girls and Lord and Lady Iddesleigh considered him to be family and had missed him terribly.

When the wagon pulled into the drive, Blythe sprang into action, crying out for Mrs. Hughes to speed herself along and dress the girls in their blue frocks. She raced from the dining room and down the hall to her husband's study, where she burst in through the doors and announced, "*Donovan is coming!*" She whirled around and nearly collided with Amelia, who had, of course, chased her down the hall, unwilling to let a moment of excitement escape her.

"Make haste, Highness!" Blythe cried, and hurried past her, down the long hall, to take care of who knew what.

Amelia looked into the study. Beck and Lila were sitting together, and Beck said, "Thank the saints, the cavalry has arrived." He stood up and strode out of the study.

Amelia followed him to the drive where footmen were helping the driver unload. She heard the driver report that Mr. Donovan had accompanied some guests to Torrington Hall and that he would be along presently.

The next two hours felt as if they were all waiting for a storm to blow through or Christmas to dawn. The girls, dressed in matching frocks, were assembled in the salon, prepared to receive him. Blythe fluttered around the staff, asking more than once if tea was ready, and even Beck walked to the front door more than once to peer out at the long drive for any sign of Donovan.

So when at long last riders were spotted cresting the road, the girls raced to the drive, falling over each other in their eagerness to line up, having forgotten the reception was to be in the drawing room. Blythe was right behind them, just as eager. Beck, Lila, and Amelia followed.

Two gentlemen arrived. Donovan was immediately off his horse; the other remained on his mount.

"What have we here?" Donovan went down onto his haunches to view the girls. "Lovely frocks, ladies. What beauties you are—a sight for me sore eyes."

"Why are your eyes sore?" Maisie asked.

"From all the tears I've shed for missing you, lass."

"We've been practicing our welcomes," Blythe said. She had a lilt in her voice.

Donovan rose up and bowed. "It is my great honor to be received in such a fashion."

Mathilda nudged Maren, who nudged Maisie, and down the line it went. The four oldest curtsied.

"My, my," Donovan said, nodding with approval. "I see

a vast improvement." He grinned, and held out his arms, and all four girls raced forward, throwing their arms around his legs and his waist. He greeted each one, a hand on top of their head or cupping their face, smiling at them as if he had brought them into this world, speaking to them in turn. And then he motioned for Birdie from Beck's arms to squeeze her in a hug.

The man was devilishly handsome. Amelia thought it should have been impossible for her to forget just how handsome he was, but clearly, she had, and she was struck a little dumb by it. She couldn't say if it was the almond shape of his eyes, or the perfect shape of his lips, or the physique that looked sculpted from marble—whatever the magic to him was, it caused her to take a step or two forward.

Donovan turned toward her and set Birdie down. He bowed low over the girls. "Your Royal Highness, I am humbled by your presence."

"Oh." She was surprisingly tongue-tied. "You remember me."

"How could I forget a breathtaking beauty?"

She felt herself flush. She took another small step forward. "Have you come to attend the ball? For if you have, I—"

"Good afternoon, Donovan!" Lila trilled very close by. "You've delivered our guests safely, I take it?"

One day, Amelia meant to tell the woman how annoying she was.

"I have indeed, madam, and all of them look forward to the ball. May I introduce Mr. Paul Peterborough?"

The gentleman on horseback, who had yet to say a word, smiled and tipped his hat to the lot of them.

"My valet," Donovan said.

"Welcome, Mr. Peterborough," Beck said. "Donovan,

have you forgotten me? I thought you'd never arrive." He came forward, his hand extended for Donovan to shake. "My wife has missed you terribly."

"It's the ball, Donovan," Blythe said. "There is so much yet to be done and my husband does not share my sense of urgency. I don't think we will ever be ready—"

"We will, on my word," Donovan said easily. He glanced up at Mr. Peterborough. "If someone could perhaps show my valet...?"

"Garrett!" Beck shouted for his butler. "Come, come— show the gentleman to his rooms. The rest of you, follow me," he commanded, and bounded into the house under the scaffolding that framed the entrance, his entourage behind him. Garrett and Donovan exchanged a few words, and with one last brief look at his companion, Donovan followed the Hawke family, scooping up a giggling Peg-leg Meg and Birdie, each under one arm, as he went.

In the salon, he fell onto the divan and crossed his feet at the ankles, very much at home. Amelia was fascinated.

For half an hour, over tea, Donovan listened to every story the girls wanted to tell, even those already told. He listened patiently as Blythe ranted about the myriad things that must be done to keep the ball from being a complete disaster, the ball which *of course* they were eager to host, but had not realized the extent of things that needed to be done.

At Lila's question, he rattled off the names of guests he'd escorted to Torrington Hall, men that Amelia supposed she was to meet. "Lord Frampton, Mr. Beasley, Mr. Cassidy, Baron Vinson. They've all been billeted."

Lila laughed. "They're not soldiers."

"In the hunt for love? They certainly are," he said, and cheekily winked at Amelia.

Amelia didn't care about the others just now—she

wanted to speak to Donovan, to ask if he had another name, and if he was married, and where did he hail from, but she couldn't seem to get a word into the conversation, as everyone was talking at once. Blythe, as usual, was simply overwrought with the idea of three hundred or more guests, not to mention the staff that would need to be brought in. "You can't possibly understand the anxiety this ball has caused me," she said to Donovan, apparently forgetting that Amelia was standing right there.

"It's a pity Goosefeather Abbey sits in ruin," Donovan said, and yawned as Birdie climbed over his shoulder to shimmy off the back of the divan. "There'd be enough room for all the bachelors in Europe to reside there in advance of the ball."

"Goosefeather Abbey," Beck said. "It *is* quite large, isn't it?"

"Massive," Donovan agreed. "But half sits in ruins." He stood up, scattering little girls everywhere as he did. He wandered to the sideboard and helped himself to a brandy. "With a bit of work, it could be made habitable again."

"Would it be large enough to house a girls' school?" Amelia asked.

Beck's head came up. "An absolutely brilliant idea, Your Royal Highness. The abbey would be perfect in terms of size and location. Why hadn't I thought of it before?"

"Perhaps because it is in ruin?" Blythe said. "You must think of the children's safety, darling."

"The hall and several of the monks' personal quarters are intact," Donovan said. "Mr. Peterborough and I had a look around while we rested our mounts."

"But who owns it?" Beck asked. "That question was put to me a year or so ago and, as I recall, the answer was not entirely clear. The records were destroyed in a fire. The whole thing is shrouded in a bit of mystery. But do you know who we might call on to—"

"Beck, darling, *really*—we must turn our attention to the ball! It's in five days."

"Right you are, my love. Donovan? We have much to do. We've made a rather extensive list."

"And we've not a moment to waste," Blythe said. She strode across the room to the door and stuck her head into the hallway. "Mrs. Hughes! Mrs. Hughes, where are you? Come and fetch the girls!"

Lila stood as the girls began to complain about being expelled from the room. "Your Royal Highness? We have much to discuss, haven't we?"

"Do we?" Amelia couldn't think of a single thing. Besides, she was perfectly content to remain and hear all that had to be done in preparation for the ball.

"We do," Lila said firmly.

It was like being with her mother again. Amelia reluctantly stood.

"We'll come together for wine before supper," Beck said as he turned his attention back to Donovan and his wife.

Amelia followed Lila out of the salon. In the hall, she said, "Well then? What is it that is so urgent we must do it now?"

"You may be cross with me, but if you had to sit through the long list of minor details that Blythe will put to Donovan you would be even crosser. Would you like to hear about the gentlemen you will meet?"

"Will Donovan be at the ball?"

Lila stared at her a moment. "I think he will be minding the girls."

"Perhaps you ought to invite him."

Lila sighed. She linked her arm through Amelia's.

"Every woman in England would like to see him invited. But Donovan…would rather spend his time with Mr. Peterborough."

It took a moment for Amelia to grasp what Lila was not saying. "Do you mean…"

"That he prefers the company of men? Yes."

Well, that hardly seemed fair.

CHAPTER THIRTEEN

BLYTHE'S NERVES WERE not improving later that afternoon. Amelia could hear her in the drawing room, her voice rising above her husband and Donovan. She was across the hall in the small salon, eavesdropping as best she could, for lack of anything better to do.

Blythe was distressed. "I hadn't wanted more than one hundred and fifty guests, but look at the list, Donovan! It stands at three hundred! We are not ready to host a ball for a princess, and really, darling, why did you ever say you would? Your sister has ties to Alucia. Not Wesloria, for heaven's sake."

Amelia stood up and walked to the open door of the salon and leaned against the frame, her arms crossed over her middle, her head cocked toward the drawing room.

"Why?" Beck asked, and there was a moment of silence while he presumably thought about it. "As a favor to Lila, really."

"*Lila!*" Blythe said hotly.

"Blythe, love." This was Donovan. "All will be well."

"Will it, Donovan?" she asked wistfully.

"Don't I always tell you the truth?"

"You do," Blythe conceded. But she didn't sound entirely convinced.

"Darling, you fret too much," Beck said.

"And you, sir, fret not enough."

Amelia didn't see why anyone needed to fret at all. What was a ball, really, but a lot of dancing and drinking and eating? It wasn't war, for God's sake. She stepped out into the hall and walked to the foyer, then up two flights of stairs to the nursery.

The nursery was a large room appended to a bedroom and dressing room for Mrs. Hughes. It occupied a significant portion of the top floor. The door was open when Amelia turned down the hall—she could see Mathilda, Maren, and Maisie on the floor with dolls. She assumed Peg-leg Meg and Birdie were napping. She stepped into the nursery and nodded at Mrs. Hughes, who was seated in a chair, hard at her needlework.

"Good afternoon, ladies," Amelia said.

"Good day," Maisie sang out. Mrs. Hughes rose from her seat to curtsy.

"Forgive the intrusion, but I was wondering who might like to learn to ride a horse today?"

Mathilda looked up from the pile of clothes she was sorting through to put on her doll. "I already know how."

"No you don't," Maisie said. "You know how to ride a pony. You don't know how to ride a horse."

"Papa showed me," Mathilda insisted. "When you weren't there. No one was there. It was just me and Papa."

"I would," Maren said softly to Amelia.

"Then come!"

"Ma'am… I beg your pardon," Mrs. Hughes said anxiously. "I—"

"It's all right, Mrs. Hughes. I'm an accomplished horsewoman. I'll have our guards accompany us."

"Yes, Your Royal Highness. I'll just speak to Lady Iddesleigh, shall I? if you don't mind."

"Not at all." The poor woman wouldn't get near Blythe this afternoon, not in her state of high dudgeon about the ball.

She watched Mrs. Hughes hurry down the hall, then turned back to the girls. "Shall we?"

The three of them agreed that they should.

Later, in hindsight, Amelia would concede it was perhaps not the best idea she'd ever had. She'd only meant to amuse the girls and herself, to pass the time. She certainly hadn't meant for things to get out of hand.

She and her guards each took a girl and set them on the saddle before them. They guided the horses to the flattest part of the road between Hollyfield and Iddesleigh House, which happened to be where the drive into Hollyfield intersected the road. The bleak mansion loomed in the background. Although, on closer inspection, Amelia decided that the house could be quite grand. A little scrubbing of the exterior and opening the rooms to light would do wonders for its tired facade.

Oter and Fabian, her guards, dismounted and set up their watch beneath the shade of a tree. Amelia had ridden the roan mare, but she took turns putting each girl into the saddle of Oter's horse, the most docile of the three. She showed them how to hold themselves in the saddle, how to hold the reins, and then led the horse by the bridle up and down the road. "Oter? Do you see these riders? Are they not excellent?" She called out to her senior guard.

"Excellent, indeed, Highness," Oter called back.

When Amelia had led each girl up and down the flat road, Maren asked, "Will you teach us how to ride like you did at the picnic?"

Amelia grinned. "It was a grand entrance, wasn't it? My sister and I used to admire a duchess who rode like that, like the wind, wherever she went. She loved horses."

"I want to ride like the wind," Maren said wistfully.

"*No*, Maren! You're not big enough!" Mathilda said.

"I want to do it too," Maisie shouted.

"Maren first," Amelia said. She called to Oter to help—she brought Maren off Oter's horse, then put herself on the roan. Oter lifted Maren to ride in front of her. Amelia had a good hold on the girl with one arm, and the reins in the other hand.

"Lean toward the horse's neck," she advised. "We'll get her to run, then give her a bit of the rein and see how fast she goes. She spurred the horse with her crop, and the roan lurched into a run. Maren squealed—with delight or fright, Amelia wasn't sure. She gave the horse more rein, and the mare began to gallop. But when she did, it was much harder to control than Amelia had anticipated. When the horse made a sudden turn onto the Hollyfield drive, Amelia lost control. No matter what she did, the horse was determined to reach the house, very nearly dumping Amelia and Maren in its haste.

Maren began to scream. Amelia thought she might, too, but mostly, all her strength was put to hanging onto Maren and the reins. She pulled hard, and the horse began to yield. But then she heard barking. A dog suddenly appeared alongside them and tried to nip at the roan's hooves. It spooked the horse.

"*Merlin!*" a male voice roared.

Amelia was reduced to clinging to the horse and Maren. A rider appeared beside her, his horse edging into the roan's side. Amelia thought he would slide right off his mount and be trampled, but he managed to lunge for the roan's bridle and forced it to slow while he reined in his horse and brought them all to a stop.

The dog who had chased the roan loped ahead, then turned and trotted back.

As the horses came to a full stop, Maren started to sob. She twisted around in Amelia's arms, her arms going around her neck and squeezing what little breath Amelia had left in her.

"What in the devil are you doing?"

She realized at once it was Marley. Of course it was. His chest rose and fell with each furious breath.

"I wanted to teach them how to ride—"

"To *ride?* You could have killed yourself and the child!"

Maren screamed upon hearing that.

"No, darling, no, no, I couldn't have," Amelia said, and glared at the duke. Whether or not she might have killed them, she didn't see the point in frightening the girl. "No one came close to being killed, I swear it. I've done this thousands of times." Not precisely like this, not out of control and fearing for her life. She soothed Maren's blotchy, tear-stained cheek.

"I want to go home," the girl sobbed.

"I know you do," Amelia said soothingly. She was still shaking from the ride, and now she needed to think of how to explain what had happened here to the girl's mother. Another shiver raced down her spine as she imagined Blythe's reaction.

Oter and Fabian reached them, both out of breath, too. Amelia could picture them running for their horses out in the meadow, then racing after her, probably certain she would die and they would be faulted for it and their heads whacked off. They looked absolutely horrified.

Marley had managed to catch his breath, but a trickle of perspiration slid down his temple and disappeared into his beard. "Is this how you guard your princess? By letting her run wild?" he admonished the guards.

"I wasn't running wild!" Amelia insisted. "It got a bit fast, *je*, but I had the reins in hand." At least she thought she had? The last few seconds were so blurry she couldn't think. "Your dog startled the mare!"

The dog had trotted back, panting for air, looking up at her and Marley, seeking approval.

"That mare was already lost before the dog ever reached her."

Oter dismounted and came forward to retrieve Maren. When he had her—her arms around his neck now, still sobbing, and oh, this would be an uncomfortable discussion with Blythe—he walked back to his horse, speaking in soothing tones to her. Amelia leaned down to pet the dog and to avoid Marley's dark stare, but she felt weak, as if the ride had drained all her strength.

"Madam, forgive me, but you are entirely too reckless."

Amelia couldn't look at him. She couldn't seem to focus at all. "Things got a bit out of hand."

"A *bit*?"

It was more than a bit. She'd been terribly foolish. She knew what might have happened—her memory of the Duchess of Tartavia riding with abandon was a fond one, but she conveniently refused to recall that the poor woman had died of a broken neck. Years after Amelia and Justine had watched her ride like the wind, they'd heard she'd fallen from a horse and had died the moment she hit the ground.

"You lost control."

She couldn't exactly argue convincingly otherwise, and besides, her heart was pounding so hard she thought it might leap from her chest. "I lost control."

He snorted with satisfaction.

"For a moment. But I would have gotten her reined in, and I almost did, but your dog scared her." Her voice sounded unnaturally high, and she could not catch her breath. Not that it mattered, because Marley was talking and hadn't even heard her. He'd removed his hat and was dragging his fingers through his hair, nattering on. "Nearly killed myself trying to stop the mare." He seated his hat and looked at Amelia. He squinted. "Are you all right?"

"*Je*," she said weakly. She tried to smile, but something went sideways in her. She watched as Marley vaulted off his horse and strode forward. He seemed to be moving too slow. Or she was moving too fast. Only then did she realize that she was tilting to one side and sliding out of the saddle.

He caught her before she hit the ground. Amelia gasped, frightened by the lack of feeling in her legs and gripped his arms tightly. "I think I'm dying."

"You're not dying, you're fainting." He held her up. "Take a breath. Several of them."

She tried, but she was having trouble focusing. Her gaze was fixed on his blue neck cloth. Her fingers were digging into his impenetrable forearms. She detected a faintly spicy and sweet scent, something she would equate with men's cologne. He did not strike her as the type to douse cologne onto his person, and she wondered if someone had doused him—and really, *what* was she thinking? She was thinking that he was remarkably handsome if one was close to him and he wasn't scowling.

"All right?" he asked.

Amelia forced herself to look up into the two mountain lakes peering back at her. "I'm..." She was wobbly, fizzy, and feeling a bit detached from her body. "I'm fine." The feeling was slowly returning to her legs. She felt a bit steadier. And foolish. But steadier.

He looked skeptical. "Can't you send one of them to fetch a carriage for you?"

And alert Blythe to a catastrophe? "A carriage!" She shook her head. "I'm not that sort of princess."

"I hope you're not the sort of princess to try and ride after that fright. You're awfully pale."

"That's my nature. My grandmother used to say she could nearly see through me, I was so pale. Especially in the winter months. There isn't much opportunity to go out into the bitter cold. I'm really fine. Just a bit of nerves, that's all."

"If you say," he said. With one callused hand, he very gingerly peeled her fingers from his arm. She hadn't realized she was still clinging to him. And why was his hand callused? That didn't make sense. "You've got an impressive grip there," Marley said.

The girls suddenly shot past them. Maisie shouted at her to see how fast they were. Maren was no longer sobbing, which Amelia considered an encouraging sign. Perhaps this would all be forgotten. Perhaps they would never have to mention it again.

She stepped back from the duke. She cleared her throat and tucked a bit of hair behind her ears. Her bonnet, she realized, had gone missing.

"It's not my place, but you really ought to have more of a care, madam," Marley said. "You might have scarred the young lass for life."

"She'll be fine! Once, when I was a girl, I was riding with the captain of the guard and was thrown from a horse and nearly trampled by a regiment, and look at me, I'm very well."

"Are you?" he asked dubiously.

"I do appreciate your assistance. We Ivanosens are not easily kicked out of the game."

"Ah. Well, I'm happy to have been on hand to intervene before I found you dead on my drive."

"I see you are determined to admonish me," she said with a bit of a smile. "But remember, to err is human. To forgive divine."

One of his thick brows rose above the other. "The words of a long-dead pope won't minimize my concern."

All she wanted was for him to stop looking at her like she'd stolen his dog. "If the words of a long-dead pope don't move you, then perhaps you would prefer the words of a poet. 'Sweet mercy is nobility's true badge.'"

"We're to sweet mercy, are we?" Marley leaned forward, close enough that she was looking into those slate-colored eyes again, and she felt a rush of heat race up her spine so quickly that she forgot what she was talking about. "'Foolishness is indeed the sister of wickedness.' How does *that* suit you, Your Royal Highness?"

It suited her in ways she didn't understand. Her thoughts felt a bit muddied. Frankly, all of her felt muddied, like one jittery mess, and she was sure it had nothing to do with the horse ride. "That's very good. Monsieur Klopec—he was our tutor—was of the firm opinion that memorization was the way to a healthy brain." She tapped her head with one finger. "I commend you."

He almost smiled. Almost. "Has anyone ever told you that you are a very peculiar woman, Your Royal Highness?"

"No. But thank you! I will take that as the compliment I am sure you intended. And again, my thanks for your assistance."

"For saving you from disaster, you mean."

"That, too." She turned to her horse, prepared to make a stunningly graceful getaway. There was just one problem with that idea, and she turned back to him. "Could you give me a hand up?"

With a smirk of superiority worthy of a king, he cupped his hands. She slipped her foot into them, and he lifted her up. She settled herself onto the saddle and took the reins. The horse was docile now, worn out by her burst of uncontained energy.

The duke put a steadying hand on her leg. "Have you got the reins?"

His touch burned through the fabric of her gown and singed her skin. Amelia smiled prettily. "Complete control." And with that, she spurred her horse into a trot, knocking his hand from her leg when she did.

But that spot on her leg burned all the way to Iddesleigh.

CHAPTER FOURTEEN

MR. EUGENE COX arrived from London at Hollyfield at precisely half past two. He was a punctual man, which Joshua appreciated. Mr. Cox was the duchy's estate manager. He was the sort of man to not care who was the duke, as long as he was paid for his work.

He entered the study looking rounder than the last time Joshua had seen him; the buttons of his waistcoat strained against his belly. He greeted Joshua as if they were old friends and plunked a sheath of documents onto the desk. He had, as previously requested, reviewed all the duchy holdings to determine specifically what Joshua could and could not dispose of.

At the time, Mr. Cox had not seemed even slightly concerned or interested in why. If he'd asked, Joshua would have told him that he needed the review so that he could make some decisions. The same decisions he'd been trying to make for two years since Diana's death.

What was to become of his life? That question kept him awake at night. Caused him to chop wood, as if trying to pound the answer out of him.

Unfortunately, Mr. Cox was not filled with good news. "There are old entails that will require further research," he said. "And considerations such as taxes that must be addressed. Not to mention the deed restrictions."

There were so many things to consider, apparently, that Joshua stopped listening.

When Mr. Cox finished listing all the reasons why Joshua was not to even consider the slightest change in the duchy holdings, he placed his hands atop his round belly and sat back, awaiting Joshua's charge.

Joshua scratched at his unruly beard as he considered his options. "I understand your concerns, Mr. Cox. Nevertheless, I should like you to determine what must be done in order that I may sell Hollyfield and vacate the title. I ask only for my own edification. It is a discreet inquiry, of course."

"Of course." Mr. Cox looked offended by the suggestion it could be anything else. He began to pack up the papers, clearly displeased by Joshua's response to his warnings. Why should he be? Mr. Cox wasn't the duke. He didn't have to shoulder the responsibilities of the title.

The gentleman hoisted his bag onto his shoulder, but he paused. "I beg your pardon, I nearly forgot. I have received an interest in the purchase of the abbey."

Joshua looked up. "Goosefeather? The ruin?"

Mr. Cox nodded. "Its location is ideal for a mill."

That was intriguing. The abbey ruin had been one of the mysteries Joshua had discovered when he'd assumed the title—no one seemed to know who it belonged to. That it was located on the border of three properties and a river didn't help matters. One could surmise that ownership had been handed off through the centuries, but unfortunately, all records of it had been destroyed in the same fire that had destroyed half the abbey decades ago.

Shortly after Diana's death, Joshua had implored Mr. Cox to do a complete search of property records, to include all the royal land grants. That had been a lengthy and costly endeavor, but Mr. Cox had at last discovered that the abbey had indeed been granted to the first Duke of Marley some two hundred years ago.

"A mill," he mused. "Would they tear down the ruin?"

"Most assuredly," Mr. Cox said.

"A pity," Joshua muttered.

"Then your answer is no, Your Grace?"

"What? My answer is absolutely yes. Sell it. Sell Hollyfield. Sell everything that has to do with the duchy. Who is it that wants the thing?"

"An Irishman. Mr. Liam O'Connor. He's made a name for himself in Ireland and would like to expand his holdings."

Joshua pondered this. A mill would bring jobs to the area, which would be a good thing. But more jobs would mean more people in this quiet part of England. More people would inevitably mean more girls in need of education.

The mill could also bring a workhouse to the area. Joshua had heard about deplorable conditions in workhouses and would not like to be the cause of that sort of misery.

He wondered idly if anyone would miss the ruin. Some people were unreasonably attached to antiquities. He was a bit attached to it. The most vivid memories he had of his brother, John, were of their childhood. Whenever they visited the duke's family at Hollyfield, they'd play medieval games at the abbey with their cousins.

Memories of his brother, John, were usually accompanied by a darkness that crept in from the edges of his thoughts. It was creeping now. All his concerns were buried under the darkness and he shrugged indifferently. "Sell it to him, then."

He noticed that Mr. Cox's jaw clenched a bit. "Yes, of

course, Your Grace. But if I may do a bit of investigation to ensure there are no holds on the abbey?"

There were no holds. The only thing Mr. Cox might find was a group willing to fight for the preservation of the antiquity. "By all means. But then sell it."

Joshua stood from his chair and walked to the window. He looked out at the road, where two carts were bumping along toward Iddesleigh House. "I look forward to word of your progress."

"Understood, Your Grace."

"Good day, gentlemen." Miles strode into the study, discarding his cloak as he did. "I beg your pardon for the interruption—I've just come from the village and asked Butler to bring tea."

"You remember Mr. Cox, my estate agent," Joshua said. "Mr. Cox, the Earl of Clarendon."

"How do you do, Mr. Cox. I'll just pop out and tell Butler to add a third."

"None for me, thank you, my lord. I was just leaving." Mr. Cox gave Joshua a curt nod and went out.

Miles watched him go. When they could no longer hear the man's heavy footfall, Miles asked, "What are you selling?"

"Lurking at the door, were you?"

"Not at all. I was walking into the room and heard you say it. What do you mean to sell?"

"This and that."

Miles waited for a better explanation.

"Hollyfield." Joshua made a lame gesture, indicating the structure around him. "This old place."

"Yes, I know which place you meant. When you mentioned it before, I thought it was the ale talking. I don't understand, Joshua—are you in debt?"

"No. Or not that I am aware. I don't want it, Miles. I don't want the bother. It's massive and costly." Joshua dragged his fingers through his hair self-consciously.

Miles's expression was one of utter disbelief. "Have you lost your mind?"

He didn't think he had, but he hadn't entirely ruled it out.

"I'll ask you again—what of the entail? Surely you can't simply sell. The entail must be rather complicated."

"Oh, it is," Joshua assured him. "Very complicated for a man with an heir. But I don't have an heir, and the entail ensures that I hold the property for subsequent generations. As there are no subsequent generations, I should think I might do what I want."

"There are no subsequent generations *yet*," Miles pointed out. "You make it sound as if you're seventy-five years old, and not the thirty-three years that you are."

"Thirty-three years or seventy-five, there will be no more Parkers after me, and therefore, no more dukes."

"Your mother—"

"Can no long bear children."

Miles snorted. "How can you be entirely sure there are no other relatives? That the line of Parkers will cease to exist? How can you predict your future with such ease?"

"I can't predict it. But I can deduce what will probably be true given the current facts."

"I think you're mad. Well and truly mad."

"Entirely possible."

Miles shook his head. "I intend to speak with your mother. I think she should know what you're about."

His mother couldn't summon enough to care. When John had died, so had all her hopes. Her surviving son had never been much of an inspiration to her. When Diana died, it felt to him as if she blamed him as much as he blamed himself. "I wish you all the luck with that, my lord."

Miles was clearly exasperated. "I don't know what's gotten into you." He joined Joshua at the window and stood with his arms crossed, his jaw clenched. He remained like that for several moments, stewing in his inability to force Joshua to his will. It was the same demeanor he'd had when they were boys, and Miles had not been able to best him in their boxing matches.

"Here come more wagons," Miles said absently.

The road to Iddesleigh House had begun to resemble a trade route what with the number of coaches and wagons that were moving back and forth. Just this morning, Miles had pointed out a set of wagons carrying crates of who knew what, headed for Iddesleigh House.

"This should be quite the ball. I wonder if the Weslorian treasury has been advised as to the extravagance of it?" Miles asked idly, then moved away from the window.

Joshua remained, watching the wagons disappear over a crest. He'd tried not to think at all about that blasted ball, but it was impossible—everyone in the village was talking about it. It was remarkable the number of things being ferried to Iddesleigh—did a ball with a royal princess really command so much fuss? Perhaps. She was terribly eccentric. For all he knew, she planned to race into the ball on horseback.

Eccentric and reckless. And also unsettlingly pretty.

"What's that?" Miles asked.

Joshua turned; Miles was pointing at a bonnet. Joshua hadn't told his friend about the mad princess—Miles already believed he complained too much about her. He'd found the hat after she and the girls and her useless guards had trotted away after that near catastrophe. What would have happened had he not been on the drive just then?

Miles picked up the bonnet. It was yellow, with little white silk flower buds appended to it in various places. Joshua knew from having examined it that two of the buds were covered in dirt. A strand of gold hair dangled from one of the bonnet strings, and he imagined her tying it up under her chin, catching a bit of hair as she did.

Miles was staring at him with a new expression. One that suggested he didn't know who he was looking at. Joshua turned back to the window. "I found it."

He recalled how her face had been completely devoid of color after she'd nearly fainted off her mount. It had struck him that for all her outrageousness, she wasn't as bold as she acted. She'd seemed fragile in that moment.

"Found it? Where?"

There was a twinge of suspicion in Miles's voice. Hardly a surprise—Miles knew him better than most. Joshua shrugged. "On the road to the village." Not a complete fabrication. One would have to take the drive from Holly-field if one intended to go to Iddesleigh.

"And you picked it up?"

Miles was gearing up for in inquisition, so Joshua was somewhat relieved when Butler entered the room with a tea service. Miles put the bonnet down.

Butler placed the service on the table between two chairs. "Will there be anything else?"

"No," Joshua said.

"Yes," Miles said over him. "Will you bring the items I gave you earlier?"

Butler nodded and went out.

"What items?" Joshua asked as he made his way to the table.

"You'll see." He poured two cups of tea, one for him, one Joshua didn't ask for. Miles sipped. "Sarah will be at the ball, did I tell you?"

That damn ball. Miles had been making his case all week, despite Joshua insisting he didn't want to go. "Why are you telling me?" He tried to sound disinterested. But he wasn't disinterested—he was confused. He had mixed emotions about Sarah now. She'd been the one person in his life he'd believed he'd loved beyond measure. But when her father had refused his suit, and she had married Wexham, and then he'd married Diana...well, there had been more than one night he'd wondered if the love he'd felt for Sarah had been as real as he'd believed it to be when in the throes of it.

His feelings for Diana had been different from the heart-pounding eagerness he'd felt for Sarah. With Diana, there had never been a consuming, burning love. But there had been mutual respect and a compatibility about some things, which, in hindsight, he appreciated more than his passion for Sarah.

He hadn't seen Sarah in a very long time. The thought of seeing her made him anxious. What if a flame still existed? Could he bear another flame on top of the inferno already raging in him?

But there was someone else who made him anxious about this ball, and that was the princess, who would surely suck all the air from the room. His anxiety had more to do with the curiosity he'd developed for her. She intrigued him in a way he was not accustomed to being intrigued.

"I am telling you because you have not as yet said definitively that you will attend," Miles said. "But I intend to see you there."

"Yes, well, thank you for your diligence...but I'm not

certain if I have the right clothing," Joshua said. "I've not worn formal attire in some time."

"You do," Miles said breezily. "Butler and Mr. Martin have been beside themselves with glee, brushing the cobwebs from your wardrobe. Ah, there he is."

Joshua glanced over his shoulder as his valet entered the room. He noticed he was holding a pair of scissors, a towel, and a razor strop. "What's this?"

"Scissors, Your Grace."

"For...?"

"Your hair, lad," Miles said. "Your beard. You require a bit of upkeep."

Joshua's hand went to his beard. "What's wrong with it?"

"Everything. It's a bird's nest. And there will be ladies present. It's always necessary to be trimmed up when ladies are concerned."

"Ladies are not concerned, Miles."

"My dear friend, all of Devonshire is concerned. Is that not so, Mr. Martin?"

Joshua shot a look at his valet. "Martin, does Lord Clarendon pay your wages?"

"No, Your Grace." But Mr. Martin didn't move. He stood there with a firm grip on his scissors.

Damnation. Joshua suspected he looked fairly awful. But to give in to this coercion was to agree to attend that ball. He glared at Miles.

Miles was smiling because he knew he'd already won.

"Bloody hell," Joshua muttered.

"There it is, Mr. Martin, as close to an agreement as you will get. Have a bath readied. You'll need to stew him a little and scrub off the grime before we tackle the thatch on his head."

"Will you stop ordering my valet about as if he is in your employ?" Joshua groused.

"You can have him back when I take my leave. Onward," Miles said, and fluttered his fingers in the direction of the door.

CHAPTER FIFTEEN

On the day of the ball, Amelia had watched wagons of flowers, additional servants and musicians, and more food and drink than seemed necessary trundle into Iddesleigh House and disgorge their contents.

At one point, she and Donovan had stood at the railing above the entry, watching things being carted in from outdoors. Donovan said this was the most highly anticipated social event Devonshire had seen in years.

"Really," she said, because she was surprised by this. If she lived here, she'd have balls every other month.

"Really," Donovan confirmed. "There are country dances and the like, but formal balls? Best you head to London for that, and even there, you'd not find more than one or two as grand as this. Beck has spared no expense."

She supposed she better enjoy it, then.

They watched floor candelabras being carried in by a procession of workmen, all turning left, marching down the long hall to the ballroom. There was an abundance of oil lamps throughout Iddesleigh House, but Blythe had said she wanted the ambiance of a formal ball, which meant elaborate gold-plated candelabras.

All the preparation made Amelia slightly anxious. That it did surprised her—she loved to attend balls and soirees. In Wesloria, she would be greeted with the smiling faces of people who had watched her grow up in the public eye, or people who had been aligned with her family for generations. She had the attention of throngs of people who had everything to gain by knowing her.

But in the month she'd been in England, the reception had been decidedly cooler.

The other difference was that in St. Edys, the extravagance of the balls she attended was a matter of course. Here, it was all just for her. She felt a little squeamish about that.

Lila had told her not to think of it, that Beck and Blythe were happy to entertain in this fashion. And that her sister the queen had seen to it that funds were approved for this sort of thing.

This sort of thing. Meaning, the marriage mart of a royal princess who had failed to make an appropriate match in her own country.

Nevertheless, despite her rare case of nerves, there was nothing Amelia liked more than the attention of gentlemen at a ball.

When it came time to dress, Mathilda, Maren, and Maisie snuck into her suite of rooms and marveled at her gown, which hung on a dress form near the window. On the dresser, Lordonna had placed all the jewelry and accoutrements befitting a royal princess.

Amelia would wear a dark green riband diagonally across her chest. It had long been the custom of Weslorians to wear a patch of green somewhere on their person as a symbol of national pride. A collar tip, a ribbon on a sleeve, or even sewn into a hem. For the royal family, the symbol of national pride was often worn in ribands. It would be anchored at her waist with the blue silk royal family order badge, the center of which was a portrait of her father, King Maksim. She would wear another royal order badge at her shoulder with Justine's likeness, and on her sleeve, the gold and diamond star with the slender green ribbon that represented the Order of the Lion, which her sister had bestowed on her shortly after assuming the throne.

The gold ruby-encrusted tiara she would wear had belonged to her great-great-grandmother and had been worn by Amelia's mother on the occasion of her engagement to Amelia's father.

The girls took turns placing the tiara on their heads and parading before the full-length mirror. Amelia could feel tension radiating from Lordonna as they did—she treated the jewels as if they were her children. Even the young maid in the room who had been sent to help Lordonna kept lurching toward the girls, as if she expected them to break it.

The jewels were thankfully rescued with a knock on her door. It was Donovan, come to fetch the girls.

"But where are we going?" Mathilda pouted. "I want to stay here." She had the riband wrapped around her neck like a neck cloth.

"I should think you are to be dressed for the ball, lass," Donovan said.

Mathilda perked up. "Mama said we weren't allowed to attend."

"Did she? Then I suppose it was a lucky thing that I spoke with her and convinced her you should be able to attend for the first hour so that you might see Her Royal Highness's entrance before you were carted off to bed."

Mathilda gasped. She turned a wide-eyed look to her sisters. It wasn't apparent that either Maren or Maisie understood what Donovan had just said, but they gasped, too. Donovan pushed the door open. "Mrs. Hughes is waiting for you."

Mathilda yanked the riband from her neck and let it flutter from her fingers onto the chaise as she dashed out of the room. Her sisters were close behind. Amelia could hear Mathilda loudly inform Maisie that she must wear the white dress and not the blue, that white was for formal occasions and blue was for picnics.

Donovan shut the door behind them and smiled at the ladies in the room. "The lassies, they are a handful, aye?"

Lordonna visibly relaxed. And the maid went back to ironing Amelia's pink petticoat.

Donovan pushed away from the door and walked to the vanity where Lordonna was putting up Amelia's hair. Amelia was no longer shocked by Donovan's free rein of Iddesleigh House. He was welcomed in all corners, from the kitchens to the attic. The man didn't know a stranger.

He paused beside Amelia and gestured at the streak of white in her hair. "I was acquainted with a man once who had a patch of white much like yours."

"Were you? I've only known the Ivanosen family to carry this trait. My sister, my father, his father...all of us with a patch of hair that won't take color. On my sister, it was noticeable because her hair is dark. And on my father, there was a circle of white, just here," she said, pointing to her temple. "When I was young, it always looked to me as if someone had hit the king with a snowball."

Donovan chuckled. "It's hardly noticeable in hair as fair as yours, is it? But it ought to be—it is clearly the mark of royalty." He leaned over and peered down at her vanity where Lordonna had arranged diamond-encrusted pins and pink satin ribbons. There was a bit of thin gold filigree wire that she would use to hold up some of the curls at the back of Amelia's head. "May I?" Donovan asked, pointing to the wire.

"Please."

He picked up the bit of filigree and examined it.

"Madam, if you will allow," he said to Lordonna, and put out his hand for the comb. Lordonna handed it to him.

"What are you doing?" Amelia asked.

"A little something special." He proceeded to expertly braid the long streak of white hair with the filigree. When he'd finished, he'd handed the end of the braid to Lordonna, who wove it into the curls at Amelia's crown. Amelia had thought it all very amusing, but in truth, the effect was striking. No one would have noticed the white had he not woven it with the gold.

"How is it, Mr. Donovan, that you know how to dress a lady's hair?"

"I suppose you might say I've had the pleasure of knowing many ladies. What do you think?"

He was the most mysterious man she had ever known, a man of many talents. "I love it."

He leaned against the vanity, his back to the mirror, facing her as Lordonna continued with her hair. "What a night for you, Highness. Tonight, you will show yourself to hundreds of guests, all of them eager to make you acquaintance. But I wonder, is there one who has caught your eye? Someone Lady Aleksander has made you eager to meet?"

"*All* gentlemen catch my eye, sir. But I've not encountered one yet who possesses what I want."

One of Donovan's brows arched. "And what, pray tell, do you want?"

Unfortunately, Amelia wasn't entirely sure. "The same as everyone, I suppose." She might not know exactly what she was looking for, but she was crystal clear on what she didn't want.

"A marriage of fortune and standing?"

Definitely not. She shook her head. "Too conventional."

"Ah. A royal princess has a right to want something more," he said.

"I hardly think *that's* true. We all want…something."

"And what is that? Kinship? Stature?"

Amelia couldn't help but laugh. "Kinship and stature? No! I can hardly explain it, but what I want is the sort of compatibility that has thus far escaped me. The sort of compatibility that Justine has with William if you want to know the truth. They are very clear-eyed with each other. I want that, too. But all my life, I've been told that I'm too forward, too exuberant, too irrepressible…" She could think of half a dozen other things about her people would find to dislike. "Isn't that so, Lordonna?"

"*Je, sund na regn.*"

"She said 'it's true as rain.' Lordonna has known me a very long time."

"I see," Donovan mused. "You seek someone who shares your exuberance for life."

"Of course I do. Doesn't everyone? Like Beck and Blythe," she said. "They are compatible with each other, but I should think neither of them particularly compatible to anyone else."

Donovan laughed outright.

"I should at the very least prefer a companion who doesn't mind my exuberance and would take me as I am." That was the sort of thing Justine had warned her against saying. "*People instantly wonder what it is they must take, darling,*" Amelia could imagine her saying.

"I'm sure I'm not making myself clear," she said to Donovan.

"On the contrary, Highness, I think you are making yourself exceedingly clear. You would like a companion who is not daunted by a woman who speaks her mind and enjoys her life and does not need to be told what to do. Someone who will stand by her even when others are disapproving. Who respects her likes and dislikes and doesn't care if they align perfectly with his. Someone who sees her spirit and matches it, perhaps even someone who likes fast horses and big dogs and long winter nights before a fire when a blizzard is roaring outside. Someone who will allow her to press her cold feet to his warm legs beneath the bed linens on bitterly cold mornings and who will think nothing of dancing past dawn. Someone who understands how you think, who you love, and how important Wesloria is to you."

Amelia blinked up at him in amazement. Lordonna stopped curling her hair to stare at him. "That's *exactly* what I mean, Donovan. But how could you possibly know?"

He smiled. "I'm rather good at guessing. And, as I said, I've been a companion and confidant to a few ladies in my life. You all want the same in the end. I wish you all the luck, Your Royal Highness. It is my experience that men are not hard to find. But good men certainly are." He winked at her. "I look forward to your entrance. And judging by the clock on the mantle, you've got a little more than an hour. The guests have already begun to arrive."

He made his way across the room. But when he reached the door, he turned back to Amelia. "For what it's worth? You deserve what you want and more. Don't let anyone tell you differently." He bowed his head and went out, closing the door behind him.

Amelia looked at Lordonna in the mirror of her vanity. "*Vanredan,*" Lordonna said.

Amelia agreed: Remarkable.

BY THE TIME Lila came for her, Amelia had forgotten all about Donovan. She'd made the mistake of looking out the window and had seen the carriages that lined the drive and the road. There were so *many*.

Lila paused in her advance across the room when Amelia turned from the window.

"Oh *my*," she said, her gaze sweeping over Amelia. "Your Royal Highness, you look...stunning."

Amelia blushed at the compliment. "Thank you." The gown, made by a French dressmaker her mother favored, fit her perfectly. The bodice was cut low, the ribboned sleeves were off her shoulders. The tiered skirt was pale green but was split in front to reveal a pink petticoat, emblazoned with dozens of tiny white rosebuds that matched those that lined the tiers of the skirt. "Has the ball begun?"

"Indeed it has. There are three hundred and twenty-four guests, which is twenty-four more than were invited." Lila laughed. "It's a perfect evening. The sun is warm, the lawn tended, the ballroom transformed."

Amelia drew a breath.

"Are you ready?"

"I don't know," she admitted.

"No? What are you missing? A fan?" Lila looked around the room and picked up one Lordonna had left for her.

"It's..." She paused and pressed her palms to the sides of her waist. She was experiencing a sudden and uncharacteristic absence of confidence. "What if they don't care for me? Sometimes people don't care for me, have you noticed? In Wesloria, they *must* care for me. I mean they must never say an untoward thing about me. They would smile and—"

"They will adore you, Highness," Lila said softly. "How can they not?"

She appreciated Lila's attempt to calm her, but she knew herself. "It is possible. My mother says that my prospects would be much improved if I didn't talk as much as I do."

Lila laughed. "You have nothing to worry about. These people have driven miles to meet you. They *want* to hear you talk. I am confident you will be much admired." She held out her hand. Amelia reluctantly took it. Lila squeezed it. "I have never seen you be anything but poised and confident. Even at your father's abdication, and again at his funeral...you held your head high. This ball is nothing compared to those moments. *This* is what you love to do. Don't let the fact that they are the English Quality and a bit stodgy dim your light."

Amelia slowly smiled. "I do love to dance," she admitted. "Truly, they can be a bit stodgy, can't they?"

Lila grinned. "Shall we?"

Amelia had waited a month for this. Her nerves aside, she was not going to miss a ball. "Yes."

Down the stairs she and Lila went, and then across the great corridor that connected the new part of the house to the old. They walked to the top of the stairs where the butler, Garrett, was waiting to announce her. Blythe and Beck were waiting for her in their formal dress. Blythe's cheeks were rosy, which Amelia had learned meant she'd had a nip of whisky. And if there was any doubt of it, Blythe gasped so loud when she saw Amelia that she felt compelled to slap a hand over her own mouth. "God help us all, Your Royal Highness. You are a *vision*. Your dress is beautiful."

"Thank you."

Blythe swooned again. "And your hair!" She was looking at the white braid.

Amelia touched it. "Donovan did that."

"*Magnificent*," she said, casting her arms wide. "Just magnificent!"

"Yes, darling, she is magnificent, but repeating it over

and over doesn't make it any more so," Beck said. "Your Royal Highness, welcome to your ball. Are you ready?"

Amelia smiled. "I think I am."

"I'll be at the bottom of the stairs to make introductions," Lila said, and slipped past them to hurry down.

"We'll be there, too," Beck assured her. "I won't have the lowly men of England swarming you like bees in a hive."

Amelia laughed. She was feeling herself again. Eager. Ready to dance, to flirt, to laugh.

Beck nodded at Garrett. He, in turn, hit a gong that caused Amelia to give a small cry of alarm. The music below ended abruptly, and behind the butler, Beck smiled at Amelia and held out his arm.

"Her Royal Highness, the Princess Amelia Katrina Ivanosen of Wesloria," Garrett called out, then stepped aside.

Beck and Amelia moved to the top of the stairs to begin their descent into the ballroom. The first thing she noticed was the brilliance of the half dozen crystal chandeliers polished to reflect millions of shards of light. The gold-plated candelabras had been spaced equally around the room so that the ballroom appeared to be glowing. Beyond that, doors were opened to the lawn, where at least a dozen torch lights flickered.

Across from her, the musicians played from a mezzanine above the crowded ballroom. The sea of guests began to surge forward to better see her. A familiar thrill raced up her spine, the anticipation of great things to come. She gazed down at the upturned faces and her nerves evaporated. This was where she was her best. She couldn't wait to meet all the gentlemen, to charm them, to entice them. Beck patted her hand and began to lead her down the stairs. They moved slowly; she felt as if she were floating on a cloud.

She looked around, soaking in the admiring looks, the curious looks, and…

And *no. No!* The Duke of Marley was *here*? But that was clearly him standing all the way in the back. His beard was gone and his hair had been trimmed, but she would know him on a dark road and she certainly knew him here.

She suddenly thought of the way he'd stared down at her when he'd caught her before she plummeted off her horse, and her heart did a funny little skip.

Damn him—he was already ruining things.

CHAPTER SIXTEEN

THERE WERE MANY aspects to Joshua's state of mind of late that he abhorred. He didn't *like* being glum and distant. He hated that he was petulant with Miles when Miles only wanted to help him. He despaired that he could be so maudlin and terse, and that he'd chopped so much wood that his hands were callused.

But one thing he was not was a liar. And he would be lying if he said to himself or anyone else that the Princess of Wesloria was anything less than beautiful.

The woman who descended the stairs was the image of a woman that most men could only dream of. Suddenly, the things he'd heard about her in the village made sense— that she was a beauty, an angel, a dream, *et cetera*, *et cetera*, *et cetera*.

Funny he'd begun to notice this about her. He'd hardly looked at her at all when he'd thought her a farm woman, which, when he thought about it, made him question his capacity for observation in general. He'd studiously avoided her gaze at the picnic when her laugh had tinkled over the proceedings and her joie de vivre had annoyed him. And he'd been so rattled when she nearly killed herself on the horse that he'd only been able to think of how fragile she was in spite of the many signs to the contrary.

One thing he had to admire about her—the princess knew how to make an entrance. Either on horseback or down a staircase, she aimed to be noticed. Tonight, she couldn't have been more notable had she toppled over on the top step and rolled all the way down in a swirl of pink and green and landed with a splat.

Like everyone else crowded into this ballroom, he couldn't take his eyes from her.

Her smile radiated to everyone as she came down on Iddesleigh's arm, moving with an elegance and bearing that didn't come naturally to most. He noticed male gazes fixed on her in lust, and female gazes fixed on her in admiration…and some in envy.

When she reached the bottom of the stairs, Lady Aleksander was there with a string of people to introduce. He watched Princess Amelia move through the crowd, stopping every few feet, Lady Aleksander leaning in to introduce people, to make some remark for them. The princess smiled warmly and spoke to each one, and the people on the receiving end of that warmth seemed to melt a little. At least it seemed so to him. He watched her until the crowd had swallowed her and the only thing he could see of her was the tiara on top of her head.

Only then did he look at the champagne glass he held and realize it was empty.

It took him some time to find a servant, as everyone was angling for a look at the princess. When he at last had a fresh glass in hand, he realized there was some commotion on the dance floor. Ah—the princess was on the verge of embarking on her first dance. Joshua rose up on his toes to see who had been granted the plum spot of being the first on her dance card. He shook his head—of course it was Miles. Always perfect in situations like these, always knowing the very thing to do, how to proceed, how to get the evening truly underway.

Joshua moved around the crowd so that he could see them. Miles smiled charmingly, made small talk when the steps to the dance brought him and the princess together. He was the consummate gentleman, Joshua would give him that. In their youth, he'd been a reckless bachelor, taking small liberties on the dance floor that were certain to get him a smile or a slap.

When the dance ended, and the princess was swept into another dance with a new partner, Joshua retreated to a corner of the room to nurse his champagne. He was studying the floor in earnest when he heard a feminine voice say his name. He knew at once the voice…but he couldn't think which female it belonged to.

He looked up and to his right, and his heart lurched. *Sarah.* How could he have not known instantly whose voice it was? He quickly straightened and looked around for some place to put the champagne, but finding nothing, turned back to her. "Sar—Lady Wexham." He bowed.

She smiled warmly. "It's Sarah. We've known each other too long to land on formality now." She put her hand on his arm.

His whole body seized at her touch. He found it…uncomfortable. Her hand didn't belong there. It hadn't belonged there in a very long time, and he didn't like that it *was* there.

"How are you, Joshua?" she asked softly. "I've heard that you…that perhaps you—"

"Had lost my mind?"

She moved her hand to her throat. "*No.* I heard that you were returned to Hollyfield."

A kind little lie. "I am well, thank you. The rumors of my demise are merely rumors. You are obviously very well." He glanced at her swollen belly. "Congratulations are in order. Your third, if I am not mistaken?"

Sarah dropped her hand to her belly and she ran her palm over it. "Yes, my third. We're hoping for a girl this time."

He couldn't help but wonder if she'd ever lost a child before birth. If she knew the sort of pain that caused. "May God bless you." An invisible hand went round his throat to choke him. *May God bless you?* What in damnation was he saying? He never spoke like that.

"Thank you." She shifted slightly closer, her hand still protectively on her belly. "I've thought of you so often, you know. What you endured is unthinkable."

It wasn't unthinkable, actually—he'd thought about it endlessly.

"I wish there were words I could offer to soothe you."

Soothe him? There were no words she could offer. The only words that would soothe him would be from Diana, and that was impossible. "It's not necessary—you really mustn't trouble yourself."

"It's just that I hope—"

"Marley!"

They both started at the sound of her husband's booming voice. Here he was, her knight, arrived in the nick of time to save his pregnant wife from her former lover's evil clutches. Joshua suspected he knew everything about the torrid love affair his wife had had with him before they were married. Or maybe he didn't know with all certainty—but there was no doubt he knew he was not the first man to know his wife. It probably ate at him—he struck Joshua as the typical sort of man to think his wife's virginity was his exclusive domain.

There was even less doubt that Wexham knew Sarah's parents had refused Joshua's offer for her hand. He looked nervous, his gaze darting back and forth between Joshua and Sarah. Joshua actually felt sorry for him—he wanted to tell Wexham that the flame for his wife had died out long ago.

"Have you come to join the list of suitors?" Wexham asked as he snaked a possessive arm around his wife.

"What? Absolutely not."

"Really? But she is lovely," Sarah said. "Quite beautiful."

The princess's beauty had nothing to do with anything.

"You should consider it," Wexham said jovially. "I understand it would be a good life in Wesloria. They've come up in the world, you know. Reforms, economic growth, that sort of thing."

"I have that sort of thing and a good life here," Joshua said. "Perhaps your brother would prefer a Weslorian life."

Wexham's gaze shifted; Joshua followed it. His brother, Mr. Wiltshire, was dancing. Joshua thought his partner was the daughter of Mr. Rowan, a wealthy landowner. That would be a good match for a son destined for the church, as he assumed Wiltshire was. He was smiling at the young woman in a way that Joshua recognized somewhere in the ashes of his soul. Wiltshire liked the lass—even with a princess in the room, his gaze was on the heiress.

What Joshua was feeling, he realized with a jolt, was longing. *Longing?* What in hell did he long for? To be part of life again? To feel those stirrings for a woman? To perhaps avoid seeing the woman he'd once loved so fully pregnant with another man's child?

"Darling, you've been on your feet. Perhaps you should sit," Wexham said. He excused them from Joshua's presence, and Sarah gave him a piteous smile which goaded him. And so Joshua moved on, strolling the perimeter of the ballroom, then slipping into the gaming room.

A couple of familiar faces enticed him into a game. He lost a few pounds and left the table. He wasn't quite sure what to do with himself, so he returned to the ballroom. It was amazing to think that he had once inhabited ballrooms across England with ease, and now he felt like a fish out of water.

He wanted to leave now that he'd made an appearance and idly wondered how hard it would be to extract the Hollyfield carriage from the long line of them. The drivers were probably deep into their own games—no one would leave for hours yet, and they would have set up their blankets to roll dice. Someone would have brought ale.

"There you are!"

This time, Joshua knew at once whose feminine voice it was. He sighed to himself and turned. "Lady Aleksander."

"I've been looking for you all night!" she said, as if they'd agreed to meet.

"Why?"

She clucked her tongue at him. "Because I want to see that you are enjoying yourself, and because there is someone I should very much like you to meet."

"No," he said at once. "I *told* you—"

"You haven't even met her! At least meet the young woman, and if you don't care for her, I'll not say another word."

"Lady—" He sighed. "Lila? I thought I was clear."

"She's a widow, too."

Joshua stared at her, dismayed. "How could you possibly think that would appeal to me?"

"I mean only that you have that in common. I am sure there are many other, more pleasant things you have in common."

"You must stop. I appreciate your concern—I do. You're not the first person to think another wife would cure my gloom. But I don't want your matchmaking. I am not inclined to marry again. So, if you please, I will wish you a good evening." He gave her a curt bow of his head and turned away, intending to march through the throng. But instead, he ran smack into Princess Amelia coming off the dance floor on the arm of a man he didn't know.

She looked as startled as he felt. Her face was flushed and there was a bit of a sheen on her forehead. But like any good princess, her tiara was firmly in place. He noticed she had strung gold leaf through the streak of white hair.

"Your Grace!" she said, surprised. "I almost didn't recognize you." She leaned forward. "You are missing a beard, I think."

"Your Royal Highness."

"The effect is very pleasing."

"Would you like a refreshment, Your Royal Highness?" asked her escort.

"Hmm?" The princess turned her attention from Joshua to that man. "Oh. No, thank you. Thank you very much for the dance."

The gentleman eyed Joshua with conceit, then bowed to the princess, and departed.

She watched him go, then turned her gaze to Joshua. "He stepped on my toes three times in the course of one dance. Why is it that people are not taught to dance properly?"

"I... I wouldn't—"

"I am surprised to find you here this evening! I must say that Lord Iddesleigh is nothing if not persistent in casting his invitations to Hollyfield."

He deserved that. "At long last, I was at liberty to attend."

"At liberty," she repeated, and laughed. "Are you enjoying yourself, then?"

He looked around them, aware that several pairs of eyes were on them. "I am not one for crowds."

A smile slowly moved her lips. "Imagine, a duke who is not one for crowds. In Wesloria, dukes are *notorious* for the crowds they draw. Either they are treasonous, or belong to the wrong political party, or are known for lavish soirees. It's part of the nature of being a duke, isn't it?"

"It's a bit different here."

"Hmm." She allowed her gaze to casually travel the length of him. "Were you speaking to Lady Aleksander?"

"We are acquainted." He paused. Surely she didn't think...that he was a possible match? His skin crawled at the very idea of being offered up as one of a long line of suitors, another cow at market. "You don't think... I should clarify..." He wasn't quite certain how to say it. He had no wish to offend. "I—I mean to speak plainly—I am not in the hunt."

"The hunt for what?"

Why was she so difficult? And why, for God's sake, did her gaze sparkle like that? "I mean that I am not here as one of your...suitors." He hadn't wanted to say it quite like that, but rather to convey that he was not on the marriage market and that she had many gentlemen who were.

However, before he could explain himself, she laughed. "*Definitely* not."

Joshua knew better than to take the bait, but she'd said it so adamantly that now he felt like he ought to be the offended one. "*Definitely* not?"

"Definitely not!" she cheerfully confirmed. "You surely didn't think that *I* had inquired about you? After you've been so..." She circled her finger in the air. "I can't think of the English word. *Tiresome*, perhaps?"

Joshua was taken aback. That sounded exactly like

something he would say to Miles about *her*. Except that he would say it to *Miles*, and not to *her*. "I beg your pardon?"

"Is that not the right word? My English deserts me at times, I'm afraid. What is the word for difficult company?"

Joshua stared at her in astonishment.

She was the picture of innocence, looking back at him with doe eyes. "I mean no offense."

"I don't see how you could possibly not mean offense." Did anyone ever tell another person they were difficult company and not expect to offend?

"Oh. I'm very sorry—"

"I'm not offended," he insisted, although he was clearly and thoroughly offended. "But I must correct your view of me—I am not *tiresome*. I am good company for the most part. And it seems rather uncharitable on your part given that I saved your life earlier this week."

"For which I was completely grateful even though we must agree to disagree whether you *saved* me or helped me. But nevertheless, my gratitude for your efforts doesn't stand in the way of me witnessing your uneasiness around me."

He was thoroughly taken aback now. There had been a time in his life that he'd been quite diverting. Ask anyone here. On second thought, perhaps not ask anyone here. "My apologies if I have been a bit tired on those occasions we have met." Bloody hell, was that his excuse? That he'd been tired? He almost rolled his eyes at himself.

"Oh, I do beg your pardon, Your Grace. I had not realized." She put her hand lightly on his arm and said, "Perhaps you should not have taxed yourself to come this evening."

He bristled, mostly because she was so pretty and clearly enjoying this exchange—and he was feeling and looking like a buffoon. Also, he was frozen with something he hadn't felt in a long time. The touch of her hand to his arm was vastly different than Sarah's. He didn't mind it. "I am speaking in general terms, madam. I don't mean to imply that I'm ill-disposed to attend a ball." Honestly, Joshua had no idea what he meant to imply, because he was and had been very ill-disposed to attend this ball.

"Then is there another reason you wish you weren't here?"

"I didn't say..." He stopped talking. He didn't know what he'd said. "That was not what I intended to convey."

"Wonderful! Now that we are agreed you are in perfect health and happy to attend the ball, you may request a dance with me."

More astonishment. As if he was waiting in line for the opportunity! As if he'd been skulking about the perimeter of the dance floor with the express hope of dancing with her! "I do beg your pardon, but—"

She gasped. "You don't mean to *decline*, do you? Why, that is *wonderful*!" She laughed with delight. "No one ever declines an opportunity to dance with me. I think you must be the only gentleman present who would even dare! I can't wait to write my sister and tell her."

The sparkle in her eye was destroying him. "I think you are the only woman present who would ask a man to dance."

"Really?" She glanced around the room, then leaned in close. "Is that peculiar?"

"All right," he said, nodding. "I see what you're doing." She was teasing him.

"Is it improper? Audacious? Probably. I'm constantly amazed at what is considered improper and audacious when a woman is involved, but very matter of course if a man is involved. Have you ever noticed it is true? Oh, but you don't want to talk about that—you're too tired! Never mind, Your Grace. If you can't abide to dance with me, I certainly won't insist."

He peered at her.

She smiled serenely. She was unperturbed. Just passing the time. Having a bit of a tête-à-tête. And in the meantime, people around them were straining their necks to hear every word.

He put out his hand. "I would be honored."

"I really didn't have that impression at all."

"I must insist."

She glanced up from his hand, and the sparkle in her eye had gone full dazzle. "I should check my dance card."

His eyes narrowed.

"You think you're doing me a kindness," she said. "And you are! But not the one you think. Mr. Caster is headed in my direction like he's leading a military charge uphill. Could you perhaps remain until Mr. Caster's advance is thwarted? Perhaps in that time you might consider the dance—it is entirely possible that even you might enjoy it. I never understood people who don't like to dance. Seems rather…boorish, doesn't it?"

"Call me boorish all you like—I've been called far worse. Where is Mr. Caster?"

She glanced over his shoulder, then leaned forward slightly to whisper, "*Standing right behind you.*" One of her brows arched in such a charming manner that Joshua was momentarily lost in it.

"*Are you certain?*" he whispered back. "Or is this your attempt to have your way?"

"Oh, I don't have to *attempt* it, Your Grace—I generally get whatever I want. At least in England, I do. Admittedly, there have been times in Wesloria that there was nothing I could do to have my own way short of raising an army and storming the palace."

He stared at her.

"Don't look so alarmed. I wouldn't have the slightest notion how to raise an army. But I will do you the honor of a dance, because now you've put us in this impossible situation and drawn the attention of everyone, and Mr. Caster is about to attack."

"I would dearly love to argue that I've put us in any situation, but I don't have the slightest idea how."

"Splendid. We'll dance!" She slipped her hand into his. Her entire body seemed to shimmer with utter delight, or maybe it was that tiara winking at him, but whatever it was, it seemed it was directly proportional to his discomfit.

He closed his fingers around a small, delicate gloved hand that felt like it couldn't possibly belong to the undaunted woman smiling back at him. He escorted her to the middle of the dance floor as the musicians began the introduction to the next dance. He faced her and bowed. She curtsied gracefully in return and rose with an aggravatingly pert smile that not only vexed him, but reminded him that she was truly beautiful. He understood why people gathered around the dance floor were practically climbing on top of each other to get a closer look at her.

He took her hand again, then placed his other hand on her back. She tilted her head back, her hazel eyes locked on his. "Please don't overtire yourself, Your Grace."

His response to that was to twirl her around with the first notes of the waltz. The movement caught her off guard— she laughed gaily, then expertly fell into step with him.

Another small truth about him was that he was a fine dancer. When he was young, his mother had insisted on lesson after lesson for him and his brother. "*I'll not have my*

sons clumping about a dance floor like country squires,"
she would say imperiously.

"You surprise me, Your Grace! I would not have guessed
you an excellent dancer. I'm usually very good at predicting
who will dance well and who won't. Do you know how?"

"No." He twirled her again, subtly pulling her body
closer to his. She nimbly adapted to his quick step, light
on her feet, her eyes still sparkling. The effect was intoxi-
cating.

"It's in the grip of my hand. A grip too tight, the less
certain a gentleman is. Too loose, and he's timid."

"And mine is just right?"

"Oh, no—your grip is too tight."

She was the most confusing, contradictory woman he'd
ever met. What surprised him was that he was not vexed
by it. He was fascinated. "I think you interpret my lack of
curiosity for uncertainty."

"Your lack of curiosity about what?"

"About princesses and wealthy heiresses. I am not one
to care about such things."

"That makes two of us." She laughed. "Why don't you
share your gift for dance with all the ladies? They would
be so appreciative."

"There are more than enough dance partners for all the
ladies," he said gruffly. "Did you hear what I said?" The
way she was looking at him was making him feel wound
as tight as a clock. And the way she felt in his arms—he'd
forgotten how incredibly soft women were, and this one in
particular felt…luxurious. A fine cashmere amid so many
spun cottons. *Good God*, he'd been taken in by a bit of satin
and silk. That's what happened when a man went without
the company of a woman for too long.

"That you don't care for princesses? I heard that very clearly."

He twirled them again.

"Why in heaven would *that* make you frown?" she asked. "Did you think I'd be distressed by it? I'm not. Royalty is not for everyone. A lot of showy pomp and circumstance when you think about it."

She was not understanding him. And he was decidedly not understanding *her*. "Allow me to speak plainly."

"By all means, Your Grace. But I think the only way you could be any clearer is to repeat it in Weslorian."

Her smile was dazzling. "I want only to convey that your time would be better spent dancing with gentlemen who have intentions. I have none."

"That must make life rather easy for you," she said as he moved them forward "I can't imagine swimming along with no intentions. *My* intention is to dance. But you mustn't fret—I won't take any more of your time than this, as I have no interest in you, either. Not the slightest."

It was a fair point, but Joshua was discovering that one could certainly depend on Princess Amelia to let every thought in her head be known. But he was unwilling to allow her the last word in this encounter between them. "If you mean to flirt, you have a very odd way of doing it."

"Flirting!" She laughed at him again. "If I meant to flirt with you, which I would never, you would have no doubt of it. Flirting is one of my more robust talents."

He twirled them again just to avoid her smile. He searched his brain for a word to describe her. *Intrepid*? Not exactly—that seemed to imply a lot of valor. *Renegade* was more like it. "There are squads of gentlemen desperate for a bit of flirting from you. For the life of me, I don't know why you aren't asking *them* to dance."

"Ah, I see. If a gentleman wants my attention, I should give it to him, is that it?"

"I didn't say that."

"Didn't you? Just when I think my English is very nearly perfect, I am stumped again. But you're right—you can't begin to guess how many gentlemen want my attention. The servants—now there's a lot who work diligently to show not the slightest bit of interest in me. You won't even hazard a guess?"

"As to what?"

"How many gentlemen seek my attention."

Was she teasing him? Because he wouldn't be the least bit surprised if she sincerely wanted him to guess. "Let's just agree there are legions of them."

"*Exactly.* I would do nothing but dance all day every day if I were made to give attention to every gentleman who wanted it."

He twirled her away from a cluster of dancers. "It must be exhausting to be in such great demand from all the gentlemen of the world."

"Mock me if you like, but I've not said a single thing that's not entirely true."

"One cannot help but wonder why you are in England searching for a match. Are there not scores of gentlemen in Wesloria who seek your attention?"

"Practically dropping out of the eaves! But a change of scenery was in order."

"Why?"

"Because…" For the first time, she looked away from him, and when she did, he couldn't help but notice the sudden absence of sparkle. "I can be impetuous. That's what my mother says. Frankly, she says quite a lot, but in this… she may be right."

He was intrigued by her admission. "Are you? Impetuous?"

"Terribly. Haven't you guessed?"

"I had guessed."

She laughed.

He wondered about that change of scenery. It was hard to imagine what could have possibly happened—she did not appear to be easily ruffled, which, he grudgingly noted, he liked about her. His guess? His, true, honest guess? That she could have her pick from the squads of gentlemen seeking her attention and would have no qualms about choosing. So something must have happened.

"Do you know," she said breezily, "that you're the only one who has *not* sought my attention in Iddesleigh? Is it because of your personal tragedy?"

He was so surprised that he almost danced her into another couple. "I beg your pardon?"

"It stands to reason."

He was stunned. What she said was true, but people weren't supposed to say it out loud, were they? He gave a laugh of sheer surprise. "I think you must be somewhat blind to your audacity, madam."

"Astoundingly, I'm not. I don't think I've said anything that others haven't thought. Perhaps you are somewhat blind to your misery."

He was flabbergasted, pushed completely onto his back heels. And he felt a small tremble of panic, that she meant to dissect his life then and there. He would not let that happen. He danced her to the corner of the dance floor and stopped. He bowed low. "As pleasing as the dance has been, you don't know me, Your Royal Highness. You're not in a position to make a single assumption about me. Thank you for the pleasure of a dance." And with that, he turned and walked away, leaving her standing there quite alone.

How dare she? How *dare* she point out how bloody miserable he was? That was for *him* to do—or Miles, in those moments he'd not admit it. Lord God, put a tiara and a royal sash with lots of medals on a girl, and don't forget the gold and white braid of hair, and suddenly, she was an expert on a man she didn't know.

He would take his misery elsewhere, thank you.

And apparently, whether he wanted to or not, he would take the memory of those shining hazel eyes and that beguiling smile.

CHAPTER SEVENTEEN

AMELIA COULDN'T THINK of a single time in her life she'd been left standing alone on the edge of a dance floor. Remarkably, it wasn't quite as traumatic as she might have imagined. But neither was it pleasant.

She did feel regretful. As was often the case with her, she had spoken without thinking. She hadn't meant to upset him or offend him, but had assumed it was perfectly obvious to him why he was reluctant to enjoy himself at a ball. She didn't have time to ponder, however, because Lila was there straightaway. Heaven forbid a princess be left alone with her thoughts for a single moment.

As her vaunted position as Amelia's matchmaker, Lila's expression was filled with concern. Her gaze followed the Duke of Marley until he disappeared into the crowd. She looked at Amelia. "Are you all right? You're flushed."

Amelia pressed the tips of her fingers to her cheeks. "The exertion of the dance. I think I should like the retiring room." What she would really like was a few moments without anyone speaking to her. She needed to think about what had happened. Or rather, how she was feeling. There was something about that man that was giving her an uncharacteristic case of butterflies.

"Certainly." Lila indicated a door just a few feet from them. "It's just through there. I'll wait for you here. Mr.

Richard Cassidy is next on your dance card. Poor man has asked me more than once if I'm certain his name is listed."

Mr. Richard Cassidy. Amelia remembered him from Lila's review of all the gentlemen who were attending with the desire to meet her and state their case. A high-ranking soldier, had come into a substantial fortune, left to him by his grandmother. Blue eyes, maybe?

Well, whatever she'd learned about him, she had not been then or was not now terribly interested. "I'll be just a moment," she said, and walked out of the ballroom, her gaze straight ahead. When one needed a moment to breathe, it was best not to make eye contact. When she made eye contact, people often mistook it for an invitation to speak.

In her experience, people at events like this fell into two camps: those who were convinced that a princess was desperate to hear what they had to say and would take advantage of any opportunity to say it. And those who were afraid of speaking at all, as if they feared they would turn to stone if they did.

She found the retiring room easily enough. When she opened the door, a silk screen had been placed to block the view of ladies inside. But at the end of the screen, she could see a line of mirrors and vanities with stools. At least one woman was seated—she could see the fabric of her skirt spilling over onto the stool next to where she was sitting. Amelia paused where she was to collect herself before entering. Whoever was inside would undoubtedly want to speak to her.

"Did you hear what she said to Lady Bricking?" a woman asked, confirming there were at least two women seated at the mirrors. "I could scarcely believe my ears."

Lady Bricking... that name sounded familiar. Amelia

had met so many people this evening she could hardly remember them all.

"No! What did she say?" The second woman sounded
eager for gossip.

"She said she understood her husband had been an admiral in the Royal Navy and that he must draw a fine pension."

Oh. They were talking about *her.* Because she'd said
exactly that to Lady Bricking, now that she thought about
it. Was she wrong? She'd heard it from an Englishman at a
state dinner in St. Edys. He'd been seated next to Amelia
and had grown more verbose as the wine had flowed. He'd
said he'd been an admiral in the Royal Navy and boasted
he could sail the world twice over with the pension he'd
received upon his retirement.

"She *didn't,*" the second lady said.

"Oh, but she did."

Amelia slowly stepped back from the edge of the screen.
She was confused—should she not have mentioned it?

"And that, after what she said to Lord Garland!"

Yet a third female voice.

"What did she say?" the eager one asked.

"She said, in front of my sister, that she thought him too
old to pursue a suit with her."

Two identical gasps of shock. "To his *face?*" one of them
asked in a voice that had turned squeaky.

"Directly! Poor man turned as red as an apple. He said
he understood and took himself away. What else was he
to do?"

"What a *horrible* thing to say. So uncouth."

Horrible? *Uncouth*? It was Lord Garland who'd made the
jest, something about he rather thought he was too old to
join the quest for her hand, and as he was at least forty years
her senior, Amelia had agreed with him. *That* was uncouth?

"She's too…cocksure, isn't she?"

"Tactless," another one agreed. "Such a contrast to her sister the queen. I met the queen, you know, when she was here a few years ago. Very graceful and subdued. Her sister, however…she desired all the attention for herself."

That wasn't fair. Amelia had desired *some* of the attention, but not all of it. Let one of them spend a lifetime with a sister who would be queen and say they didn't want at least some of the attention!

"I remember that she had a way of stepping into a conversation when her sister was engaged and taking over. It was all very… I don't know. Untoward?"

Amelia could feel the blood drain from her face. That was not true. They didn't know that Justine had been plagued with crowd fright all her life. Or that Amelia had learned at a very early age to step in and spare her sister the agony. Justine had welcomed it! She was much better in crowds now, of course, as she was queen, and she had William at her side, but there had been many years that the heir presumptive could hardly step into public without being attacked with nerves, and Amelia had always been able to do it with ease.

"Lady Iddesleigh confided that she doesn't endear herself to them at all."

Amelia folded her arms. She'd have to inquire of Blythe how she might go about endearing herself, then, as Blythe seemed fit to mention it to everyone.

"Well, it's obvious why they've sent her all the way to England to find a match, isn't it? She's probably affronted all the bachelors in Wesloria."

That remark was followed by some giggling between the three of them. Amelia could feel her heart sinking.

"My prediction is that she won't find her match here,

either. Gentlemen do not care for ladies who are so forward, no matter their title. And it's not as if she's a princess of France or England, is it? I don't think I could point
out Wesloria on a map."

"Forward? I think you mean rude, darling."

"Off-putting. That's it," said another one.

"Yes, that's it," one of the ladies said, and the three of
them giggled.

Off-putting. As if she had a smell about her. A pungent
smell of rot.

The door suddenly swung open, and a woman swept in,
nearly colliding with Amelia. "Oh! I beg your pardon, Your
Royal Highness! I didn't see you there."

"Please," Amelia said, and gestured for the lady to pre-
cede her around the screen and into the room. And when
the lady moved, Amelia slipped out the door before any of
them could feign ignorance or try and convince her they
didn't mean what they'd said. She could feel the burn of
tears, thick and hot, in the back of her eyes.

"Your Royal Highness?"

She didn't know which woman called after her, and she
didn't want to find out. She'd never meant to offend anyone. Why was everyone so easily offended!

She hurried away from the direction of the ballroom,
searching for a place she could recompose herself. If that
was even possible. All her life, people had chastised her
for the things she said, and damn it if she could understand
why what she said was so troublesome.

At the end of the hall there was a half staircase up onto
a landing. She picked up her skirts and ran up the stairs.
A darkened balcony was just ahead, the doors open to the
night air to help cool the house. She slipped out onto the
balcony and paused, put her hands on her waist, and drew

several deep breaths. It was dark up here, but there was light below. She drew a few more breaths, wiped away the few tears that had managed to escape. She went to the railing, gripping it with both hands.

On the lawn, couples milled about beneath the torches. Happy people. Presumably people who did not offend others with their mere presence as she seemed to do. She wished Justine was here. Justine would put it all into perspective for her, but without her sister, Amelia was at a loss to do it herself.

She leaned over the railing and drew more deep breaths to keep her tears at bay. Crying accomplished absolutely nothing. Her feelings were hurt, but she wasn't going to ruin her powder and her evening with tears.

She was six and twenty. *Six and twenty*, and still hoping for the very thing she could not command: Love. A husband! She couldn't command children, or a purpose for living. Was it really so difficult to find someone who loved her and didn't find her off-putting? In her mind, she was personable. Easy company. A truth teller. It hurt that people thought ill of her. It hurt that she seemed to easily alienate people. She thought herself refined, but she didn't understand all the rules of civility, quite obviously.

A movement caught her eye, and she glanced down at the lawn. There, in the shadows, behind a hedge that separated the lit part of the lawn from the rest, were two figures. At first, she was uncertain what she was seeing. But her sight adjusted to the dark, and she realized it was a couple dancing in the light of the moon to the faint sounds of music drifting from the ballroom. It was terribly romantic, and it pulled at her heart. She bent over the railing to have a better look at the slow, sultry waltz. She thought it odd that they would both be clad in black.

And then she understood why. It was not a man and a woman as she had assumed, but two men. And not just any two men. She heard one of them laugh and knew instantly it was Donovan. The other was Mr. Peterborough. The two of them were engaged in a very private bit of dancing behind a hedge.

Amelia moved back from the rail. She couldn't help but be a wee bit envious. That made three gentlemen here tonight who could not be less interested in her: Marley, Donovan, and Mr. Peterborough. Her prospects were dwindling before she'd even begun.

The tears were burning in her eyes again. She wiped one from her cheek and made up her mind to go back to the ballroom. Face the crowd like a warrior. Dance as she liked to do. Meet the rest of these blasted suitors with her head held high. She was a princess, for God's sake.

"Perhaps she is up here?"

She recognized that voice as belonging to one of the women in the retiring room. They were looking for her. Amelia was paralyzed with fear that she'd be found with tears after their comments. That was unacceptable. It was one thing to be wounded, and quite another to let anyone know.

"Shall we try the balcony?"

Her heart leaped. She didn't think she could summon up the devil-may-care easy mien for them. She began to back up, tiptoeing to keep her heels from making a sound, keeping her eye on the doors to the balcony as she moved. Their voices and footfalls were drawing closer. Amelia held out her hands to keep from hitting a wall or toppling over the railing. Just as one of the ladies stepped onto the balcony, Amelia stepped behind a potted tree—and into the unmistakable body of a man.

CHAPTER EIGHTEEN

SO MUCH FOR HIDING.

He'd just wanted a moment of peace and quiet, to avoid idle banter for a space, but now he found himself in an untenable situation. Joshua caught the princess's arm nonetheless and pulled her deeper into the shadows before she could cry out and alert everyone that she was in a dark corner with a man she hardly knew. He was reminded that one should never stand in darkened corners on balconies, because this *very thing* could happen. Who knew what trouble would come for you?

What the devil was she doing here, trying to hide on his balcony? Why wasn't she off somewhere being admired? And what had caused her to take such heaving breaths? He took them quite often, but generally it had to do with his general despair. She possessed no despair that he could detect. Why wasn't she at this very moment laughing in a circle of admirers or relating some fantastic royal tale?

When she'd stepped onto the balcony he had, naturally, thought to tell her that he was there, too, but he'd hesitated, certain she'd think he was following her, which would mean he was in the hunt, which he had expressly told her he was not, and he was *not*...but before he could say it, she'd been drawing those breaths and, if he wasn't mistaken, wiping away tears? And then, just like that, she was tiptoeing backward.

It wasn't until the women stepped onto the balcony that he understood why, and he'd pulled her deeper into the shadows.

Naturally, the princess had opened her mouth to shriek or shout at him, but he quickly pressed two fingers to her lips and shook his head. Then, with his chin, he silently indicated the women.

She understood him, but batted his hand away from her mouth, and silently pushed him away. Then, as if they had discussed it, the two of them at the same moment stepped deeper into the shadows of the corner. Which was how Joshua found himself pressed against her behind a tree that scarcely covered them, the fronts of their bodies touching in all the wrong places.

The princess glared at him, almost as if she thought he had a choice other than to smash himself against her. Surely she could see that he didn't? That close to her, he noticed something else in the light of the moon—the very faint, but certain track of a tear streaked down her cheek. He leaned forward to have a better look. She pushed him back with a little too much gusto. He put his finger to her lips again. She batted his hand away again.

"I feel absolutely wretched," one of the women said. "I never thought she'd overhear."

"It's not your fault, darling," said another. "You can hardly be blamed for noticing what everyone else has noticed. She's very blunt."

Joshua could feel the princess stiffen beside him.

"I would like to be so blunt with my husband," said another one.

"Please, Mary—you could never be so presumptuous or rude."

"Perhaps the princess will teach you," another one said. The three women giggled.

Joshua was confused. They were clearly talking about the princess. What could she have possibly said to warrant this discussion?

"Frankly, as much as Robert vexes me, I should never like to speak to him so indelicately. He doesn't deserve cruelty."

Cruelty? The princess said each and every thought that popped into her head, yes, but she was not cruel.

The princess's mouth dropped open, and there was a flash of true dismay on her face that Joshua hadn't ever seen before. She reminded him a bit of a wounded puppy. She drew a breath and he realized that she meant to speak. He caught her wrist and squeezed. She glanced down at his hand, and then at him, frowning. He shook his head. He put a finger to his lips to indicate she should keep quiet.

"I wonder..." one of the ladies said, but her voice trailed off.

"Wonder what, dearest?"

"I really shouldn't say it."

"You're among friends."

"Do you think her sister sent her to England to be rid of her? Imagine having her underfoot when you're trying to rule a country."

The princess froze. And then she made a move as if she meant to step out. Or lunge. Joshua had no idea what she might do, but could imagine her flinging herself at them, or worse, saying something that would be repeated far and wide. Not to mention, any attention she drew to herself she would draw to him. He wasn't thinking clearly, but he had the idea that there was only one way to keep her quiet until the magpies had left. He caught her chin and forced her to look at him. And then, as if in a mad dream, he touched his lips to hers.

Actually, he did more than touch. He pressed, molded, nibbled her lips with his, and the sensation of it rocked him. He hadn't expected her lips to be so velvety soft. He hadn't expected his hand to go around her nape and draw her into him. He certainly hadn't expected her to kiss him back, her lips parting beneath his, her chest rising to press against his, her hand sliding up to his neck, her fingers caressing his ear.

He circled his arm around her waist and pulled her closer. He was torn between wanting to hold her as close as possible and bending over to brace himself and gasp for air. Could she feel his heart slamming against his ribs? Could she taste how long it had been since he'd kissed a woman? Forever, that was how long.

But whatever she thought, her kiss was just as needy, and she had a grip on his body. Not an entirely physical one but binding just the same.

He moved his lips across hers and felt every inch of her body against his, soft and pliable, and yet full of strength. The pressure of his kiss intensified, and she must have sighed, because his tongue was suddenly in her mouth, sweeping her teeth, her tongue, and the valleys of her cheeks. He cupped her face, his thumb stroking her cheek in the very spot he'd wiped away mud just days ago.

He'd gone round the bend. He couldn't stop kissing her, and she showed no signs of wanting it to stop. He was kissing this woman like there was some arrangement between them, like she had agreed to be his lover. And she was kissing him back like she would a fiancé, giving him the sort of kiss that was dripping with the promise of what would come on a wedding night. *Oh, God, he'd lost his fool mind, he really had*, and he thought he might explode in that corner with all that want.

Her body curved into his, melting against him, and he heard the other women leaving, still talking, talking, talking. They could talk all night and he would kiss the princess all night. It was the most arousing kiss he'd ever had, and if there was any doubt of it, his body was hard and pressed against her belly, and he could feel himself slipping away into the grip of unparalleled desire.

But just as the ladies left, he heard the tinkle of her tiara, finally dislodged, tumbling onto the floor of the balcony.

He reluctantly lifted his head and gazed down at her face. Neither of them spoke; he ran the pad of his thumb over her bottom lip.

She was gazing at him as if she hadn't realized who had been kissing her until this moment. "What was *that*?" she whispered.

An excellent question. "I didn't know how else to save you."

"*Save* me?" She sounded incredulous, as she should be.

"If you'd made a sound, they would have seen you hiding in a corner. With a man you hardly know. You may trust that word of it would have reached the ballroom and everyone in it before you righted your tiara." He bent down and retrieved her tiara. He brushed it off, pushed that white streak braided with gold back from her temple and fixed the tiara on her head. She watched him as he did it, for once entirely speechless. He wouldn't have thought it possible.

The tiara sat a little crookedly, but he was satisfied it wouldn't fall again. Unless…well. He wasn't going to kiss her again, quite obviously. That would send the wrong message.

The princess was slowly nodding, as if she'd just come

to understand something. As if she was seeing an apparition. Maybe he was seeing one, too, because he couldn't take his eyes from her, either. He was surprised by how luminous she was in this moonlight, how her hair looked silver and gold, and there were so many thoughts tumbling in his head that he couldn't put together a coherent thought. Such as how his body had responded in a way it hadn't in years, and how tightly wound it left him. Jesus, he wished he could chop some wood right about now.

The worst of it was that he didn't know what to do next, how to extract himself from the experience of that kiss in the moonlight. How did one stroll away while the sensation of it still thrummed in him? But what alternative did he have? To stay was to invite familiarity. To go was to save himself.

That was what he would do. But he couldn't stop himself from brushing his knuckle against her cheek before he went. And when he dropped his hand, she touched the tips of her fingers to the bit of skin he'd touched.

"They are probably looking for you," he said.

"Let them."

"If I may offer a piece of advice?"

She said nothing, just stared at him.

"Don't listen to them. They're very wrong about you. They can't hide their jealousy for your looks or your position."

Her luscious lips parted and he was reminded of that kiss all over again. "Do you say that to be kind, or do you really believe it?"

"I not only believe it, I know it." He didn't dare say more. Anything more would open too many doors in him that needed to remain closed. "It looks as if the balcony is clear. I'll go first. Good evening, Your Royal Highness." He stepped out from behind the tree. She looked almost wild-eyed as he walked away, and just before he went through the door, he looked back over his shoulder.

She was still staring at him. But she had righted her tiara.

CHAPTER NINETEEN

THE AFTERNOON AFTER the ball, while servants cleaned the hall, and linens were washed and hung to dry, and the wilted flowers taken to the church yard to be distributed among the graves there, Lila met the princess to review the evening and the acquaintances she'd made.

She'd wanted to have tea so that she could casually go over her notes, but the princess was on the lawn in her plain brown gown and walking boots. So Lila tucked her leather notebook under her arm and went out to meet her. She was feeling good about things—Princess Amelia had laughed companionably with Mr. Beasley and had danced twice with Monsieur Archembeau. She'd met a host of other gentlemen, so if either of those two gentlemen were not to her exact liking, Lila still felt they'd had a promising start to the summer. She had no doubt that Amelia Ivanosen would be affianced by the time she returned to St. Edys.

She was convinced until the moment she saw the princess up close.

The woman was always impeccably turned out, but today she was sporting dark circles under her eyes. And she had not dressed her hair, letting it fall in a golden curtain down her back. She was holding a walking stick that she kept jabbing into the ground.

"Good afternoon, Your Royal Highness! It's a glorious day, isn't it?"

Princess Amelia hardly spared Lila a glance. "*Je*, it is."

"Oh dear. Are you a bit under the weather?"

"What? No." The princess looked at her curiously. "I am perfectly well. But I mean to walk. Will this take long?"

The princess's patience for reviewing gentlemen had suffered a precipitous decline in the last week. It was remarkable—the woman who loved to be surrounded by gentlemen didn't want to talk about them. "That depends on you," Lila said. She gestured to a bench beneath an elm tree. "Shall we sit?"

The princess shrugged and walked to the bench, stabbing her walking stick into the ground with every other step.

"If I may," Lila said, settling in beside her, "you do seem a bit out of sorts. Did you sleep well?"

"I'm a bit tired—it was half past two when I left the ball."

"A pity that—the ball was still in full throes. I think the last guests departed at dawn."

"Oh, I'm aware," the princess said, settling against the back of the bench. "I heard the reverie all night."

She was exhausted, that was all. Who could blame her? She'd been the center of attention all night, had danced almost every dance.

"May I ask you something?" the princess asked, twisting in her seat to face Lila. "Do you find me off-putting?"

"What an absurd question! Of course not."

The princess rolled her eyes and settled back against the bench again. "I don't believe you. I don't even know why I asked."

"I am sincere! Why would you ask such a thing?"

The princess shook her head.

Someone had said something to her. Something she probably had misconstrued. Her English was excellent, but every so often, she would misuse a word, or misinterpret one. "Did you...perhaps...say something that might have been perceived wrong?"

She gave a bitter laugh and looked heavenward. "I couldn't say. It seems so much of what I say is perceived wrong. I've concluded that the English are easily offended."

It seemed to Lila that most people were easily offended by one thing or another. Everyone had a cross to bear. "Did a gentleman—"

"No, nothing like that," she said, and glanced away. "The gentlemen I've met are all quite proper and polite. Very eager to charm. What does it mean, *cocksure*?"

Lila laughed, but at the princess's direct gaze, she sighed. No subtleties or innuendos for this lady. "It means...overly confident. A bit arrogant, perhaps."

The princess nodded. "I suppose that describes me, then."

Lila couldn't imagine who had the gall to say such a thing to her. "I think it describes all of us at one time or another."

The princess shrugged.

"Did one of the gentlemen suggest it?"

"No."

That was a small relief. Lila would have flayed any of them who would dare to say such a thing to Princess Amelia. Yes, she was unpredictable and said things that other people were certainly thinking. But she was also charming and lively and really very beautiful, and more importantly, she meant well. Lila had a soft spot for her. When she'd first met her in London two years ago, she'd thought then that the princess had everything a man could possibly want, but needed some time learning how to live in a world that was not full of privilege. To experience what others endured to find love.

"I'm glad to hear it. Speaking of the gentlemen you met...did you find any to your liking?"

"Not a one," the princess said flatly.

Well, that was disappointing news. Lila thought she'd assembled some of the best candidates on her list. But this young woman was a hard one to match, and Lila was not daunted. Yet. "I am astounded!" she said gaily. "I was certain at least one or two would stand out. Surely one or two did? You danced and danced, and I thought you were quite taken with Monsieur Archembeau."

The princess arched a brow at Lila. "Archembeau's uncle is my mother's cousin. We are practically brother and sister."

"Fortunately for us all, that's not how familial relations work. But do tell me what you found lacking in the monsieur?"

"Nothing! I found nothing lacking in any of the men you introduced me to. Every last one of them was perfectly polite and eager to charm, as I said."

What the devil was annoying her so? "What about Mr. Cassidy? His family is well known across Europe."

The princess rolled her eyes.

Lila suppressed a sigh. "Lord Frampton?"

"Who?"

"Ma'am—surely *someone* stood out to you. I don't mean to suggest that you found the man you wish to marry, but I would think that you would have found things to admire, someone to have piqued at least a bit of interest. The more you can tell me, the more I can narrow the list to introduce you to someone who meets your desires."

She snorted. "The only one who stood out to me was the Duke of Marley, and not for the reasons you would like.

Please explain to me why you insist on inviting someone like him to the ball or any other social event. That man left me standing on the edge of the dance floor. And that was after he attempted to decline to dance. He has made it very plain he is not a suitor. He's gloomy."

Was this a spark of interest? No one had stirred that sort of emotion in Princess Amelia at all. That her response was not flattering to Marley was neither here nor there—what mattered was that her feelings were strong. "Well, he's experienced—"

"A tragedy, I know, I know. He has no wish to be here, so I don't see why he was invited at all. Don't invite him again. Please."

"Oh, I won't," Lila said. "But I didn't invite him."

The princess frowned and glanced at Lila from the corner of her eye. "Can't you ask Beck not to invite him, then?"

"Of course!" she said brightly. She wouldn't—she'd be a fool to ask that, to ban the only man the princess had spoken of since arriving in England. "I will certainly *try*. But…they are neighbors."

"I don't care. I don't want to see him."

"But… Beck might." In fact, Lila thought the perfect thing to do in this situation was to suggest a supper party with Marley prominently on the invitation list. Beck would be delighted. There was nothing he enjoyed more than a good meal with good wine and good company. Marley wasn't particularly good company, but that wouldn't deter Beck. "Is there *anyone* you would like to see again?"

The princess sighed so wearily, one could imagine she'd been dragging a plow around a muddy field. "I don't know, Lila. They all seem the same. I don't mean to be troublesome—I truly don't. One seems as good as the next, but quite honestly, I'm disappointed. I had hoped someone would leap out at me and capture my wildest imagination."

Lila didn't know if anyone would ever capture the princess like she desired, but she hoped she would at least find someone who would, over time, capture her. "It's all right. I have so many in my book—"

"There must be something wrong with me. The only men who have ever appealed to me are all wrong. All I want is someone who excites me, but perhaps more important, *esteems* me, Lila. *Me.* Not my position in a royal family, but me. Unfortunately, I am off-putting and cocksure."

Lila wished she knew who had said such a horrible thing to Princess Amelia. She smiled sympathetically. "You are not off-putting or cocksure. I think that people expect you to be one way, and you're another, and they aren't sure what to make of it. You're a princess, and they have ideas about what that is. But they long to meet you, and to be you, and to see their ideals in you. They may not recognize that you are your own person and you can't possibly please them all."

The princess folded her arms and gazed across the lawn.

Lila understood her disappointment. Princess Amelia was no different than any other young woman—she wanted someone to love her and hold her in high esteem. She wanted someone who would accept her as she was. The princess despaired of finding that man, but Lila had no doubt there were scores of gentlemen who could love her. The real problem here was not the lack of suitable men— it was that the princess desired someone complicated and exciting. Or, as she put it—the wrong person.

But Lila knew very well that sometimes the wrong person was actually the right person. And as much as the prin-

cess couldn't see it, someone had stood out to her at the
ball. Just not in the way she'd expected.

The more she thought of it, the more a match between
Joshua and the princess would be lovely for both of them.
She could hardly wait to speak to Beck about a supper party.

To a Resident of Devonshire, Concerned,

*We are in receipt of your letter concerning the unac-
ceptable events of Monday. It was indeed one of our
young students whom you saw "with your own eyes"
open the gate of the Harrington estate to allow the
cows to wander onto neighboring property. The student was adamant that the cows clearly wanted to be
set free and she didn't feel that she was in a position
to deny their wishes. How fortunate we are that you
were on hand to witness the entire affair! Otherwise
we might not have known how the cows came to be
in the wrong meadow. Naturally, we offer our apologies that your dog was enticed to join in our student's
bad behavior, but I suppose dogs are happiest when
chasing children and animals and balls.*

*To your question as to whatever happened to the
old wisdom, to spare the rod spoils the child, we can
offer no explanation, but will observe that perhaps
that there are other more effective means of prevent-
ing children from being spoiled. Is it possible that
parents desire spoiled children? Or has the sheer
number of offspring worn them down? To take a single child and mold her into a model of discipline is
quite the challenge. To take two or more to mold at*

the same time must be overwhelming. It therefore stands to reason that spoiling children may be impossible to prevent. A disappointing truth.

We've been thinking quite a lot about disappointment of late. Have you ever considered that no matter how hard one might work to avoid disappointment, in the end, it simply cannot be avoided? It's as if some people come into our lives to astound us, and others to disappoint us. The circumstances of our individual lives might leave us vulnerable to a host of disappointments. A sobering thought and, we will confess, one that has left us feeling a little down at the mouth.

Yours kindly,
The Iddesleigh School for Exceptional Girls

—

To the Iddesleigh School for Disobedient Girls,

In fairness, I must apologize for the dog's behavior. I had not anticipated a complete breakdown in discipline.

I read your letter with much interest. We share this thinking, as I, too, have thought quite a lot about disappointment. Especially the sort that comes as a result of one's choosing. I think the single most abominable crime of our nation is that we present each child with such high hopes for happiness and prosperity. Why do we tell ourselves that life will be grand? Who can promise this? Will not every person encounter sorrow and heartache at some point in life? And yet, we harbor such lofty expectations, which leads to the crushing disappointment at the slightest catastrophe. You may think me cynical, but life has taught me this invaluable lesson. We would do our children a service if we taught them to expect happiness, but to know that they will, at some point, be disappointed. It's how we persevere that serves us best.

I suppose we ought to take care not to create expectations that lead to such high hopes. I harken back to the wisdom that the only thing we may sway to our will in this world is our own conduct. Life is to be lived moment to moment, day to day, and not in some sunny future of the mind. Joy is found in the everyday part of living, if only we'll look for it. Perhaps we ought to resolve to live for each day as it comes, and hope for the best.

My sincerest wishes that you are released from the doldrums of your personal disappointments.

In the meantime, I strongly urge you to explain to your students the concept of private property.

A Concerned Resident of Devonshire

CHAPTER TWENTY

MORE THAN ONCE in the last few days, Joshua had pondered the headmaster's dismay at life's disappointments. He felt a certain kinship with him—he imagined they were two men who had expected something different than life had handed them and were struggling to right their little ships.

And then again, he might be reading far too much into a single letter. But he felt their camaraderie and hoped he'd been successful at offering some encouragement.

Then, in hindsight, he wondered if he'd been too pessimistic. Life was not worth living without *some* hope. He would make a point of that the next time he wrote.

Remarkably, he'd found a glimmer of hope in the last place he would have believed. It had arrived in the form of a kiss and had shocked a budding desire to root in him. He'd felt alive again. He'd felt parts of his body he hadn't felt in an age. He had the very rusty thought that maybe he could emerge from the misery he'd created.

It was raining today, or he'd be at his wood, chopping away at these unexpected feelings. He glanced at his dogs, the two of them lying on their sides before the hearth, facing each other. Artemis had settled on Joshua's desk, making himself at home on top of the estate ledger and purring loudly.

At least Joshua had the three of them. And a good horse. He had his three companions, a good horse, an estate, and quite a lot of money. Otherwise, his life would be truly disappointing, wouldn't it? He couldn't image a life of poverty on top of his general malaise.

"What are you doing? You haven't opened the drapes."

Miles's entrance into the study disrupted the silence that Joshua and his companions had become accustomed to since his return from the Continent.

The dogs awoke with a start. Bethan began to bark in the direction of the bookcase.

"Bethan!" Joshua scolded, and the dog turned around, saw his favorite person, and loped toward Miles to join Merlin, who had already presented his belly for a rub. Once again, Joshua doubted the utility of his dogs as protectors. Even Artemis was enlivened by Miles's presence—he rose and stretched, and then, presumably because he was feeling good, batted at an empty candlestick until it toppled off the desk.

Miles went down on one knee, as was his standard greeting to Joshua's dogs.

"You're still at Hollyfield, I see," Joshua drawled.

"You know that I am. We dined here last evening. And again this morning at breakfast."

"I thought surely after you'd had your opportunity to meet the princess and come up wanting, you'd have gone home."

"How do you know I came up wanting?" Miles asked as he came to his feet and brushed dog hair from his legs. "I might be at the very top of her list."

"If you were at the top, Lady Aleksander would be pounding on our door at this very moment."

Miles laughed. "And did you come up wanting, too, after your dance? I was surprised to see that you're still a fine dancer. There is an elegance to you that I thought you might have lost. I must commend the tutor your mother hired to teach you and John. It was money well spent."

"I will pass along your congratulations to her. And by the by, the princess forced me to dance with her."

"Forced," Miles scoffed.

"Never mind," Joshua said. "I'm not thinking of the ball." Which was a terrible lie, as he hadn't thought of much else. Except that kiss, of course. That had been burned into his brain.

"But you brought it up."

Joshua grunted. He didn't know why he was so annoyed that she'd managed to entice him to dance when he was against it. There was a time he would have done the same or worse. He'd made a game of flirting and enticing young women to do as he wanted. He supposed he didn't like being beaten at his own game. And then she'd said the thing that cut through all else. She'd said the truth. That he was the way he was because of his loss.

He'd felt so exposed when she said it. But everyone knew it was true. And if Miles knew what she'd said, he would take the opportunity to drive the point home.

Speaking of Miles, he was staring a little too intently at Joshua this very minute, probably trying to see inside his head. "Again, why are you here, Miles?" he blurted. "Surely the Earl of Clarendon has business that needs tending, a house that must be looked after, tenants that must be heard."

"Your hospitality is, as always, deplorable. You are right, I do have affairs that need tending, but like any man with substantial holdings, I have the people in place to ensure things carry on while I'm away. If you would like to know why I have not left you to rot in your darkness, it is because I have developed more than a passing interest in Miss Allison Carhill."

Joshua looked up. "Allison Carhill. The one with the muddy brown hair and pale skin?" He turned in his chair toward Miles. "That slight little thing?"

"No, the one with the hair the color of tea, the luminescent blue eyes and the alabaster skin. *That* Allison Carhill."

Funny how two men could look at the same woman and see two vastly different beings.

Just then, Butler entered the room. He was carrying that blasted silver tray, on which was a thick cream envelope. Joshua shook his head. "Take it away, Butler. I don't want it."

"Well, I do," Miles countered, and plucked the envelope from Butler's tray. He held it up with a smile. "As it happens, it's addressed to me."

"You're getting your post here, now?"

Miles ignored Joshua's grousing and opened the letter and read the contents. He smiled. He looked up at Joshua. "We have been invited to dine."

"What do you mean, *we?*"

"I mean you and me, obviously. Would you like to know who has issued the invitation?"

Joshua snorted. "Hardly necessary. Iddesleigh can't let a week pass without issuing an invitation to one thing or another."

"His sister, the beautiful Lady Caroline Hawke, and her husband, Prince Leopold of Alucia, will be arriving at Iddesleigh on Thursday."

Joshua groaned. Devonshire didn't need any more royalty to arrive and cause more rumpus. The countryside was supposed to be pleasantly bucolic and quiet, not teeming with royalty. "I beg you explain to me why the man will not take no for an answer? I scowled the entire time I was at the ball. What more does he need?"

"Oh, I wish I understood it, too. If it were me, not only would I have ceased to invite you, I would have barred my door to you. But he seems an affable fellow, willing to forgive and forget. You should greet this invitation with enthusiasm."

"Why?"

"Because you're all cleaned up now, and Butler and Mr. Martin have gone to great lengths to revive your wardrobe. I understand you have new shirts coming."

Joshua glared at his butler.

Butler lifted his chin ever so slightly.

"Who gave you leave to toddle off and spend my money?"

"You did, Your Grace."

Joshua glared at him some more. That was true. Butler had leave to purchase whatever was necessary and Joshua trusted him completely. "No one asked you to freshen my wardrobe."

"I beg your pardon, Your Grace, but Lord Clarendon adamantly requested it."

Miles grinned, clearly pleased with himself.

"I have no intention of attending a bloody supper party so that I can remark on the weather and the crops for an interminable time."

"But you must," Miles said. "Carhill will be inclined to believe me a suitable match for his daughter if I come in the company of a duke. You know how these fathers are—they must see the connections and *feel* the connections if a man is to have a chance with his daughter. You, sir, give me the standing I need."

"My presence doesn't help you, Miles—have you forgotten that everyone thinks I'm mad?"

"Everyone does *not* think you're mad. *I* do. Although I wouldn't be surprised if Iddesleigh thinks it as well. Nevertheless, Mr. Carhill has not yet been exposed to your current state of mind, so we have a bit of time before he forms an unfavorable opinion of you." He smiled and handed the invitation to Butler. "Please send our warmest regards and affirmation that we will attend."

"Wait just a bloody minute," Joshua said, but his rotten butler had already turned and walked crisply from the room. The dogs trotted along behind him, as if they suspected Butler would lead them to a bone or two. Would no one consider his wishes?

He glowered at his oldest friend. "You have to stop this, Miles."

"Stop what?"

"Managing my life. Directing my servants. Receiving your post here and freshening my bloody wardrobe."

"You want me to stop so that you can continue to wallow in misery?"

"I lost a wife and a child!"

"You lost them two years ago, Joshua. Two years you've sat in sorrow, and with a life yet to live. I will say what no one else will say to you, because I love you as a brother— you are wearing their deaths like a shield. I don't know if you even realize how thoroughly you've settled into this melancholia, but as your friend, I will do whatever I can to see you out of it."

"I've not settled into melancholia. I happen to be planning a trip to the Province of Canada." He wasn't planning such a trip, *per se*, but the thought had just occurred to him.

Miles looked confused. "Canada?"

"Canada."

"Why?"

"To hunt. Bears. They have bears there."

All right, he didn't know what all was in the province,

and he'd never given a single thought to hunting bears. But he'd recently read a travel journal by a gentleman who had traversed a great bit of the Canadian province, and *he'd* described the bears. It seemed exciting. It seemed remote. It seemed perfect for someone who wanted nothing but his dogs and cat and to be left alone.

He expected a lecture from Miles, but instead, his friend's face was filling with glee. He could hardly contain himself. And then he couldn't—he burst out laughing. "You're not going to hunt *bears*, Joshua. Bloody hell—"

"I can't do this anymore, Miles!" Joshua suddenly surged to his feet. He was embarrassed—he knew he sounded ridiculous. He dragged his fingers across his scalp. But how did one admit he didn't know what to do with himself?

"You can't do what? *Mope?* Brilliant—you are agreeing with me, then."

"I am talking about this," he said, casting his arm around the study. "I can't be a duke. I can't be expected to produce an heir. I can't attend balls and supper parties and pretend that I'm perfectly at ease in this house and in this life."

Miles's expression softened. "You might be perfectly at ease if you would just live your life. You might find another love, someone with whom you could bring an heir into the world. But you won't even try, Joshua. You rarely leave this house. You roam the countryside at night—"

"Who told you that?"

"It doesn't matter. What matters is that you can't continue like this. You, of all people, have the best reason to dine with your neighbors. Because if you don't start to live again, you'll die. And I, for one, will not idly stand by and watch it." He turned and walked out the door, done with the conversation. Miles was at least as headstrong as Joshua.

Joshua stared glumly at Artemis, who stared back, unimpressed. He reached out to pet him, but Artemis hissed and batted his hand away, then jumped gracefully from the desk and walked out after Miles, his tail high in the air.

Even his cat was against him.

Joshua went to the window and opened the drapes. Then the blinds. He stared out at the wet, dreary day. He thought again of the dance with Princess Amelia. Mostly, he thought of the way she'd felt in his arms. So damnably soft. And her hair, that mix of gold and cream and white. He thought of the things she said, of the way she spoke with such truth. He thought of that kiss and felt his blood stirring all over again. He sighed, pressed a hand against the frame of the window, hoping the pressure would push his desire back into its coffin.

Who was she considering as a match? Which opportunist would pursue her? She might come with a royal title and wealth, and she was comely...but that woman clearly had a mind of her own. Some men found that disconcerting. Usually the peacocks.

Personally, he liked that about her.

But he didn't *like* her.

CHAPTER TWENTY-ONE

May, 1858
England

To Her Majesty the Queen, Justine,

Dearest, I apologize for not responding to your recent letters before today, but nothing of note has happened since the ball and it would have been a very short letter. But today, Lord I's sister, Lady Caroline, and her husband Prince Leopold of Alucia, arrived for the weekend. The girls were so stirred by their arrival that they turned into little whirling dervishes like the ones we saw a few years ago when the sultan visited Rohalan. Unfortunately, all the shrieking prompted Birdie to cry, and then there was such a commotion that it was fifteen minutes before the pair were properly introduced to me.

Lady Caroline is beautiful and quite charming, and she spoke to me as if we were acquainted. She said that we had met at her brother's house in Mayfair many years ago, which alas, I do not recall. Her husband, Prince Leopold, claimed to have made my acquaintance when I was still in swaddling, at the Kestrotov Summit. He said Papa was proudly showing me to all who had gathered. Isn't that the summit where our father and the Alucian king could not come to terms over that spit of land and departed in anger? I believe that was the start of the Brezlin War, was it not?

I told the prince that while I would not recall that meeting, I felt as if I knew him because his reputation lived long in the halls of St. Edys. I meant only that everyone remembered him, but Lady I very nearly fainted. His Highness laughed and asked if his reported reputation was good or bad, and I told him it depended on who one asked. He laughed again, but Lady I muttered something to Lila and I don't think it was very kind. I truly don't understand her nerves, on my word.

We went in for tea, and Lord I joined us then, his neck cloth undone. He said he was in the bath, and that Lady C had said they would arrive late. She countered that she'd meant they'd arrive late morning. She was wearing a bonnet, and this she took off and tossed onto a chair, and when she did, one of the footmen who had accompanied her stepped in to pick it up. As he was directly in front of me, I smiled at him, and he smiled back. He was tall and handsome, and his uniform fit him very well. Isn't it a pity that all men are not made to wear uniforms of some sort? I particularly like the uniforms of the Weslorian soldiers. Remember the one who stood outside Papa's chambers? You made me pretend to be him so that you could pretend to marry him. I laugh as I write this. I know you'd not want anyone to know of our silly games when we were girls.

I should have liked to have looked at the footman a bit longer, but who should appear as if by magic but

Lady A. She stood just between me and the footman and exchanged many pleasantries with the prince and Lady C, and then someone asked about her husband, and she said he wasn't coming for a few weeks because of some elections in Denmark, and then rattled on quite long, all because she wanted to stand between me and the footman. She is determined that I will not flirt with another servant. She's a killjoy, and I swear, Jussie, I think you've put her up to it.

After she finished her soliloquy on Danish elections, everything seemed to descend into chaos. The girls were bouncing around, demanding attention, and Lady I was in her usual state of panic that there was so much to be done for the supper party this weekend, but then Donovan arrived to quell all anxiety and announced that tomorrow's supper was well in hand. It seems that all he must do is say it, and everyone believes it is true, whether it is or isn't.

He greeted Lady Caroline and her husband warmly, and she threw her arms around his neck and hugged him. She asked if Peter had come, who is Donovan's valet, but he's not really a valet. He told her he'd heard from the Tricklebanks, and they had sent their warmest regards and hoped that Lady Caroline would come to visit again.

Then Lady Caroline inquired as to what I've been about since my arrival in England, and I dutifully reported that I had walked quite a lot and helped some at the girls' school. Lady I said she thought it wasn't good for my skin to be so often in the sun, but I said I had quite a lot of bonnets, and then asked what else I ought to do, as everyone else was well occupied, and if one more person suggested I read a book, I might scream, as I had read so many in the last two years that surely I ought to be deemed a scholar of something.

Prince Leopold said he'd done the same when he'd come to England, all that reading, but that he rather liked reading, and had just finished a tome about the fall of the Roman Empire, and had anyone else read it?

That was when it was collectively decided that everyone would retreat and rest up for the evening meal.

Naturally, Lila followed me to my suite with her journal. You should see it, Jussie—it's quite fat, stuffed with vellum and paper, and bits of ribbon and old quill feathers marking various pages. Who knows what she's really written there? She wanted to tell me of the special guest who would come to dine this weekend, and I suppose I yawned, and she said pretending that it was all tiresome would not keep her from her duty. She said of particular note was Mr. Swann. I asked why and she said that he was handsome, and his mother was an Indian princess, and his father a wealthy landowner from the Lake District. She said he is a scientific man and, at his leisure, he developed an improved method by which kerosene is distilled from coal. Lila was quite pleased with this fact.

I said I couldn't imagine what that had to do with me. Lila said it had made Mr. S a very rich man and that she thought I would like him very much, and I said probably so, as I happen to like *all* gentlemen, but had yet to find one to esteem for more than an evening. That made me think of Lady C's footman. Why do I always think of men who are so wrong for me? Perhaps because it is more exciting than kerosene.

I hadn't wanted to say this, because I had pinned such high hopes on it, but the ball has left me disillusioned. I feel as if I am spinning like a top here. Is it possible I am destined to be alone all my life with only you and William to care for me? Or perhaps I was meant to do something more meaningful than to love someone and bear children. Perhaps I should study things like distilling kerosene from coal or some such that everyone would appreciate. Something helpful to mankind. Hopefully something more interesting than kerosene.

By the grace of God, Lila finally left my room, and when she did, I reread a letter I received at the school. It was written by an old woman, and she said our high expectations are the cause of our disappointments. It makes sense, doesn't it? I think I am so impatient to meet someone who would be with me for life, and I expect it as I am a princess, and therefore, I am constantly disappointed because he hasn't come along yet.

Really, I think it may be too late for me, Jussie. I'm six and twenty, well past the age most ladies are married. I've met some lovely gentlemen here, as lovely as all the gentlemen in Wesloria. But not one of them has incited even the slightest bit of feeling in me. Not a single spark or rainbow or bolt of lightning. I've not been breathless or eager in ages, and in fact, the only time I've been breathless since arriving at Iddesleigh was...well, once when I was almost run over on the road and my heart very nearly quit with shock. And for a few moments when Marley took me in his arms

on the dance floor and spun me around. That felt ex-
hilarating. ~~And then on the bal~~

Stupid man, why must he be so morose? I seem to
think of him instead of the gentlemen who have come
to make my acquaintance. I can't imagine why that
is, other than he vexes me.

If he is in attendance at the supper party this weekend, it will ruin everything. I can hardly think about
some rich kerosene man with the duke's gloomy presence draping over the room. But you mustn't worry—
as long as he is not seated next to me, I will survive.

My regard to Mama and William. You will soon
be presiding over the flower festival! It is my favorite thing in the spring. I miss Wesloria and the dogs.

Your sister, A

CHAPTER TWENTY-TWO

AMELIA WAS NOT seated next to Marley as she feared, but worse—she was seated directly across from him.

She'd almost convinced herself he wouldn't come at all, that he would refuse the invitation as he liked to do, and she would escape his oppressive presence, and thereby also her prurient curiosity about him. That's all it was—she liked to be kissed, and she hadn't been kissed in quite a long time, and his kiss had only stirred up all those things she liked to feel.

It couldn't possibly be more than that, as he was clearly another one who was all wrong for her. She sincerely hoped he wouldn't come so she might turn her full attention to Mr. Swann and his kerosene—heaven save her—but then at the last possible moment it felt as if a bad gust of wind swept him and Lord Clarendon into the house and settled his dark mien over the drawing room.

She was certain that Lila had worked her sorcery and brought him here—there was something about the little smile on her face when the two men entered the room that made Amelia immediately suspect her. She tried to stare more daggers in Lila's direction, but Lila was a master at avoiding her gaze when she wanted to.

The guests gathered in the drawing room for wine before supper, and Marley stood apart, his back to the wall, his clean-shaven, impossibly strong jaw clenched. Clarendon had deserted him to speak with Miss Carhill, a tiny thing who had come in the company of her tiny little parents. How did small people survive a cruel world? Amelia hoped Miss Carhill was never caught outside in a storm, because she would be washed away like an ant.

She didn't give voice to her thought. Blythe could breathe a sigh of relief.

Mr. Swann was, as promised, a handsome man. When he was introduced to her, he'd smiled at Amelia with eyes as warm and brown as hot chocolate. But then he was immediately engaged in conversation with Prince Leopold. The two of them stood near the hearth laughing at a private jest like they were old friends.

Amelia stood with Lady Caroline and her brother, listening to the two of them argue about Maisie. From what Amelia could glean, while visiting her aunt, Maisie had been forbidden from taking porcelain china down to the river to make a boat of it, and had then used words that were inappropriate for a proper young lady.

"I can hardly be held responsible for *that*," Beck had complained. "There are *five* of them, for God's sake, Caro. Who knows the things they hear?"

Amelia imagined what the old crone would have to say to that—she'd be beside herself with indignation. She smiled into her wineglass, thinking she might just write and tell her that at least one parent claimed he could not teach his children properly because there were too many of them.

"You sound as if they appeared at your door and you had no idea how they came to be there. I told you this would happen," Lady Caroline said. "I told you that three children were far too many for an old bachelor."

"Speaking of inappropriate talk," Beck sniffed.

Lady Caroline rolled her eyes, and then shifted her gaze

to Amelia. She frowned. "Are you all right, Your Royal Highness?"

"What?" Amelia looked down at herself. "*Je.* Why do you ask?"

"You look a bit sad."

"Oh. I...your banter makes me realize how much I miss my sister, I think."

"Darling!" Lady Caroline put a comforting arm around her shoulders. "All you have to do is pick one of the gentlemen Lady Aleksander is presenting to you and voilà, you can flit off to St. Edys immediately afterward."

Amelia laughed. "If only it were that simple." She looked across the room, and her gaze inadvertently landed on Marley. To her great surprise, he was looking at her, too. It startled her, and the heat that rushed through her unbalanced her. She turned back to Lady Caroline and forced a smile.

"I understand," Lady Caroline said. "I was very particular in my time, wasn't I, Beck?"

"I can think of words more apt than *particular*," he groused. "*Stubborn. Headstrong—*"

"Yes, all right, you've made your point," his sister interrupted. "What I mean is that I didn't like to be told what to do and desperately needed someone who would *not* attempt to tell me what to do. But really, what I needed was someone who wouldn't be *afraid* to tell me what to do. Do you see what I mean?"

"Ummm... I'm not sure that I do."

"My lord." Garrett, the butler, had sidled up to Beck. "Supper is served."

"Excellent. Ladies, prepare to have your tongue tickled and your belly satisfied." He stepped into the center of the room. "Ladies and gentlemen, supper is served. We may go through to the dining room."

The promenade was quickly arranged—Beck and Blythe, of course, as the hosts. Lady Caroline and her prince. And much to Amelia's chagrin, she was to be escorted by the next ranking person in the room: the Duke of Marley.

He wordlessly bowed and presented his arm.

"We meet again. In a well-lit room, and without the benefit of music. It's a new world," she said.

"The world looks very much the same to me. May I see you to your seat?"

She put her hand lightly on his arm. She couldn't touch him without thinking about that kiss. She could feel the flush of memory creep up her neck and onto her chest. Did he think of it? Or was that a service he went around performing at all the country balls?

They began to walk, neither of them speaking. It was absurd, strolling along like an old married couple with nothing to say. Amelia couldn't stand it. "Have you nothing to say this evening?"

He kept his gaze fixed straight ahead. "Is there something you would like me to say?"

"I thought you'd at least make an attempt at the civilities. Inquire after my health. How long I intend to be in England, if anyone else has kissed me. That sort of thing."

"You look in perfect health, Your Royal Highness. The picture of youth. And Lady Aleksander has told everyone from Cornwall to London that you will be at Iddesleigh through the end of summer. The rest of it is none of my affair."

All of that was true. But it was the polite thing to at least *inquire*. Amelia should have left it there, been grateful that for once she didn't have to make small talk. On the other hand, she'd never been grateful for men not paying attention to her. Nor was she one to allow silence to fill a promenade. The question at the back of her mind tumbled out of her mouth. "Why were you looking at me in the drawing room?"

He glanced at her. "Pardon?"

"In the drawing room. You were looking at me."

"I wasn't looking at you. I was looking into space for wont of something better to do and you happened to occupy that space."

She stared at him. "Do you really expect me to believe that?"

One corner of his mouth tipped up. "I certainly would hope not. All right, I was looking at you. I was looking at you just as was everyone gathered in the drawing room. You are, after all, a beautiful woman."

The compliment was unexpected and made her blush again.

"And I wondered what had happened to your tiara."

Amelia was tempted to touch the top of her head to assure herself she wasn't wearing one. "It seemed like a lot of trouble for an intimate gathering."

"Everything seems like a lot of trouble for an intimate gathering," he said under his breath as they entered the dining room.

"Is it really so awful?"

"What?"

"Dining with your neighbors. With friends. With *me*."

"Dining here with friends and neighbors and even you is not at all awful. Here is your seat." He dropped her hand and pulled out the chair.

"But you don't enjoy it. You don't find it diverting."

"No."

She gathered her skirt and sat. "If you don't find these occasions awful or diverting, then how do you find them?"

He pushed her chair in, leaned slightly over her shoulder and said, "Enjoy your meal, Your Royal Highness." He walked away from her chair.

That was when it occurred to Amelia what was left. "*Boring*," she murmured to his departing back. He was *bored*.

She watched him skirt the table, looking for his name card, and finding it, and the dawning realization of where that put him at the table. He glanced up. Amelia smirked.

He sat down, directly across the table from her.

People were still moving around, finding their places. Amelia leaned forward. "You're bored."

The Duke of Marley cupped his hand around his ear, pretending not to have heard. Amelia refused to repeat herself. When she would not, he leaned back, shrugged indifferently, then turned to speak to the tiny Miss Carhill, who had just been seated to his right.

Verdammt, as her mother would have said. *Damn him*. Amelia was highly piqued, but also highly intrigued because she herself was uninterested, and she couldn't imagine how the two of them, as opposite as night and day, could be the same in this.

Whatever the answer, she was now full of interest and pique. And it was wildly inexcusable that she couldn't seem to think of anything else, particularly as no one else appeared to have noticed him and his ennui.

It was especially aggravating because Mr. Swann was everything Lila had promised him to be. He had thick black hair and lashes, brown skin, and brown eyes. He surprised her by speaking Weslorian to her. He was a student of languages, he said. He was not at all dry as she'd feared, but far livelier than one might expect of someone who spent a lot of time with kerosene. He was well traveled, he loved horses, said he'd once attended the Royal Lentkin in Wesloria, an annual event featuring horse racing and trading.

"It was a few years ago, admittedly," he said in his deep, silky voice. "But I recall seeing you there, in the royal box. You were the beauty of them all."

The overserved compliment quelled Amelia's curiosity about him a notch. It was what everyone said and had said all her life—Justine was the queen; Amelia was the beauty. Her looks defined her in her own country, her attributes and talents and anything she might actually offer the world boiled down to that. She had long passed the point of being able to demur and blush as her mother would have liked when someone remarked on her appearance. But in moments like this, it made her wish that *she'd* been the one to squeeze kerosene from coal. Imagine that conversation. *Thank you. Did I mention that I improved the method of squeezing kerosene from coal?* Or however that was supposed to be stated.

"That is very kind," she said, and mustered a smile.

"However, if I may be so bold, I'd like to know more," Mr. Swann said. "Beauty in a woman is certainly appreciated, but there is so much more to a person than the casing, wouldn't you agree?"

Had he just been inside her head? "I would."

"Perhaps after supper we might stroll the grounds and you can tell me more about yourself," he said to her in Weslorian. "I understand there is to be a lunar eclipse this evening." He smiled.

"*Je*, perhaps." She smiled back.

Lord Clarendon took the opportunity to ask Mr. Swann about his scientific endeavors.

The charming Mr. Swann had everyone's attention while he explained how he'd improved the process. His response was rather convoluted, and one would have to be keenly interested in coal to keep their mind from wandering. And Amelia found her mind wandering to the girls' school. Why *not* teach them how to do things like distill kerosene from coal? Why were improvements like that always left to the male sex? The simplicity of girls' education by comparison seemed so ridiculous to her, as if the world—rather, *men*—thought girls were incapable of thinking scientifically. Girls were expected to learn how to be good wives and mothers, and boys were expected to change the world. It was even worse if one's family lacked privilege—there was even less for a girl to learn. Read, write, and learn your figures, then sweep and cook and launder clothes and don't forget your needlepoint.

She thought of the girls who came to school at the old cottage. They were bright and creative, full of curiosity about the world around them. She wished they could grow up to be scientists and mathematicians and parliamentarians. She imagined them in blue gowns with white aprons, wearing monocles around their necks and gathered around beakers, studying the findings of their scientific experiments. Wouldn't it be wonderful if the girls in Mr. Roberts's care presented Queen Victoria with findings that revolutionized an industry? A new way of doing something from which the whole world would benefit, thought of entirely by girls?

Mr. Swann was describing new machinery that was currently being developed, but it was apparent to her that the charming man had lost his audience. There was an art to a supper party, and that was the ability to engage one and all. Amelia was rather good at that sort of thing, and she could have saved him. But she didn't feel like wresting this moment from him. She suppressed a sigh and glanced at her plate, then happened to look up—right into the gray-eyed gaze of Marley. He was quietly but impassively studying her, like one might study a fish they'd just caught to determine if they ought to toss it back.

She leaned forward. "You're looking at me again," she whispered, just as Mr. Swann reached the crescendo of his machinery talk.

He shook his head, and with his chin, indicated something behind her. Amelia turned. The only thing behind her was the painting of a fat man. She turned back and arched a brow at him.

He arched one back at her, but his was less inquisitive and more challenging.

"What are you two going on about?" Beck asked suddenly, his voice booming.

He was speaking to her and Marley.

Mr. Swann stopped midsentence and looked around, surprised that anyone had been talking during his address.

"I beg your pardon, it is my fault," Marley said. "I was admiring the painting just behind Her Royal Highness. She must have thought I was leering at her."

"Not at all," Amelia said lightly.

"The second Earl of Iddesleigh, I think?" Marley said to Beck.

"The very one," Beck said. "A great-great-great-... uncle?" he said uncertainly and looked at his sister for confirmation.

"Cousin," Lady Caroline corrected.

"Ah, yes. Our cousin's legacy lives on. He had a fondness for port and horses and excessively sought them both."

"Isn't he the one who originally expanded Goosefeather

Abbey?" Mr. Carhill asked. "I seem to recall some history about it."

"Very good, Mr. Carhill. But he wasn't the one to expand it. That would have been his son, our..." He looked to Lady Caroline again.

"Cousin."

"Cousin. This one," he said, pointing at the portrait, "sought to tear down the abbey. Didn't like the geese, you understand. There was a time they roosted there every year and made a terrible mess."

"Darling! Please, we are dining," Blythe said.

"But it's the truth, dearest. Or it was. The abbey doesn't get many geese now."

"What happened to them?" Lord Clarendon asked.

"The geese? I reckon they've gone the way of everything to do with that abbey—it's a mystery. The place must be cursed or haunted—but we intend to change that."

"Change what?" Marley asked.

"The abbey." Beck motioned for the butler to refill wineglasses. "It borders your property, too, Marley. Do you know anything about it? Perhaps who it belongs to?" he asked curiously.

Marley picked up his glass and swirled the contents. "I wager I know as much as you, my lord."

"We intend to purchase it if we can get to the bottom of who owns it."

"Whatever for?" Marley asked. "It's a ruin. A hazard, really."

"Yes, but my man thinks it could be revitalized. He assures me that at least part of it can be made useful."

The duke brought his glass to his lips. "Useful for what?" he asked just before he sipped.

"For the Iddesleigh School for Girls. Our little school has been such a success that we must expand."

Marley suddenly coughed, nearly spitting out the wine. Lady Caroline, on his right, put her hand on his back. "Goodness, Your Grace. Are you all right?"

"Yes, thank you," he said hoarsely. He looked, Amelia thought, like he would be ill.

"A girls' school," Mr. Swann said. "How interesting."

"My brother and his wife founded the little school down the road when it became clear that options for properly educating their daughters were lacking," Lady Caroline explained. "It's proven so popular that many wish to send their girls there."

"Bravo, my lord, my lady," Mr. Carhill said. "I applaud your efforts. We had a devil of a time finding a proper tutor for Allison and her sister."

Beck bowed his head in acknowledgment. "We are in need of more teachers and more room. As the abbey sits empty, it seems the perfect location. It's on the road between Iddesleigh and Hollyfield, not far from our present location. And it intersects the main highway north and is convenient to the train. We would like to make it a boarding school."

Amelia hadn't heard about the boarding school. "But that's marvelous!" she said. "I always wanted to attend a boarding school. I thought it would be the happiest of times to be surrounded by girls my age. Alas, my father the king was firmly against it. Our tutor said we were already at a boarding school, in that we lived in a separate part of the palace than our parents for most of the year. But it wasn't the same."

"I think you were fortunate to be in St. Edys, Your Royal Highness," said Prince Leopold. "I was sent to a military school in Fondaven, in the north of Alucia. I've never been so cold in my life."

Several of the guests laughed.

"We should very much like to have a boarding school," Beck continued. "But first, the mystery of the ownership of the abbey must be solved."

"Why is it a mystery?" Amelia asked.

"The property records were lost in a parish fire many years ago."

"Well, I think it is commendable of you to devote such thought to education for girls, my lord," Amelia said. "What do you think, Your Grace?" she asked innocently.

The duke jerked his gaze to her, clearly startled by the question. "What do I think of...?"

"The school," Amelia said. "Or, more generally, girls' education."

He glanced around the table. "I think it is necessary."

Such a bland answer. "*Je*, and?"

"And...?" He eyed her curiously. "I'm pleased that Iddesleigh has taken such an interest in it."

"Do you think girls should be educated as thoroughly as boys?" she asked.

"No," Mr. Carhill said flatly.

Amelia glanced at his daughter, whose gaze was on her plate. She wondered what Miss Carhill thought. "May I ask why not?"

"I should think it obvious," he said. "There is no need for it. Girls will become wives and mothers. There is no need for them to study subjects they won't use in their daily lives. They don't need to know how to, for example, distill kerosene from coal." He nodded at Mr. Swann.

Mr. Swann nodded in agreement with Mr. Carhill,

"Some subjects, I think, are overly complicated for the female brain."

Lord. What did these two gentlemen think? That the female brain was a tiny little pebble rattling around in their heads? "How interesting!" she said brightly. "Do you believe the female brain is inferior to the male brain?"

"Well, in some ways, yes," Mr. Swann said. "Our Creator has made our minds differently, hasn't He? The female brain is inclined to nurture and give life. The male brain is inclined to protect and provide, to solve problems."

"I beg your pardon, Mr. Swann, but that is ridiculous. I can solve problems as easily as you," Lady Caroline said.

Mr. Swann's smile was a bit patronizing. "Yes, of course. I'm not speaking of anyone here. I'm speaking in general."

"But don't you think, given the same education, that females could also solve complex problems?" Amelia pressed. "My sister and I were taught subjects most girls are not taught, because she would be queen one day. She solves problems frequently. Much bigger than problems any of us here might have."

"I've no doubt she is a talented and resourceful queen," Mr. Swann said. "But she has male advisors and a husband to protect and defend and to guide her."

Amelia's pulse quickened. Justine didn't need men to tell her what she had learned at her father's knee.

"I know I speak only for myself, Highness," said Blythe, "but if I had to keep the accounts of Iddesleigh straight, well…" She laughed, and Mrs. Carhill and all the men joined in.

Amelia looked at Lady Caroline. She frowned back at Amelia, then shifted her gaze to Lila, who was staring ponderously at Blythe.

"I never really had a head for figures," Blythe said airily.

Amelia wouldn't press the issue. Beck seemed to think differently than his wife, and that's what mattered in this house. She settled back and smiled prettily. "All the same, I think we can all agree that it's a boon for Devonshire to have a school for girls."

"Absolutely!" Mr. Carhill said. A few nods in agreement, a *Hear! Hear!* or two. Amelia glanced at the duke. He was looking at her with an expression she couldn't quite read. He probably thought she'd weighed in on a subject for which she had no right to have an opinion. He probably thought that the sooner she was married with someone to tell her what to think, the better. She frowned at him.

"Speaking of girls and education," Blythe said. "Our oldest girls have been at their music and have a musicale planned for your entertainment." She beamed as if she was introducing a London opera. "Let us have our dessert and then we can retire to the drawing room."

Amelia smiled, the consummate guest, not here to ruffle feathers. She happened to glance at Marley again. He was still looking at her, one corner of his mouth tipped up ever so slightly in something that, on any other man, might have indicated a smile. On him, she wasn't certain, but she had the distinct impression it was a smirk. He'd enjoyed the conversation and her exasperation. She wasn't as good at hiding it as she thought.

But if there was any doubt, *he* was the bore. Not her.

CHAPTER TWENTY-THREE

IT WAS JOSHUA'S worst nightmare come true—a girl's school, a *boarding* school, practically right outside his door. He stared at the old earl in the painting. *Why didn't you take it down, you old fool?*

He could imagine the agony—the noise, the high-pitched girlish voices alternately crying and laughing and then, all the talking and singing. He imagined them trampling gardens and setting cattle and sheep free from their meadows and wreaking havoc up and down this valley.

"What are you doing?" Miles whispered to him as the gentlemen stood to join the ladies.

He was so lost in his imagining of an infestation of little girls that Joshua hadn't even noticed the command from Iddesleigh to assemble in the main drawing room. Everyone was already out of their seats, their cigars smoked, their ports drunk.

He roused himself and followed them from the dining room.

The ladies were already seated, and before the hearth, a man Marley thought looked vaguely familiar was arranging the Iddesleigh daughters according to height. There were five girls in all, the youngest no more than two years, and that one bouncing around in bare feet. The other four were wearing identical blue frocks, their golden red hair bound in curls at their crowns.

Miles stepped up to where Joshua was standing and leaned in. "Try and look like you enjoy it, at least," he whispered. "The children are not deserving of your scowl."

He was scowling?

Miles strolled to stand behind Miss Carhill.

"All right, then, Mrs. Hughes?" the man said.

A middle-aged woman in a lace cap appeared and hurried to the piano. She sat on the bench, arranged her music just so, and placed her hands on the keys. Ready.

The man stepped forward and bowed. "If I may, I am Mr. Donovan, friend of the family, and uncle of sorts. And this," he said, stepping back and gesturing with his arm to the girls, "Is the Hawke chorus."

Everyone in the room clapped. Joshua, too—he wasn't an ogre. But he had a feeling this performance would be excruciating.

Mr. Donovan gave Mrs. Hughes a nod and the music began. The girls missed their opening note. Mr. Donovan put up his hand, Mrs. Hughes stopped playing, and he walked to the line of girls. He went down the row, leaning over, whispering to each of them.

"But Birdie will ruin it," one of the smaller ones said with a stamp of her foot.

Mr. Donovan heeded that caution and picked up the youngest child and returned to his place. The music began again. This time, the girls began to sing on their mark. And, remarkably, *dance*. Mr. Donovan put the littlest girl down and began to mimic the movements the girls were supposed to make, guiding them through it.

"*Little Miss Careful whenever she wish-es*" the girls sang while moving arms and legs here and there. The two oldest girls had clearly practiced their steps. The next two watched the older ones, copying their moves, a beat or two behind. And the little one, Birdie, hopped around the piano on both feet like a chicken, clapping her pudgy little hands and singing a song that only she knew the words to.

"May play with her best tea party dish-es..."

The singing was just like what he'd heard coming from the school—horrendously out of tune. And yet, something came over Joshua. A tingly bit of warmth, the feeling one had when surprised or titillated. It started in his belly and moved slowly up, wrapping around his heart and squeezing the soot from it. It spread to his limbs and crept up his neck. He tried to shake the feeling loose, but watching those girls so earnestly sing their song and dance their dance, he was helpless. The feeling flooded into him and squeezed out his eyes.

These girls, these rowdy little angels, the ones responsible for the noise and the garden trampling and the cow releasing, had caught hold of his heart with their terrible singing. The memory of what he'd so desperately wanted from Diana, the overwhelming desire that had driven him to convince her to try again to bear his child when she'd suffered two miscarriages, was climbing out of its vault.

It was the one thing he'd wanted in his life. *Truly* wanted. To be a father. He wanted to be Iddesleigh, with his beaming smile, glancing around at everyone to see if they appreciated his perfect daughters as much as he did. And when that hope had been taken from Joshua, he'd pushed his desire for it so far down, it couldn't breathe. He'd smothered it. Snuffed it out. Despised it, loathed it, blamed it.

And now, here he was, the one place he didn't want to be, not four feet from those little girls, feeling it rise up like a phoenix in him. Bloody rotten hope, all fresh and new and sprouting into a dull ache.

The first performance was completed. The audience

clapped, and the girls, led by the oldest one, clasped hands and bowed.

"Is that all?" Iddesleigh asked eagerly. "Haven't you another song prepared for us?"

"Yes, Papa," said a girl who looked to be the middle child. Maisie, Joshua thought he'd heard.

"Are you certain? We've not practiced another one," Donovan pointed out.

"*Yes*," Maisie reminded him. "It's one we sing in the nursery, Papa."

"Then by all means, let us hear it," Iddesleigh said, and once again, looked around proudly at his guests.

Mrs. Hughes knew the unsanctioned song and began to play. The girls grabbed hands and began to slowly circle. "*Ring around the rosie, a pocket full of posies, at-shoo, at-shoo, we all fall down.*"

Only one fell down.

"Not *yet*, Meg," said the oldest one.

The princess laughed.

"Oh dear," said Lady Iddesleigh. "Donovan? Shouldn't we do something?"

"All right then, lassies, we've had our—"

"*The king has sent his daughter to fetch a pail of water at-shoo at-shoo, we all fall down!*" Meg yanked Maisie's hand, causing her to fall. Maisie shrieked and hopped to her feet and promptly pulled Meg's hair.

"Tilly, no!" cried Lady Iddesleigh as the biggest girl took a swing at the back of Maisie.

Iddesleigh stood from his seat and faced his guests. "Regrettably, the performance has come to an end." Behind him, Mr. Donovan, Mrs. Hughes, and Lady Iddesleigh were working to separate the participants in the brawl while the princess laughed, clearly delighted by the melee.

"Didn't you say we may see a lunar eclipse this evening, Mr. Swann?" Iddesleigh asked loudly.

"Yes! If we may walk onto your lawn?"

"I think we best walk somewhere, and the sooner the better," Iddesleigh said, and led the group out of the drawing room and away from the arguing girls.

They walked out onto the terrace. The lawn below was dark; only a pair of torches dimly lit the grass. "This is most excellent," Mr. Swann said. "We should be able to see all the stars. If you will follow me?"

He jogged down the steps to the lawn. The ladies slowly made their way in the moonlight, a couple of them grabbing onto the arm of a man nearby. Once they had all made it to the lawn, Mr. Swann went forward and stood on a fountain wall. "You will want to spread out," he said, using both arms to demonstrate how they should disperse. "I find stargazing is best accomplished when you feel like you are the only one on earth."

Joshua rolled his eyes, but he did as requested, moving away from them all...and Miles and Miss Carhill in particular.

"Now then," Mr. Swann said. He began to point out some constellations. Lady Aleksander seemed the most interested of all of them and peppered the man with questions. Joshua, however, was not particularly interested in Mr. Swann's cosmological lecture, and moved deeper into the shadows, toward the hedge.

"Attempting an escape?"

The feminine voice startled Joshua and he twisted around. There was the princess, up against the hedge. Her pale blue gown practically blended with the moonlight. "Are you?"

"Not yet. I would like to see a lunar eclipse—I've never seen one. Have you?"

He shook his head and looked heavenward. The stars were brilliant this evening. He lowered his gaze to her. "Are you capable of understanding the eclipse? Or will it require interpretation?"

The princess gave him a sharp look. Joshua couldn't help himself—he smiled.

She peered curiously at him. "I must be dreaming. Was that a *jest*, Your Grace? A bit of humor?"

"I think it was."

"Now you see, when the earth rotates…" Mr. Swann was instructing loudly from the fountain. He was obviously a very learned man. But the sort of learned man who was convinced that everyone around him wanted to learn from his knowledge.

Joshua looked up at the moon. He could see no sign of an eclipse. "I expected to see a shadow."

The princess looked up, too.

"What do you see when you look at the moon?" he asked curiously.

"A hare."

"A *hare*?"

"*Je*, look." She pointed at the moon and traced a shape that did not look like a hare to him. "Do you see?"

"No. Nothing in the moon resembles a hare."

"But it does!" She shifted closer to him and pointed again. Joshua moved behind her and tried to follow her finger. He was distracted by the smell of rosewater in her hair, the sweet fragrance of her perfume.

"Just there is the Orion constellation." Mr. Swann's voice carried over the lawn to where Joshua and the princess were standing. "Named for a hunter in Greek mythology. You can see his club, his shield." He pointed skyward, gesturing.

"Now do you see it?" the princess asked, ignoring Mr. Swann's speech.

"No."

She sighed with exasperation and glanced over her shoulder at him. "Then what *do* you see?"

"Two things. I see a man."

"Where?"

Joshua stepped closer. He didn't know what made him do it, but he settled one hand on her waist and leaned his head over her shoulder. "He's a bit lopsided, but see the two dark spots there," he said, pointing out what looked like depressions in the moon.

The princess leaned her head against his shoulder and looked up. Her hair tickled his nose. He didn't know what to do with this odd little bit of intimacy between them. But he didn't stop pointing, and he didn't nudge her away, because he liked the way she felt against him. It felt natural. It felt like she ought to be leaning against him all the time.

The crypt inside him began to rumble. He ignored it. "And the nose just beneath." He pointed, tracing the air like she had.

"Ah," she said.

"Do you see it?"

"No."

"What else do you see?" she asked, and lifted away from his body, stepping forward, folding her arms across her middle.

He was keenly aware of the space she'd just occupied. It felt empty. Exposed to the elements. "I see infinity."

"What do you mean?"

"I mean that the moon goes on and on, appearing every

night, disappearing every morning. Nothing to do but orbit the earth. On and on and on. Seems tedious, doesn't it?"

She snorted. "You are describing life, Your Grace. We go to sleep, we rise the next morning, and we do it again. The same thing every day." She turned her attention to him. Her gaze moved across his face, then lingered on his mouth. His blood stirred—she was thinking about that kiss as much as he was. "Does it follow that our lives are tedious?"

"Would you have it any other way?" he asked. "The alternative is grim."

She laughed softly. "There is no other way I may have it. I sleep at night, and I rise the next day, and I dress and maybe I ride and maybe I read, and maybe I have visitors... but mostly, I wait. I wait and I wait and I wait. The only thing that makes all that waiting bearable are the surprises that come along when I am least expecting them."

"You must experience many surprises, Your Highness. Not the least of them a steady march of gentlemen admirers for you to entertain."

Her smile was charmingly lopsided. "There you go again, assuming that because they admire me I must entertain them. The steady march of them is hardly a surprise. I expect men to admire me. It's predictable. And boring. Unsurprising."

"Hmm," he said, admiring the curve of her neck. "You make all that admiration sound unpleasant."

"It's not unpleasant at all. I rather like it. But it's not surprising." She shrugged. "We are all born to a certain path."

"Are we?"

"*Je.* I was born to be admired, and you were born to be sullen. And we are those things until we are surprised." She tilted her face up to smile at him. Her features were illuminated by moonlight, and he knew she was teasing him, but he'd been miserable for so long he didn't know how to respond. His desire was to surprise her now, to kiss her again, hold her again. He wanted to feel his blood flowing and his heat rising and his heart beating. In other words, he wanted to feel part of the living again.

"I wish I could surprise you," she said. "I wish I—"

"Your Royal Highness, have you seen? The shadow is beginning to cover the moon."

And here came Mr. Swann to ruin the moment, crashing into their midst to draw her attention away from Joshua and to the sky. What did she wish? *What the bloody hell did she wish?*

He was not surprised that someone had come along to ruin the moment.

But he was surprised that he cared.

CHAPTER TWENTY-FOUR

A FEW DAYS after the supper party, Lila and Blythe stood on the drive at Iddesleigh House and watched Mr. Swann and the princess ride away, her guards trailing behind. Mr. Swann had arrived earlier with a broad smile and the gift of a horse for the princess. "I have heard it said you are an accomplished rider," he said as he presented her with the Arabian.

"I am," she confirmed without hesitation. She looked at the horse, then at Mr. Swann. "Thank you, Mr. Swann. Your gift is quite thoughtful...but too extravagant. I'm afraid I can't accept—I couldn't possibly transport the horse to St. Edys, and even if I could, he'd be swallowed up in stables with all the other palace horses."

Mr. Swann clearly hadn't anticipated this response and looked rather stunned. He probably thought he would be lauded up and down Devonshire for his gift. But as he was a clever man, he smoothly pivoted. "Then perhaps we might consider him a loan for your convenience whilst you are in England."

Amelia looked at the horse again. "I rather like the roan mare I've been riding."

Mr. Swann's smile fell.

"Mr. Swann, you are so very generous," Blythe said. "My husband and I should be delighted to stable the horse for Her Royal Highness during her stay." She looked pointedly at Princess Amelia, but the princess was stroking the horse's nose and murmuring to it.

An hour or so later, when the pair of them at last rode away, Blythe sighed wearily. "She doesn't have to be unkind."

"Was she unkind?" Lila asked. "I thought she was well within her rights to say it was too much. Who brings a *horse* as a gift? A dog, a kitten, perhaps. But a horse?"

"*I* thought it was charming. He obviously esteems her."

Lila clasped her hands at her waist. "I wouldn't be so certain of that, Blythe. It's been my experience that the ones who try too hard are often more concerned about winning than anything else."

Blythe looked at Lila with confusion. "Well of course he is. There is a great advantage to the winner of this particular contest, isn't there? Why did you invite him here if that's not your intent?"

"Because it has also been my experience that one never really knows the sort of suitor one will be until he's met the lady." She shrugged. She couldn't be right about all of them. The few times she'd met Mr. Swann, she'd thought him charming. It wasn't until the supper party that she'd realized how pretentious he was.

"I think he seems a perfect match for the princess."

"Perhaps he is. But she has yet to indicate what she thinks of him."

"Oh?" Blythe asked eagerly. "What has she said?"

Princess Amelia hadn't said much, and that was the problem. "That she had no complaints about him, and she would consider him." In fact, the princess never had any complaints about anyone but Marley. She said the duke had annoyed her by implying he was bored with the supper. But then, later that evening, while Mr. Swann was pointing out stars and constellations and the beginning of an eclipse, Lila noticed that both Princess Amelia and the Duke of Marley were nowhere to be seen. She'd wanted to kick herself for her lapse in attention—she should have had her eyes on Princess Amelia, gauging how she responded to Mr. Swann. It was her own fault—she'd been enamored of the night sky, and Mr. Swann did seem to know a lot.

That was the other problem—Mr. Swann wanted as much attention as Princess Amelia and had managed to command it.

When Princess Amelia had reappeared with Mr. Swann— and Marley trailing behind them—she smiled and told them all about a Russian astronomer who had come to the Weslorian court with a powerful telescope. "It seemed almost as if you were standing on the stars," she said. "He named a star for me. One for my sister, too."

"How wonderful," Mr. Swann had said. "Where is the star?"

"In the sky, sir."

Everyone had laughed.

"I think you should try and convince her, Lila," Blythe said. "She is not the easiest person to like, is she? But Mr. Swann seems to take her in stride."

Lila thought Princess Amelia was probably very easy to like if Blythe would just try and understand her. But Blythe was like others in that she had a firm idea of who a royal princess was to be, and Princess Amelia did not fit that ideal. Lila couldn't blame them—all of England was presented with the ideal every day—Queen Victoria's daughters were the apple of the queen's eye.

But Princess Amelia fit her own mold and she was not willing to be someone she was not. One had to admire a woman devoted to being true to herself.

At least Lila did.

"I will speak with her again," she said, only to appease Blythe. But it was painfully obvious to her that she was going to have to make a new list of potential suitors. Her husband, Valentin, was coming to London from Denmark in the next few weeks and she was desperate to see him. She wondered if perhaps another change of scenery would be good for Princess Amelia. They could go to London. Most people she would want to introduce to the princess were packing up to head to the country for summer months. But the princess liked to shop, and she generally liked meeting people who weren't being assessed as a potential match for her.

Lila caught up with the princess the next afternoon to present her plan. Princess Amelia had gone to the school this morning with the girls, but instead of coming back in an hour or so, she'd stayed away the whole day. She was wearing her brown walking gown and had left her hair in one long tail down her back. The sun hat she wore was so big that Lila could only see her chin. This, too, was unlike the princess. In the years Lila had known her, Princess Amelia had always been meticulous about her appearance. In the last couple of weeks, she'd stopped worrying about petticoats and hairstyles altogether.

"There you are!" Lila said, coming down the drive to meet her. "I've been working on a new list of suitors for us to review."

Princess Amelia sighed.

"There are two gentlemen I have in mind who I think will spark your interest."

The princess removed her hat and looked at Lila with her light hazel eyes. "Do you really think that two more from your list will be any different than the ones who have come before them?"

Lila hesitated. "You've lost faith."

The princess laughed. "*Je*, in every possible way. They all know precisely what to say—they will mention their connections, think all they must do is admire my looks to make me esteem them, and smile and be chivalrous and boast of their accomplishments while they imagine all the gains that could be made from marrying me."

"Good Lord," Lila said with a surprised bit of laughter. "How cynical you've become, Your Royal Highness!"

"Please, Lila. It's Amelia. There is no need for formality between us. Not now, anyway."

Lila didn't know what she meant by "now," but clearly she'd crossed some threshold.

"You know what I say is true," the princess continued. "Privately, these men think I am inferior to them by virtue of my sex, and assume they will rule me once we are wed, for isn't that the way of marriage, royal or not?"

The conversation about female brains had been awfully vexing—Lila had dashed off a letter to Valentin to complain about it that very night. "Mr. Swann's opinions are hardly the opinions of *all* men."

"But aren't they, really?"

She couldn't argue with that. Mr. Swann did hold views that squads of men held. Lila considered herself the luckiest woman on earth that Valentin was not one of them. "You are describing the push and pull between men and women. Both sexes have a unique view of the other, and their views don't always align."

"That makes it even worse," Amelia said as they reached the terrace steps and walked up. "And the worst of it is, I'm at a terrible disadvantage because of their good behavior.

How am I to know if they are unique in any way? It's impossible. And really, Lila, I am beginning to question the need for it at all."

"The need for what?"

The princess paused to look at her as if she thought she was being purposefully obtuse. "*Marriage.*"

Her state of mind was worse than Lila had anticipated. "There is *every* need for it. Don't you want companionship and family? Love and fidelity?"

The princess shook her head and continued up.

Lila caught her by the arm and forced her to stop her ascent. "You're not being fair. You've only met a few people thus far."

"I know, and I was so eager to meet them all," she said wistfully. "I truly believed I would find something or someone new and exciting in England. But they're the same here as they are in Wesloria. They're *always* the same."

Many years ago, Lila had tried to match an heiress who could not be satisfied with anyone she met. She lived with her parents to this day, and from what Lila had heard, she had become bitter from the experience.

She did not want Amelia to be like that heiress.

"Baron Hancock of Ireland is due to arrive next week, and I think you will find him delightful. He's an equestrian!"

The princess shrugged.

"Your Royal Highness—"

"Amelia! Honestly, even the honorific sounds insincere here."

"Amelia, then. What is really troubling you?"

Amelia looked heavenward, as if she'd explained this time and again. "I am the problem child everyone wants to see married as soon as possible so they may go about their business, aren't I? But I'm not a child, Lila. I know what I want. My family would be grateful for anyone that met the most basic of criteria, but I can't agree. And in the meantime, I am entirely useless. Blythe doesn't want my help. Gentlemen don't want me to do any more than look pretty. The only person who seems to value me for something other than my title is Mr. Roberts. I can hardly marry him."

"But we can find someone like Mr. Roberts."

Amelia's face darkened. "Where, Lila? In your leather book, with all the names and bits of paper stuck here and there? You realize, don't you, that it's the expectations we create that cause our disappointment?" She began to stride up the terrace steps.

Lila hurried to keep up with her. "I have an idea. Let's start fresh! Clearly, you've not seen the one who would spark your interest, so let's go over it all again. What you like, what you don't like—"

"Nothing has changed! What have I not said to you? I want someone who surprises me, someone who is not what is expected. Someone who is surprised by *me*."

It was hard to fathom that the poor woman didn't realize she was describing Marley. In that moment, Lila knew what she had to do. But if Marley was too intractable—and Lila feared that could very well be so, as he was both haunted *and* stubborn—she had to have another plan. "What if we went to London in a few weeks?"

That drew the princess up. She turned to look at Lila. "London?"

Lila nodded. "I'll need to speak to Beck, of course, but... there are some gentlemen in town I think you might like to meet before everyone leaves for the summer." She smiled. She expected the princess's face to light, for her to gasp with excitement. When Amelia had visited England a few years ago, she'd found every way she could to be in London society, in London shops, in London drawing rooms.

But she did not gasp with delight. The idea actually seemed to deflate her. "*Je*," she said. "Of course. Why not." And then she carried on inside the house.

Lila stood at the top of the steps, watching as she disappeared inside. The situation was becoming dire, wasn't it? She couldn't imagine anything worse than sending the problematic princess back to Wesloria without a match. She knew what would happen if she did—a twenty-six-year-old princess who had not found a successful match in Wesloria or England? Word would spread quickly through all royal and noble households. Lila was certain that notwithstanding her title and wealth, all the wealthy, titled men worthy of her hand would not want someone they would naturally assume was problematic.

She wished Valentin was here to help her think her way out of this impending disaster.

To the Iddesleigh School for Too Many Girls,

I have heard in the village that the number of girls to be educated will be expanded to include more ages. My good man, have you lost your mind? Have you any idea what that will do to our little spot of England? A larger school should be situated in a larger community such as Plymouth or Exeter, but not here in Iddesleigh, if you please.

I beg you do not misunderstand me—you are to be commended on the success of your school. Education in all its forms for all students is important to the health of our nation. But I must urge you to think through your plans. How will all this traffic be accommodated? We hardly have the roads necessary for all the coming and going. Your decision is simply incompatible with our quiet countryside, and as such, I must assume you've allowed your emotions to guide you without considering the larger consequences of your decision. You bring to mind a man who makes a decision to marry without knowing how compatible he truly is with his intended or considering the full range of consequences of his decision. That is the way of marriage, I suppose—we are nat-

urally inclined to attach ourselves to someone based on emotion rather than fact.

You, sir, need someone to stop you from making hasty decisions on the basis of emotion rather than fact.

A Concerned Resident of Devonshire

—

To A Resident of Devonshire, Concerned,

Thank you for your support for the Iddesleigh School for Exceptional Girls. We are pleased to announce that we do indeed seek to expand our student population so that more girls will be properly educated. You may rest assured that will not happen until we have adequate space to accommodate them all. Our girls are practically standing on each other's shoulders as it is.

We find your notion of marriage quite interesting. We note with curiosity that you fail to mention love as the true reason for marriage. "Love looks not with the eyes, but with the mind," wrote the bard, Shakespeare. He was very much an observer of love.

What is your opinion if one can't find a like-minded person to attach to in the state of happy matrimony? Does one retreat into books and carry on alone, making decisions without anyone to remind us to consider the consequences? It seems so desperately lonely, does it not? Then again, one cannot imagine a worse tragedy than marrying someone only to find you are not the least compatible in thought and mien after all. The quandary of it all!

Recently, we had to say farewell to a pair of young sisters relocating with their mother to the north. It was a terrible circumstance in which the parents experienced an infidelity so great that one banished the other. In this particular case, one can reasonably assume that love looked with the eye and not the mind, and perhaps found it wasn't love at all. Lust is deceitful. Let it be a reminder to us all that the dangers of marriage are fraught. Unless, of course, one can determine compatibility before marriage, in which case, surely the rewards of marriage must be great.

With kindest regards,
The Iddesleigh School for Exceptional Girls

—

To the Iddesleigh School for Absent Girls,

I will admit you raise an excellent point that love should enter into one's calculation of marriage. Perhaps my own cynicism has gotten in the way of my thinking. I have tried, and failed, to earn that distinction and it has perhaps left me wary. I stand firm, however—proof of compatibility must come before marriage, and a decision should not be made on emotion alone. If not, the risk of failure is too great. Obviously, compatibility in all things cannot be known before marriage, and I think you understand what I mean. But many things within a marriage can be improved if there is a meeting of the minds to begin with.

Sincerely,
A Concerned Resident of Devonshire

CHAPTER TWENTY-FIVE

June, 1858
England

To Her Majesty the Queen, Justine,

Dearest Jussie, please forgive my late reply to your last letter. I will be brief, as I am expected at the school and am dashing off soon to put this in today's post. You are right to assume Lila's efforts have not been successful, but I can't give you a solid answer as to why. Mama has sent three letters urging me not to be stubborn. I swear to you that I am not. But with everyone Lila brings, I find I am less interested in knowing them. I feel an ennui that I've not felt before.

I can't fault Lila's selections—all of the gentlemen have been good, laudable men. It reminds me very much of when she presented you with so many candidates for your hand and how, after a time, they began to blend together. Do you remember how weary you were of it?

The only person who has been the slightest bit interesting is the one I thought to be the Grim Reaper. He is much improved since he shaved his beard and trimmed his hair. He has the most astounding eye color I think I've ever seen, a grayish blue that brings to mind winter and summer at the same time. Can you believe it, but he is not the least bit curious about me? He has even said so and has stated more than once he would not pursue my hand. It's as if he doesn't see what all the others see and cannot be enticed by my title, or my inheritance, or anything about me at all! I am at a loss to know how to greet such disinterest, as it is unlike anything I have ever experienced. I am not vexed by it, but rather, I find it remarkable.

Lila said we may go to London soon. I should like to visit the shops, but when I think of more parties and balls where I am to be presented as the one who cannot find a match, I don't care to go. Nor do I want to leave the school. Mr. Roberts needs me desperately, and Lord I is in search of a larger facility. Once that is determined, there will be so much to do, and I will be needed. I would hate to leave now just so that I may don a tiara and smile and laugh and allow men to assess me for marriage and ladies to whisper how I don't endear myself to them. I have never understood the desire to pretend to be sweet when I am not.

Oh dear, the time has gotten away from me. I really must be off, darling. I promise I will write more when I can.

Yours, A

CHAPTER TWENTY-SIX

ON A MORNING when the air was so thick it felt as if one could slice it with a knife, Amelia finished her work in Mr. Roberts's office for the day and gathered her shawl. She could hear the girls in the classroom. Mr. Roberts was teaching the Greek classics and today's lesson was about the Greek deities. The girls had taken a particular liking to Athena, as she was a warrior. Mathilda said that she would one day be a warrior goddess, and her father would give her a sword. Predictably, Maren and Maisie said they would be warrior goddesses, too, and *their* father would also give them a sword.

It went downhill from there.

It was the way things went with little girls, Amelia was discovering. What one had, they all wanted. Much like grown women.

Amelia put on her sun hat and waved at Mr. Roberts through the open door of the classroom, but he didn't see her. She walked outside and stood for a moment.

She dreaded returning to Iddesleigh House. She didn't want to hear Blythe and Beck bickering over fabric selections for their renovation. She didn't want to see Lila's hopeful smile, either—although that one was due to leave for a few days, which came as some relief. Amelia had no doubt she was striking out to round up some new prospects for her. Amelia liked Lila, and she appreciated her desire to help. But she was weary of this endeavor. Indifferent to the possibilities. To her astonishment, meeting bachelor gentlemen had become a chore.

She walked to the arch and looked down the road toward Iddesleigh and Hollyfield. She then looked in the direction of Goosefeather Abbey. She and Mr. Swann had ridden there the afternoon they'd gone out, at Amelia's insistence. But Mr. Swann had been impatient and said he agreed with Marley, that it didn't stand to reason they'd put a boarding school there. But he opined that the land looked like it might be well suited to another endeavor. Something agricultural, he mused, as if he was also an expert in land use.

Amelia was enchanted by the idea of a girls' boarding school and wanted to have a closer look at the abbey. She was beginning to think there might be a way for her to be useful to this world. She could help bring it to life, couldn't she? If nothing else, she ought to be able to bring in some funding for it. She decided to have a better look than she had with Mr. Swann and struck out in her sturdy walking shoes.

At first, she enjoyed the walk, alone with her thoughts. But after a half hour or so, when there was no abbey in sight, she began to worry she had misjudged the distance, or had confused the right road. The humidity was high, and her plain gown was sticking to her. This had to be the right path—she and Mr. Swann had not ridden more than three quarters of an hour before happening upon abbey, and they'd passed the present school on their way. So, she carried on, unnoticing of the clouds gathering overhead.

After an hour, the light was being squeezed from the sky by the clouds. But she'd spotted the standing spires of the abbey and continued. After another quarter of an hour, she realized the abbey was farther away still.

She was exhausted by the time she reached it, and yet pleased that she'd made it. She spent a bit of time walking around, stepping over stones, looking into intact rooms. She pictured the entire boarding school in her mind's eye—the girls would sleep where the monks had slept. In the missing parts of the abbey—large rooms from what she could judge—they could build a dining hall, and a chapel. There were other rooms, too big for personal quarters, and too small for dining halls, that could be used as classrooms.

She could hardly wait to speak to Beck about it. Her head was spinning with so many ideas when she started back that she still hadn't noticed how thick the clouds had become. Not until the first fat raindrop hit her hand.

And then another one.

And then the deluge came. "*Verdammt!*" she cried, and pulled her shawl over her head as the skies opened up. She ran down the road for a time, her lungs burning, until it became clear she couldn't outrun the storm. She considered dashing into the trees to seek shelter, but the rain was coming down so hard, she didn't think she would be spared even there.

When her legs refused to run, she tried to walk faster, but the road had turned muddy, and her shoes were sinking into the wagon tracks. One of them sank so deep that it came off her foot. She stopped to pull it from the mud. She was soaked through, and freezing, and if she hadn't been so angry at herself for her carelessness, she might have cried. Might have flung herself facedown onto the road and sobbed until her entire body sank into the mud.

And then, by some miracle, she heard a muffled shout. Clutching her muddy boot, she turned, hoping for a carriage. It was a rider coming toward her, the horse's hooves churning up the mud in a way that didn't seem possible. She

recognized that black cloak instantly—*that* was the Grim
Reaper. He drew up and stared down at her, rain coming
off his hat in streams. "What the devil?"

Fortunately, Amelia didn't have to explain herself then
and there, as she would have been at a loss. He leaped off
his horse and grabbed her by the waist. "Where are your
guards?" he demanded, but once again, he didn't wait for
an answer—he picked her up before she could speak and set
her on the horse, then swung up behind her. He anchored
her with an arm around her waist, smashing her against
his hard, warm chest. He pulled his cloak around her then
spurred the horse on.

It was hard going—the horse stumbled a couple of times,
but plodded on, head bobbing, wanting out of the rain as
much as she did. Amelia was unable to see much of anything in that torrential downpour, but she was aware that
he led the horse off the main road and onto a trail that went
through the woods. They eventually emerged at the back
of the mansion at Hollyfield. The horse picked up its pace,
loping for the open doors of the stable.

The horse trotted inside and stopped in the middle of the
stable. Horses in their stalls snorted and whickered at them.
Amelia realized she was panting, unable to catch her breath.

A groom appeared and took hold of the horse's bridle.
Marley dismounted, then lifted Amelia down. But as she
was still clutching her boot, she couldn't brace herself
against him, and he lifted her in a way that her body was
pressed against his, sliding down the length of him until
she landed lopsided, still clutching that damn boot as if it
was everything she had in the world.

He stepped back, looked her up and down, and noticed
the boot. Then he lifted his gaze to hers, slowly placed his

hands on his hips, and his eyes narrowed accusingly. "What in God's name were you doing out in this storm?"

Did he think she'd gone out in it intentionally? She was shivering so hard that her teeth were clattering. "Oh, just out for a stroll."

He opened his mouth as if he meant to shout, but then quickly clamped it shut.

"For heaven's sake, it came up while I was out. It wasn't my *intention* to be thoroughly soaked."

"Pardon my skepticism. I think we can agree that one never knows with you."

"We can agree to no such thing. I *always* know. Thank you, incidentally, for coming to my rescue."

He was still looking at her with a confused expression. Like he didn't understand her at all. Like she was some sort of creature he had never in his life seen before this moment.

"Why must you look so confused? I walked to the abbey, but I didn't realize how far it was by foot, and by the time I did, it was too late." She rubbed her free hand against her arm.

Marley's expression darkened. "You need dry clothes. Come with me."

"I best go on to Iddesleigh. I can walk the rest of the way—"

"The devil you can," Marley said. "Look at that storm," he said, gesturing to the deluge they could see falling through the open doors.

It was a daunting sight, all right. "They will send out a search party."

Marley nodded. He looked at the young groom. The young groom's eyes nearly popped out of his head, because he, too, could see the storm, and apparently, he could see what his lord was thinking, as well. "Well then, Theo—today is the day you are a hero."

"Your Grace?"

"Take care of him," the duke said, pointing to the horse. He shrugged out of his heavy cloak and draped it over the stall gate. Then he removed his hat and balanced it on top of the cloak. "When you've brushed him and given him a bucket of oats, take my cloak and hat and go to Iddesleigh House. You are to tell Lord Iddesleigh that Her Royal Highness was caught in the rain but is safe at Hollyfield and will be returned as soon as the storm passes."

Theo's eyes rounded even more.

"And you will remain there until the storm passes. Iddesleigh will see you are fed and kept dry. Do you understand what you are to do?"

The apple in Theo's throat moved up and down with his swallow. "Aye, Your Grace."

"Good lad." Marley turned back to Amelia. "You. Come," he said, and began striding for the open door.

Amelia hobbled after him. "Where?"

"Inside, of course."

"Inside your house?"

Marley looked back at her with obvious exasperation. "Contrary to your earlier observations, my house is not abandoned. It is a house, it is reasonably dry, and at least some of the rooms are warm." He reached for her hand. "And presently, madam, it's the only option you have." He wrapped his fingers around hers and tugged her into moving with him, striding forward as she hobbled along behind him.

But at the open doors, they paused. The rain was coming down so hard she could scarcely see the house. Marley's grip—a very large and strong grip, she couldn't help notice—was tight. "Can you run?"

"I think so."

He looked at the boot she held. "Bloody hell," he muttered. "Please oblige me by not resisting."

"What?"

He abruptly picked her up and tossed her—*tossed* her—over his shoulder. And then he ran.

Amelia shrieked and grabbed onto the back of his coat with both fists. "This is hardly necessary!" she shouted into the void as he ran across the grass toward a door. It was a side door, not a true entrance. He put her down with an *oomph* as roughly as he'd picked her up. He slammed against the door twice with his shoulder to force it open—it popped free of its swollen frame and he pushed her inside to a narrow hall. He was right behind her and used his shoulder again to force the door shut.

"Need to have that repaired," he said, more to himself than to her.

Amelia realized she had dropped her boot somewhere between the stable and the door, and was looking around her, trying to see in the dim light of the hall, when she heard a racket that sounded as if the house was coming down around her. She turned just in time to see two dogs racing toward her. She shrieked and hardly managed to get her arms up before they both leaped at her. She was certain she was going to be mauled...but the only thing she felt was the rough lap of their tongues as they licked the rain from her face, their bodies wiggling with excitement.

"Bethan! Merlin! *Off!*" Marley roared.

The dogs instantly backed away from her and sat, their tails wagging furiously, their expressions eager, as if they were expecting to be praised for their excellent greeting.

Marely stepped around her, putting himself between her and the dogs. He pointed down the hall. "*Go*," he commanded them, and the dogs obediently trotted away.

He shook his head and looked at her. "Are you all right?"

"*Je*. Wetter than I was, but I'm fine," she said, and with the back of her hand wiped dog drool from her cheek.

"I beg your pardon for it. Those two were models of discipline until Miles ruined them."

"Who?"

"Lord Clarendon," he clarified. "He's been my guest, lo these many weeks or months or years. Let's just agree it's been an eternity. All right, come on," he said, and they were moving again, down the dark hall, emerging into a larger, grander hall. She noticed, as she tried to keep stride with him, that the doors in this hallway were closed. And there was hardly any light at all—she would have thought a servant would have lit the lamps by now.

They entered another empty, dark, and cold hallway, this one much wider, and after another long walk, they reached a drawing room. A warm, pleasantly lit drawing room she was happy to see. She almost cried with relief.

But as she walked in behind him, she noticed that most of the furniture was covered with dust cloths. Was it a storage room?

Marley went to the hearth to stoke the fire. Amelia wrapped her arms tightly around her middle and took in the covered furniture. Even the paintings on the wall had been covered, except for one over the hearth. There were two chairs, a divan, and a small table with two chairs on one side of the room that were uncovered, giving the impression that only part of the room was inhabited. It made no sense. "Are you leaving Hollyfield?"

"Yes." He stood up from the hearth and discarded his

coat. Then his waistcoat. Then his neck cloth. Then he turned around to face her. His shirt was soaked through and clinging to his chest. His skin, and every long curve of muscle, was visible through the wet fabric. Amelia was stunned into speechlessness. He looked...*he looked—*

"You're shivering," he said.

"What?" She blinked. She was shivering from cold in part, but also from the sudden racing of her heart. "*Je*, I am."

He walked to where she stood, put his hands on her shoulders, and steered her to stand before the fire. "Stand here and don't move. I'll be back in a moment." He strode from the room.

He returned a few minutes later with a man. "This is Butler," he said. "He is my butler."

"Pardon?"

"It's confusing, I admit," he said. "Mr. Butler is my butler." He looked uncomfortable. Uncertain. He said to Mr. Butler, the butler, "Her Royal Highness, Princess Amelia of Wesloria."

The butler bowed.

A woman hurried into the room like the dogs were chasing her. Her mouth dropped when she saw Amelia.

"Don't let flies settle on your tongue, Halsey. Her Royal Highness, Princess Amelia of Wesloria, has been caught in the rain." He spoke as he dragged his fingers through his hair, flinging droplets of water everywhere.

The woman audibly gasped. But she quickly closed her mouth and curtsied.

"Miss Halsey is my housekeeper. You mustn't hold the state of Hollyfield against either of them. It's not their fault, it's solely mine."

What was he talking about? The dust coverings?

"If you will kindly follow Halsey, she will give you dry clothes and help you with…whatever you need."

Amelia was so miserably cold and wet she wouldn't argue or ask any questions. She pulled her soaked shawl around her and followed Miss Halsey.

They went through another long hallway, and then upstairs. Down another hallway where more lamps were unlit and more doors were shut. It seemed as if the entire wing was closed, and she assumed Miss Halsey was leading her to a storage closet. But they arrived at a large bedroom.

This room was obviously inhabited and darkly masculine. Embers glowed in the hearth, the bed was made, and a cat was lying on the foot of it, watching impassively as Miss Halsey bustled in, leading Amelia. Someone had placed a pair of Hessian boots in the corner, and an array of male toiletries was spread across the top of the bureau. A pair of trousers were tossed carelessly across a chair and a morning coat was hanging neatly from a coatrack.

"Whose room is this?"

"It is the duke's room. The other rooms in this hall are not open, and he bid me bring you here, as the hearth is lit. Will you wait here?"

Amelia nodded, and the housekeeper disappeared through an interior door into an adjoining room. She felt conspicuous, standing in his room. It was too intimate somehow. Like she was seeing a part of him that he kept hidden from the world. She noticed a couple of books on a bedside table. *Tendency of Varieties to Depart Indefinitely from the Original Type.*

She considered her English to be excellent, but she couldn't make sense of that title. The book beneath it was *A History of Phillip II.* The only Phillip II she knew of was a long-dead Spanish king.

She looked around the room, her gaze falling on a single leather-bound chair and a table near the windows. On the table was a pocket watch and a riding crop. Amelia moved to the foot of the bed and stroked the cat's head. At first, the cat meowed, rejecting her attention. But then it lifted its head and began to purr.

Miss Halsey appeared again with a towel and some gowns. She laid them carefully on the bed. "These belonged to the late Duchess of Marley," she said. "I brought three for you to choose from, if you like."

Amelia picked one up and held it up to her body. The Duchess of Marley had been considerably smaller than she. She glanced up at Miss Halsey, who was seeing the same conundrum. "I don't think I can possibly fit into them."

"She was such a tiny thing," Miss Halsey agreed. She stared at the gown with a perplexed expression. "But we have no other ladies' clothes, Your Royal Highness."

"Perhaps then, one of the duke's shirts and..." She glanced around the room, trying to think. Her gaze landed on the trousers. "Trousers."

Miss Halsey looked at the trousers. Her cheeks turned red. "Oh my. I don't...that doesn't seem—"

"Miss Halsey, I am soaked through to the bone and freezing. Look." She held up her hand. The tips of her fingers were blue, and she couldn't stop shaking. "I must have something very soon. Please."

"Yes, ma'am." Miss Halsey curtsied and went into the adjoining room again. She returned with a pair of canvas hunting breeches, a lawn shirt, and a hunting jacket.

Amelia had never in her life donned men's clothing, had never even dreamed of doing it, but when she'd dressed, she wondered why not. She didn't care—as long as whatever she put on was dry and covered her, she was satisfied.

It felt strangely sensual to put her body into clothes where his body had been. The faint smell of clove and cardamom was soothing to her.

But mostly, she was relieved by the warmth of dry clothes.

CHAPTER TWENTY-SEVEN

IT DIDN'T OCCUR to Joshua until the princess left with Halsey that she would return in Diana's clothes. He was slightly startled that he would feel anything about it, but his heart did a couple of pirouettes in his chest at the thought of seeing his dead wife's clothes on an unruly princess.

He should have gotten rid of them. Given them to Mrs. Chumley's daughter, sent them to his mother—but he'd left them languishing in her dressing room, just as he'd left everything languishing after she'd died.

He heard Halsey's determined footfall and drew a breath to steady himself. He turned from the fire in the hearth and…and he was speechless. Truly speechless. Of all the things he could have imagined, it would never have been her wearing *his* clothes.

Her wet hair was braided in one thick tail. She had donned a pair of his hunting breeches, which Halsey had secured with a cord tied around her waist. She was also wearing one of his lawn shirts. It was voluminous on her, tied in a knot at her waist, and buttoned to the neck. Over that, she wore one of his older hunting coats that hung to her knees.

He looked to Halsey, confused as to why she would do such a thing. In return, Halsey looked as if she would be ill.

The princess looked at Halsey, then at him. "Before you say anything, I must explain that your late wife was considerably smaller than me. I couldn't fit, Your Grace. And as I didn't think I could bear another moment of shivering as I was in my wet clothes, I asked Miss Halsey for your clothes rather than searching the grounds for a suitable gown. I hope you won't think too ill of me."

Joshua should have minded that she'd donned his clothes, but he didn't. He couldn't—he was too mesmerized by it. There was something quite alluring about a woman in men's clothing—specifically, *his* clothing—so much that it took his breath away. Thankfully, the storm raging against the windowpanes covered the sound of the actual catch in his breath.

"Thank you, Halsey. If you would be so good as to tend to her clothes?"

"Aye, Your Grace." She gave him an awkward curtsy, and took a hasty retreat from the drawing room, probably scandalized by this turn of events.

The princess looked much smaller in his clothes. Almost meek, which was not a word he would have thought he would ever use to describe her. She walked into the middle of the room in bare feet and gazed at him curiously. "You've donned dry clothes, too."

He realized he was staring. Gaping, really. He glanced down. He'd changed into dry trousers and lawn shirt and had put on a coat for some warmth. He, too, was barefoot. "Yes, I...was wet," he said. He cleared his throat and gestured to the table. "Butler has brought some tea and biscuits." He walked to the table and stood behind one of the chairs, intending to hold it out for her. She looked at the chair, then looked at the hearth, where the flames were blazing now. His impossibly lazy dogs had stretched out on the rug before it to warm their backsides against the heat coming from it now. "Would you mind terribly if we took tea there?"

"Where?"

"There," she said, and pointed to the dogs.

"You want to sit with the dogs?"

"Is it too improper for you? I've gone all the way through the door into impropriety by borrowing your clothes, so I don't think it could be worse. All I know is that I can't shake the cold. It's gone into my marrow."

"Then we'll have tea there."

He watched her study the dogs, neither of which had in mind to move. She stepped over one to stand in between them, and then gracefully floated down to sit cross-legged between them. Bethan shifted around so he could lay his head in her lap, like they were old friends instead of new acquaintances. Merlin lifted his head off the rug to see what the fuss was about and seeing nothing to cause alarm, laid it down again with a heavy sigh.

"I'm afraid my dogs think everyone is here to accommodate them. I apologize."

"Please don't—I am very fond of dogs, in all shapes and sizes." She casually stroked Bethan's ear. "My family has dogs at Rohalan Palace. Mig and Roo, they're hunting dogs. Bess, she's terribly lazy and likes nothing better than to sleep in the sun. Tava, he's old and blind, but Lulu leads him about. She loves him." She sighed. "I miss them all so much."

Joshua would add dog lover to the list of things for which to commend this woman.

He poured tea, handed her a cup, then poured another for himself. He picked up the plate of biscuits and stepped into the pack on the rug. Why not join them? He was fond of dogs, too. But he didn't go down as gracefully as she had and managed to spill a bit of tea on Merlin. Merlin took no offense.

She smiled as he settled in, their knees practically touching. "Isn't it strange how we always seem to find ourselves in peculiar places?"

"Passing strange indeed. What on earth compelled you to try and walk to Goosefeather Abbey?"

"I wanted to have a closer look." She sipped her tea and wrapped her hands around the cup. Her fingers were slender and elegant, and he imagined them on a piano.

Or on him.

He immediately looked down. Unwelcome thoughts like that would only make this afternoon even more interminable than it was. Except that it wasn't as interminable as he'd been prepared for. It wasn't interminable at all.

"I had gone once to the abbey, on a ride with Mr. Swann. But he was impatient. He said he didn't care for ruins, that they were in the past. He said he liked to look forward."

Pompous bastard. Where did Mr. Swann think the ability to look forward came from? From learning about the past. What made men so bloody stupid? "So you went alone?" he asked.

"Why not? I like to walk, and Devonshire is the only place I've ever had the freedom to walk wherever I please."

The wandering princess. He looked at the tea he'd poured for himself, but he didn't want it. This august occasion seemed to call for something a little more substantial. He set the tea aside and gained his feet. He went to the sideboard and picked up a decanter of whisky. He held it up so the princess could see it. "Would you like?"

Her face lit with a smile. "An excellent idea, Your Grace."

He poured generous portions into crystal glasses and returned to the hearth with them. She took a healthy sip; he added that healthy sip to his mental list of things to commend her on.

"Thank you. Nothing warms the heart like whisky, does it? I mean...besides love and that sort of thing."

"Exactly." He sipped, too. "I'm curious...what is your interest in Goosefeather Abbey?"

She seemed surprised by his question as she picked a biscuit from the plate and nibbled. "The girls' school, of course." Her gaze moved idly around his drawing room, taking it in. "You recall, don't you? Lord Iddesleigh hopes to make a girls' school of it and I would like to help. I wanted to see it for myself."

That damn girls' school again. He sipped his whisky. "How would you help?"

"I don't know as yet," she said. "But I would like to. Why shouldn't girls be educated like boys? Why shouldn't they be the ones to discover how to brew kerosene from coal?"

He chuckled. "I don't think it's a brew."

She waved a hand at him. "I'm not suggesting we discuss the education of girls again. The opinions of men were made quite clear at supper."

His opinion wasn't made quite clear. But there was no way for him to reconcile his belief that girls ought to be educated like boys with his firm desire not to have it occur near him. He had his reasons, as misguided as they might be.

She stared into the fire thoughtfully, and he noticed how the firelight caught the white streak in her hair and made it more noticeable.

"The abbey...it has given me such hope for a purpose."

"Pardon?"

She winced slightly. "That must sound mad. It's difficult to explain, but I… I need something to hope for. A means to making my life meaningful in some way. And if I don't find purpose, there's nothing for me—I'm nothing more than an ornament. And the abbey…it would be such a wonderful thing to benefit my sex." She looked at him. "I could be of use. *Real* use."

"In what way?"

She smiled. "To start, I know a lot about girls. And I know scads of wealthy people who could become patrons of the school. All I need is the chance to prove it."

He could imagine her persuading monarchs and aristocrats to contribute to the school. She would be charming and beautiful, and they'd not be able to resist.

"Where are you going?"

"What?" He'd lost his train of thought.

She fixed her clear-eyed gaze on him. "You said you were leaving."

"Ah." He sipped his whisky and constructed his truth, whatever it was at that particular moment. And the truth was, he didn't really know. "I've not yet decided. The Province of Canada, perhaps."

"Canada? It's a wild territory, isn't it?"

"Parts, yes." He hardly knew himself. "I think I'll start in Toronto and carry on from there." Or rather, he thought that in this moment. Who knew what he'd think tomorrow? His mind was careening all over the place.

She munched her biscuit, eyeing him. "But why there, if I may? It seems awfully far to go just to be away."

"Just to be away?"

"From Hollyfield and the memories here? Isn't that what you intend?"

It still astounded him that someone who was not part of his family could so directly question him. Miles did, of course, but Miles considered himself family and believed he deserved answers. Not even his mother could broach her son's feelings on the death of his wife. Which was why, probably, he didn't have a very good answer at the ready when he was asked why he was leaving. It wasn't clear even to him. But what *was* clear to him was that he didn't need to be away from Hollyfield as much as he needed to walk headlong into his misery.

He said simply, "I have noticed, Highness, that you have no qualms about mentioning the death of my wife."

"Oh." She blinked. "I apologize. I—I don't mind when someone mentions the death of my father. I'm rather relieved they remember him."

"It's a bit different for me. In answer to your question, I am leaving because I feel restless here. That's it, nothing deeper than that."

"I know that feeling well," she said. "That's the reason I'm in England you know—I was too restless in Wesloria. Or rather, I was bored, and when I'm bored, I have a tendency to do things that are not in my best interests." She paused and looked at him sidelong. "According to the rules of my family, that is. Not necessarily according to mine."

What did *that* mean?

She didn't explain further, but finished her biscuit. He couldn't help his gaze meandering to his lawn shirt she wore, visible through the open coat. He imagined he could see her breasts through the fabric.

Another unwelcome thought to give him a bit of a start. He forced his attention to the flames. Honestly, he couldn't remember the last time he'd thought of breasts, or touching them, but they were suddenly looming in his mind. Big ones, small ones, pert ones, soft ones, white ones, brown ones.

Bloody hell, he could hardly sit here with her and think of breasts.

He had to focus on conversation. Something. "Perhaps your boredom will be eased once you've finished your search for the perfect companion?" he blurted.

She laughed. "I never said I was searching for the perfect companion."

Wasn't that everyone's search in the end? "Are you not?"

"That would be lovely, but I really don't have the luxury." She reached for another biscuit. "Because I am my sister's heir at present, and a daughter of Wesloria, my companion must be acceptable to Wesloria."

He knew that was true. Even in his small corner of the world, marriages were made for advantage. "Have you had any luck with your search?"

"It's going about as well as one could expect."

An interesting answer that made him all the more curious. "What did *you* expect, if I may?"

"That it would be better than this. Easier, maybe? At least diverting. But it's not been easy or diverting. I'm a princess with passable looks, but it hasn't been easy at all, and I don't know why not."

"Hasn't it?" It seemed easy from where he was sitting. She came down the stairs in a beautiful gown, and men gathered around her.

"It has not," she said breezily. "Surely you've noticed that I am not the sort to be easily matched."

Joshua laughed with surprise. "I haven't noticed any such thing. I'd wager you are an easy match—by your own admission you come with a title and are quite comely."

She smiled with pleasure. "Thank you. *I* said I was passable."

"You're *quite* comely, and I think you know that you are. I'll say it another way—you're unique in every respect."

"*Je*, because I am a princess!" She laughed. "Apparently, that is the only thing to recommend me, but there really is more to me lurking beneath the tiara. And by the by, please call me Amelia. The royal address sounds so stilted here and so…" She made a circular motion in the air with her hand. "*Unnecessary.* In fact, I insist. Amelia."

"I suppose it does seem unnecessary when one is sitting on a rug with dogs and dressed in men's clothing. But if you insist, then I must, too. I am Joshua."

"Joshua," she said softly. She smiled. "It suits you."

What suited him was hearing her use his given name. "By the by, I didn't say you were unique because you're a princess. I said it because you simply are."

"Do you really think so?"

"You're a person who speaks her mind and, I think, appreciates the same frankness in return. Not many people can boast of either attribute. It also seems to me that you have a unique way of viewing the world."

She smiled with gratitude. "You're being kind. I don't."

"You do. Almost as if…you are the audience to a play we are all performing for your benefit."

Her smile broadened. "I'm sure I ought to be offended by your description, but I'm flattered. And yet it astounds me that you've come to any conclusions about me, as you can hardly abide me." She spoke gaily, as if that amused her.

"That's not true." What he couldn't abide was himself. It was a pity that he couldn't boast about speaking *his* mind. "I admire that you speak to what you observe and think. No one can say there is any varnish to your views."

She laughed at that. "No one can. My poor, dear mother has tried her best. I can't count the times in my life I've heard, 'Don't say that, don't sit like that, fold your hands, lower your eyes, Amelia, and for God's sake, be quiet.'" She sighed. "It's exhausting to fight my true nature. I don't understand why I must. I am not easily offended, and I don't see why I must care what society wants from me. I will never be queen. I'm just someone living in a palace. Shouldn't I be guided by my own conscience?" She popped the rest of the biscuit in her mouth and washed it down with the rest of her whisky, then turned her attention to stroking Bethan's head while that dog gazed at her with slavish devotion.

"Are you feeling better?" he asked.

"I am, thank you." She glanced up from the dog. "Look at you, Joshua. You've gone from nearly running me down like the Grim Reaper to rescuing me."

He smiled a little. "Three times. Not that I'm keeping count."

"Three! I will grant that today you were my savior. I can't bear to think what might have happened had you not come along when you did."

"You would have been washed away, or struck by lightning, or caught your death of cold. I also rescued you the day your horse went wild, lest you forget."

"Ah," she said, holding up a finger. "I will never forget it. And I will grant that you were indeed helpful, but you didn't *rescue* me. I had almost gained control."

"That is what everyone will say who has ever suffered a broken limb after being thrown by a wild horse."

She laughed. "True. And the third instance of rescue?"

There was a bit of a shine in her eyes—she was silently challenging him to say it. "The night on the balcony...or have you forgotten?" He had just chastised himself not to think about breasts, and here he was, resurrecting that kiss.

A smile turned up the corners of Amelia's mouth. "I will never forget that, either." Her eyes sparked gold with the firelight dancing in them, or, maybe, Joshua had developed a fever and was imagining things.

She pulled her legs up and wrapped her arms around her knees, then rested her head on top of her knees, her gaze on him. "But I don't believe you were rescuing me. And I don't believe you do, either."

He was suddenly filled with the uncomfortable but determined urge to touch her. To stroke her hair, or her back. He wanted to whisper in her ear that he'd rescued her from exposing herself and he wanted to rescue her from doing it again. "Perhaps not," he admitted.

She didn't look away. Neither did he. He couldn't play these flirtatious games anymore. He was rusty. Stiff. And she knew it, judging by her soft smile.

He looked down. "You were saying," he said at last, and dragged his fingers through his hair in an attempt to return to himself. "Lady Aleksander has not yet found the gentleman to make your prince."

"Was I saying so? I don't think I did. Because Lady Aleksander has introduced me to any number of gentlemen who would satisfy Wesloria and the crown, *and* my mother. But none satisfy me."

"I take it that none of them have surprised you," he said, harkening back to their all too brief conversation the night of the lunar eclipse. "Not even Mr. Swann."

"Mr. Swann? Not at all."

"No? I should think the intimate knowledge of kerosene would be a bit surprising." He could feel the corner of his mouth tip up in a slight smile.

"*Very* surprising, but in an academic way. I prefer my

surprises to be a bit more risqué than that. He did, however, surprise me with a horse."

Joshua blinked. "A horse."

She nodded against her knee. "The gift of a whole horse. But I didn't accept it. What am I to do with a horse?"

What, indeed? Had no one ever told Mr. Swann that gifts of jewelry or expensive perfume were generally more suitable when a gentleman wanted to make an impression? "Now I understand. You don't wish to be surprised for the sake of surprise. You want it to be meaningful."

"Well, of course. No one wants a bad surprise, do they? Although I've had plenty of them in my life. Once, when I was a girl, and my father was on tour in the southern region, near the sea, the palace there had not been used in some time. I insisted on having the nursery opened. I was quite bored, I think, and Justine was off learning her history lessons and whatnot. They opened the nursery for me, but there was hardly a thing to entertain me, and I was young enough that I was still inclined to tantrum when I was displeased. I fell to the floor in a fit of pique and was bitten by a spider. It made me quite ill. My father said he thought I was lost to them and commanded that the entire palace be swept by hand."

"I am sorry to hear it."

"I was sorry for the spider, really. I surprised it by falling on it." She smiled a little. "Accidentally."

"Of course."

"Funnily, the incident did not curb my appetite for tantrums. Not then, anyway. It wasn't until much later, when I understood that young gentlemen didn't care for them and my mother threatened to send me to Astasia Castle in the mountains until I was married. A fate nearly worse than death, I assure you. I suppose we all grow up eventually."

He smiled. "Eventually. What of my good friend, Lord Clarendon? Did you find him surprising?"

"Lord Clarendon." She wrapped her fingers around her bare toes. "Not surprising. But I found him to be a kind and decent man who desires Miss Carhill above all others. Didn't you see the way he looked at her over supper?"

"I couldn't avoid it no matter how I tried."

She giggled. "Where is he now? You said he was your guest."

"He is my perpetual guest, stopping in when he pleases with no regard for my convenience," he said with a wry smile. "At long last, he has gone to see after his own estate. But he threatens to return by week's end in time to escort Miss Carhill to Sunday church services."

"What a kind and decent thing to do." She yawned. "And terribly predictable."

Joshua wanted to yawn, too—he couldn't imagine a more boring or proper courtship than the one Miles was intent on performing. Amelia was right—it was predictable. "What about Mr. Cassidy? Or Lord Frampton?"

"Mr. Cassidy was too timid, and Lord Frampton was unremarkable. I can't even recall what he looks like."

Joshua privately agreed with both assessments. "I never thought Mr. Cassidy timid. I would say he is a quiet man."

"*You* are a quiet man. He is timid one. Maybe not when it comes to sporting or gaming...but I doubt very much he would have had the courage to rescue me on the balcony."

He could feel something like an invisible rope wrap itself around them and tether her to him. It felt fierce, like a swollen river current carrying her toward him so fast that if he wasn't careful, she would slam into him. "There is something to be said for timidity," he said quietly. "Or a lack of impulse."

"How boring life would be if we were all timid and lacking impulse."

The pull grew more taut. Joshua felt hot. He was too close to the fire, that was what. Hot on one side, cold on the other. A little fuzzy in his brain, too. But the rest of him—the rest of him was alert, ready to spring at the slightest provocation.

The princess pulled the old hunting coat more tightly around her.

"Still cold?" he asked.

She nodded.

He was grateful for an excuse to move. He stood up, walked to the divan, and picked up a lap rug. He brought it back and squatted down before her. They were so close now that he could see the flames of the fire dancing in the reflection of her eyes. He could see a tiny freckle at the corner of her mouth, and more of them scattered across her nose. He could see how darkly gold were her lashes and how plump were her lips. He draped the lap rug around her shoulders and tucked it in beneath her legs. She remained perfectly still, watching him. And when he was done, he lingered there, looking at her, fighting off the urge to kiss her. His gaze moved to her lips. Plump and full and begging to be kissed. Or was that him, wishing lips could beg? Wishing he could find the courage to kiss her again? Wishing he was a different man?

A strong gust of wind followed by a sharp bang against the window startled them both and broke the spell. The dogs bolted awake, Merlin crashing into Amelia in his surge to his feet. They began to bark and Amelia put her hands over her ears.

"Quiet!" he said loudly. He walked to the window to see what had happened. A shutter had come loose and was banging against the window. Joshua opened the window, which prompted the dogs to bark even louder. In a blinding rain, he caught the shutter and fastened it to its mooring. "It's really raging out there," he said as he shook the rain from his sleeve.

The dogs were still unsettled, pacing around the room, whimpering. "Pardon me," he said to Amelia, and to the dogs, he pointed at the door. "Come." He marched them to the door of the drawing room and opened it. "Butler!"

Butler did not answer.

With a sigh, Joshua went out into the hall and, seeing no one, walked on to the kitchen, the dogs trotting behind him, their concern with the window forgotten.

He found Butler in the kitchen, placing pails beneath two roof leaks while Mrs. Chumley mopped around him. Joshua looked up at the ceiling and frowned. "We should see that repaired." Nothing like stating the obvious to two people in the throes of cleaning up. "Do something with these dogs, will you?"

"Of course, Your Grace."

With a curt nod, Joshua turned and walked back to the drawing room.

He expected to find Amelia still sitting before the fire. But she was lying on her side, curled up under the lap rug, her head pillowed on a bent arm. He moved closer and looked down at her. She was fast asleep.

He went down on one knee and tucked the lap rug around her. The only thing free of the cover was the long braid of hair. His eyes followed the trail of white from her crown, as it wended through the braid all the way to the tip. He lifted his hand—hesitated—then ran his fingers along the braid, dusting off the memory of what it felt like to lose oneself in the silk of a woman's hair.

This was madness.

He stood up and went to the divan and sat. He braced his arms against his knees, then covered his face with his hands for a long moment, trying to will some perspective into his brain. And when that didn't work, he sat there watching the gentle rise and fall of her breath, the way the gold in her hair caught the light of the fire.

It had been so bloody long since he'd held a woman. He'd put away that want, had buried it under all the ashes in him. He hadn't even thought of it until now, and suddenly, everything in him was burning with need.

It had been so bloody long since he'd talked with a woman. Really talked—a full conversation. A glimpse into something beyond the polite and superficial.

This longing was a familiar feeling, one he knew well. But it was not a comfortable feeling. The last time he'd felt the need to be with a woman had been Diana.

He'd killed her with that need.

CHAPTER TWENTY-EIGHT

AMELIA WOKE WITH a start, the result of a numb arm that had begun to burn. She sat up and looked around her, uncertain for a moment where she was, trying to piece together her surroundings while rubbing her arm back into use.

But when she turned her head, she saw the Duke of Marley in one of the chairs, quietly reading. He glanced at her over the top of his book.

Marley. *Joshua?* Was it really so informal between them now? Had she really fallen asleep on the floor? "What…" she said thickly. "What am I doing?"

"You were sleeping. And rather soundly at that."

"How long?"

"An hour or so."

The full day's events were coming back to her. She didn't hear the storm, but when she looked to the window, it seemed awfully dark outside. "Is it still storming?"

Joshua shook his head. "It's passed. Nothing but heavy rain."

Iddesleigh! Lila would be beside herself with worry, and Lordonna—oh dear, the poor woman would faint with fear for Amelia. She made a move to stand. "I have to get to Iddesleigh House." But her legs were stiff and uncooperative. "They will be sick with worry—"

"Don't fret—Theo returned with a message from Iddesleigh. His lordship bids you stay the night, as the road and paths are impassable at present. He'll fetch you in the morning."

Morning? She could almost hear her mother's shriek across Europe at the idea of her unmarried daughter sleeping overnight in a man's house without a maid or lady chaperone at her side. "I can't possibly," she said. "The imposition is too great. And people will say—"

"It is no imposition, and no one will say a word. Who will know? It's not as if I picked you up in a crowd. No one, save my staff, knows you are here. And Iddesleigh is right—it is too dangerous to attempt to return to his house in the dark in this rain."

Her heart was racing, but she could hear the rain slashing against the windowpanes. He was right, of course—she couldn't ask him to see her back in this weather. She glanced down at herself, only then remembering she was in his clothes. She could hear her mother shriek again.

"I've asked Butler to prepare a light supper."

Supper. "Ah... I have nothing to wear."

"I would beg to differ. My clothes have never looked as good as they do on you."

There went her heart, pitter-pattering in her chest. Amelia stood up. She felt a little off-balance, her legs a pair of unbendable logs. How far had she walked?

Joshua lowered his book. "Is there something I might get for you?"

This was all too comfortable between them. She was wearing his clothes and sleeping on his rug. She had talked about her suitors and he had talked about leaving Hollyfield. She could imagine her mother and her sister if they could see her now. Justine would beg Amelia to please stop turning up in places she ought not to be and her mother would accuse her of being reckless. All fair points.

Joshua put aside his book and stood. He went to the sideboard and returned a minute later with a glass of wine. "This might help."

She reached for the goblet, but she didn't pull it from his hand. They stood there a moment, both with a tenuous hold on the goblet, their fingers a bit tangled around the stem. She noticed his callused hand again. "I'm sorry."

He frowned. "Whatever for?"

"For…everything. For requiring a rescue and wearing your clothes and falling asleep."

"There's really no need to apologize."

"I thought I knew how far it was to the abbey, and it was too late when I realized I was mistaken. I've no idea how far I walked, but my body feels like it must have been miles."

"I'd say at least seven, if not more."

"*Seven?*" And she thought she'd walked two miles at most. And now she just felt silly.

"Do you want the wine?"

She still hadn't taken it. She was thinking of his eyes, and the way he'd looked at her earlier. She was thinking of the glimpse she'd had of his body, and how it had stirred her. She was thinking of the way she'd felt before the wind blew and the dogs barked and she fell asleep. She was thinking of the spark she'd felt, that definite, dangerous spark of pure attraction and how she had hoped he would kiss her.

"Amelia…are you all right?"

He'd said her name, and it felt like the most intimate thing anyone had ever said to her. "*Je*, thank you." She slowly pulled the wine free. "There is a saying in Weslorian: *Rumlus er vesas to tarken.* Which means, folly is the teacher of the wise. I think I've been taught a valuable lesson today."

"Ah. Then perhaps the day was worth it in the end?"

She smiled. "Perhaps." She was feeling better now. Stronger. She carried her wineglass to the hearth and looked up at the only uncovered painting in the room. It was of a family. The woman was in pink satin, the gentleman nearby on a horse. Three children in last century's dress were romping beneath a tree with a pair of spaniels. "Ancestors of yours?" She sipped her wine.

"Probably so. I've not inquired."

He'd not *inquired*? "Weren't you required to learn art history? One summer, I was made to go around all of Rohalan Palace and learn the paintings we have there. Who painted them, the subjects, the year, the meaning...and all of it to be committed to memory in the event I was ever to entertain guests. Except for the painting of my great-great-aunt the Duchess of Dunreese. My tutor said that my mother the queen had expressly forbade him to teach me about her, as she'd had a torrid affair with a lady-in-waiting." She giggled, recalling how eagerly her tutor had taken her up the servant's staircase to show her. "He delighted in telling me the story all the same."

Marley smiled.

She turned her gaze to the painting again. "Have you been the duke very long?"

"Only a few years," he said. "But I didn't receive any instruction as a boy. I wasn't meant to inherit the title."

"What do you mean?"

"My cousin was the duke. My father an earl, my brother a viscount. I was the youngest, which meant I was destined to be wealthy, but nothing more than that." He smiled sheepishly. "There had been some talk of the clergy, but I think my father recognized early that the Grim Reaper was not a suitable candidate for the cloth."

Amelia laughed and groaned at the same time. She

couldn't believe she'd called him that—and to his face! Her mother was right—sometimes she should not speak. The impression she'd had of him in the beginning couldn't be more different from the one she had now. "How did you accede the title?"

"A series of calamities. My brother died suddenly. His heart gave out. And that proved to be too much for my father—not six months later, he followed John to the grave. I assumed both titles. A few years later, my cousin was accidentally shot during a hunt. He had no issue, and his title would have passed to his uncle, and then to my brother. But it passed to me."

"My goodness," Amelia said. "That's a *terrible* way to become a duke."

He nodded. "It was. But that's generally the way these things work, isn't it? We're all players on a chessboard—someone dies, and you advance."

"It sounds positively medieval when you put it like that." She paused. "Is your family gone?"

"My mother is living in Hampshire."

"You're all alone in Devonshire, then?" She couldn't imagine such a lonely existence. She would be in terrible despair if she had to inhabit Hollyfield by herself. Where was the fun?

"I'm not alone. I have Merlin and Bethan. And a cat wandering these halls that will sometimes grace me with his presence."

She went to the divan and took a seat. She sipped the wine, watching him as he studied the painting. "Do you like being a duke?"

"Do I like it?" He turned from the painting to consider her. "I've never thought of it like that. It's a duty. Quite a lot of responsibility. The estate is vast."

"But...if you weren't the duke, what would you have done?"

He settled his hands on his trim waist. "I don't know. I once fancied myself a painter."

"A painter!" She grinned.

"What...do you think that odd?"

"No! I think it's a marvelous surprise. Imagine, the Grim Reaper a painter. He creates lovely art by night then rides like the devil by day."

He smiled, amused.

"Do you have any of your art?"

"There are a few stored in the north attic, I think. I lost my appetite for it once I assumed the title and married."

Butler appeared at the door. "If I may, sir, supper is served."

"Thank you. You may put it on the table."

Butler opened the door wider, than wheeled in a cart.

Joshua said to Amelia, "The dining room hearths are cold. Will you mind taking your meal here?"

She gestured to her attire. "Not at all."

Butler set the table with china and crystal. He had a platter covered with a silver dome that he set in the middle of the table. Joshua told him to leave it, he would do the serving.

Amelia hadn't realized how hungry she was until she smelled the food. Joshua held out his arm to her and escorted her to a seat at the table just as if she was wearing crinolines and jewels. He poured more wine for them, then removed the silver dome. In the middle of the platter was a roasted chicken, surrounded by small potatoes. "It's not your usual fare, I'm sure, but given the storm..."

"It's wonderful. Thank you."

He carved the chicken with ease, and she imagined him

with his wife in the formal dining room, carving a chicken or beef, her leaning forward, watching him with admiration and love. "May I ask you something?" she asked.

"Yes, of course."

"Do you miss your wife?"

He abruptly stopped carving. He slowly looked up, his gaze piercing hers. He looked as if he expected an accusation.

"Is that something else I should not have asked?" Probably not—that was the bane of her existence, always saying out loud the questions and thoughts that should be kept in her head. "But you haven't remarried, and I wondered if maybe...you missed her too much."

He dropped his gaze and resumed carving. "What I miss... I miss what might have been."

Which meant to Amelia that he missed her terribly. That he had thought of a long and happy life with her that he would never have now. It really was tragic for a man as young as he was. "It seems your marriage was all you expected it be."

He put some chicken on her plate and then some potatoes before he answered. "What does anyone expect from marriage, really?"

"Happiness and love, I would hope. But so many don't take the time to determine true compatibility before they determine love, I think."

Joshua stilled, his knife in the meat. He slowly looked up. "What did you say?"

"I've said it poorly. I meant that we should endeavor to determine compatibility before we enter into marriage for love."

"No, you..." He stared at the chicken for a long moment. "You've said it perfectly."

"Hmm," she said, watching him. "I'm asking too many questions and saying too many things, I think. I really don't mean to pry, but I'm dying of curiosity. I wonder if you knew how compatible you would be with your wife before you married. Doesn't it seem that so many are caught up with the emotion of courtship and don't consider how compatible they are to one another, really? Or perhaps you loved her straightaway, because it seems to me you loved her so very much. She was a fortunate woman, I think. And love is…it's hard to find, isn't it?"

Joshua looked stricken by her words. She really had to learn when to stop talking. "I beg your pardon—I've offended you."

"No. You haven't. I…think perhaps I have offended myself."

"Pardon?"

He looked at her, his gaze intense, like he was trying to find something in her face. "If I may, Amelia, I would rather not speak of my late wife. It's too painful."

"*Je.* Of course." Amelia could feel a flush in her cheeks and dropped her gaze to her plate. "The chicken is excellent." She hadn't even taken a bite.

"Amelia…"

He was going to explain that he'd loved his wife beyond imagining, and it was excruciating to revive her memory, and Amelia suddenly didn't want to hear it, to know that he'd had what she desperately wanted and would probably never have. "It's my fault—I've been thinking about so many things because I'm to find a match and be married," she blurted, interrupting him. "And I can't imagine a marriage without love or felicity, but I fear if I put off making a choice any longer, I will be left with no choice at all. Oh

Lord, I beg your pardon." She put down her fork. "I really must stop talking."

"No, you're fine," he assured her. "What will you do if you don't settle on a match?"

"Return to Wesloria as the vanquished princess. I think there is no worse fate than that as far as my mother is concerned. And then she will cast her net wider, toward more undesirable options."

Joshua looked confused. "Such as?"

"Such as…two Russian princes she has in mind, but she hasn't wanted to include them on any list because she fears the family's eccentric history."

He looked at her blankly.

"So she claims." Amelia dropped her gaze and forced herself to eat the chicken. Her mother feared so many things, half of which seemed nonsensical to Amelia.

"I see."

"Do you? Because I never have. All I've ever really wanted was to be like everyone else. When I was a girl, I used to stand at the windows and watch visitors to the palace come in through the gates. I would imagine becoming one of them. Just…abandon my body and enter one of theirs and return home to a cottage in the forest. I would have family and friends and attend country dances on the weekends and bear my children with a midwife and look forward to the summer harvest."

"The summer harvest, eh? Why a cottage in the forest?"

"Because it sounds simple and carefree to me. No music lessons, no tutors, no heads of state or dinners to attend. Free to choose my friends and my lovers. No reason to worry about living in Russia with strangers who my mother has warned me are eccentric, whatever that might mean."

He laughed with surprise. "If you were other than you

are, you might be surprised to find your lovers were not the sort of men you're accustomed to. A simple life in a cottage would require the fruits of your manual labor. After your summer harvest, you'd have to cook. You'd have to break the necks of chickens and iron and wash and sweep."

"I could do all those things," she insisted.

He cocked his head and smiled dubiously.

"I could! I'm almost certain of it."

His smile turned more dubious.

"Fine. I'd like to imagine that I could."

He laughed. He took a bite of chicken, but he didn't seem to have much of an appetite. "When I was a lad, I would imagine packing my paints and my easel and traveling the world, painting what I saw. Unfortunately, I made the mistake of casually mentioning that dream to my father."

"What did he say?"

"He struck me across the mouth and said to never say such a ridiculous thing again in his presence."

Amelia gasped.

But Joshua shrugged. "My father was not the sort of man to engender warmth. He had a certain idea of how young men ought to behave and demanded it of us."

"He and my mother would have gotten on well, then. My father, however, was very kind. And understanding. He used to tell my mother that I was an Original, and to leave me be."

"King Maksim sounds like he was a wise man."

Warmth filled her. "He was. He was a benevolent king. Some thought him weak, and more than one attempt was made to overthrow him. But he cared about the people he governed and especially about me and Justine. He taught Justine all that she knows about being a sovereign, and she has proven herself to be an excellent queen. Oh, but I miss them both so." The tears that filled her eyes startled her. She quickly picked up her napkin and dabbed at her eyes, appalled that she would lose control so easily and for so little. "Goodness. I'm not generally so sentimental." She put down her napkin. "Forgive me."

"There is nothing to forgive. You sound a bit homesick?"

"I am, a bit." She loved her freedom here...but she missed her family and her dogs.

She settled back in her chair and looked at her unlikely host. "I hope you won't mind me saying so, but I find you fascinating, Joshua. You're not who I thought you were."

"I should hope not—you thought I was the Grim Reaper."

She rolled her eyes. "I should never have said such a thing. In my defense, you seemed rather cold and unfriendly and foreboding."

"I can be those things."

"It wasn't fair of me. I mistook your quiet for something else. My sincere apologies for having judged you unkindly."

His smile was indulgent and warm, and she could feel it swaddle her. "It was fair. I didn't strive to be neighborly. And I judged you, too."

"Yes, well...people often don't care for me, so I'm not surprised."

"I didn't say that I didn't care for you, Amelia. But my initial impressions were incorrect. I thought you were spoiled and entitled."

She laughed with delight. "I *am*!"

"You're not. You're true to yourself and from what little I know, you seem rather clear-eyed."

The warmth settled and held her closer. "You're being kind."

"I'm being honest."

They ate in silence for a few moments, but she didn't

have much appetite. The warmth she'd felt was beginning to flutter in her belly. "When are you leaving Hollyfield?"

"I haven't decided. By the end of summer, I should think. If I can put my affairs in order."

"Who will look after Hollyfield while you're away? Lord Clarendon?"

He chuckled. "He'd like that, I've no doubt."

"I admire that you mean to take a chance in this life and go on an adventure. It sounds thrilling."

He laughed and reached for the wine. "Clarendon thinks I am mad to consider it."

"Really? But you're so lucky to have the freedom and the means to do as you please. You can experience this world in ways most of us can't."

"Us? Surely you don't include yourself in that number. I would think you've experienced quite a lot."

"*Je*, but the experiences I've had have been what others have proscribed for me. Not the adventures of my choosing."

"Interesting." He poured more wine into her glass. "I'm curious—what adventure would you choose?"

"You'll be disappointed in my answer after all the talking I've done. But my great adventure would be a family. Not a royal one, where the children are kept separate or are brought into the world for succession. But a *family*. I can think of no greater pleasure than to have a home filled with children. Like Iddesleigh House."

He looked utterly perplexed, as if those words coming from her made absolutely no sense. Of course he did—what an odd thing to desire when she could desire anything in the world. But she thought it curious that his expression seemed almost sad. "Why are you looking at me like that? Is it so strange?"

"I thought… I thought you'd say something else. I had the impression you enjoyed a bit of danger and would choose something more along those lines."

"Oh, I do! I feel very much alive when I teeter on the edge of disaster." She laughed at herself and absently traced her finger around the rim of her wineglass. Perhaps she'd had a bit too much of the wine. Her thoughts were fluid, she was at long last warm, and she felt amazingly comfortable in his presence. She thought they might have been friends in another life. "It will sound mad when I say it, but my truest wish is to be like everyone else. I wear the finest gowns and priceless jewelry and dine with royalty, and all I want is to be like everyone else."

"I don't think it's mad at all."

His gaze had softened, and she felt herself blush. "And you? What do you want from this life?"

His smile was wry. "Not that."

"You don't want to be like everyone else?" she teased him.

"I think it is best for all concerned if I am left alone."

"Alone! But what about family? Children?"

He pressed his lips together. "That is not for me."

Disappointment stabbed at her. She realized that she'd wanted him to say the exact opposite.

The rain suddenly began to come down in torrents. They both looked to the windows. "I asked that a room be prepared for you. It should be warmed by now. Would you like to see it?"

She was not ready for the day to end. She wanted to spend more time with him and tell him everything—who was her favorite dog at the palace, where was the secret place in the palace gardens she went when she wanted to be alone. How many men she'd kissed—probably imprudent of her to say, but still. She felt entirely at ease with him. There was no one else she'd felt so comfortable with here. It was a bit like talking to Justine—she felt as if she could confess everything to him.

There was no point in lingering. It would only give rise to a hope for something she couldn't have. "Please," she said at last. Maybe she was learning to be a spinster now. Talking and talking and revealing too much, then saying good-night when one wanted so much more.

He picked up one of the candles from the table and cupped his hand around the flame and walked to the door.

"Are there no lamps?" she asked as she rose from her seat. It seemed so odd to have a house like this without lamps.

"I've gotten out of the habit of having them lit."

The dogs were sprawled outside the closed door and came to attention the moment the door opened. When Joshua stepped into the hall behind Amelia, the dogs turned and began trotting ahead of them, the path familiar to them.

Amelia walked along with the duke in her bare feet, down the large hall, up the stairs again, and into the hallway she'd seen before. But this time, instead of following the dogs all the way to the end, Joshua stopped at an open door about halfway down.

A fire was glowing in that room, making the yellow wallpaper seem even brighter. The dust cloths that had obviously covered the furnishings were folded neatly and stacked in a corner. She walked into the room and looked around.

"Will this suit?" he asked.

She turned to look at him. He'd not stepped over the threshold, but was leaning against the door frame, one hand in his pocket, the other holding the candle.

"Was this your wife's room?" She needed to know. She didn't want to be in her room, God rest her soul. She couldn't be thinking about him while in a dead woman's room.

"*No*," he said, aghast.

She was astonished by how relieved she felt.

Joshua hadn't moved, but he was looking at her in a way that made her heart skip a little. She thought she recognized a bit of yearning in his look. She felt it, too, waving through her.

"Well," he said, and straightened.

Amelia was suddenly loath to have him go. "Thank you," she said quickly before he could leave her with the candle. "I don't think I've talked about so many things to one person in ages."

He withdrew his hand from his pocket, and Amelia thought the moment was passing her by—she impulsively reached out and touched his fingers with hers.

Joshua froze.

She stepped closer and laced her fingers through his. She could feel the roughness of his palm against her hand. He didn't resist her but he watched her warily. She wrapped her fingers a little tighter around his, then turned his hand over and looked at his palm. She touched her finger to the calluses. "Why are your hands like this?"

He looked at his palm for a very long moment. "I like to chop wood. I find it to be a better salve than a bottle of whisky." He lifted his gaze; it settled on her mouth, stirring more trouble in her. She traced a line over his palm.

"What are you doing, Amelia?"

"I'm teetering on the edge of disaster." She let go of his hand, then took the candlestick he held and set it aside. She was teetering, all right, and she would fall, and there could be no hope of saving her, and worse, she didn't want to be saved and she wanted to take him with her. And he wasn't doing anything to stop it.

Her thoughts felt like a million different pieces. Was this thing between them compatibility? Had she discovered it in Joshua when it had eluded her with everyone else? Could this feeling be more? It *felt* like more. He was seeing her as she truly was, and only Justine and her parents had ever seen her like that.

She reached up and touched his face. "Before you say anything, I know I am wrong to touch you. But something happened to me today."

"Quite a lot happened today."

"I mean that a window was opened that has been sealed shut all my life, and I… I don't want to close it." She tugged his hand, forcing him to step over the threshold. He moved stiffly, as if he didn't want to enter the room. She ran her hand up his chest, to his neck.

Joshua bent his head and looked her directly in her eye. "You are issuing an invitation and you should know now that I will not accept the offer."

"Why not?"

"For all the obvious reasons. I am not in your queue. I have no desire for an entanglement or anything beyond that. You have very clear desires and a virtue and a duty that I don't share. What sort of man would I be if I took advantage of that purely for my personal pleasure? Do you want me to go on?"

"For heaven's sake, please don't." She couldn't bear another word of denial from him, especially when she could plainly see his regard in his gaze. She wasn't imagining it—she could feel it filling up the room around them. She rose up on her tiptoes and touched her lips to his. He didn't resist her; he moved his lips against hers, accepting the invitation to at least a kiss.

She sank her fingers into his hair, then moved her hands to his shoulders, sinking her fingers into muscle. He could say what he liked, but she could feel his body harden against hers.

Then he slipped his arm around her waist and drew her tighter against his body and kissed her back. He kissed her like a man who would give everything up for pleasure, and she pressed against him, letting him feel that she would, too.

He cupped her jaw with his palm, and a thousand flutters of pleasure winged through her. He held her so tightly that nothing was left to her imagination. With one hand, he pushed the coat she was wearing from her shoulders and she let it fall. He cupped her breast, kneading it through the lawn fabric. She was beginning to drown in a powerful desire—she wanted to be beneath him, to feel his weight on her and in her. She wanted to give her body everything it had been craving.

He moaned, dipped down to kiss the hollow of her throat. She was completely disarmed—he could have his way with her, do whatever he liked, and she would come along for the thrill of it. She raked her fingers through his hair, pressed against him, tried to convey that she wanted him to surround her and take her on his adventure tonight, to places she'd never been but was desperate to know.

She was ready, too, her trunks packed, her mind already at the train station. But when she reached for the cord that held the breeches on her, he caught her hand. He pulled it away so that she had to let go of the cord. He cupped her face in both hands and kissed her tenderly, then lifted his head to the ceiling and let out a loud groan.

He slowly dropped his hands from her and stepped back.

She was dizzy with want and she couldn't think for a moment, couldn't grasp what was happening.

Joshua rubbed his nape. He gazed at her with an expression of pure torment, taking her in from the top of her head to her bare feet.

Amelia understood how these things worked. She understood why he refused to be her lover even though he obviously wanted to *be* her lover. She folded her arms across her chest. "I won't pretend I'm not disappointed."

He smiled sadly and touched her cheek, caressing it. "I won't pretend, either." He brushed his fingers against her temple. "You really are quite beautiful, Amelia. If I was any—"

"Please don't say it," she said, before he could make an excuse. "Please?"

He sighed. He took her hand and brought it to his lips, let his kiss linger a moment too long. "Good night, then." He turned away from her and walked out the door, shutting it quietly behind him.

Amelia stood there for a long moment, trying to will him back. He was right to leave her, of course he was, but tonight, she didn't care about propriety and decency. It was just her rotten luck to want the one man who refused to be, as he said, in her queue. He didn't care that she had a terrible regard for a virtue she'd been taught to protect with her life until some magic moment she was supposed to leave it behind. She just wanted that man. She wanted to be with someone who could abide her, who clearly wanted her, too. She wanted to be set free to run unbridled, with abandon.

CHAPTER TWENTY-NINE

THE NEXT DAY was bright and crystal clear, without a single cloud in the sky. Iddesleigh and Lady Aleksander arrived at Hollyfield at half past ten in a carriage to fetch their royal ward.

Joshua met them on the drive, dressed to go out, his intention to exit Hollyfield and clear his head as soon as possible. He'd not seen Amelia this morning—he'd instructed Butler to serve her breakfast in her room. Last night, he had come dangerously, perilously close to doing something he would sorely regret, and he would not allow himself to be tempted like that again.

He exchanged the usual pleasantries with Iddesleigh and Lady Aleksander—yes, the storm was a bad one. Yes, the day looked to be a fine one. No, it was no imposition to have hosted the princess, he was only relieved he'd come across her when he did.

When she appeared on the entry landing, her gown cleaned and pressed, she looked remarkably fresh. Her hair was still braided, and she was still barefoot, her shoes having suffered the worst of the storm. Joshua had a sudden image of her in a cottage in the forest, picking wildflowers, leading a group of children from one patch to the next.

But she looked...fatigued. He wondered if her night had been as sleepless as his.

"*Bon dien*," she said. "Good morning."

"Good morning." He offered his arm to her, but she picked up her skirts and glided down the stairs on her own. Butler followed, carrying her shoes.

"There you are, Highness!" Lady Aleksander trilled, her voice reminding Joshua of the morning birds—bright, cheerful, and too much noise at first light.

"Here I am," she said.

"Your Grace, I must thank you for taking in our guest. We were worried to death when she didn't return before the storm as we expected," Lady Aleksander said.

"My fault," Amelia said instantly. "I thought I might walk to Goosefeather Abbey."

"Walk!" Iddesleigh said. "But that is too far!"

"Yes, my lord. Regrettably, I discovered that yesterday." She smiled thinly.

"How lucky you are that Marley was—"

"I was very lucky indeed," she said, interrupting Lady Aleksander before she could launch into a speech about good fortune. She glanced at Joshua. "Very lucky," she said again. "I can't thank you enough for rescuing me, Your Grace."

"It was my pleasure." His undiluted and thorough pleasure. As well as his agony. He bowed.

"You must be exhausted, darling," Iddesleigh said. "Let's get you home. The girls have been asking for you. They were caught in the storm, too. By design, I might add. Nothing like a good downpour to tempt a few silly girls to dance in the rain."

One of the coachmen opened the door to the carriage. Joshua watched Amelia walk down the last few stairs and then pick her way carefully across the drive. She stepped up into the coach and Butler handed her shoes to the coachman holding the door.

Just before Amelia disappeared into the interior, she glanced back at Joshua.

She may as well have touched him with a hot fire poker—he felt her look sizzle through him.

Lady Aleksander followed her into the coach.

"Careful on the roads, Marley. Parts of it have washed away," Iddesleigh said. "Thank you again. We are in your debt."

"Not at all," Joshua said.

Iddesleigh tipped his hat and entered the coach.

Joshua remained standing on the drive as the coach rolled away, bouncing and lurching through the new chuck-holes created by yesterday's storm. He remained standing there long after the coach had disappeared.

He was a terrible host. He should have invited them in. But he couldn't bear to be in the same room with her, fearing all his feelings would be instantly understood by them all.

What he couldn't fully grasp was what had happened to him yesterday. He didn't understand the storm, or her wearing his clothes, or the time spent in the drawing room, talking so freely about so many things. He didn't understand when she kissed him and he kissed her, and it didn't really matter, did it, because either way, he was in pieces.

All night and all morning he'd felt his jaw clenching against his desire and his confusion over who and what he was.

But there was another question looming front and center in his mind. Who was *she?* How in the bloody hell had she repeated what he'd written to the headmaster? She'd said it, the very thing he'd written, that one must find compatibility before love. She'd said it nearly word for word. He could only surmise that she'd read his letter—or worse, Mr. Roberts was sharing the contents of them far and wide.

Were they laughing at him? Reading his letters and howling at his complaints and his observations? He thought he and Mr. Roberts had struck up an alliance. He'd thought Mr. Roberts was possibly his friend. He'd imagined having an ale with the man.

One way or another, he would discover how she had come to read his letter.

But the worst of it, the absolute *worst* thing to have happened was that Princess Amelia had managed to capture him. She'd taken her flimsy butterfly net and had swooped him up like a fat slug. He had believed himself to be untouchable, and moreover, that she was the very last person in the world who could touch him. And somehow, she'd done it—and he hadn't even known it was happening. She'd forced his surrender with hardly a touch, had pulled him in with her smile and her beauty and the outrageous things that she said, and it was *unfair*, *unfair*, *unfair* that he'd turned into such a pitiful man.

She was lush—her lips, her body, all of her—irresistible in a way that no one had ever been. Never Diana. Not even Sarah. Her mouth was as succulent as he'd remembered from the night on Iddesleigh's balcony. The kiss last night had been utterly molten—a volcano melting him from the inside out. His desire had erupted, spilling hot throughout his body, and before he knew what was happening, he'd pulled her into his chest and was kissing her while his thoughts raced through all the ways he wanted to kiss her, all the places of her body he wanted to taste.

And she'd arched into him because she knew that he wanted her, and she'd bent her knee, pressing against him there, too, feeling his raging hardness for her. He was bewitched, out of his mind, his abstinence having created a monster in him that had clawed its way free.

Thank God his corrupt conscience had somehow fought through the fog and stopped him from doing harm. *Tremendous* harm. What in the hell did he think he was doing, entangling himself with a foreign princess who was here for the sole purpose of finding a husband? He was not that man. *He was not that man.*

He was as far from that man as he could possibly be.

He'd killed one woman already.

He'd spent hours tossing and turning before his common sense had slowly returned to him and began to reconstruct the wall he'd painstakingly built over the last few years. A wall his lust had very nearly torched to the ground.

He was to meet with his solicitor, Mr. Darren, today in Iddesleigh. Tomorrow, he was going to pay a visit to that school to get to the bottom of how she had come to know what he'd written.

CHAPTER THIRTY

THE DRIVE TO Iddesleigh went exactly as Amelia expected—Lila full of questions, Beck amused by it all. Lila wanted a full accounting of what had happened yesterday. How had he come upon her? What did they do once they were safely at Hollyfield? What did they talk about? What did they eat? Where did she sleep?

Amelia answered all the questions with calm indifference. She said the entire experience was tolerable, when it had been the most astounding thing to ever happen to her. She said they didn't do much but wait out the rain, when she'd let her guard down and talked about so many things to someone who was not family. She said she went to bed early as she was exhausted, but then had lain awake all night, thinking about him.

And as they rolled up to Iddesleigh House, she feigned exhaustion and asked that she be left alone for a few hours to rest.

She didn't want to talk about it anymore.

The whole thing had left her feeling more restless than she'd ever felt in her life. She couldn't think of anyone but him, didn't want to meet anyone else but him. Every other gentleman on Lila's list looked flat and lifeless in comparison. That man, that duke, was not despicable after all, but surprising and exciting and all the things everyone wanted her to feel for Mr. Swann. Things she couldn't possibly ever feel for Mr. Swann but felt so easily for Joshua.

What was she to do? Joshua had made his intentions quite clear. He was not her suitor. He was leaving. He had loved his wife deeply and he'd kissed Amelia but he'd left her and it was quite obvious to her that was the end of it. He'd told her very plainly that he wanted to live alone. That children were not for him.

And Lila was talking about London again.

Amelia wanted to go home to Wesloria. Except that she didn't. She wanted to go to London. But she couldn't bear the thought of all that small talk and polite drawing room conversation. She wanted to bathe and change clothes and go to Hollyfield and ask him why. *Why not her. Why was it so wrong. Could he really never love again, was it even a little possible?*

She wanted desperately to talk, but she had no one to talk to. Justine was too far away. Blythe? Never—Blythe would flutter anxiously about and insist Mr. Swann was a perfect match. Lila would read too much into anything Amelia said, and then would want to help her solve her problems or point her to an available man.

Amelia didn't want that sort of help.

What she wanted was to understand what made a man love a woman.

There was one person she could pose the question to: A Concerned Resident of Devonshire.

This afternoon, she was to go to the village with Lila and Blythe to pick up some gloves and shoes. Afterward, she would write her letter and leave it at the school.

THE PRINCESS'S FATIGUE was not from walking several miles in a blinding rain, Lila had decided on the drive into Iddesleigh. There was something else on her mind, and if Lila was a betting woman—and she was—she would bet that it had to do with a dark and morose duke. Unfortunately, Lila couldn't get to the bottom of it because Blythe had come along for the ride into the village today.

"I ordered the gloves ages ago," Blythe was explaining as they drove into the village. "Donovan was to bring them out, but they weren't ready when he went to pick them up."

The princess stared out the window as Blythe talked on about her history with this particular pair of gloves. She didn't seem to hear a word that was being said. Not that she missed much—Blythe seemed not to notice that no one in that coach was interested in hearing the very long tale.

In Iddesleigh, the princess perked up a bit in the dressmaker's shop. There was hardly anything to the village of Iddesleigh, but there was a dressmaker who'd set up shop in the front of her thatched roof cottage. She had just received new silks and satins that caught the princess's eye, and she and Lila went through them, holding up finished dresses in the mirror, then both selecting fabrics for new gowns.

When Blythe determined she would like a new sun hat, Lila and the princess stepped out to the street for a bit of air while Blythe perused the various hats for sale. Lila was trying her best to make conversation, but the princess seemed miles from where they were. Until the moment she suddenly straightened, her gaze locked on something up the street.

Lila followed her gaze. The Duke of Marley had just come out of Mr. Darren's offices. He was walking purposefully toward a horse, but he happened to look up and his gaze fell on the princess. He faltered, midstride. He tipped his hat to the two of them then carried on to his horse. In a few moments, he'd mounted and was riding away.

Next to Lila, the princess physically deflated, sinking back against a wall.

"What is the matter?" Lila asked, even though she suspected she knew full well what was the matter.

The princess shook her head and folded her arms, her reticule dangling from one wrist.

Lila watched the duke disappear down the road. "Did I tell you that Mr. Swann has asked if he may call?" She hadn't told her that because Mr. Swann had not asked if he might call. He had expressly told Lila he was to London to do some important scientific work. Or rather, that was how she had heard his long-winded explanation of why he wouldn't be calling again. She had to give the man credit for knowing when the game was lost.

"I don't want to receive him," the princess murmured.

"Then shall we carry on with our plans to go to London?"

"I don't want to go to London, either."

At last, the perfect opening. "If I may, Highness…what *do* you want? My every suggestion is met with resistance. I feel as if there is something or someone holding you back."

The princess looked down at her hand, stretching her gloved fingers wide, then closing them in a fist, as if she was suffering from a rheumatoid pain.

"I've never had anyone turn quite so uncooperative—"

"I don't mean to be. The problem, Lila, is that what I want, you can't give me."

Now they were getting somewhere. "If I don't know what it is you want, how can I possibly?"

The princess sighed.

"For someone who prides herself on speaking her mind, you seem terribly tongue-tied at the moment."

"All right," the princess said with great exasperation.

"What I *want* is someone who is most unsuitable for me. Someone who will not enter the race for my hand. Someone who would like to be left behind or, at the very least, alone."

Lila feigned confusion. "Who could that possibly be? I would think every gentleman in Britain and throughout Europe would want the opportunity to vie for your hand."

"Please," the princess said with a withering look. "It is glaringly obvious that's not true. I'm referring to Marley."

"*Marley?*" Lila attempted to sound as confused and surprised as possible.

"Yes, Marley. Why do you look so…amused?"

"Pardon. It's just you've despised him since your first meeting."

"I know, and I have. I *did*. But…but my feelings have changed. Once I spoke to him—"

"Yesterday?"

"Before yesterday," the princess said impatiently. "Does it matter when? My feelings have changed, but his have not."

All he might need was a healthy push. It was certainly worth exploring. Then again, Lila wanted the princess to understand that sometimes people held beliefs about themselves that were intractable. Marley, well…she wasn't sure. "Ah," Lila said with a bit of a shrug.

"Ah what?"

"It's nothing—"

The princess straightened from her slouch. "Has he said something?"

"No, no…but he has suffered a great loss. He lost a wife and a child, and I think he has not yet come to terms with his grief."

The princess's face fell. "Who can blame him?"

Lila gave her arm a sympathetic pat. "Grief has a way of overwhelming us."

"Do you think he was terribly in love with her?"

Lila knew for a fact that he was not terribly in love with Diana, and neither was she with him. She thought all that could be said for their union was that it was amicable. "I think...he feels her loss."

"*Je*, of course. But don't you think that sometimes grief can open closed doors?"

That was not an observation Lila would have expected the princess to make and looked at her with genuine curiosity. "How so?"

She rubbed her forehead as if it pained her. "I've suffered a great loss, too. I've grieved beyond anything I thought was imaginable. It's a wretched thing, to realize that life will never be the same. That my father would be forever missing from my life. But if he'd lived, Justine would not be queen. And she's a brilliant queen, Lila. And had she not become queen, I would not have lost my way in Wesloria. I would not have come to England. My father's death opened another path in my life, and I'm not sorry that I've embarked on it."

"Perhaps you should share this with the duke," Lila suggested.

The princess shook her head and looked down. "I could never presume—"

"There you are!" Blythe's voice rang out. She had exited the small dressmaker's cottage, a sun hat in hand. "It's rather plain, but she assures me Mrs. Wilson, who lives near the old Bakerley Chapel, will dress it. We'll just swing by there, shall we?"

The moment was lost, but Lila was, as always, optimistic. If the princess was reluctant to tell him, Lila was not.

In fact, it might be better coming from the duke's favorite matchmaker than Princess Amelia.

When they arrived back at Iddesleigh House, the princess retreated to her suite to take care of some correspondence. And Lila retreated to her rooms to write her husband and plot her next move.

There was not much that delighted her more than two people who were obviously meant to be together, except, perhaps, having a hand in bringing them together when they couldn't manage to get there on their own.

To A Resident of Devonshire, Concerned,

You will no doubt be astonished to find a letter waiting for you, as that has not been our arrangement. But we have come to rely on your considered opinions and find ourselves facing the most egregious dilemma. Nothing to do with our most excellent students, who, by the by, are determined to have a garden of their own. You will be happy to know that the Mr. Puddlestone has agreed to oversee this endeavor himself, and just this morning brought round some shovels to be used in tilling the soil. Unfortunately, one of our younger students thought the shovel could just as well be used for some pretend swordplay, and struck another student, quite by accident, but hard enough to break the skin. Her father came to collect her and warned us that such mishaps will not be tolerated. Of course they won't. We don't pride ourselves on bringing up students who are likely to bean each other on the head with a shovel, but accidents do happen.

As for our need for your sound advice, we find ourselves in the untenable position of having developed esteem for someone who has not returned it in kind. You will be shocked, as you might have suspected that, like you, our desires did not trend toward esteem and companionship. We can only say that it happened by chance. We had developed strong opinions that were proven to be unfounded, and now, we don't know what to make of our feelings, as we have discovered a compatibility with this particular person that we did not think possible. Truly. We can't help but wonder, when does one know that compatibility has turned to love? Is there a signal? A feeling, a single moment one recognizes as love?

And if such feelings are not reciprocated, what is one to do? How does one go about the daily living? It seems as if it could become intolerable.

Your advice is, as always, very much appreciated by the Iddesleigh School for Exceptional Girls.

CHAPTER THIRTY-ONE

HE APPROACHED THE school carefully, glancing around him to see if anyone was near. Anyone who would see him enter the small, plain building would wonder what he was about.

And then he looked for an escape if one became necessary. With so many children potentially underfoot, a quick exit could very well become urgent. He could hear the children through the open door, their voices raised in song. *Again.* Why were girls always singing? What made them think that life was joyous? Maybe it was joyous for them now, but one day, they'd not sing so much, would they?

Joshua had to dip down to step into the narrow entry. He doffed his hat and stood anxiously, expecting someone to greet him. A girl, Mr. Roberts—anyone. Surely one couldn't simply walk into a school. And yet, no one came to see who was calling. Remarkable.

He moved a little deeper into the old house to a point where he could see into what he assumed was the main classroom. But the girls and Mr. Roberts were not there. He heard their voices again, and realized they were outside, somewhere in the back garden. He rolled his eyes. It seemed to him they were constantly outdoors. He walked past a tidy, but cluttered office, stuffed with books and papers, umbrellas and rain boots. He had to pass through the classroom to reach the back door. In this room, a variety of crude tables and crates were squeezed in beside each other.

Around the room were slates and books. Drawings were tacked to the wall opposite the windows. A large chalkboard stood at the front of the room, onto which several arithmetic equations had been written.

Joshua followed the sounds to the back garden. The girls had stopped singing, thank the saints, but now they were chattering. How did they do it? All of them talking at once, over and around each other. Did any of them hear anything another said? And then the one, lone male voice rising above them to pay attention and to keep their hands to themselves. *Excellent advice, sir.*

He dipped through another low door and emerged into a bright sunlight garden. There they were a dozen or more girls milling around. Some held shovels. A few held spades. And then there were three of them with nothing in hand but who were chasing each other in a circle, shrieking with laughter.

"Children! Children, I will have your undivided attention!"

Mr. Roberts, Joshua presumed. He'd never met the headmaster.

The girls—most of them, anyway—gave him the attention he sought. There were one or two who didn't. There were always one or two in any crowd, weren't there?

"What did Mr. Puddlestone advise?" Mr. Roberts asked.

A hand shot up. "That the rows must be straight!"

"Precisely. Thank you, Miss Roth."

Miss Roth looked around smugly at her classmates.

"Now then, does this row appear straight to any of you?"

The girls inched forward to have a look. "Yes," said several of them at the same time some said, "No."

"It is not straight," Mr. Roberts said. "Miss Waverly, will you please take the end of this string and—" The man happened to look up and noticed Joshua standing there. "I do beg your pardon, my good man. I didn't see you there. Good day."

"Good day."

The girls whipped around, almost as one, staring up at him.

"How may I help you?"

"That's the Grim Reaper," said one of Iddesleigh girls.

"Lady Mathilda!" Mr. Roberts said sternly. "Apologize at once."

Joshua lifted his hand. "It's quite all right. There was a bit of a misunderstanding at the Iddesleigh house, not of her making. I am Lord Marley of Hollyfield."

Mr. Roberts's brows rose with surprise. "Your Grace, welcome. Children, the Duke of Marley has come to call."

"Oh. You're to curtsy to a duke," Lady Mathilda informed them. She and two girls Joshua recognized as her sisters curtsied. They were joined by one or two more, but mostly, the girls continued to stare curiously at him.

And two of the more industrious students began to dig. Not at the row they were trying to make, but just in general. Joshua couldn't help himself—he pointed at them. "That's not…that's not the proper way to dig dirt. Or to hold a shovel."

"We're still learning," Mr. Roberts said, and smoothly took the shovels from the girls and leaned them against the fence.

Joshua's curiosity had gotten the better of him, and he took a few steps to see the row the girls had dug. If it was indeed intended to be a row. From what he saw, it was a mess of overturned dirt. "What is this?"

"We are creating our own garden," Mr. Roberts said proudly. "It will require a bit of reconfiguring."

"It will require being redone. Why not have one of Iddesleigh's men do it?"

"That would defeat the purpose of the hands-on experience, Your Grace. At the Iddesleigh School for Girls, we believe in using our hands as well as our minds to promote educational growth. If you'd like, I'd be happy to schedule a time we might discuss the curriculum—"

"No, thank you." He was making an ass of himself, questioning the digging of a gaggle of little girls. And really, why did he care how they dug a row? "I don't..." He didn't know what to say, really. "Need to know."

Mr. Roberts nodded politely. "Is there something else you need, then?"

Yes, he needed to know who Mr. Roberts had shared his letters with. Who he had deemed fit to read letters that Joshua thought were private. "I, ah...there has been some talk of Goosefeather Abbey."

"There has indeed, Your Grace. The old abbey is the perfect location for our growing school."

"Yes," Joshua said. "I wanted to see the school for myself."

Mr. Roberts did not question why. He was beaming at the mere mention of the abbey. "Then perhaps you might like to observe our botany lesson. Miss Waverly? The string, please."

Miss Waverly walked as far as the string would allow her.

"Do you have a daughter?" A girl standing nearby directed the question at him.

"No."

"Then why did you come here?"

"I wanted to see the school."

"Is your daughter going to come? We haven't any room," said another one.

"I don't have a daughter."

"But she can come when we move. Mr. Roberts says we'll have more room, then," offered another. "What's her name?"

It was to have been Carla. Carla Parker.

"He doesn't *have* a daughter, Penny," said one of the girls.

"Then why is he here?"

"Children!" Mr. Roberts said sternly. "Do you see the string Miss Waverly and I are holding?"

They all agreed that they did.

"I will ask again, does the row appear to be straight?"

The girls studied the row for longer than was necessary—even a quick glance would convince the dullest of creatures the row was not straight. They all agreed it was not, except for two lone holdouts, who stubbornly held on to their original yes votes.

"Is he the *gardener*?" one of the smaller girls asked.

"When is it time for tea?" asked another one.

"*Tea, tea, tea,*" shouted one of Iddesleigh's girls, jumping up and down with each utterance of *tea*.

"Enough of that," Mr. Roberts said sternly. "Is this how you will behave when we have a distinguished guest?"

"No, Mr. Roberts," they sang at him.

Joshua had to leave. He had to get out of here before his heart exploded with grief. But he still had to think of a way to broach the letters with Mr. Roberts. It had seemed so simple when he'd set out this morning, but nothing seemed simple now. He was looking at a sea of cherubic faces with pink cheeks. They were bright and so trusting that life would bring them joy. He suddenly had an answer to one of the questions he'd posed to Mr. Roberts—adults promised children joy, because how could they look at these faces and wish for anything less? It was an expression of sincere hope.

And hope was all an adult would have when they discovered that these cherubs couldn't dig a hole to save their precious lives.

He shrugged out of his coat. "If I may, Mr. Roberts. This row has been dug too deep in some places. Furthermore, it's too long and too crooked. And there is no indication of where the next row may be. They must be spaced at a proper distance. Has anyone thought of that?"

"I did," said one small girl, and Joshua believed that she had.

"Very good," he said. "If you will give me your shovel, I will demonstrate."

"Your Grace! That's not necessary," Mr. Roberts tried.

"Why not? I'm here, and you are clearly in need of assistance."

Mr. Roberts looked set to argue, but he didn't say more.

Joshua began to repair their first attempt at making a row. The girls were absolutely no help at all, which he might have guessed, but he'd given Mr. Roberts the benefit of the doubt and thought perhaps they hadn't been trained any better.

The girls peppered him with questions while he worked. Where did he live? What was a duke? Could they be dukes, too?

He asked what they intended to plant. From their answers, there didn't seem to be any sort or plan. Some said flowers. One girl said pinwheels. He explained a pinwheel was not a plant, but lost the argument when she and her friends agreed that if it was *planted in the ground* it must be a *plant*.

"You need to plant food," he said. "How do you intend to feed your family with flowers and pinwheels?"

"My husband will do that," said one girl.

"No, Molly, you'll have a *butler*," one of Iddesleigh's girls corrected her.

"I think not everyone will have a butler, Lady Maren," said Mr. Roberts.

"Really?" Lady Maren inquired, perplexed. "Why not?"

As Mr. Roberts explained that butlers cost money, Joshua carried on, straightening their row and filling it back to a proper depth. But when he picked up the first seedling, Mr. Roberts asked him to stop. "It is important for the students to do the planting."

Joshua thought it was painfully obvious they would do it wrong and kill the seedlings, but Mr. Roberts hastily continued, "And I'd not like to steal Mr. Puddlestone's moment in the sun. He will be here on the morrow to help with the planting."

Another of Iddesleigh's daughters very primly put her hand out for the seedling he held. Joshua reluctantly relinquished it to her open palm.

"We are going to continue our botany lesson inside," Mr. Roberts said. "You are welcome to—"

"No. Thank you." He felt like a fool. He'd gotten caught up with these girls, had spent an hour pretending what might have been. He picked up his coat.

"Is there anything you'd like to speak to me about privately?" Mr. Roberts asked.

Joshua looked at the girls, at their now-dirty faces and hems. How several of them had gathered around a caterpillar inching its way along the garden path.

"No, thank you." He tried to smile but couldn't seem to manage a proper one. It felt like his mouth stretched out and was on the verge of a scream. He thanked Mr. Roberts again and walked out of the school, passing the overstuffed classroom, the tidy-but-cluttered office. He walked out the open front door and paused to drag breath into his lungs.

He'd just spent an hour with a dozen or so young girls and had survived. The children were...adorable. He glanced back, trying to make sense of the pain in his gut. But when he looked back, something caught his eye. He leaned to his left. It was a bit of cream paper.

He walked to the door and leaned again, peering around the edge. No. It couldn't be. But it *was*. It was a letter, addressed to "A Resident of Devonshire, Concerned." When did Roberts do this? While he was repairing the row? Before that? Joshua glanced all around him to see if anyone was watching. He yanked the letter free of its tack, shoved it into his pocket, and strode quickly to his horse. And then he rode like the devil away from that school.

At Hollyfield, he stormed inside, eager to read the contents. He was intercepted by Miles, who wandered out of the dining room with Joshua's dogs escorting him. "There you are. Where have you been?"

"You're returned to us so soon?" Joshua asked. He glared at his dogs. They would let a band of thieves into the house.

"And a good afternoon to you, too, sir," Miles said with an exaggerated bow. "I was just about to have lunch. Care to join me?"

Normally, Joshua would have joined him just to remind him that he didn't actually live there, and therefore could not summon up a lunch at his whim. But the letter was burning a hole in his pocket. "I've got something I need to do."

Miles shrugged and smiled. "As you like." He went back into the dining room, and his two canine sentries turned and followed him.

"They are my dogs!" Joshua yelled through the door, then stomped to the stairs. He took them two at a time, strode to his master suite, shut the door, looked at it, and locked it. He didn't trust Miles not to stroll in.

He removed the letter from his pocket, broke the small seal, and read the contents.

He read it again.

And then he sank slowly to the edge of his bed, forcing Artemis to leave his patch of sunshine with a meow of disapproval. But Joshua didn't hear him. He was staring into space, his mind trying to understand how this had happened. This letter was about *him*. And now he knew that Mr. Roberts hadn't been writing the letters all this time. *She* had.

How was it possible? And yet, she clearly thought he was someone else. She didn't know she was writing *him*.

He read it again. And once more. He had to respond.

How did he respond? How did he tell her that he didn't know the answer to her question and wanted to know the answer, too? How did he say that maybe compatibility is a form of love, and it only grows deeper with time? How did he say that she'd bewitched him, confused him, and he'd wanted so much more, but was unable to give her more?

How did he tell her that he was terrified of reliving the same fate with another woman? How did he carry on, knowing her feelings, suspecting his own, and after having seen those girls today?

Joshua slid off the bed and onto the floor. He felt almost in a daze. He loved, he wanted, and yet he held himself away from all that he needed. His breath grew short.

His heart pounded in his chest. He tried to stop the burn in his eyes, he *tried*. But when the first tear fell, the rest rained down on him.

He sobbed for what he'd lost and what might have been. He sobbed for Diana and Carla, for all the mistakes he'd made as Diana's husband. He sobbed for Amelia—golden, unique Amelia. He sobbed for his broken heart and spirit, he sobbed for those beautiful girls, those perfect, exceptional girls. He sobbed until he couldn't draw a breath and thought he might suffocate, and then Artemis climbed on his lap and began to claw his leg.

CHAPTER THIRTY-TWO

AMELIA HEARD ALL about the duke's visit to the school the day before—she figured she must have just missed him, as she'd had been there earlier, answering correspondence. And leaving her own, tacked to the door.

"The Duke of Marley?" Blythe asked a second time over breakfast. She was as incredulous as Amelia.

"Tilly made us curtsy," Maisie said. "You're to curtsy to dukes. Everyone knows it."

"Sariah didn't know it," Maren said. "Sariah didn't curtsy. She doesn't know how."

"But what would the duke be doing there?" Blythe asked Beck.

"What does anyone do at a school? Observe, I suppose. I really haven't the slightest idea." Beck held Birdie on his lap, and she kept trying to grab his nose.

"And he dug a hole?" Blythe asked her oldest daughter again.

"Not a *hole*, Mama. A *row*. That's what you call it when you put plants in it," Mathilda informed her.

"Mr. Puddlestone is coming today and we're going to put the plants in," Maisie added.

"I want plants, Mama," Peg-leg Meg said, pouting.

"We'll make our own row, shall we?" Blythe said to her, and Meg nodded. "But I can't imagine him doing any such thing," Blythe continued to Beck.

Amelia could imagine it—she'd seen his rough hands, had felt them on her skin. She could imagine him doing any number of things with them. Mostly she imagined those hands on her body. He chopped wood, he said. A better salve than whisky. She wondered what else he might find a better salve than whisky.

She shifted in her seat and glanced down.

"What have you planned today, Highness?" Beck asked as he put Birdie on the floor.

"I thought I'd write my childhood tutor and ask if he knows an educator who might like to come to Devonshire. And I want to explore raising funds for the school."

"I am pleased you've taken such an interest in our school, and I should be delighted for your assistance in all things. But perhaps we ought to wait until we've secured the abbey. As it happens, I have a meeting with Mr. Darren today— he said he has news about ownership."

"Wonderful," Amelia said.

"Won't you be traveling to London soon, Highness?" Blythe asked.

"Lila has suggested it."

"I think you ought to take her advice. There are so many more gentlemen to choose from in London." She smiled in that way someone might smile when they kicked you out of a house and then mockingly asked you to come again. "Oh dear, it's time for school," she added, looking over Amelia's shoulder at the clock on the mantle.

Amelia could imagine Blythe pestering Lila every day about when they'd take their leave. But Blythe couldn't pretend she hadn't grown accustomed to Amelia escorting her daughters to school every day. "*Je*, look at that," Amelia agreed.

When the girls had their hats and shawls and their slates

and books, they set off down the road. Mathilda and Maisie raced each other for a time, putting themselves ahead of Amelia and Maren.

Maren slipped her hand into Amelia's. They both looked at Hollyfield in the distance as they passed it. Funny, the grand house didn't look so foreboding to Amelia now. She thought with a bit of cleaning and opening of windows it would look like a bucolic country estate.

"Are you going to marry someone?" Maren asked.

Amelia shifted her gaze to the girl. "What makes you ask?"

"I heard Mama talking about it. She said she didn't know if you even wanted to marry someone."

"Did she," Amelia drawled.

"Do you?"

"I do."

"Then who are you going to marry?"

Amelia glanced skyward. "That's a very good question, Maren. I don't know who. I'm still meeting gentlemen."

"But do you like them? Mama said you don't like *any-one*."

Lord, she would be happy when she was no longer Blythe's guest. "Your mama is mistaken. I like all the gentlemen I've met, very much. But if I am to marry a gentleman and stay by his side for the rest of my life, well…he must be the perfect man for me, mustn't he? That's a very long time to be with someone who isn't perfect for me."

"I don't think it will be very long," Maren said. "You're already old."

Amelia laughed. "There are days I certainly feel that is true."

One of the girls shouted at Maren to come have a look at something they'd found on the road. Maren pulled her hand free. "I hope you find the perfect man!" she said as she ran ahead.

"Thank you," Amelia said softly. "I think I might just have." He'd crept in when she was least expecting it. She could feel her esteem for him growing. The more she thought about him, the more she believed how perfect he was for her. Surprising, adventurous, not easily offended. Handsome and strong and astoundingly attractive. A duke, a man of the world, someone who would understand her position in life. How could anyone compare?

How could she persuade him to see it? She felt almost desperate in her hope that the old woman had written her with the advice she needed.

But there was no letter tacked to the door when they arrived at the school. Amelia tapped down her disappointment—there could be any number of reasons why, although generally the old crone could be depended upon to respond right away. Still, Amelia was certain the letter would be there on the morrow.

But there was no letter the next day, either. Or the day after that.

"You are to be commended, Miss Ivanosen," Mr. Roberts said cheerfully. "I think you've finally rid us of our bothersome midnight caller."

Like so many other times in her life, that had not been her intent.

She felt her despair swallowing her regard for the duke, threatening to suffocate all hope.

CHAPTER THIRTY-THREE

WHAT HAD STARTED out as a beautiful sunlit day had rapidly descended into a hellish one for Lila.

She'd had her morning stroll, enjoyed a hearty breakfast, and was sitting down to write some messages to people in London when the post arrived. There was a letter from her husband, Valentin, which she eagerly opened first. The news was not good—his trip to London to see her had been delayed indefinitely. He wrote to ask when she would be home, told her that he missed her, and asked why was it that the royal matches always took the longest when it stood to reason they would be the easiest. Didn't everyone want to marry a prince or princess, he asked?

No, darling. Not everyone.

The next letter was from Baron Hancock, who wrote to regretfully inform her that he could not come to England after all, that business kept him at home.

She was terribly disappointed. For the first time in many years, she felt herself running out of options. But Lila was not one to concede. The letters from Valentin and the baron only strengthened her resolve to find Princess Amelia a proper match as quickly as possible. And given the princess's mood the last few days, she thought her only possible hope was Marley.

Unfortunately, she hadn't yet thought of a clever way to bring him around.

From there, Lila went down to lunch with Blythe and Beck and their two youngest daughters. The older girls were at school with the princess. Lila was surprised to sense a palpable tension when she entered. Peg-leg Meg and Birdie were playing with a little rolling cart, stuffing their dolls into it, then pulling the cart around the dining room table. Blythe's face was pinched, and Beck looked thunderous. Lila had never seen him in any mood less than affable. She hesitated at the door and thought she would quietly back out, but Beck beckoned her in. "Come, come, Lila."

"I don't—"

"Yes, please come in," he said firmly.

Lila slowly entered the room and took her seat at the dining table.

"Girls, it's time for your lunch. Come to the table please," Beck said.

"I don't want to," Meg said.

"You will do as I ask," Beck said.

"But I don't *want* to—"

Beck's hand hit the table so hard that the dishes and glassware bounced and rattled. "You will do as I tell you or you won't have lunch at all, Margaret! Do you understand me?"

Meg understood, all right. She began to cry. Then so did Birdie.

Lila was astounded. She'd never heard Beck raise his voice to his daughters, his wife, or anyone else, for that matter. And clearly, neither had they.

Blythe stood from her chair. "Mrs. Hughes!" she called. She scooped up Birdie and grabbed Meg's hand, pulling her to the open door. "Mrs. Hughes, you are needed!" She took the girls out of the dining room.

"I beg your pardon," Beck said as he slowly sank back in his chair. "It has been a trying morning."

Lila remained silent.

Blythe was back in a moment and resumed her seat. "Our apologies."

"Yes, yes, our apologies," Beck agreed. "I beg your pardon, darling," he said, reaching for his wife's hand. "I didn't mean to snap."

Blythe smiled sympathetically. "Who can blame you? After such news."

What news? Lila wanted to shout.

Garrett calmly began to serve lunch while Beck drummed his fingers on the table. He turned his frown to Lila. "As I'm sure you've gathered, I've had some rather distressing news."

"Your sister is well?"

"Yes, of course, nothing like that. It's the abbey. It might not be a possibility after all."

"Oh. Why not?"

"Because it has just been sold to an Irishman who means to build a woolen mill there. He intends to raze the abbey."

"Oh *no*," Lila said. "But everyone seems to agree it's perfect for the school."

"It is absolutely perfect. I'm as distressed as you are, Lila. I mean to see if I can stop it, but I doubt I'll be able to. But it is the circumstances of the sale that have made me so bloody angry."

She glanced at Blythe, who looked disgusted by something. "Why?"

"I have learned who the owner of the abbey was, prior to Monday when the sale was made."

"Someone you know, I take it?"

Beck fixed his gaze on her. "It was Marley."

"Pardon?" Lila asked. "The *Duke* of Marley? *Our* Marley?"

"Our Marely, Lila—the very one. He is—he *was*—the owner of the abbey."

Lila frowned. "But he never said so! Here, at your dining table, with all the talk of the abbey, he never mentioned he owned it."

"Indeed, he did not, and that is a terrible disappointment," Beck said. "I would expect more from him. I mean to speak to him about it."

"Oh, darling," Blythe said. "Do you think you ought? I wouldn't want there to be any discord between us."

"I don't care if there is. What he's done is abominable."

"What will you do?" Blythe asked.

"I don't know," Beck said. "Appeal to him. Demand an explanation. Garrett, where is the meat?"

The butler moved to a platter of roast beef on the sideboard. He served Beck first, then Blythe. But Lila waved him off before he could serve her and stood.

"What's the matter?" Beck asked.

"I'm afraid I've lost my appetite," Lila said.

Beck blinked. "That's not like you."

"Very true, my lord. But I find my stomach has turned. Please excuse me." She strode to the door and went out before anyone could utter a word.

Suddenly, everything felt as if it was falling apart, and now, she wouldn't have her lunch. As if this day could get worse.

And yet, she would soon discover that it could.

CHAPTER THIRTY-FOUR

JOSHUA HADN'T BEEN sleeping much, and what he'd lost in sleep, he'd made up in drink. But there wasn't enough ale in the world to fill the void in him. He was disgusted with himself. He couldn't make sense of his conflicting emotions, about Amelia, about children, about his life. So he chopped wood. He swung the axe over and over again, and with each strike, he let out a primal roar.

That's where Miles found him. He made him put down the axe. He pointed out that Joshua's shirt was soaked through and his hands were bleeding. Joshua glanced down, surprised by the open blisters. He hadn't felt them. Miles took a handkerchief from his pocket and wrapped it around Joshua's hand. "You have to stop this madness. You realize that, don't you? Come, let's have some whisky and clean this up."

Joshua knew Miles was right, but he didn't know how to stop. Life had prepared him for many things, but not how to face his darkest moments. Someone ought to have taught him.

In the drawing room, Miles poured two whiskies, then rang for Butler. "We'll need hot water and soap," he instructed, "and clean towels." When Butler went out, Miles looked Joshua up and down. "What in bloody hell is the matter with you, lad?"

"That's an excellent question," Joshua said. "I don't have

a satisfactory answer for you." He felt sick to his stomach. He felt his head was exploding. Everything he thought and felt was wrong. He wanted to explain that to Miles, but he didn't know where to begin. He was in love? That was almost laughable after the last two years. He didn't know how he could feel it at all, given his state. But he could. It had knitted into his sinew. He was in love and frightened of it. Which meant that on top of everything else, he was a damn coward.

Butler returned several minutes later with the clean towels and water. "I beg your pardon, Your Grace, but Lady Aleksander has come to call."

She was the last person Joshua could tolerate. "Jesus, not now," he said, and picked up a towel.

"Mr. Butler? I won't be turned away!" That was Lady Aleksander, shouting from down the hall. Miles looked at Joshua with confusion. "What's happened?"

"I have no idea. But I can't abide her cheerfulness just now."

Miles sighed. "Bring her in."

"For God's sake, Miles, stop—"

"What do you want me to do?" Miles snapped. "Watch you drown in despair? If you have another suggestion for how I may help you, for the love of God, tell me!"

Joshua opened his mouth to argue, but Miles threw up his hand. "Don't speak, Joshua. Just look at you. *Look* at you!"

Joshua didn't have to look to know what Miles meant.

Lady Aleksander swept into the drawing room behind Butler looking a little like a wild cat that wanted to claw someone's eyes out.

"Lady Aleksander?" Miles said. "Is everything all right?"

"Ask your friend, my lord."

"Believe me, madam, I have tried. What is the matter?"

"Where shall I begin? With his worst offense?"

"His offense? I don't understand—"

"Lord Iddesleigh has discovered who owns Goosefeather Abbey." She glared at Joshua.

The abbey. Joshua's muddled brain tried to pull a thought from the pile of neglected thoughts.

"And?"

"You don't know? The Duke of Marley owns Goosefeather Abbey. Or, I should say, he *did* own it, until this week, when he sold it to an Irishman. Who wants to tear it down and build a mill."

"Oh my God," Joshua said. The thought he'd been trying to extract exploded into the forefront. He'd completely forgotten about his instruction to Cox to sell the abbey. What had he said? He'd told him to sell it, but—

"What?" Miles looked at Joshua with even more confusion, if that was possible. "You own the abbey?"

Joshua needed to gather his thoughts, to *remember*. But it was difficult, because all he could seem to recall was Amelia talking about the abbey. Her purpose. It gave her purpose. It gave her hope. And he'd just knocked that out from under her. What had he said to Cox? He'd instructed him to sell it. What did he think would happen? He thought someone would protest, surely, some group that wanted to preserve antiquities. He'd so cavalierly told Cox to sell it with the vague notion it would not sell, that it would be as difficult as selling Hollyfield.

"What about the girls at the school? What about their education, their chance in this world?" Lady Aleksander demanded.

He thought of the girls in their garden, and his stomach clenched with nausea. "They deserve it," Joshua said. "That and more."

"Then *why?* How could you do such a thing? You sat at Lord Iddesleigh's table and listened to him talk about his hopes for the abbey and you never said a word!"

Yes, he had done that, and at the time, he'd had no remorse.

He had buckets of it now. He had to fix this. He needed to speak to Cox at once. He had to go to London, now. Today. He needed to see Amelia.

"Will you not speak?" Lady Aleksander asked.

"Lila… I don't have an answer you will accept. I'm certain of that."

She gaped at him.

"It's grief," Miles said, throwing up his hands in defeat.

"What?" Joshua said at the same time Lady Aleksander said, "Pardon?"

Miles gestured at Joshua, at his attire, his general state of disarray. "Can't you see?" he asked Lady Aleksander. "Tell her," he said to Joshua. "Isn't that why you are seeking to sell Hollyfield as well?"

"Oh my God," Lady Aleksander whispered, horrified by the thought.

"He wants to sell it because he can't bear to be where he lost his wife and child," Miles finished.

Joshua's gut twisted harder. "That's not true."

Miles snorted. "Isn't it? Tell us why, then, if you can do it without dissembling."

"I don't *grieve* them," Joshua bit out. "I am one man, and this duchy, this title, is more than a single man. I have no heirs, no *desire* for an heir," he said, choking on the word *desire*. It was a lie, a terrible lie. "There is nothing that keeps me here. Nothing here that I deserve to have."

But Amelia deserved the abbey. He had to fix that, to do something to repair the damage he'd done.

"Well that certainly explains the rest of it," Lady Aleksander said tartly.

"The rest of what?" Miles asked.

"He is denying his feelings for Princess Amelia."

"What?" Miles groaned to the ceiling. "I need a drink." He stalked to the sideboard and poured a whisky, and tossed it down his throat. "Anyone else?"

"You don't know what you're saying, Lila," Joshua said, ignoring him. "Leave it be."

"I won't leave it be! You have suffered a tragedy that I can't possibly imagine. But you can't give up on your *life*, Joshua. You have a chance for happiness, to love again. You *must* allow yourself to love again."

"I didn't *love* Diana, I *killed* Diana!" he exploded.

Lady Aleksander gasped.

Miles slammed down his whisky glass. "What in the hell are you saying?"

Joshua's confession was burning a hole in his chest. It felt like it could burn down this massive house. He'd never said it out loud, had never admitted to anyone what he'd done. "I wanted—"

His voice caught. He felt on the verge of being sick and gulped down a swell of nausea. He took a breath.

"I wanted a child. An heir. No, that's not…it was more than that. I wanted a half dozen children. I wanted to fill this house to the rafters with them. Dogs, children, laughter, love. Diana had two miscarriages before the last pregnancy. She didn't want to try again. She was afraid—she said she couldn't bear to lose another one. Do you understand what I am telling you? *She* didn't want to try, but *I*, in my selfish desire, convinced her because *I* wanted it."

Lady Aleksander's mouth gaped. "But you didn't—"

"I *pleaded* with her. I reminded her again and again of our duty to bear an heir. Of our marital arrangement—her freedom for my child!" He was shouting, he realized, but the confession was ripping out of him, and he couldn't lower his voice. "She agreed. And then she conceived, and…" He couldn't say the rest. He couldn't bring himself to utter the words out loud.

Miles said it for him. "And she and the baby died."

"Oh, Joshua," Lila whispered. "Oh dear God, you poor thing. You're not responsible for their deaths."

He abhorred the sound of pity in her voice. "I know what I did," he snapped at her. "I live with it every day."

"Are you God?" she asked. "Do you divine who lives and who dies? Isn't it possible you were a man who simply wanted a child? Who wanted to love, as you said?"

The room felt as if it was shifting under his feet. He dabbed at his hands with the towel. He'd done so many things wrong—he could never make them understand.

"Haven't you punished yourself enough?" Lila asked, her voice softer. "Can't you give yourself another chance? Because you have a chance for *true* happiness. She loves you, Joshua."

Love? The room shifted even more. *The abbey. That* was her hope, not him. He had to fix it; he had to get the abbey back for her. What was he doing, standing there?

"What did you say?" Miles asked.

"Princess Amelia loves him," Lila said.

"She said those words?" Miles asked, his voice full of reasonable disbelief.

"In so many words, yes. Don't look so skeptical, my lord. I know these things. She's told me he is the only man she will consider."

Miles's jaw dropped. Joshua's heart was beating hard. Of course he knew Amelia esteemed him, but...*love*? He felt as if he could shatter into pieces. He loved her, too. Of course he did.

"Joshua—don't be a fool, man," Miles said.

He needed to breathe. To hit something. He needed to get an abbey back. He tossed the towel aside and started for the door.

"Where are you going?" Lila cried. "Don't walk out, please! If you let her go, you'll regret it all your life."

"I can't talk now, Lila. There is something I must do right away."

"She's leaving!"

He stopped, midstride, and looked back at Lila. "London?"

Lila shook her head. "*Wesloria.* She's going home, unless you stop her."

His gut felt caught in a vice. Joshua turned and walked out. He had to think what to do, and he couldn't do it with an audience.

He had finally succeeded in turning everyone away, just like he'd wanted. Even his dogs preferred Miles to him now. He was free to wander the earth, to continue his deserved isolation.

So why, then, did it hurt so much?

CHAPTER THIRTY-FIVE

THERE WAS STILL no letter.

Three days had passed without a response. Three days! Had the old crone died? Had she lost patience with the correspondence? Had she moved, taken ill, run out of paper, started sleeping at night? What possibly could have happened to make her suddenly silent?

Amelia paced the small school office. She held one hand against her waist, the other pressed to her forehead as she walked four steps one way, four steps back, over and over again, trying to think.

She'd been irrationally angry the first two days when no letters had arrived. Who did the old crone think she was? But today, she was worried for her friend.

She turned sharply and accidentally knocked over a stack of books. She stooped down to restack them. This pacing was pointless—she'd been at it all day, hiding in this little office, nursing her wounds, thinking of Joshua, hoping for guidance.

Maybe the time had come to admit that an anonymous old crone was not going to solve her problems. Maybe it was time to take matters into her own hands. She'd never had trouble speaking her mind before—why did it suddenly seem so daunting? What was wrong with declaring her feelings to Joshua? What was the worst that could happen?

Well, obviously, the worst was too horrible to even contemplate.

Amelia grabbed her shawl. She stepped out of the office, waved at Mr. Roberts, and went out the door into the sunshine. She paused to draw in a deep breath. *Courage.* It was as if her father had whispered it to her from the beyond. He used to whisper that word to her and Justine before they'd walk into receiving rooms or stand on balconies before thousands of people. *Courage.*

She began the walk to Iddesleigh.

She pondered how she would make her declaration. Should she send a note to Hollyfield, requesting an audience? *I must speak with you straight away.* Or should she take the more direct route and knock on his door? She'd never in her life walked up to a door and knocked. Her arrivals were generally prearranged and announced. Furthermore, she understood it was frowned upon for unmarried women to go knocking willy-nilly on unmarried men's doors. But she often did things that were frowned upon, and really, what did she have to lose? She'd be bound for Wesloria soon enough, no matter his response.

All right—if she were to knock on his door, what would she say?

Good afternoon. My feelings for you have grown.

No. Too bland.

I have come to declare my intentions.

Well, she wasn't proposing marriage, and she wasn't inviting a duel, so that wasn't right, either.

As she mulled it over, she came upon the path that Joshua had taken the day of the storm. It went through the forest and skirted along the river. It was almost midday. She paused, considering that path. If she arrived at Iddesleigh now, she'd have to take lunch with Beck and Blythe, and she couldn't bear even the idea of that in her current state.

She turned onto the path and continued walking. She recalled there was a point in this path where it turned toward Hollyfield, a bend very near the river. When she reached it, she noticed a large, flat rock. It was such a fine, warm day, that Amelia decided to continue her rumination here. She spread her shawl over the rock and lay on her back under the warmth of the sun. She closed her eyes, thinking through all the things she could say.

And imagining what it would be like to love him. To live a life with him. She pictured the two of them at supper. Or riding. Or fishing. Or pretending to argue about silly things, like who was the better dancer. She imagined their bed, and the way the firelight would dance on the ceiling while they came together.

I think I'm in love with you. Except that I know I'm in love with you. I know I am in love with you because I realize I have never really loved anyone until I met you.

The clank of a bridle made her sit up with alarm. She looked to the path and saw the rider coming from Hollyfield. It was as if she'd summoned him—Joshua came loping into sight.

He was startled by the sight of her on that big flat rock. He pulled up on the reins and stared down at her as if he was trying to understand how she had come to be there.

"*Bon dien,*" she said.

He came down off his horse without a word. He took off his hat and dragged his fingers through his hair. "Are you all right? What are you doing here?"

"Walking. Well, actually, resting. I came from the school."

He said nothing, just stared at her.

"I heard you called on the school."

He swallowed. He looked at the ground. "I did." He lifted his gaze to her again, and his eyes looked full of sadness. And something more. Something softer.

Amelia stood up from the rock. "Lady Mathilda claimed you dug a row for them."

"Well... I repaired a row they had dug. The lot of them are exceedingly bad at digging."

She smiled. She stepped up on the path toward him. "What are you doing here?"

He shrugged lightly. "Thinking. Avoiding others. I can't seem to escape Lord Clarendon, and I—I need to think."

"Oh." He seemed so serious. She looked at the river. *Courage.* "I've been thinking, too." She turned her gaze back to him.

He looked suddenly uncertain. As if he might speak, but wasn't certain what he wanted to say. Well, she knew what she wanted to say, and this seemed her moment—either she'd speak, or she'd go home to Wesloria and nurse the biggest regret of her life. "Joshua... I've been thinking about you." She stepped closer. "I've been thinking so *much* about you."

"Amelia." He held up his hand. "Before—"

"Please, I need to say this."

He was suddenly moving, striding toward her. She didn't understand his intention and took a step back, but he caught her hand and pulled her into his embrace. He roughly caressed her face, held it in his callused hands and searched her eyes.

"You are—"

He kissed her before she could say he was what she wanted. He kissed her so deeply, so fervently, that she was immediately lost in the sensation of it. All her thoughts flew out of her head and all her emotions turned raw.

The kiss turned passionate; he moved to her neck, to her ear. Amelia wrapped her arms around his neck and pulled him to the rock. Joshua braced himself above her.

Any inhibitions between them evaporated. The desire was as mutual as it was intense. Their hands roamed each other's bodies as they kissed. He slipped a hand into her bodice and freed one breast of the fabric of her gown, and with a groan of want, took it into his mouth.

The pleasure was almost more than she could tolerate, and Amelia dug her fingers into his shoulders as he moved his attention to the other breast. She felt like she was undulating, her body liquid against his. She pressed her thigh against his erection, and explored his shoulders, his arms, his back with her hands.

His slid his hand down her body, caressing the flare of her hip, then down her leg, to her ankle. He slipped his hand under her skirt. Amelia's heart raced with anticipation; she put an arm around his shoulders and found his mouth as he began to slide his hand up her leg again, between her legs. Her breath quickened and she moved beyond rational thought when he slipped his fingers into her sex. Her head fell back as he began to move his fingers on her, in her, around her. She could feel the desire building to a crescendo. She gave a strangled cry as her body released into her desire, throbbing with the deliverance. He kissed her, withdrew his hand. He rolled onto his back and brought her to lie on top of him, kissing her again. She could feel he didn't want to let her go. Her heart was so tender toward him, and she felt everything she'd ever imagined she could feel for the man who would be her husband.

It was magnificent, that feeling of contentment and love.

Joshua cupped her face, traced her bottom lip with his thumb. He kissed her once more, then sat up. She sat in his lap and draped her arms over his shoulders. "I must tell you something."

He shook his head. "Don't." He kissed her once more, then set her aside and stood up. He straightened his clothes and took her hand to help her to her feet.

What had just happened? "Joshua, I need—"

"Don't say it, Amelia. Don't." He took both her hands in his. "Don't say it, because I can't respond in a way you'd like. I want to be who you want. On my word, I do. But..." He winced, as if the words were causing him pain. "I can't be who you want at present. And I fear there will come a time very soon when you won't want me."

"What?" He was confusing her. What had just happened between them? Why would she ever stop wanting him? "I don't understand."

He kissed her again, then bent down, picked up her shawl, and put it around her shoulders. "Go to Iddesleigh, I beg you. I am to London."

"*Now?* why?"

He stroked her cheek. There was a desperation in his eyes that made no sense to her. He seemed desperate to stay and desperate to go, and she couldn't grasp what was happening. He kissed her forehead, her cheek. "Go home now."

She grabbed his hand. "What's wrong? What have I done?"

"Nothing. It's me, Amelia. I've made a dreadful mistake and I must go to London." He took her into his arms once more and held her tight. "You've been perfect, do you hear me? You are perfect." He put his hands on her shoulders and set her back. "When I can tell you, I will."

He stepped away from her, backing up to his horse, his gaze still locked on her.

Something in her faltered. Lost its footing, broke off, floating free of her brain. It was her heart, she realized. It was breaking in two. She looked almost blindly at the river. "I don't understand," she said helplessly.

"I hardly understand myself at times." He took the horse's reins.

"Is it because you lost your wife? I understand! I lost my father, and it was devastating," she said, pressing a hand against her chest. "I live every day with my grief...but I'm not ready to die for it."

"It's not as simple as grief."

She assumed he was talking about love. "Do you think you're the only one to have experienced the death of a loved one? I *know* you loved her, and it must—"

"I didn't love her!" he exclaimed skyward.

Amelia gasped softly.

He shook his head. "It wasn't love that we had, Amelia, not in the way you believe. Ours was not a great love story, and my loss is not as deep as yours."

He was confusing her even more. "Then...then what's wrong? Please tell me. I can't bear not knowing."

He looked up the path for a moment. "You may hate me...but believe me when I tell you I am doing what is best for you."

Her heartbreak turned to fire. "How dare you to presume what is best for me? I have spent twenty-six years determining what is best for me. I don't need you to tell me what that is." She suddenly realized he was right—she would hate him. She hated him now. And when she was through hating him, her heart would ache with the yearning for him.

So many emotions were tangling up in her—she had gone from disappointment, to hope, to love, to despair. If she stood here another moment, she would collapse. She began to walk, making her arms and legs work to carry her to Iddesleigh House.

"Amelia." Joshua reached for her as she passed, but Amelia pushed him as hard as she could.

"This is what you want," she said, and continued to walk until that wasn't enough, and then she began to run. She paused once to catch her breath and look back. He was where she'd left him, staring after her, his expression dark and pained and…full of *love*.

Did he think she couldn't see it? What a bloody fool he was.

And she was an even bigger fool for having fallen in love with him.

She strode to Iddesleigh House, fighting tears with every step she refused to let fall. And as she was walking up the drive, Lila came out to meet her.

"No, Lila," Amelia said, and tried to brush past her. "I don't want to hear about your list or your plans for London."

"It's about Marley."

Lila stopped walking. Her hands fisted at her sides and she slowly turned around. "What of him?"

Lila looked at her with such pity that Amelia wanted to scream. "What is it?" she demanded. "Speak, woman, or I—"

"Marley is the owner of Goosefeather Abbey."

It took a moment for Amelia to arrange her thoughts. "What?"

"He *was* the owner. But he sold it earlier this week. To a man who means to tear it down and build a mill."

Amelia stared at her. "*What*?" she said again, her voice

weaker. How could he? How could he listen to her talk about the abbey and what it meant to her and say...*nothing?*

Joshua was right—she hated him.

CHAPTER THIRTY-SIX

June, 1858
England

To Her Majesty the Queen, Justine,

Dearest Jussie, I am writing to beg you to bring me home to Wesloria as soon as possible. This trip to England has not been successful, and I can't possibly abide another moment of being here. I've no doubt that Lila has sent word of how wretched it all turned out, although I think she is loath to admit that she has failed. She insists she has not given up, but as I pointed out to her, it hardly matters, because I certainly have.

I trust you will keep this between us, promise me, but I've never been so despondent, not even when Papa died. I don't want to rise from bed in the mornings. The girls, who have been my great joy these weeks, bring me no cheer. I despair that I likely will never marry, as no one suits me. And then my chest fills with fury that the one I thought suited me perfectly should prove to be so deceitful. It is my burden in this life to be drawn to ones who are so very wrong. Happiness will elude me all my life.

I will never forgive Lord M for what he made me

feel both in happiness and despair. I beg you never say his name to me. I can't bear to hear it. I know you will want to know what happened between us, and of course I will tell you, but at present, I can't think of him without feeling ill.

I'll write more when I'm able. At present, even the pen feels too heavy a burden for me. I miss you terribly. I miss my dogs. I even miss Mama. Please don't tell her I said so, or she will write and tell me to lift my chin, that I am the daughter of the great King Maksim and have absolutely no reason to weep when I do.

Yours, A

CHAPTER THIRTY-SEVEN

LILA HAD BEEN at the business of matchmaking for nearly two decades. In all that time, she could count on one hand the times she had failed to make a successful match. And never had she been unsuccessful with a member of a royal family.

She had written Queen Justine and Prime Minister Robuchard to tell them that the princess desired to return to Wesloria, that she'd not found any of the suitors to her liking. The prime minister responded right away to say he was disappointed in the outcome, but hardly surprised. The queen responded with a heartfelt request that Lila take care of her sister. She wrote that Princess Amelia may not seem to be tenderhearted, but she was, and she was distressed to learn her sister had not found love.

The queen wasn't the only one who was distressed by the turn of events. But what bothered Lila most of all was that the Duke of Marley and Princess Amelia were perfect for one another. She rarely had two people so perfectly suited.

It didn't help that Joshua left Hollyfield for London almost immediately after the sale of Goosefeather Abbey was known. She could hardly persuade him to see his way to the princess if he wasn't here.

Princess Amelia was due to leave in four days. Lila was packing to leave, too. Donovan was bringing Valentin to her, as their plans for London had been scrapped, and the two of them intended to carry on to Scotland, where the heir to a substantial fortune wished to speak to her about her services. She missed her husband terribly, so it was jubilation she felt when she heard the jangle of horses and the creaks of a coach on the drive.

She dropped what she was doing and ran down the stairs and out onto the drive and didn't stop running until Valentin caught her in his arms. "My love," he said, laughing, and kissed her unabashedly in front of everyone.

But then he set her back and with a smile said, "I think you ought to look around."

Lila looked around. There was Donovan, of course, who had been kind enough to fetch Valentin. And standing next to him, looking stiff and uncomfortable, was Marley. He had dark circles under his eyes and the shadow of a beard. What was he doing here? She turned around to look at Beck, who stood at some distance, his expression grim. "Lord Aleksander, you are most welcome. I'd walk over and shake your hand heartily and inquire after your journey, but it would appear I have an unexpected visitor and my good humor has evaporated."

"Fair and deserved, my lord," Marley said. "But I've brought you something I hope will restore your good humor."

Beck snorted. "Unless you've brought me Goosefeather Abbey, Your Grace, my good humor can't be restored."

"Beck, darling," Blythe said.

"I am speaking the truth. He has deceived us all. He didn't give us a chance."

Marley reached into his pocket and withdrew a paper. "You are quite right. I was terribly remiss in failing to mention my involvement. My reasons would mean nothing to you, so I won't take your time to offer them. The point is that I had instructed my estate agent to sell the abbey before I knew of your interest in it. My agent is nothing if not efficient, and did as I asked more quickly than I would have thought possible. The first I heard the sale had transpired was when Lady Aleksander brought it to my attention."

"Pardon? You can't expect us to believe that," Lila said. "Your agent would not have made a sale of property without consultation from you."

Marley's jaw clenched. "One would think. But he and I have had a different sort of arrangement the last few years. He did have consultation with me, and my instructions were to proceed by any means possible. Believe what you like, but it's the truth." He turned his attention to Beck. "When I heard about the sale, I went to London immediately to see what could be done."

"What could be done?" Beck asked, throwing his arms out. "Nothing!"

"Correct. I couldn't stop the sale," Marley admitted.

Beck snorted and looked around at the others, clearly angry. "Why are you here? To tell me what I already know?"

"I am here because there was something else I could do."

"And what was that, Your Grace?"

Marley held up the folded paper. "I could buy it back. Which I did, and for a dear sum. One is not in a position to strike a fair bargain when the other man holds all the cards. Nevertheless, I bought that ruin and I've signed it over to you, my lord. You will find everything in order. You should have your school."

Everyone on that drive stared at him as if they were waiting for him to finish the joke. It had to be a joke.

Marley, clearly uncomfortable with the attention, cleared his throat. He walked forward and held out the paper to

Beck. "Mr. Donovan was very good to bring me from the train station. Please take this, Iddesleigh. I made a wretched mistake, and for that I apologize. But I hope I have righted it in your eyes."

Beck took the paper and looked at it. "It's the property papers," he said, his voice full of incredulity.

"Well then. I will leave you to your guest." Marley touched the brim of his hat. "Good day." He walked away, in the direction of Hollyfield.

Lila was astounded. Simply, truly, astounded. She looked at Valentin.

Valentin smiled uncertainly. "What was that about?"

"Come in my good man, and we'll tell you all about it," Beck said. He suddenly laughed. He picked up his wife and twirled her around. "Can you believe it? Come, everyone. We must have a drink to celebrate." He and Blythe ran up the steps into the house. Donovan followed them.

Lila hugged her husband again. "Oh, darling, I'm so happy to see you. But there is one thing I must tend to."

She'd told the princess she wasn't giving up. And she wasn't. She took Valentin inside to the drawing room and excused herself. Then she hurried upstairs to tell Princess Amelia the extraordinary thing that had happened.

CHAPTER THIRTY-EIGHT

EVERYONE AT IDDESLEIGH was in fine spirits after the gift of the abbey was made clear to Beck. When Lila had brought Amelia the news, she'd run to the window to catch a glimpse of Joshua, but it was too late—he'd disappeared into the forest.

"Did he say anything else?" Amelia asked. "Did he ask about me?"

"Well, no, but that was hardly the place," Lila said.

Amelia's shoulders sagged. He hadn't changed his mind, then. She turned away from the window. "I still hate him."

"Oh, my dear—"

"I have to finish packing," Amelia said, cutting her off before she could offer some bromide that would make Amelia want to break something. She went to the door and held it open. "Thank you for bringing me the news. I am truly happy about the abbey."

Lila slowly walked to the door, but she paused there. "Do you still intend to visit the school tomorrow?"

"*Je*," Amelia said. As if she could leave England without saying goodbye to Mr. Roberts and the girls.

"Will you come down for tea? Valentin has come."

"Of course." Amelia fluttered her fingers at the open door, indicating Lila should go.

When Lila had gone, Amelia collapsed into a chair. She felt so tired.

Later, she went down to tea. And then to dinner. She talked, she laughed, she told a story or two about her time in Wesloria. One about losing her dog Bess in the crowd. Another about a play she and Justine staged when they were young girls, and that, of course, inspired the Iddesleigh girls to throw together a play for the adults at the last moment that made no sense to anyone.

All the while, she kept looking out the window to the drive. She kept waiting for him to come. Did he have nothing to say to her? Could he not bring himself to say goodbye? She would be on a train Thursday, leaving Devonshire. Possibly forever.

The next day, she remained in her rooms for breakfast, unwilling or unable to abide the girl's cheerful faces. But she dressed to walk them to school for the last time. They were waiting for her, practically bouncing around the foyer. Maren took her hand as they started out. "We have a surprise today."

"I love surprises," Amelia said.

"You're sworn not to tell!" Mathilda scolded her sister. "I'm telling Mr. Roberts."

"I forgot!" Maren shouted at her.

Amelia already knew the surprise—the girls had been practicing a song the last few days, and she suspected it was for her.

On the road to the school, they walked past Hollyfield. Amelia couldn't help but look at it. She wasn't certain, but it looked to her as if many of the windows had been cleaned and opened. And there were four chimneys smoking this morning.

Her eyes began to water.

"Are you crying?" Maisie asked.

"No. The wind has stung my eyes."

The girls looked at each other. Probably because there was no wind. It was a perfect summer morning.

When they reached the school, Mathilda stopped several feet from the door. "You're to wait here."

"Am I?" Amelia asked.

"Mr. Roberts will come when we're ready for the surprise."

"Don't tell her!" Maisie shouted.

"I didn't!" Mathilda insisted, and in the three girls went, bouncing off each other.

Amelia could hear quite a lot of commotion inside the school. Anne Waverly arrived late and darted past Amelia into the school. After a few minutes, it sounded as if they girls were moving into the back garden. There was a lot of giggling and girls telling girls to hush. Eventually, Mr. Roberts came out, perspiring, but his face was beaming. "You've heard the news?" he asked excitedly.

"About the abbey?"

He laughed. "Isn't it wonderful? He held out his hand. She slipped her hand into his. "Miss Ivanosen, or, Your Royal Highness, as Lady Mathilda has informed me, I can't thank you enough for your help. You will be dearly missed. The girls have prepared a surprise to see you off."

"Oh." She smiled tremulously. The damn tears were threatening to fill her eyes again.

"Would you like to see the surprise?"

"I can hardly wait."

"I must ask you to close your eyes. I'll lead you."

She closed her eyes and put a hand over them. Mr. Roberts guided her into the school, down the narrow hallway, and into the back garden. Amelia could sense the girls gathered around, could hear them giggling and moving.

"All right. Open your eyes."

Amelia opened her eyes. The girls yelled, "Surprise!"

The back garden was filled with flowers. Dozens and dozens of beautiful flowers. Amelia stared at the sight, her mouth agape. "How did you...?"

"We had an accomplice," Mr. Roberts said.

He pointed. She looked to her right, and her heart climbed into her throat. Joshua had come. He was standing in the middle of all those girls. One of them held his hand. Several of them jumped up and down with excitement. "He's a duke!" one of them shouted. "You're to curtsy to a duke!"

Amelia couldn't think. She couldn't breathe. She curtsied.

He came forward, the girls moving with him, getting in between them.

"You brought the flowers?"

"I had considerable help from Lady Aleksander and Mr. Puddlestone." He looked around them, as if searching for something. Then at her. "You're leaving."

"Tomorrow."

"Before you go, I have something for you." He held out a piece of paper. It was thick cream vellum, and she recognized it at once. The old crone had finally written her. But how...?

She took the letter. It was addressed to The Iddesleigh School for Beautiful, Extraordinary, Exceptional Girls.

She broke the seal and opened the letter.

From a Concerned Resident of Devonshire,

I hope you read this letter, but if you prefer to burn it, I will understand. I beg your pardon for taking so long to respond to your last letter, but I wasn't certain what to say.

A shiver of surprise ran down her spine. Amelia glanced up to search his face. "You're the old crone?"
"Pardon?"
She continued to read.

I might answer with the story of a man who had the world. For many years, he had no cares but to drink all the wine and to woo all the women. One day he met a woman he thought he might like as a wife. But his past behavior had been so reprehensible that her family wouldn't allow a match. It happened that later, he unexpectedly became a duke. He needed an heir. He married another women whom he didn't love, and who didn't love him. They had an agreement— she would be a duchess in exchange for children. Not just the obligatory heir, but a house full of children. The man wanted the children and a family more than anything else in the world. He didn't want to tour the Continent, he didn't want to game. He wanted to be with a family at his hearth.

Amelia looked up. He steadily returned her gaze. She continued reading.

The duchess tried to meet her end of their bargain. Two of the children were lost before they were fully formed. The man convinced her to try again and when she appeared reluctant, he pressed home the issue and reminded her of their agreement. But this time she and the child were both lost. And the man decided he could never love again, as he could never risk something so precious as another life again. He couldn't even bear to hear the sound of children, because it reminded him of his loss.

But then he met someone who turned his world upside down. At first, he was afraid to admit his feelings. Then he was afraid to act on his feelings, for fear of losing her, too. But as time went on, he realized that he'd allowed his life to turn fallow. There was nothing left in him. The moment love touched him, his hope began to grow again, like the garden you see here.

Amelia looked around at all the flowers. She could feel hope growing in her, too.

To answer your question, maybe compatibility doesn't lead to love. Maybe compatibility is love, and it only grows stronger. How do you know it is love? When you find the courage to face your fears because she is the only thing that matters.

You are the only thing that matters, Amelia. Allow me to love you. Allow me to take you to Wesloria, or wherever in this world you want to go. Allow me to listen to your stories and tell you mine. You were not expected. You have surprised me. You endeared yourself to me the moment we met on that road. And I can't bear to lose you, too.

Allow me to be with you, always,
A Concerned Citizen of Devonshire

Amelia's heart was beating out of her chest. She could feel tears burning in the back of her eyes as she calmly folded the letter. She felt on the verge of hysterical laughter or a scream or maybe even an impromptu dance—her heart was so full she could hardly contain it. She looked into his gray eyes, and she could see the love swimming there.

Joshua slowly went down onto one knee. Then the other. "Will you allow me?"

"*Je*," she said. "Be with me, always."

His smile was full of relief.

"Are you going to kiss?" one of the girls asked.

"Miss Frame, that is an inappropriate question," Mr. Roberts said.

"I most certainly am," Joshua said, and hopped to his feet, wrapped his arms around Amelia, and kissed her fully on the lips, much to the frenzied delight of all the girls gathered.

Amelia laughed when he lifted his head. "I can't believe *you're* the old crone," she said incredulously.

"What?" he asked again, confused, but Mr. Roberts had stepped forward to congratulate them, and the girls were shrieking with delight that he'd kissed her, and even more of them were racing around the garden with joy.

Their delight was nothing compared to Amelia's.

To Her Majesty the Queen, Justine,

Darling, darling Jussie, you are so kind to have written me about Roo and Mig's new puppies. I was so looking forward to seeing them, but I've some news! I won't be coming home as soon as I had planned after all. Something wonderful has happened, something so extraordinary that I can hardly contain myself. Lord M has confessed his true feelings to me! I have decided to stay on at Iddesleigh House so that he might pursue a proper courtship, one that will meet the approval of Mama and the PM. But it hardly matters what they think, for I have found that one person in all this world who can bring me happiness. We are compatible in every way, except he says at times I am too reckless on horseback. But he doesn't care that I speak my mind, he is not offended by the things I say, and he thinks I am beautiful. *Je*, I know that I am, but it hardly matters until the person you want to think you are beautiful finds you so.

Lady I has been trying desperately to keep me under lock and key. She said it was important that her girls see proper courtship behavior. So I've taken to strolling late at night, and no one is the wiser. Except Lordonna, who looks at me with great disappointment, just as Mama would do if she were here. I can't possibly stay away from him, and the societal rules for courtship here are oppressive.

I will confess to only you that I now understand the happiness you find with William in all respects. You won't say a word to Mama—she would ban me from St. Edys until she has been taken to the grave. And don't think to scold me, either. I am six and twenty and haven't any time to lose. I'm not waiting anymore.

I must dash away—we are all to the abbey today to begin planning what work must be done. I've already talked with Lord I's sister, Lady C, to plan an event to raise funding for the school. We mean to go to London for it, and hopefully, soon thereafter, all the arrangements will have been made so that I can bring Lord M to St. Edys.

Oh dear, the girls are hopping around me, eager to be on their way. Peg-leg Meg has a birthday tomor-

row, and she has requested a donkey as a gift. Lord I
is beside himself, as he can't imagine where she got
the idea. But he has a special surprise for her—their
dog, Alice, is getting a sister!

Oh, Jussie, how can I ever thank you enough for
banishing me to England? It's the best thing that ever
happened to me. I am so very happy.

I'll write as soon as I can. With much fondness, A

EPILOGUE

It was a winter afternoon with a heavy mist in the air, which meant all the hearths were blazing in Marley House in Belgravia. Lord and Lady Marley had come to London to seek the services of a doctor. They hadn't meant it to happen, but it appeared that Amelia was with child. Again.

They were delighted. It hardly mattered that they already had two twin boys and a baby girl.

In fact, Joshua insisted they remain in London to celebrate the first birthday of his daughter, Annika. They were hosting a luncheon for their friends to fete her. But John and Maksim, who were now three and proper little terrors, thought the party was for them. In the interest of maintaining a happy household, Joshua and Amelia decided the party could be for everyone.

Donovan had arrived to help prepare for the celebration and had brought his helpers, ladies Mathilda, Maren, and Maisie. Peg-leg Meg and Birdie came along with their parents. The twins were fascinated by Birdie, who commanded them in the same manner her sisters used to rule her. The twins didn't seem to mind.

Lady Annika had not yet made her appearance. Amelia had left her in the care of her father, and had disappeared with the boys, who had begun to shout with excitement the moment they heard Donovan's voice.

Lord and Lady Clarendon had come, too. Miles had been successful in his suit of Miss Carhill, and Joshua and Amelia privately marveled that tiny Lady Clarendon had given birth to a ten-pound baby boy. Lady Clarendon really was quite lovely and had been of particular help to Amelia in her quest to raise funds for the Iddesleigh School for Girls.

Despite Lordonna's stubborn insistence that she dress Annika, Joshua had shooed her away. After all, he'd bought her birthday frock. She would be dressed as a cherubic Greek goddess, complete with a gold leaf laurel. The baby was playing with a wooden duck Joshua had carved for her while he tried to fasten the costume. He rarely chopped wood anymore. Carving toys soothed him now. John and Max had little horses and a canon each.

Annika ignored her father as she played with the duck. When he'd fastened the costume he picked her up and held her out to look at her. The baby smiled at him. He smiled back. "I know your mother is a princess, Ani, but you're the real princess here." He winked.

"Duck," she said.

He put her down and put the gold leaf crown on her head. She immediately reached up and took it off. He put it on her again. She took it off again, then held it out to him.

He sighed. "You realize, don't you, that without the crown, our guests may not understand you are a Greek goddess and think I wrapped you in a sheet."

"Duck."

"You're very much like your mother in that I can't deny you a bloody thing, can I?" He put the tiny gold leaf crown on his head.

So it was that he was wearing a tiny gold leaf crown

perched precariously on his head when he carried the Belle of the Hour into the main salon. She was greeted with such cheers and applause that she immediately started to cry and buried her face in Joshua's collar. He couldn't calm her, not like her mother could. He kissed her head and handed her off. Amelia smiled at him with such warmth and tenderness that he felt a little queasy.

He looked around at the room. At his friends, who were like family. At his children, all of them blond, all of them with a tiny bit of white in their hair where the strands would not take color, just like their mother. He looked at his wife, the love of his life. He looked at his warm hearth and his lazy dogs, sprawled in front of the flames, with no regard for the activity around them. Well, he supposed Bethan was aware that Birdie was draped over him like a rug, but it didn't move him.

And even there, on top of the wrapped presents for Ani, was his cat Artemis. He'd meant to leave the cat at Hollyfield, but the boys wouldn't hear of it. The cat's tail swished violently as he cast his judgmental eye at the lot of them.

As the guests came forward to coo at the birthday girl, Joshua acknowledged that it was times like this that he couldn't believe this was his life. He had what he'd always wanted, what he'd feared he'd never have. And it touched him so that he could feel tears welling.

Amelia put her hand on his back. "Steady, darling," she whispered, and smiled up at him. "It's just a birthday party."

He smiled gratefully at her. She was the light of his life and he was the luckiest of all men.

To her Majesty the Queen, Justine,

Dearest Jussie, I hope this letter finds you well. I am still reeling over the news that Robuchard has been dispatched and Fedoro is your new prime minister. I always thought him a bit humorless. I should not like a PM who lacked a sense of humor.

How fares our future king? William has written that little Rolli is quite impressive on a horse, and he's only four years! I won't need to warn you that his baby brother, Vincent, will strive one day to be a better horseman—that's the only amusement a spare has, you know, trying to best the heir.

We are all aflutter here as Ani has four words now: *mamma*, *papa*, and *duck*. Joshua swears she says *peas* for *please*, but I think he is overly proud of his children.

We announced our happy news to our friends and children that I am expecting another child by the end of summer. They are all delighted, of course. Our Maksim is insistent he be provided a baby brother and claimed his sister cries too much. John said he would like another sister, as Ani thinks she is a boy and she is *not*.

We were pleased to celebrate Ani's first birthday Saturday last. In attendance were Carhill and his lovely lady and son. Naturally, Lord and Lady I, their children, and Donovan would not miss the occasion. We had quite a lovely time. Even Lady I was tolerant of me and made not a single remark about my mothering up until we found Ani on the floor, fast asleep with the dogs again.

The most curious thing happened just as the footman was serving cake. Butler announced that Miss Harriet Woodchurch had come to call. No one knew who she was except Lord I, who said he couldn't imagine why she would have any reason to call on my husband. We were all dying of curiosity, and we asked that she be sent in.

I expected a grown woman, but she was a girl! She held her hands tightly together to keep them from shaking and, when Joshua asked her how he could help, she said she was in search of employment. We were all astounded by this. Joshua told her that we had all the household staff we needed, and she thanked him, but said she had something very different in mind and asked if he might have need of a secretary or perhaps a solicitor's assistant! Can you imagine?

Joshua was very kind to the girl and told her he had a solicitor and a secretary, and he wished her luck and sent her on her way. It was amusing to all but Lady I, who said she would hope to never see her daughters in such a situation of having to beg for employment. I said I immediately had in mind that the girl ought to be at the Iddesleigh School for Exceptional Girls. I like ambition in a female, don't you?

Beck said I should come around and see him if that was my idea, as he had information about young Miss Woodchurch that I might like to know. He made it sound very ominous, and then Blythe asked if the girl wasn't the daughter of that odious man? Beck agreed that she was. Naturally, my interest was piqued, and I'll go round tomorrow with the children.

My husband is calling me, darling, and so are my sons. I think their voices must be the best sound in all the world. All my love to you and William and the boys. And Mama. And of course, the dogs.

A

* * * * *

Don't miss the first novel of

Julia London's

sparkling series: _Last Duke Standing._

Charming. Cheeky. Cunning.

Be sure to connect with us at:
Harlequin.com/Newsletters
Facebook.com/HarlequinBooks
Twitter.com/HQNBooks

HQN

HQNBooks.com

PHJL9820MAX